These Thousand Hills

OTHER BOOKS BY A. B. GUTHRIE, JR.
IN THORNDIKE LARGE PRINT

Arfive
Fair Land, Fair Land
The Last Valley

THESE THOUSAND HILLS

A. B. Guthrie, Jr.

THORNDIKE PRESS • THORNDIKE, MAINE

Library of Congress Cataloging in Publication Data:

Guthrie, A. B. (Alfred Bertram), 1901-
  These thousand hills.

  Originally published: Boston : Houghton Mifflin ;
Cambridge, Mass. : Riverside Press, 1956.
  1. Large type books. I. Title.
[PS3513.U855T45 1984]   813'.52   84-16202
ISBN 0-89621-576-8 (lg. print)

Large Print edition available through arrangement with
Houghton Mifflin Company.

Cover design by Holly Hughes.

To
Theodore Morrison

No man of our day can write about the West of
the 1880's without reading about it. If he is
very lucky, as I have been, he may remember
vestiges of that vanished period and he may
have friends among the few aged old-timers
who will help fill him in.

For me there was Teddy Blue Abbott, whose
life story as taken down by Helen Huntington
Smith is one of the very best of the cowpuncher chronicles; there was Con Price, who
wrote two wonderfully humorous and right
stories about Montana; there was Charlie
Russell, the artist, sculptor and storyteller, and
there was also James Willard Schultz, the white
Indian of still older experience. There were
these and other old-timers, living and dead,
published and unpublished, from whom I have
borrowed again and again. I am immensely in-
debted to them, as I am to the Montana State
Historical Society, whose staff members have
been ever helpful.

Part One

1

These three old men would sit and smoke and let a word fall and pause to hear the echoes of it as if they owned all time to speak their little pieces in.

Lat Evans shifted his seat on the ground, finding patience in the thought that their talk didn't matter now, and looked off to where dusk was putting a dull shine on the river. It was good and lonely water once, the Umatilla was, before people had begun coming in to spoil it, bringing plows to rip up pastures and cattle to graze ranges already overgrazed and sheep to make affairs still worse. That was the trouble with all Oregon, here and elsewhere even more — too many people, too much stock, too many homestead claims, and so wild life was disappearing and cows were poor in flesh and price, and streams ran tame and clouded. Some cattle ranchers talked of spaying all their she stuff.

"We came to Oregon in 'forty-five, and none of us was ever sorry for it." Pa spoke as if he'd never said the same before, as if by saying it again he held tighter to a thought he didn't want to lose. He sat on a block of wood like the other two men, an elbow resting on his cocked knee, the upheld hand fixed to his pipe.

It came to Lat, looking at him, that he might be seeing him for the first time now that he himself was about to say goodbye. Here, under the burden of leave-taking, Pa was all concern and sadness and unsaid love, and it was these that counted, not the fits of sternness, not the hard and sudden angers that no one could explain and no son aged twenty keep on living with. It was a wrench to watch him, to feel the slow eyes turned between the bits of talk and see them drop before the fact. Pa's face was lined and old, though at fifty-odd he wasn't really old. It was struggle, it was struggles of some kind or another that made him look that way. It was the hard times of the last ten years. He would have done better, maybe, if he hadn't tried his hand at ranching, if he had stayed on the Willamette, a grower of fruits and berries and small grains, on land that he and Grandpa staked in those first years. But the Lord knew best. That was what he said. Always the Lord knew best. The Rock. The

Salvation. Ma said so, too.

Lat turned to Grandpa and then to Colly on his left, wondering if, as in the case of Pa, he'd ever really noticed them before. In the growing dark Grandpa's beard shone white as a duck's tail. The eyes that were just pockets of shadow in this light would be misty or vacant, as they often were now, though people still called him Senator and listened to him out of old respect. Colly was a couple of bones in an old shirt and worn pants. He couldn't clamp on to his pipe, not having teeth that matched, and so kept a finger curled around the stem. He looked too scrawny to hunt the hills for gold.

Pa sucked on his pipe and took it from his mouth and sighed. "It's so far from anything."

Colly asked, "Like what?"

"Like any kind of order. Like civilization."

A grin made a crooked half-moon out of Colly's mouth. "Oregon wasn't so goddam civilized when you whoaed up."

Lat felt Pa stiffen at the curse. Few but Colly would have dared it. He felt himself stiffen on account of Pa. In that discomfort they were silent.

Sunday school. Church. Prayer meeting. Bible reading. Grace. No working on the Sabbath, except what couldn't be avoided. No play. No card playing, ever. No dancing and no

13

drinking. The Lord was a jealous Lord. And Pa was a jealous father, a jealous lord himself, who, like the Lord, had kind and sunny moments made dearer by comparison.

You couldn't figure Pa. You couldn't know what made him stormy one time and peaceable the next. You couldn't tell ahead what little things might set him off. Ma said he was always sorry afterwards, that never a night did he go to sleep without apologizing if he had been unreasonable. So you loved him and you kind of hated him, and you had to get away.

It wasn't just this last case that had done it, though it stood big in mind. It was the sum of things. It was the grim and unaccountable commandments of the years, it was the losses of temper, the dark angers; inside yourself it was the overhanging feeling of uneasiness around him, of uneasiness and even fear, which, being fear, you had to fight against, which you had to deny sometimes by going against his rules. Like slipping to that dance two weeks ago and drinking whiskey and coming home to find Pa up and ready for a rampage.

"Disgraceful!" Pa had ended up in that flat voice that made the stomach sick. "No excuse at all! Get to bed! I'll talk to you in the morning when you're not under the influence."

It wasn't whiskey that answered. He hadn't

had enough of that. It was all the sores coming to one head at last. "No, you won't! I'm leaving here, and you can't hold me."

There was that moment of will against scared will. Pa's spaced words broke it. "The next thing you know!" He turned and marched upstairs but halted at the landing and turned back, his face as bleak as stone. "Go then! But remember, the next thing you know!" He went on up.

The next thing you know? Temptation. Weakness. Transgression. Sin. Sins. The dark and secret sins that lowered even Pa's voice and haltered the words of warning he had tried before to give.

Sin or no sin, it was time to light out, right now, but for a moment he had waited, hearing upstairs the rumble and under-breath of conversation and then Ma's tread on the steps.

She came down in her wrapper, seeming smaller than he knew her, around her face and eyes such lines of burden as to squeeze the heart. It struck him before she reached his arms that she was always burdened, all her brave and smiling life, burdened by Pa, by the crazy moods of Pa, burdened by anxiety, by the steady need to soothe and talk sense to him and keep the household happy as she could.

She pressed her head against his chest and

15

said, "Please, son," and he broke out, "I don't know why you put up with him!"

Her voice was a little cry. "No! No! You don't know what you're saying. He loves us. That's what you have to understand. Above everything he loves us, and we love him."

"Just the same—"

She didn't let him finish. "It's all right for you to go. He knows so, too. It's best maybe, we think, now you're almost twenty-one. But don't leave home mad! Don't break away! We couldn't live here after all we've stood for, all the things we thought were right. We couldn't look people in the face. He loves you. Try to understand." The words came on a rush of breath.

"If he'll be reasonable," he said, but she was crying now, and he blinked against his own tears and felt his will and anger melt almost to nothing. "I have to go, though."

"Yes," she said and pressed him close. "Son. Son."

Here, seated on the ground, listening to idle talk, he felt himself wrenched again. He shook that other time out of his head. "I'm not sorry we came to Oregon," he told the men for lack of something better.

"Sorry?" Grandpa chuckled. "You wasn't even born yet." He kept on chuckling, finding

16

some humor there that the others missed.

Grandpa Evans had been a man to remember before time played its slow trick on his wits. Grandma Evans, too, though she was dead and dim in memory. No one had much to say about Ma's parents, McBee by name. They'd quit the trail to Oregon in 'forty-five and traipsed off to California and there apparently been lost; but Ma couldn't be what she was if they hadn't been people to remember, too.

When no one was talking Lat could hear the little whine of the mosquitoes that pestered him and Pa. The others didn't seem to mind. He imagined Grandpa was too old and leathery and Colly too dried up to draw a bite. A light blossomed inside the house and sent a beam out the window, blinding him to the twilight shine of the river.

"For all that Lat's going, we got things nice here," Pa said, not in the tone of argument. He hadn't argued since Ma had talked to him nor had he mentioned that one night, but had accepted with good grace and offered help and, helping, joshed around. "Neighbors are good people. God-fearing people, most of them. And our Indians here in Oregon aren't anything to worry much about, not since Chief Joseph's been shipped off."

"Brownie," Grandpa said to Pa, "you mind

17

the time the Sioux treed you on Independence Rock, and you just seventeen years old?"

Pa paused to say, "I do so," as if here was a subject he'd never be allowed to forget. Then he went on. "Times can't be bad forever. Every road has a turn. We got things to be thankful for."

Colly quit sucking on his pipe. "All a man could want," he said and let the words hang there.

Again there was the silence and the mosquito hum and, overhead, the whistle of a wing. Out somewhere in the shadows, Tip, the half-hound, was snuffing through the grass. The stars were beginning to come out. One blinked east like a signal fire.

"Those Sioux were bad medicine," Grandpa said. "How many was there, Brownie?" He scratched his head. "I swear, my mind's not as long as a minute."

"Let's talk about Lat and the trip now."

"Lat?" Grandpa answered. "Why, Lat was named after Albert Gallatin, and Albert Gallatin was Treasurer under President Jefferson and President Madison and Commissioner to England after the War of 1812, and he did a lot for Oregon. Smart enough for them Britishers, you bet. Hadn't been for him, might not be any Oregon. I mind it like yesterday."

Colly looked at Pa and then at Grandpa, and Lat thought he saw a little twist at the edge of the broken mouth. "And now you got Oregon, which is all a man could ask. An' I bet there was people thought you was crazy leavin' Missouri back there in 'forty-five."

For a little while nobody answered, each one maybe wondering, like Lat himself, just what it was that Colly meant. Then Grandpa shrugged as if to get his mind away from Gallatin. "It was a movin' time," he said and stopped and said again, "A movin' time."

"For you." Colly spoke more to Pa than to Grandpa.

Grandpa went on. "We was young then, and so was the country. A man likes to grow up with the country. And when he gets growed up, he likes the country growed up, too." The old voice stopped, letting the old mind think on the words. "Or maybe he does or maybe he don't. Some ways one way, some ways t'other. But it was a movin' time."

Colly said, "For you," again, but Grandpa had sunk into himself, thinking of those young days on the trail or maybe thinking of nothing at all.

Pa picked up the talk with Colly. "It beats all. Once we couldn't get west fast enough, nor far enough. What'd we want with places like

Nebraska or Wyoming, not to make mention of Montana that's worse yet to hear tell it?"

Colly gave Lat his broken smile, saying by it that they knew things Pa didn't see.

Pa sighed. "We been such a close family," he said in the way of someone talking to himself. "The Lord saw fit to take our first two young'ns, and then Lat came, late, and I guess we overdone it. He's past twenty." His voice trailed off.

Lat put his hand out and laid it on Pa's knee. "Pa, you take on so, like we'd never see each other."

Pa sighed and didn't answer, but it was as if the current of his love ran strong and clear, unmuddied by his bile. Ma was right. The love had always been there, often clouded over, sometimes shining out, but always there. Remember, for one instance, how Pa smiled when someone said his son took after him. For that matter, love from each to each, seen at this time and prized as not before. A person had to be himself at last, but it was a proud, supporting thing to know his father was a man, a poor man maybe but so solid in his ways, so upright in the sight of men that men looked up to him. A person had to be himself, but it was hard to go.

Colly said, "Lat'll do all right."

"That don't worry me," Pa answered. "He's bound to."

Grandpa was snoozing on his block, snoozing the light, frail sleep of age that was close to sleep itself. His head would bob, and he would straighten, half awake, and look to find out where he was and then begin to sag again.

"She's cold as the nose on a froze dog." Colly changed the subject as he turned to Lat. "Not like here, and you can bet your boots on that."

"I don't mind cold."

"And when you think it can't get any colder or stay cold as it is without puttin' hell out of business, then maybe a warm wind, a chinook, starts puffin' from the mountains, and glory be!" Colly broke off for a minute. "Might be something in that for a cattleman."

"What?"

"Closer the bone the sweeter the meat, that's all. Put your brain to it," Colly said, and Lat knew he was grinning to himself and wouldn't give a better answer. He might have put more questions even so, but there was the sound of a horse's hoofs out in the front and then the barking of the dog, the whine of the yard gate, the jingle of spurs. A figure grew out of the dark.

Lat got up. "It's you, isn't it, Mr. Butler?"

"Right, suh." Mr. Butler gave good evening

21

to the others. He was a big man but not fat, seeming even bigger in the dark than Lat remembered him by day, a man big and businesslike for all his soft-voiced slur. He wore a wider hat than people did in Oregon. The blacker shadow on his hip would be a gun. "If you all will pahdon me for interuptin'," he said and turned to Lat, "we'll staht at foah in the mawnin'."

"That's fine."

"Got my business tidied up. Just wanted to tell you."

"I'll be ready. This is my father, and Mr. Collins there, and my grandfather."

Grandpa had woke up. He put out his hand. Mr. Butler shook with him and the others.

"Set, won't you?" Pa said, getting up so Mr. Butler could have his seat. "We been talking things over. Lat, he's never been on a drive before, you know."

"Thankin' you, but foah comes early." Mr. Butler spread his hand toward Lat. "He'll make out."

"If you want a rider, put him on a bronc," Colly said.

Lat told Colly, to hush him, "They'll all be good riders."

"He's fair, all right," Pa had to put in. "Can't keep him off of horses. Never could."

"That's good." Mr. Butler spoke as if he'd have to see. "I reckon we can accommodate him. We have some broncs at Boise with the cattle. Thing now is to reach theah."

"Two hundred miles or more," Pa said. "You'll set out right away, I mean from Boise?"

"I'm hopin' so. The boys should have the cows all gathe'ed and road-branded."

Grandpa stirred himself to say, "Watch them British at Fort Boise."

"There's no British there now, Pa, nor no fort, either. You're thinkin' on another time," Pa answered.

"Oh," Grandpa said. He might have been ashamed. "Yes. I s'pose so."

Mr. Butler looked at Lat. "I'll be waitin' theah in town."

"All right."

"Plenty room for you here," Pa said. "Why don't you take the night with us?"

"I'm right thankful, but my plundah's all in Pendleton. I'll say good night." Before he turned and made off to the jingle of his spurs he bobbed his head at Lat. "In the mawnin', then."

Over east, the signal star still blinked.

23

2

They were five days on the trail before they swam the Snake and half a morning more before they reached the trail herd gathered outside Boise City, five days of long and steady going, backwards along the road that Pa and Grandpa had helped grind out so long before — from Pendleton up into the Blues and down into the hole of the Grande Ronde and on through Baker City and to the river breaks.

Mr. Butler had been waiting in the lifting dark, his saddle horse saddled and his pack horse packed, when Lat rode into Pendleton with is own gear lashed on board a mule that Mr. Butler had provided when they had made their deal. "Mawnin', theah," he said and mounted and shook himself before heading out. "Cows and conscience is two things that don't allow for sleep." His eyes swept over Lat's outfit.

The gear was little enough but still enough.

It consisted of a blanket roll, some underwear, a change of pants and shirt, socks, red bandannas, a reefer for the chill of mountain nights. These, along with a razor, a comb, a chunk of soap and two towels, Lat had loaded on the mule, after wrapping in the middle the Colt revolver that Pa had surprised him with and Ma had pleaded with him not to wear because accidents would happen.

"Why, Mother, a man needs a gun," Pa had said and winked at Lat as if to say they both knew the gun would come out once Ma was lost to sight.

Outside the pack, tied behind his saddle, he had a yellow slicker and an old suit coat and, strapped below the horn, a sea-grass lariat. These were all except the clothes he wore — the pants of California cloth, the blue wool shirt, the scuffed-up chaps that might become too hot before the day was done, the spurs, the open vest, the too small, too soft hat of belly gray. The list ticked through his mind while Mr. Butler looked.

Mr. Butler nodded and heeled his horse, and they creaked into motion, away from the sleeping settlement, along a road left pocked and rutted by the travel which had followed the heavy flood of spring. Nowhere was any sound except the squeak of leather and the scratch of packs and nowhere any lights except the shineless coming-on of day.

Up the long climb to the Blues the thought kept dodging in that he didn't look the cow-puncher, not with his worn-out piece of saddle and his little hat and old, cheap boots. He should have strapped the Colt around him, though people mainly didn't carry arms in Oregon. But it had been hard enough to say goodbye without saying no to Ma, hard enough to listen to Pa's reading of Psalm Twenty-Three and Ma's little prayer last night. It had been hard enough, at the extra-early breakfast she was bound to fix, to see her anxious eyes above the mouth she made to smile, to listen to the little jokes Pa cracked to cover up.

Grandpa had made things easier. He had heard the sounds of breakfast and got out of bed, dotty from age and lack of sleep but excited by the goings-on, and sung out of tune but word for word an Oregon song remembered from old times.

Then hip-hurrah for the prairie life!
Hip-hurrah for the mountain strife!
And if rifles must crack, if swords we must
    draw,
Our country forever, hurrah! hurrah!

26

He had beamed, and they had smiled at him, relieved to have this little thing to smile about.

It was time to go then, and they went out to the horse and mule, and Pa, who couldn't afford a gun as a gift but had bought one just the same, extended his hand. "God bless you, boy!" With his lower teeth he worked for an instant at his upper lip. "You'll do all right. You'll make a name for yourself one day." One corner of his mouth smiled. "We know that, naturally."

"God bless you, Pa!" Lat said and shook fast with Grandpa and gave a quick, blind kiss to Ma and climbed aboard. Not till they couldn't see his face did he turn around to wave.

Climbing to the Blues with Mr. Butler now, he couldn't bring Ma into focus. She was just mist and gentleness and a kind mouth begging him to take along more truck — clothes and blankets, medicines, a pillow for his head.

The day got up slowly, as if it didn't like to face itself. First there was the dull flush and then a band of red in the east and then the eye of the sun half open above a bank of clouds. Mr. Butler had gone along humming to himself or whistling low while Lat rode by his side, the road being more than wide enough for two. By and by he quit his humming. His gaze swung over, to the beat-up saddle and to the runty hat.

He nodded slowly. "Fancy tackle makes tom-fools," he said.

"How's that?"

"Give a boy a new hat and pretty leatheh an' he spends his time alookin' at his shadow on the grass. Can't spot a down cow on account he's struttin' in his head with the girls in Dodge or Abilene." He looked off into the distance as if he might be seeing them himself. "Girls like Roundup Rose or Oklahoma Annie – or anyone of a passel that's obligin'." As his gaze came back he gave one of his rare smiles. "You wouldn't know as yet, I reckon."

"This saddle isn't much, but I'm used to it."

Mr. Butler nodded. "It's your tail on it, boy. Us Texans ain't strong for a single cinch, likin' double rigs, but tastes got a right to diffeh." He was silent for a while and might have been turning the thought over in his head, but when he spoke it was to say, "That hoss you got, now?"

"Chief's old all right, but steady."

"Not faultin' him, but mostly it ain't good when a trail hand has his own. Means he can quit because of any piddlin' reason and hightail it to town wheneveh he's a mind to. Means he might be easy with the hoss he owns himself and fag the string that ain't his."

"You ne'en to worry about that."

"I reckon not." Mr. Butler let the words out

28

quietly, as if here was a subject met and settled.

They camped that night on the east slope of the Blues, near where the Grande Ronde River slowed for its journey through the hole, and ate a chunk of meat from Mr. Butler's pack and bread baked in a frying pan tilted up to face the fire. Before they went to bed Mr. Butler said to call him Ram like everybody else. "Ram for Ramrod," he said while he looked into the fire. The fire picked up his forehead, nose and thrust of chin, leaving in shadow the twin nooks of his eyes and the twin lines that edged his mouth. "You know ramrod means trail boss." He flicked a twig into the little blaze. "In standin', it's a little up from sheep dog." He paused again. "One of these days I'll buy some cows my own self and settle down to ranchin', God and all the little godalmighties willin'."

Never before had he spoken of himself, never opened up at all, and Lat kept silent, shy to answer, for it was as if the distance that divided them was shortening. It was as if this knowing, older man found something in a greenhorn.

Ram climbed to his feet. "Mawnin'll be on time, barrin' a miracle," he said.

Lying in bed, hearing the steady crop and crop and now and then a sneeze of the stock they'd tethered in the mountain grass, Lat jumped the years. Like Ramrod, he'd own cat-

29

tle, and by the thousands, and have range for them in the new land of Montana, and men would come to him to ask advice, all brands and breeds of men, including some who wouldn't go to Pa; and Pa would smile a proud, small smile, since he hadn't done as well, and say, "We knew it from the first, son," and Ma would bake an apple pie, remembering how he had loved it before he fared so high, and Grandpa would break into a song.

He went to sleep thinking of Grandpa and Pa and Ma and Ram and cattle branded LAT and men filing to his door to find out how he thought, and when he met them he was Ram himself, with all the green rubbed off.

Fair weather favored them, favored them and the emigrants they passed who were wheeling on to Oregon or Washington from Kansas or Nebraska or other eastern states. Some of the emigrants drove oxen and others mules or horses, and some trailed cattle that showed milk and Durham strains. One outfit had hitched a saddle horse and steer to a cranky wagon that a hatch of young ones chirped around. How far? the drivers asked. How far to towns they could call home? How far? How far? As if getting there was all that mattered. As if these final miles brought tears at night when all the camp was sleeping and nothing lived to take the mind

30

off reaches lying ahead.

But still these people had it easy compared to older times. A road so wide and plain a man could follow it at night. Soldiers here and there. No Indians much to guard against except for petty thievings. The Sioux were scattered, those that hadn't given up. The Shoshones liked the whites, or anyhow put up with them. So far he and Ram had seen just some Umatillas, who were fairly tame these days and didn't range too far from their reservation there by Pendleton. Eighteen-eighty wasn't eighteen forty-five.

They had it easy sure enough, these later travelers, had it easy until the very last when they would find not milk and honey the land they strained for now. It never had been, for that matter, else Pa would have some money, wouldn't he? Else Ma could fix and prettify the house like she'd always wanted to and like she would in time, for he was back home now, after stirring years away, and his hand was in his pocket, and he was saying to Ma, "Do everything you want, Ma, and in the way you want it. Money is no object." And, standing by, Pa seemed shaken in his belief that it was hard for a rich man to enter the Kingdom of Heaven.

These westbound men need have no worry on that score. They'd find the good soil taken up, the ranges worked, cabins here and there and yonder, the cows and sheep they drove at so much pains not worth the trailing, and no grass to feed them on to boot. So the last would be the worst, the measly answer to the toilsome hope.

"You got it wrong, a little anyway," Ram said after they had passed a train of four ramshackle wagons. "It's new land to 'em and so won't be a come-down for a spell. Most folks don't like to stick. What's yondeh beats what's nigh."

"But still?"

"It's only by and by that what they left looks good, and then because it's wheah they ain't."

"But what's in Oregon?"

"It's Lat's eyes lookin', boy. They'll see things different."

How, then, as they rode along, did things appear to Ram, the things they both could see, the Powder and Burnt rivers, the dusted sage, the roll of hills, the camping place at Farewell Bend where the Snake bulged out to touch the trail? Stretch the idea far enough, and what was one thing to one set of eyes might be opposite to others, like hills and valleys. And if no eyes saw it? But common sense could tell when land was crowded and unpromising, or green and open, waiting to make cattle fat.

Ram pulled leftward from the trail and took it slow along the river side, his gaze measuring the stream which here ran almost level with its banks. It looked wide and green and full of purpose.

"Some folks would hunt a ferry, but me, I love to spend my money on impo'tant things," Ram said. He checked his horse. "This, now, looks good enough. See that landin' place downstream? And it ain't all swimmin' wateh."

He sat quiet for a minute while he gauged the crossing, then slowly began to unbuckle his cartridge belt. "You a swimmah?"

"Fair."

"How about the hoss?"

"Never swam him that far."

"All right, likely. It's them thin-backed, steppy hosses can't swim for drowndin'."

With his cartridge belt Ram took a wrap around his saddle horn, then made sure his revolver was cased safely. Lat did the same. As he finished, Ram said, "If the hosses swim too low, we can grab fo' the artillery an' hold it up."

They swung off then and took off boots and chaps and stuck them under the lashings of the packs. "Good thing to loosen up the cinches, too." Ram began on his. "Swimmin', any animal needs breath to keep him floatin'."

Mounted again, the horses took to the river

without too much urging, stepping out and holding up to drink and then going on with little snorts while the water rose and swelled against them. Ahead, Ram bent forward in the saddle and brought his feet up high behind. His horse lined neck and head out and changed gaits, from a shambling walk among the boulders to the gentle single-foot of swimming. Ram's pack horse pulled against the lead rope, and Lat used his rein ends on his rump, and he cast off, the light pack riding high. Then Lat's Chief was swimming, and after him the mule, pointing upstream like Ram's two and, like them, being carried down. Ram kept glancing back, his face serene but watchful, too.

There was nothing to it, no need to slide off in the water and hang to tail or saddle leather. Just hunch ahead and keep as dry as possible and watch the Colt and hold the horse on course and let him do the work.

The horses found bottom and climbed for shore and pulled out streaming at the spot that Ram had sighted from the other side.

Ram vaulted off, to keep from getting wetter than he was, and knocked his unprotected toe against a rock. He hopped around, holding the toe with both hands and cutting loose with curse words that would have stiffened Pa. "Somethin' in nature got it in for a man," he said as the pain eased. "Damned ambusher, that's what she is."

"She's a goddam son-of-a-bitch, all right," Lat answered. The words came out unnatural, but Ram didn't seem to notice.

"It ain't half a ride to wheah the cows is at, but s'posin' we find a tidy place and take the night." Ram began getting back into his rigging. "Be late by the time we get to camp, and the cook asleep and red-assed if we woke him up to get a bite. Them two wild chickens we shot should be just right for us."

They hadn't far to look. Upstream a hundred yards they found firewood and handy water and good grass and a bald spot by some trees to roll their beds on.

It seemed to Lat he'd hardly put his head down, hardly filled himself and stretched out and sunk deep in sleep before Ram was cracking branches for the breakfast fire. He swam awake and floated on the surface. The sky had darkened and the stars dimmed out, as if they knew they couldn't hold a candle to the coming sun. The campfire played its little licks of light against a tree trunk. Overhead, leaves he didn't see whispered to a touch of air he didn't feel.

"Mawnin', boy," Ram said. It was as though he knew exactly when Lat came awake. He put more wood on the blaze he'd started. "Best eat a bait and get to movin'."

It was full daylight but cool yet with the night's dew drying on the grass when they spied the cattle grazing outward from the river and, farther off but closer to the bank, two wagons and a tent shining in the long rays of the sun. All around was good feed, untouched by the gaunted livestock of the pilgrims whose road passed to the north. Two riders watched the grazing herd range out. Close by the wagons, blurred in the distance, was a swirl of movement and of color. "They still got the hosses up," Ram said and dallied the packhorse rope around his saddle horn and heeled into a trot.

The swirl grew into horses, fenced in by lariats strung from front and back wheels of the coupled wagons and held by men on foot who kept them twitching so's to discourage any breakthrough. The open side was closed by other men who swung rope ends to keep the bunch inside. A couple of horses, saddled but riderless, had been turned loose and were nipping at the graze. Beyond the buldge of the forward wagon, half out of sight, a man was tying up another.

Ram raised a hand to the men who weren't too busy to watch him. "Hold 'em," he said to one and rode on to the rear and the cook fire around which three others stood. "How? Any coffee left? And how's the troops of the Potomac?"

A small, lean man with crinkles around his eyes spoke up. "Takin' things in order – How? Ask Sally. And war is hell." He spat and grinned. "Knew you'd be ahead of yourself, but you ain't caught us settin'. We got the cows all trail-branded and shoes on some of the cayuses."

"Good." Ram slid down from his horse. Lat got off, too. Ram wagged a thumb at him. "It's Lat Evans here. From Pendleton. He's goin' along."

The men nodded shortly, while Lat waited for Ram to name their names. The middle one, standing back behind the fire, he guessed was cook, for he carried a paunch and wore suspenders and had a dab of dried dough above a scraggly mustache. The third, off a little to the right, looked like an ordinary hand, but extraordinary because his eyes and mouth were extra small and smaller yet by contrast with his length of face. It passed through Lat's mind that nature could have staked more ground for them and had a better layout.

The little man stepped forward, smiling, and held out his hand. "Ram don't know my name. It's Carmichael, Mike Carmichael."

"I know the name all right," Ram said. "It's

the face I couldn't place." His eyes showed he was funning. "Mostly, you can't tell wheah you'll meet it at." He glanced at Lat, then pointed to the paunchy man behind the fire. "The cook goes by the name of Sally when he don't get ringy and demandin'. Then it's Jacob Schmidt."

Sally didn't come around to shake. He said without smiling, "Just don't kick your goddam dust into my makin's, Evans, like some I could spit on, and don't bellyache about the grub, and we'll team up all right."

Lat nodded. "All right."

Ram turned to the man with the squinched eyes and squinched mouth. "And you, suh?"

Before the man could answer, Carmichael spoke up. "I was gettin' around to that. Meet Mooman, Harvey Mooman." They shook hands. Carmichael went on. "He's lookin' for a place, and I asked him to hang around just on the chance." His gaze swung over to Lat.

"I thought, with Evans, we'd make out, Mike."

"Full crew then?" Mooman asked.

Ram spent a minute thinking. "You a rider?"

"I ain't walkin'."

"I mean a man can stick the real rough ones? We got fo'ty broncs or so to gentle."

Mooman looked at the ground. "In my time I guess I got my guts shook up enough, not meanin' I won't take my string as it comes."

"Well?" Ram said and fingered his chin. "Nobody's quit, Mike?"

"Nope."

Mooman said, "I'll mosey on then."

"No need to busy away," Ram told him. "Let's have some coffee, and me'n Evans got to pick a string for him."

Each poured his coffee from the giant, blackened pot. Seeing Ram let himself down and sit cross-legged on the ground, Lat did so, too.

From yon side of the forward wagon had come a tapping and now and then a "Whoa, there!" and now there stepped around the rear a man about of Lat's age, a dark-skinned man with blue-black roots of beard on jaw and chin and a forelock like a crow's wing fallen from underneath his pushed-back hat. "For shoein' horses," he said to all, "a man should get a medal."

"It'll be a horseshoe, and we'll tack it on youah face to keep that nose from bruisin'," Ram answered. "The trails you take, you need protection. Howya, Tom? 'Bout through?"

"Howya, Ramrod? One to go, and I bet he'll be a double distilled son-of-a-bitch net."

"Meet Lat Evans here. Lat, Tom Ping."

Ping came over and put his hand out as Lat scrambled up. He took a long look. Then his heavy mouth spread in a smile that showed large, even teeth.

"A hossman, so I'm told," Ram went on. "He's j'ined us."

"Well, Jesus Christ and glory!" Ping said. " 'Bout time we had some young blood here to keep me company." His hand waved toward the other men as he spoke to Lat. "These old bastards are so dried up they don't know tit from tether or give a good goddam, what's worse. Most you can say for 'em is they've learnt their ass from a hole in the ground."

"Tom's ma never had to spank him to keep him from holdin' his breath," Carmichael said.

"The wind you blow! And it meant for the other end!"

"It ain't always this windy, Lat," Ram said and gulped his coffee and got up. "We'll unpack and then pick you a string."

He led the way around. They unloaded the pack horses and dumped the packs inside the bed wagon. Afterwards Ram said, "You might as well unsaddle and try one of the string." His eyes turned with a question in them. "Huh?"

"Sure."

"We'll just turn these hosses loose to graze,

40

except I'll keep my own up. I'll be needin' him directly."

Lat unsaddled and put the rigging down and untied his lariat. His six-gun would be a nuisance on board a bucking horse. He unbuckled it and stuck it in his bedroll.

The man at the rope corral had caught their horses up and were just idling while they kept the rest inside. The rest were solid colors mostly, and some looked good and some just middling and a few of them plain bad. Together, they added up to maybe seventy. The best of them, Lat figured, had come from Oregon. They were the largest and had better heads and feet and showed less of mustang blood. Good and bad bunched up, heads raised, eyes watchful for a chance to break around, as he and Ram stepped toward them.

"You bein' the last to join, youah string might be a little rough," Ram said. It was as much a question as a statement.

"That's all right." He was pretty used to rough ones, though maybe not so much so, nearly, as these older hands. Still, for Pa and neighbors, he'd ridden out a few.

"You want to try an unbroke, ornery one?"

"I guess so. Can't do more than pile me."

Ram gave a slow nod. "That knot-headed sorrel, he'll need a heap of breakin'. And the big

41

black with the blaze, they say he's broke to lead. The buckskin is the truck, a night hoss from away back, that I been keepin' from the boys." Ram went ahead to get the bunch to moving. "That Roman-nose bay, see?"

"I'll catch up the sorrel then, and the black?"

"Just try the sorrel now." Ram watched as Lat played out a little loop. Outside, others watched, too, men known and unknown, Tom Ping, Carmichael, Sally, more, most acting as if just idleness had brought them there.

The loop sailed clean and neat. The sorrel was halter-broke. He pulled up, snorting.

Lat took the horse outside and led him up and tied him to a wagon wheel, feeling eyes turned to him as he moved, the strange and not yet friendly eyes of men who wondered what his caliber might be, .22 or .45 or in-between or maybe only squirt gun. He got a glimpse of Ping, looking on with open interest, and then of Mooman, pulling on a cigarette that seemed to cork his mouth.

The sorrel disliked the bit and humped up as the saddle hit him but from the ground led out all right as Lat stepped him around to let him get the feel of things. Then, quickly, Lat swung up.

Two pitches, and he knew he'd stick. The bronc was strong but ignorant of tricks, a highpoler, not a gut-twister. All he knew was jump and thump, and these were not enough.

Not enough. Not near enough. Each jolt told him so. And then he was sailing, riding air, above the sorrel and to one side, with the saddle still between his legs. He landed hard and somersaulted, tangled with the leather, and got up shaken and looked down and saw the cinch had torn loose from one ring. He took the saddle by the horn and dragged it toward the fire, still feeling eyes upon him, reading in the men's fixed soberness of face an inner ticklement.

Ram said, "You hunkydory?"

"Yah. Another cinch around?"

"Extrys in the bed wagon. I'll catch that bronc back up." Ram made for his horse.

Tom Ping helped dig a cinch out, saying, "You had the bastard topped, weren't for that accident." The other men were drifting off.

Lat squatted by his saddle to undo the latigos. He was still working with the first one when he heard a snicker. Another and another followed. It was Mooman, letting loose with little choking brays that rounded out his bullet hole of mouth.

Tom Ping turned and took a step. "What's so goddam funny?"

Mooman's laugh died to a smile. His gaze

43

went to Ping as if he hadn't heard right. "Didn't he look comical, ridin' air?" Then his smile died, too, and his eyes slid away from Ping, and it hit Lat that the years had cheated him, not making him a sure man. "Didn't mean to het you up, or Evans, either."

"All right, Moo Cow," Tom said and moved toward Lat, "but I bet if he'd busted a leg, you'd've laughed your face off."

Lat said, "It doesn't matter."

Tom winked and spoke low. "Nope, but it just kind of r'iled me. Outsider bustin' his goddam gut. Stick together is my motto." He smiled. "Bein' as you're not hurt, it was kind of funny, you goin' ass over teakettle."

Lat said, "Yeah," and glanced up and saw Ram coming with the sorrel in tow. "Saddle's ready."

"Maybe you ain't feelin' like anotheh sashay," Ram said, pulling up.

"Why not?" Lat took the sorrel's reins and tied them to the wheel and swung the saddle on. Carmichael and the cook lagged up as he cinched and stepped back with the others as he boarded.

There was buck left in the sorrel, but again not near enough. Lat raked him hard. He kicked the last jump from him and wrenched him around and brought him back and got off.

"Good enough," Ram said.

"Except, by God, you'll have grit in your mulligan," the cook put in. "A man can't seem to climb a horse around here without one foot in the grub."

"Hush now, Sally!" Ram's gaze swung from Lat to Mooman. "Now a good-enough man could maybe fight them broncs and still do the day wranglin', or some of it, anyhow. A good-enough man. It ain't a job for weaklin's or wet ears. The pay would be the same as a top hand's."

"I ain't weak, and I'm weaned," Mooman said as if hurt pride demanded that much, "but you can look somewheres else."

Ram smiled easily. "I wasn't talkin' to you." His eyes came to Lat. "Would you accept? Mooman's out of office and will second the nomination so as to step into your boots."

"You think I can?"

Ram's hand reached out and rested on Lat's shoulder. His smile deepened the lines around his mouth. "We'll see, but I vote aye, and the ayes have it."

3

Carmichael dished himself some breakfast and sat down, feeling sleepy yet and dull. A man oughtn't to get up before the sun itself got up. Then he, for one, felt more like shining, even on hot, dry days like these they'd had. He'd remember as a story to be told, though, how Slim George Stevens lifted his sweat-dirty face and, sober as a sore-tailed judge, asked the noon sun yesterday, "Where the hell was you last January?"

At this hour most of the men were quiet or grumbling low in the manner of Old Oscar who had just said, "I'd like to waltz into the buzzard that put the name of fruit to prunes." Sally was busy at the pot rack frying sourdoughs and didn't hear him. Ram Butler got up and poured a cup of coffee. Unlike the seated men, who hadn't quite come to, the kid, Lat Evans, had finished up and was dragging in a chunk of wood for Cookie. Good kid, he seemed like.

Willing anyway. Busted out with kid's ambition. In the east the coming sun was kicking up red dust. Soon be time to line 'em out. Time now for the last watch to come in, and here came one of them, the flank man, Mexico.

Mexico rode up, not close enough to ruffle Sally, and got off and came over and helped himself at the pot rack, not speaking until he had let himself down. Then he said, "Calf out there."

Ram turned to him. "A calf!"

"Bull."

"A bull calf!"

"I got so I can tell a calf, he or she, pret' near every time."

"It's supposed to be dry stuff, all dry stuff."

"Wisht you'd told me," Mexico answered through a full mouth. "Too late now to shoo him back." He swallowed and grinned at Ram. "Want me to tell all them other big-bellied cows it ain't legal?"

Ram got up. Carmichael could feel his small and quick impatience with such nonsense. "All? It won't be funny if we slipped on many, eh, Carmichael?"

"I seen 'em closer'n you," Carmichael said. "Some I received when you was gone." He liked this Texan and maybe understood him. A conscientious man always was overloaded. He

47

gave a smile intended to be easy. "You got so many worries, Ram, you got to build up more. One cow with calf slipped in, that's all." He was a fairly conscientious man himself – which maybe was a reason he shied off from responsibility. Being Ram's second on the drive was a mite more than he cared for.

"I reckon so," Ram answered, nodding slowly. "Mexico, wheah they at?"

"North of the bunch a piece."

Ram sighed, still nodding, and patted his chaps with his fingertips. "Carmichael, you mind disposin' of the calf? I'll help get things movin'. Lat Evans can go with you."

"And neck the cow to a heavy steer, huh?"

"No. Not time now. Take the bed wagon and dump the calf inside. It'll keep all right today, and the cow'll follow. Tonight we'll neck her."

Carmichael lapped the last of his syrup and got up. "Ready young'n?" he said to Evans who had been standing close enough to hear. "I'll take the bed wagon. You come with a horse, a ropin' horse, not one of them catamounts you love to scratch."

It was a calf all right, a red-and-white, still-damp calf with the wide and trusting look of all new calves. It had found its feet and stood tottery by its ma, its licked hide catching gleams of light like silk. Carmichael whoaed the team and got down from the wagon and wrapped the reins around the hub. The cow tossed her head and let out a low bawl and licked the calf again. Carmichael waited by the wheel. Damn it, there was this chore to do, the common-sense, the ordered chore! Baby things died by thousands, didn't they?

"That cow won't be a barnyard pet," he said as Evans rode up. "Have to dab a rope on her."

Evans threw an easy loop and drew it tight and strained the cow off from the calf while she bucked against the line and threw her head, bawling through the choke of rope.

Carmichael went to the bed wagon and got out an axe. One little blow would do it, one tap between the newborn eyes. So would a shot, but the sound would reach the herd and just might spook them.

He walked over to the calf. The cow strangled out a bawl. The calf looked up at him and mouthed an unsure bleat. He raised the axe and let it down and rested on it with one hand on the handle while he spoke to Evans. "What was them orders, now? To dispose of the calf, wasn't it? Just to dispose of it?"

"That's what he said."

The kid didn't look in love with this deal, either, which set him up a peg. Kids could be awful cruel, crueler far than need be in a business cruel enough. "Dispose?" he said. "That could mean a pile of things. Means put away, don't it? And if I put the calf away in the bed wagon, ain't I disposed of it?"

He didn't need an answer. He scooped the calf up and carried it over and found a place for it. He walked back toward Evans then. "Let Ramrod do his own baby-killin'." He rubbed his moist hands on his shirt. "The cow'll be on the peck. You know the trick of gettin' off the rope? Ride fast around, circlin' her with your lariat, and pull away and down she'll go."

"Yes," Evans said and spurred his horse. With her front feet the cow cleared the circled rope, as Carmichael knew she would, but she couldn't clear behind. She thudded down, her hind legs yanked out from under. Evans jumped from his horse and ran up and slipped the noose from her neck and ran back and climbed aboard almost before she got untangled.

"Skookum," Carmichael said and edged back toward the wagon. She wasn't on the prod, though. She just went smelling for her calf.

For an instant Carmichael stood by the front wheel, wondering what Ram would say but not caring much. There were jobs and jobs.

Evans pulled up alongside and began to coil his rope.

"You know," Carmichael said, "the nighthawk might not like it, bein' the wagon is his day bed, but what's a little calf shit to a wrangler?"

From a rise a mile or so ahead of the herd, the point was all that Butler could make out, the lead cows and the riders at the sides and behind them nothing but a long, thick, creeping worm of lava dust. Here, looking back, a man could almost believe the leaders pulled the worm, as if hitched to it and bound forever to have it on their heels.

It was hell for men behind, hell for swing and flank and double hell for drag, and the riders would be riding masked by their bandannas but still the dust in mouths and noses, dust in ears and hair, on cheeks and lashes, dust powdered, layered, streaked by tears and slaver, dust in the deep-split lower lips that were better left unlicked.

Butler put a finger to his own, wishing it would heal, wishing axle grease or bacon grease or a leaf of chewing tobacco would cure it, as some believed before a trial. If anyone complained, the boys said to use the inside lining of an egg, and then they grinned their sore-mouthed grins, for who could come up with an egg? Eggs, States' or plain, were town and city

51

fare, and just the thought of one brought water to a man's mouth and made his split lip worse.

Well, to hell with hell. They'd seen the bigger part of it and made good time regardless — Camas Creek, Big Wood River and then this lava desert where, back a piece, they'd heard the earth's guts rumbling and sniffed at hot and cold air that its holes let out. To the sinks of Lost River then, to Birch Creek, to Mud Lake and on to Beaver Creek. Fair camps. Poor camps. Heat. Dust. Physic water. But things were all right just the same. Cattle trail-broke. Men in good spirits, cracking jokes, laughing though it hurt, singing to the herd or singing just to be singing, singing songs that stayed in the head, old songs, strange songs, bits of song that rolled around with thought.

> *Your grub is bread and bacon*
> *And coffee black as ink;*
> *The water is so full of alkali*
> *It's hardly fit to drink.*

Now, here, upstream on Beaver Creek, he could see the Tetons and the Rockies rising, rising clean and cool and snow-patched, purple in the purple distance. There the worm would die, there on the climb to Monida Pass, and they'd cough up this corruption and breathe air that wasn't two-thirds snot.

You will never get consumption
By sleeping on the ground.

He had to find a place to water and then a place to camp, but before going on he looked back of him again. The mess and bed wagons were rolling up, following the traveled trail from Salt Lake to Montana that they'd struck just north of Mud Lake. Behind them were two distant clouds of dust that he guessed were freighters' wagons or stages. This empty country had a railroad, too, that now and then he spotted, an uncompleted narrow gauge reaching for Montana. The saddle-horse band ranged to the west of the herd, a smaller, paler, not-so-dusty worm. That would be Lat Evans at the tail, hazing them along.

Butler clucked to his horse. He'd played in luck in rounding up a crew. Carmichael. Stevens. Mexico. Sally. The partners, Drury and Codell. All of them, even the two youngest, Ping and Evans, who tended to pair off because of age, different as they were except for it. Ping for a known fact could spot Evans a half a dozen years or more of rough experience — Texas, up the trail, here and yonder, getting educated fast, too fast maybe for the taste of

53

older men. He'd lost the greenhorn's eagerness to please, like by seeing things to do beyond his set job. Or was it just the greenhorn in Evans? The young wishing? Hard telling. People changed or got changed, by themselves and time or the little godalmighties. Might turn out one way, might another. Anyhow, that Evans sure as hell could ride.

> *My love is a rider,*
> *Wild broncos he breaks . . .*

Some day for the fun of it he'd tally all the little godalmighties. The men you met and what came of it. The way cards acted. The weather that could break you. The price of cows. The badger hole that threw your horse and got you tromped to death. The hankering that took you to a chippie that took you for your roll and maybe left a little something to remember her by. The friend you trusted. The way cards acted. Add them up and what did you have?

All the same, now that he was pressing thirty, he should be putting out some plans. By and by he'd quit this hiring out to others, this buying cows and driving them for men who sat at home and enjoyed the taste of liquor while he got wages and a cracked lip. Take this bunch of unbroke horses that he'd mostly gathered up

54

himself and wouldn't get a dime out of except maybe for a bonus that would last one night in town. He knew where he'd locate there in Texas. Just let those pasteboards act right once!

Ahead was a good-enough watering place, and it was now late afternoon. Best bring the cattle to the creek and let them get their fill and push on then two miles or more. That way, they'd be ready to bed down and not be waterlogy from drinking in the morning. Any damn fool knew that much, but some didn't.

He stood in his stirrups and twisted around and signaled with his hat and saw a point man answer, his movement like the moving feeler of the dust worm. He watched a little while to see that things were right and then turned back around and tapped his horse, hoping he could find a little grass to put the cattle on. The chances didn't look too good.

Out of the rolling in his head one of the scraps of song came to his lips, and his horse cocked back an ear to listen.

> *Come close to the bar, boys,*
> *We'll drink all around,*
> *We'll drink to the pure,*
> *If any be found . . .*

That would be Fort Benton, not sooner.

55

Camp near a town and not only did the damn town dogs worry the herd but most of the boys, including some of the best ones, got a big thirst on. They did even at trading posts where whiskey might be alcohol and water flavored with pepper or a plug of tobacco or soap to make the Indians sick and so show them they had drunk the real stuff. The trick was to dodge such places, as he had dodged a post called Junction, or to give orders when you couldn't, for whatever good they were. Boys would be boys. Not as you blamed them much. But you had to get a trail herd to Montana before snow closed the mountains. You had to meet a set time. Jubilate when you got there.

"Just amble to some feed," he said to his horse, and again the horse bent back an ear. "That's all we're needin' now." Just grass and rest. Just grub and easy sleep. The cows were in good shape. They hadn't stampeded even once. They'd made their twelve to fifteen miles a day and maybe even gained a little flesh. And they had cost per head just fifteen dollars!

He was a Texas man, and Texans stuck up for the long horns, but they were wrong. These Oregon cows, these hefty reds and roans were better. Carried more tallow, had more sense, handled quieter. Too tame, boys like Ping complained, forgetting how it was to turn a herd

56

that picked the dead of night to run in. On your horse then and after them, to the clatter of horns that you might not see at all, to thunder that rose out of the ground, drowning out the higher thunder that often caused a run. Watch out, hoss, watch out! Watch out for varmint holes and cut banks, watch out for rocks and stumble blocks, else what's left of us is hoof jam!

It wasn't likely that these cows would ever stampede now, not after being under herd so long and never in a run and quiet-natured to begin with. Around two thousand head of good mixed stuff, of steers and dry cows, plus a wet one. That's what they'd deliver at Fort Benton.

He could laugh at himself now. Back there he sure had climbed a nightmare, multiplying one calf into a hundred or a thousand and seeing the miles ahead and snow deep on the pass before young legs and anxious mas could cross. One calf? Calves? The Territory of Montana? He knew it for a crazy notion then, but still he couldn't shake it.

The one calf was a fact, though, and for once he'd wished for Indians, for the draggle-tailed root-diggers who had begged for beef before. They would have liked it fine. Heap good, this pale flesh, soft as jelly yet. With the calf knocked in the head, there was still the goddam cow. She would bawl her jaw off and keep seeking, always seeking, breathing at the tailgate until the carcass was pitched out and then straining back and trying to turn, necked to a steer that dragged her on.

A sure-fire, all-round nuisance, that's what she would be, and more so when they got her necked and she balked against the rope. That's what she was that first day. She trailed the wagon close, mooing, mooing, looking, smelling, her bag swinging to her steps. A damn squaw grieving couldn't beat her bawl and bawl. A good mother, if something in her favor must be said. Worth all of fifteen dollars, too much to put an end to or to leave behind. She could bawl then! She could whiff and seek and stumble in her hurry! Montana left no time for birthings.

He hadn't seen much of her then, but noon and morning were enough. The job of trail boss in uncertain country kept the boss out front. Let her bawl!

All day that way, and then he had found a fair bed ground and signaled back and ridden back while the wagons with the cow behind rolled on to set up camp.

When he rode in with the boys, Sally had supper on the way. Jerome, the nighthawk, his sleep finished, had climbed down from the bed wagon and was rolling up a smoke. Old Oscar had tended to his team. The riders swung off one by one and just stood there as if no chores were left to do. The cow nosed at the tail of the bed wagon, nosed and bawled and bawled and nosed. After a day of it, a man would think she'd lose her voice.

"We'll neck that cow now," Butler said.

No one moved.

"What's trumps here? Someone tell me."

It was Carmichael who had answered, on his face a little asking smile. "I went accordin' to my definition, Ram. Dispose, you said."

"I don't get this loco talk."

"We named him Slips," Jerome put in. "Doin' smart, too. He didn't need to add, "Just listen!" The feeble blat from the bed wagon spoke for itself.

They looked at Butler, all of them, like men waiting a decision, like hopeful men, and the fact dawned on him as he glanced from face to face. They wanted the calf to live. They would go to the time and trouble of nursing it along, each of them, Carmichael, Jerome, Oscar, Evans, others. The fools! The crazy fools! A crazy little flood ran in him.

He unforked his horse. "Thing now is to get him with his ma," he said.

Looking back, it hadn't been at all bad. He'd

done all right, that Slips. Got so he could travel some and not be always in the wagon, though Jerome seemed actually to like him there. Regular pet he was, a little boost to tired spirits.

Ahead now was some grass, a place to bed on that was as good as any they would find this day. Time to call a halt, too, to let the cattle rest, to make a fire and burn some mulligan and give the calf a chance to suck.

Butler reined his horse around and waved a circle with his hat to show this was the spot. The wagons had speeded up as suppertime drew near and weren't more than two rifle shots away. A breeze was tattering the lava worm. Lat Evans, riding some jug-head bronc, had brought the horses close. Good enough. Good enough.

You'll be rounded up in glory by and by.

4

Lat Evans lay on his back, putting off for a moment the business of getting up and stepping away from his bed. He guessed it must be nearly midnight, for he could hear the cattle stirring. The moon was right for midnight, too, being a hand span west of plumb. Any minute now he'd be routed out for the twelve-to-two watch that had fallen to him when they drew straws last. Not much use to go back to bed once he'd got up, though he ached for sleep. Fourteen hours on the trail and then a two-hour watch, and no one got rest enough. Carmichael had said all he wanted at the end of the line was six solid months in the soogans.

He sat up. The mountains they had trailed through stood to westward, silver-purple in the moonlight. North and east was one long shine of land, leading to the Shonkin and the Musselshell and other ranges maybe still unnamed. He shivered a little, not from cold, shivered a good shiver while he waited for his need to prod him up.

The chuck wagon, its tongue pointed toward the North Star that the moon had since drowned out, bulged pale against the western slopes. The lantern hanging from the tongue was a ground star to guide the night shifts in. Underneath the wagon was a hump that would be Sally, for in these fine days they didn't pitch a tent for him — Sally maybe dreaming of the time he needn't cook. Out from the gray-coal fire the other sleepers lay, their bodies under cover making mounds like newly spaded graves. The night horses, staked out or tied up to the bed wagon, drowsed on their feet. One of the men — Moo Cow, it was — was snoring a long, hard, worn-out snore. Out of that little mouth so much, like a calf out of a heifer. Off somewhere a coyote lifted a call that was answered somewhere, distant as the echo of an echo. A cow lowed and another and another. By listening hard a man could hear the splash and plop the herd made before settling back to rest. He could catch the soft singing of the men on guard, the cavvy jingle in the sleepy distance where the nighthawk would be napping in his saddle.

There were these sounds and over them a silence that was a sound itself, a ringing in the ears that might be time or distance or wind around the moon. Or the breath of prayer from loved ones far away and too often lost to mind. Poor Ma, who'd worked so hard. Poor Pa, too, high in the right but low in worldly goods. At this distance, in this freedom, Pa's moods went for nothing against the total size of him. So little had the pair had and yet stood stout, and so little now was left. Nothing much except himself and the hopes they pinned on him and he would satisfy, God willing, the kind God there who rode the moon. He'd show Pa yet!

He rolled out of bed and stood up. Maybe the cows hated to get up, too, though they had the best of it, being always ready-dressed. How would they feel in skin feet and underwear for hides?

By accident he brushed a shrub, and, off a little toward the wagon, Tom Ping came alive in his covers, the black head rearing up and one hand feeling for the old Sharps that he always took to bed.

"Just me," Lat said, low-voiced so's not to wake the rest. He walked a little further and unbuttoned and let go and, seeing Tom still sitting, stepped that way.

"That damn moon!" Tom said.

"What's wrong?"

"Injun moon." Tom scowled up at it as if to put it out. "You ain't never seen Comanches, but just let the moon shine bright —" The thought made him silent, the thought perhaps of other nights down south and the sky lit up and then the sudden, fierce, hi-yi of Indians, and the earth-pound of the running herd.

"Oregon is all I know."

"Hmm. I come up from Texas ten years ago first time. Just a cub, o' course, and scared like blue be-Jesus." His eyes left the moon and fixed on the hump that was Moo Cow. "We used to fight shy of a snorin' gent. He'd give away your camp to a dead Comanche out of hell. I even knowed a man the law caught up with just by his pardner's snore."

Lat waited to see if he was done. "Tom," he said then, "what you aiming to do when this job's done?"

It always took Tom a little while to face a change of subject. "Why." he answered, grinning, "find me a woman. What you aim to do? Squirt on the moon?"

"I don't mean that."

"I s'pose it ain't on your mind, too?"

"All right. Sure," Lat said. Tom was forever bringing women in, as if a man could think of nothing else. "I mean afterwards."

"Afterwards?"

64

"I'm not going to die poor, Tom."

"Lived poor so far, is that it?"

"We had enough to eat. You too?"

"Never so much as a pot. Goin' to live rich, are you? By bein' real nice? By extry flunkyin' like you been doin'?"

"Like what?"

"Need wood? Want the teams unhitched? Anything I can do? Sure, glad to do it."

"Why not? Someone has to."

Tom took a deep breath and hitched his seat on the ground. "Lat," he said and stopped, as if the thought was heavy. "You ever see a badger and a coyote pardnered up? Good friends, they say. Pards from away back. But I taken notice that the badger can dig and the coyote can't. The badger he digs out a prairie dog or gopher, and the coyote grabs it and slopes off, bein' a faster runner."

"Meaning what?"

"Workin' men is badgers."

"You think so?"

"Even Ram, the goddam fool! Workin' for coyotes. Knows cows, knows trails, knows how to manage, and winds up with a little stake that coyote gamblers take and has to go back to his diggin'."

Sally's yell cut off an answer. "Will you sons-of-bitches shut up!"

The yell stopped Moo Cow's snoring.

Tom called back, "A man has chores to do."

"You got to make a party of it every time you piss?"

"First two gents to the right of the ring and swing Sally Goodin," Tom sang in a whisper.

Lat walked soft back to his bed, shivering a little now that the night air had fingered to his skin. He could see the other men shifting, getting set for more sleep after being disturbed by Sally's yell. Off in the darkness one of the night guards was singing, just loud enough to be heard:

> *Eyes like the morning star,*
> *Cheeks like the rose,*
> *Jennie was a pretty girl,*
> *God Almighty knows.*

Maybe he had time for another wink after all. He tunneled back into his bed, hearing Moo Cow settle again into his strangled rhythm.

So Ram was a badger, but he had led them through the desert and up the mountains and down this side, down Red Rock Creek to the Beaverhead, through a bob-tailed town or two and by the bigger town of Helena, across the Dearborn River, beyond the Sun, and here they were close to the end. All along he'd shown his

66

savvy, in handling men and animals and the hungry Indians who had begged along the way for whoa-haws, which to them meant cows. And to Tom he was just digging for coyotes!

Two days or so, and then goodbye, so long, good luck. Ram and others of the crew were striking south, maybe never to be seen again, soon after the cattle were delivered; and this time, this work, this life they'd had would small down to the leavings of a dream.

But north, not south, was the country for a man. It had opened like the Promised Land after the brown lava, the gray sagebrush, the heat that dried the juices up. Down from the pass the air blew clean and streams ran cold and hills and benchlands riffled with grass like growths of grain. "My lip feels betteh just from lookin'," Ram had said and smiled as others, topping the divide, had thrown up hats and fired off guns and yelled the Rebel yell and the cows moved on with purpose, too eager to be scared.

This was even better, though, this country now around, this giant spread of land, this plain on which the herd had spilled out from the hills. Everywhere but to the mountained west it flowed forever. Farther than a man could think, beyond buttes blued by distance, floating in it, the earth line lipped the sky. And hardly anything, any living thing, to see. Wolves, coyotes, prairie foxes, gophers and the like of these, which didn't count. Now and then a bunch of antelope. No buffalo so far. Cattle to be counted on the fingers except back on the Sun where early ranchers had a scattered few. Beyond them, here, just emptiness and open sky. Air like tonic, days like unclaimed gold. And grass and grass and grass. Grass beyond the earth line, which wasn't any line but just the farthest reach of eye. World without end, that was it. Ma reading from the Book. "World without end." She closed it and looked at him and smiled her mother smile, so gentle that it turned the heart. She put her hand on his shoulder, and her voice came out as gruff as a man's, "Your watch, kid!"

5

Ram Butler paid off in gold, standing at the bar and counting time and money and afterwards buying drinks for all. The saloon was a long, low box with a false front and a sign that said HERE'S LUCK. Inside were a poker table and a wheel and two lamps hanging from the ceiling and a barrel of whiskey on a butcher's block behind the bar. The bartender was fat and solemn and untidy and kept a Henry rifle on a deer-horn rack behind him. It couldn't be a top place, Lat thought as he sized it up. It was just one they'd happened on and entered, being too eager to be finicky.

It was early yet for business. Besides the crew there wasn't anyone around, barring two who stood silent and apart. One of them was a tangle of whiskers that a face might lie behind. He acted pretty drunk and even at a little distance gave off a smell like souring hides. The other was an old man who had looked

69

them over openly as they came in and then stared straight ahead. The first of them mouthed "How" to Ram before he poured the drink into his whiskers. The other gave one bob of his head.

"To Texas, wheah a boy don't freeze his pa'ts," Ram said and drank his drink and called for more. Now that he'd got the herd delivered, he seemed like a different man.

"I seen icicles a foot long hangin' from my horse's bit down on the Yellowstone," Slim George Stevens said. "Slobber ice. And I seen the time with no snow on the ground but cold as Christmas just the same that I would kick a steer up so's I could lie down on the spot he'd warmed."

"I made out through a heap of winters." It was the old man, speaking slowly, looking at them out of eyes that seemed to speak old times themselves. "Since 'sixty-five I made out."

"And all the time you could've been in Texas," Tom Ping butted in. He smiled up and down the bar as if joined with the rest in having fun at ignorance.

"Texas ain't to my taste."

"It makes a man real sorry for you."

"Texas?" The old man thought about it. "It's all room and no furnishin'. Just bare room from line to line, and all your jawin' don't

70

make it any different, thank you kindly."

Tom glanced at the faces right and left as if to read there what to answer. He answered, turning, "It would be kind of dangerous for you to talk that way if you was half your age." Just the last track of his smile remained.

"I ain't had to call for help yet." The old man still spoke slowly.

Tom shouldered from the line so as to have no one between. The old man twisted around and raised his face, asking what came next. Nobody interrupted, not Ram, not Carmichael, not any of the older men that Tom felt bound to show his mettle to.

Lat stepped to Tom. He put a hand out. A saying of Ram's came to his tongue. "Tastes have a right to differ." It wasn't like himself to speak up so. He made his tone soft. "Come off your high horse, pardner."

Then Carmichael said, "Can't convert the heathen, Tom."

"It's a free country," Ram added quietly, "and that means people's free to pick the sho't end of the stick."

They smiled at Tom, and he smiled back uncertainly and in what seemed a little flood of relief turned back to the old man. "Hang on to your principles, Pop."

"Yup."

Tom ordered up another round. While it was being poured, the old man gazed on and off at Lat, his mouth unsmiling.

Two breeds came in the door. Tom motioned them to belly-up. They smelled of willow smoke and grease.

"Any girls around here?" Tom asked the bartender. With his long black hair and long black beard he didn't look like company for girls; he looked like something from a cave.

"Some."

Slim George was going on about Montana weather as if they'd had no hint of trouble. "And the days get so short it's like the sun come up just to say good night. In a month now the whole damn country'll be freezin' up."

The old man didn't show he'd heard.

Tom kept staring at the bartender, his question in his eyes. The bartender pulled out his watch as if the doing of it was a chore. "Likely they'll parade later. Generally they do."

Lat asked Stevens, "There's a warm wind they call a chinook, isn't there?"

"A chinook is a windjammer's name for a wind that don't blow. It's like the answer to a prayer, mighty slow a-comin'."

"I might go callin'," Tom said to the boys down the bar. "Hey, Lat?"

"Men've been known to." The bartender

spoke as if there wasn't much men hadn't been known to do.

"Damn you, Tom!" Slim George said. "We get lined out on a nice, elegant subject like the weather, and you start bawlin' for the hookshop!"

"My mind just tracks that way," Tom said and gave a grin around as though this hunger, being a shared thing, was an open subject. "Where my mind goes, I go."

"You can't be goin' far," Sally Goodin told him.

There was a twinkle in Carmichael's eye. "You got the cart before the horse, boy. It's your mind bein' pulled, I couldn't guess by what."

Tom grinned. "It don't matter which goes first, the cart or horse, just so we both get there."

One of the breeds plucked at Tom's arm. "One dollar. Good. Heap good. I show."

Tom pulled away. "I don't need no guide."

"Them goddam pimpin' breeds." The bartender's voice was louder than before. "Like as not it's his wife, or anyway some old hay bag." His eyes swung from breed to breed. "Git out, both of you! You ain't got a dime between you. Git!"

The one breed backed off from Tom. "Good. One dollar?"

73

The bartender yelled, "Git!"

"Guide! With the compass that Tom has already!" Sally said.

"Now if I aimed to take me courtin'," Ram told Tom as the breeds shied out the door, "I would cut off a ya'd or so of beard and wash down just to that second coat of lava dust. It would be right risky to scrub it all off in this climate."

Tom stroked his whiskers. "My papa said never to grow on your face what grows wild on your tail." He asked the bartender, "Barber got a bath?"

"Two bits. And dump your own slop."

"Take along a shovel." The advice came from down the line, from Drury, who'd been talking on the side to Codell. "That water ain't goin' to pour."

Old Oscar spun a gold piece on the bar. "Thirst comes first. Your old man tell you that?"

Tom didn't answer. He was looking toward the door. A tall man with a clipped mustache and a nose like a curved blade stood there. The face and height of him alone first struck the eye, and then the light gray hat without one sign of wear, the shirt small-checked of red and blue, the fancy vest, the pearled revolver, the dress pants tucked in shining boots.

The man was in no hurry. He gazed around and turned and closed the door, softly, and, turning back, said, "Howdy, gents."

"Howdy, Jehu," the bartender answered. "Stage on time, huh?"

Jehu stepped up to the bar, nodding to the others' nods. He was an inch or two taller than Ram. "Since when haven't I pulled that outfit in on time, Fatty?" The mouth was pleasant under the high curve of nose.

"I ain't got opportunity to count," the bartender answered. "See me when I ain't busy."

"Fatty can do anything better than anybody else just as long as he don't have to do it," Jehu announced to no one in particular. "There's something about slopping drinks that makes a man smart."

"It's the company. It's the goddam smart company. The house'll buy, gents, seein' Jehu can't get his hand in his pocket."

Jehu had moved in close to the whiskered drunk, and now he angled his head and looked out of the corner of his eye while his thin nostrils sniffed. Then he edged away. "It ain't the season," he told Fatty.

"Ever know a hide hunter to clean up?" Fatty asked with a glance at the drunk. The drunk was hanging by his elbows to the bar and didn't seem to notice. "Sons-of-bitches come in here,"

75

Fatty went on, talking to the crew, "and the last one to pick a louse off his carcass has to buy the drinks."

"Nice, clean subject," Jehu said as if to put a stop to it. "Excuse me, gents." He turned away from them to Fatty. "My man show up?"

Fatty shook his head.

"His name was Turpin."

"You told me that a'ready."

"He promised he'd be here."

"Promisin' man, huh?"

Jehu let out a disgusted sigh. "Got scared, I guess. That's today for you. I can remember, back there, when I could've done it myself, or found a dozen salty men for nothing."

"Yeah. Yeah." Fatty's tone was jeering. "You ought to use that fancy six-gun on him like I said before."

"And get my wife down on me and give a hole-card ace to her father and the rest! I told you he was a gift."

"Hell of a gift. Your wife's pa must want to make a widow of her."

Jehu said, "Uh-huh," and fell to thinking and after a minute looked up and said, "Sorry, gents. I didn't mean to bust your party up. Have a drink."

"We was only talkin' women," Ram replied, "and theah's a field that's grazed aplenty." He held his shot glass up and studied it. "Shootin', as you say, suh, is a last reso't."

"He's not just a gift, but more'n that, a kind of pet."

"Could a man ask what it is, suh?"

"Sugar by name."

Fatty added, "He-devil by nature."

"Suh?"

"A goddam outlaw," Fatty said.

"A hoss? A saddle hoss?"

Jehu answered, "S'posed to be. I thought I had a fair man hired, one good enough, but he ran out on me, seems like. You know how it is these days — good men too old and young too soft." He got tobacco and papers out of his shirt and started working on a cigarette, frowning down at his hands as he did so. "Maybe it's just as well. He'd probably been piled and hurt, being what they brag of as the younger generation."

"It's your pride," Fatty told him. "You can't stand for your old lady's old man to have the laugh on you, not as I blame you much, him bein' such a cacklin' bastard, but still I'd get shet of that horse."

"When I haze him off, damn if he don't beat me back to the gate."

Ram's gaze swung to Lat, and Jehu's, quick to follow, touched him and moved on. "Good-looker, too," Jehu went on. "Bred up from Oregon. Heavier than most cayuses and faster, I'd say, with the kinks ironed out."

"Purty is as purty does," Fatty said.

Jehu shrugged. "Oh, well." He moved out from the bar. "Palaver doesn't get the chores done. So long, you gents."

Ram let him get almost to the door. Before he spoke, he flicked another glance at Lat. "We got a little ol' boy can sometimes stick a hoss."

Jehu smiled over his shoulder. "No," he answered. "No. Forget it." His hand went to the doorknob.

"That bronc's a son-of-a-bitch and no mistake," Fatty said.

Ram wagged his head and looked at one of the hanging lamps and said to it, "My mistake then. I was thinkin'—"

Carmichael cut him off. "We was thinkin' this animal had hair on. Our boy'll fork anything with hair on."

Jehu came back from the door. "Who is this champeen peeler?"

Ram pointed. "That little ol' boy theah."

Jehu looked and shook his head. "He's got a mother someplace."

"Likely."

"I wouldn't want to be to blame." The searching eyes came back and after a long instant moved to Ram. "No offense, but ain't you pushing your boy? It's not his meat, as you can see. He's kind of tallow-faced a'ready."

"How about—" Ram began, but Tom's voice drowned him out. "You goddam shorthorn!"

Jehu put out his hand as if to calm a wave. "Easy, son! I'm thinking of your pard. I wouldn't let a scared boy climb old Sugar. To be feazed is to be froze, you know yourself."

"How about it?" Ram asked. "Not meanin' to impose, but how you feel, Lat? Game?"

They waited for an answer. Just plain sense answered no. He said, "But why should I?"

"Fo' hell and education. Jehu needs 'em both."

"Why? What's in it, though?"

"Oh, I take Jehu for a sportin' man."

Mexico added, "Just like all of us."

"Show him who's so smart!" Tom said.

Jehu put his hand on Lat's shoulder. "Go low if your gizzard's weak, I tell you."

"How about it, Lat?" Ram asked again.

Sharp with the question, the eyes of all of them were on him. "Yes," he said and repeated, "yes," because the first one sounded small.

Ram bobbed his head and said to Jehu, "Would a hundred dollahs salve that conscience?"

"A bet?"

79

"Salve fo' you."

"Money talks, but I swear I don't like to listen. Now, boy, own up, ain't you scared?"

"Feaze and freeze him first, eh, Jehu?" Sally said. "I ought to take a cleaver to you."

"Not of a horse," Lat answered. The words came out too small again.

"I could salve your conscience some myself," Carmichael said and added, "not that I think it's so awful saddle-sore."

Sally squeezed a hand into his pocket. "Same here."

Jehu spread his arms. "Why, gents, I never figured it would come to this."

"But seein' it has?" Ram asked. The gold he brought out rattled on the bar.

Jehu looked from man to man. "You're asking for it. Is the rest of you as reckless?"

"Recklesser," Tom said and shied a smile at Lat. "Double or stone-broke." He started putting out his money.

Oscar wanted in, too, and Drury and Codell and each and every one of them.

Of a sudden Jehu was all business. "Call all bets. Fatty can hold stakes. But no cinch hooks, gents." He looked down at Lat's old spurs. "And no spade bit. Riding to be done in the open, not in a corral."

"Yes, suh," Ram said while he stacked his

80

money, "but for a man that don't want my boy messed up, you talk right bloodthirsty."

The old man, quiet since his clash with Tom, moved around to Jehu. He slid a poke out on the bar. "This bet's on the the boy, or ain't you game?"

Jehu looked at the man and then at the poke and then at the bartender. "What's it worth, Fatty?"

Fatty brought a pair of scales from underneath the bar and blew the dust off and sprinkled raw gold from the poke. "Ten ounces, about. Make it two hundred dollars."

"Match it," the old man said.

Jehu was fingering the gold. "Much of that where you come from?"

"Match it."

"Must have a nose for it?"

"Gold don't stink, which ain't all I might say."

"You're a feisty old bastard."

"The right name is Godwin."

Jehu turned away. "You want to pair off the bets, Fatty?" His hands worked inside the checked shirt and brought out a money belt. "There's plenty here."

While Jehu raked coins from the belt, Fatty found a sheet of paper in the money drawer. "That damn pencil must have legs," he said as he cast about for it. "Well." He took the Henry from the rack and levered out a cartridge and made ready to write with the nose of it. Ram handed over the pencil that he carried to keep time and tally with.

Fatty nodded and announced, "Names, gents, and what you're bettin'. We don't want no misunderstandin'." Under Jehu's eyes he stacked one pile against another and moved each set to a little shelf behind him and slipped a scrap of paper underneath.

"All up?" Jehu looked around. "What about you there, bronc-fighter, or did your money get scared, too?"

Tom muttered, "Aw, the goddam shorthorn!"

"Fifty," Lat said.

"Fifty is right. Stack it up and make it out, Fatty, and then we'll have a drink."

Ram shook his head. "Thankin' you, but not now." He gave Jehu a small, one-sided grin and went on, speaking soft. "You and Fatty got a real sma't act. Us foolish flies is tangled in youah web. Let's see now can you eat us."

Jehu grinned. "It tuckered me, that act. And I bet you'd've took me up regardless."

"All I said is true as Jesus." Fatty turned to put the last bet on the shelf. "Wisht I could go along. That's the trouble with keepin' bar. Always tied up to a barrel."

Don't cry in the whiskey," Jehu told him. "Cut 'er down any more and people'll be asking you where Missouri River water got that funny tang." He started for the door. "Come on, you high-rollers. Happens I got Sugar in a catch pasture just a step away."

"Fo'tunate, ain't it?"

They followed Jehu out, all but Fatty and the drunk, who tried a step as if to come along and looked down at his leg and dragged it back to place and had to clinch the bar to keep from falling.

Lat brought up the rear. As he reached the door, Ram crowded past him going back in. Ram put both hands on the bar and fixed Fatty with his stare. "Suh," he said, "I take you for an honest man, but once theah was a tinhorn that run out on us. We caught him in the Nations." He paused. "Sometimes I wish the boys had only shot him."

Fatty didn't try to answer. He stood still, his eyes wide, and finally bobbed his head.

Ram wheeled around and came back and took Lat's arm. Tom was waiting and took the other one as they moved out to the hitch rack where the men had gathered. "Win or lose," Ram said and smiled an easy smile, "no man of us will fault you."

"Your best is good enough for us, pard."

Tom gave a playful push. "We're just havin' fun, you old web-foot. It ain't a funeral."

"I'll hoof it," Jehu was saying at the hitch rack. "It's just yonder. You that want to ride can ease along." He started out, trailed by old man Godwin, while the rest untied their horses.

A man came out of a store across the street and yelled at Jehu, "Where's your posse bound?" A wagon driver whoaed to hear.

"After an outlaw name of Sugar."

"Hell you are! Wait up!" He poked his head back inside the door. Some other men came out.

There was the known sky, just as in Oregon, the known sun dancing, the known earth waving under hoof, the companions once known on the trail. And this was Fort Benton, Fort Benton, Montana Territory. This store, this house, this hall, this river, this steamboat and its waiting cargo, these people watching, they were Fort Benton. It was a ground breeze that fiddled with the dust. It was wood smoke that lifted from a cabin.

Jehu had turned west. He strode along with Godwin keeping pace, strode straight along as if someone had aimed him, out of town, into the open, toward a barn and a fence and a pole corral. Fort Benton from here swam with the river and, swimming, still stayed still. It was a herd that watered there, a little thirsty herd of wood and brick bunched on the bank. Out of it were coming a rider and another and a wagon and a handful of people on foot.

Now from the barn ahead a horse trotted. It grew into a big dun that stopped to watch and stood quiet and high-headed like a statue. The ground breeze fanned his tail.

Jehu twisted around to say, "You wouldn't think it to look at him, but just wait!" He walked on to the gate. "If some of you'll come in and corral him, I'll go to the barn and get my rope. He's partly halter-broke."

They held up to watch a minute. The horse looked at them out of big and innocent-appearing eyes set wide above a straight nose. He came closer by a couple of easy steps, his nostrils widening as he tried the air.

"Good head," Ram said. "Damn good even if the horse is no damn good."

"Good all around, or maybe could be," Carmichael answered. "Chest. Barrel. And look at them legs! Too bad he's spoiled."

Codell and Moo Cow rode through the gate and got behind the horse and hazed him toward the pole corral. He made straight for it, striding long, as if he had the sense to know it was no use to try to break around.

"Action, too," Carmichael said and dismounted with the rest.

Jehu came out of the barn with a rope. "Won't take but a minute," he called out. Codell was closing the gate of the corral.

Tom put an arm across Lat's shoulders. "You've rode worse. Just keep that in your noggin, and damn that shorthorn! He wouldn't call me scared!"

Half seen through the poles of the corral, a noose sailed round the horse's neck. Jehu snugged the rope and held it up to Moo Cow, who took a dally on his saddle horn. The gate opened. Moo Cow rode out slowly. By turns the horse behind him balked and yielded to the rope. Jehu came out on foot and curved around and came ahead. "No snub in that corral," he told them at the gate. He put his hand on the gatepost. "We'll tie him up right here."

"No sense in makin' things easy," Ram replied.

Behind them a voice rose. "Don't get in a lather, Jehu! More's comin' to the ball." The first of the followers were pulling up.

Moo Cow brought Sugar to the gate. Lat turned away. It was time to peel the gear from his own horse. From the side a stranger said, "Money says that nag'll pile you."

Tom and Mexico were taking off the rigging. "Here," Lat said.

Tom swung the saddle down. "Can't let our meal ticket fag himself doin' piddlin' chores. Come on." He tucked the saddle blanket under his arm and lifted the saddle by the horn. Mexico brought the bridle.

Sugar was tied short to the gatepost. He stood quiet except for a fine trembling that riffled his hair like a touch of breeze.

"A man like you won't mind to cool his heels," Jehu said to Lat. "See?" He motioned. The tail end of the little procession that had trailed them was still a piece away. "Soon enough the time will come, my boy. Now let me see that bit."

Mexico held it up. It was a plain bar bit with only rings for side pieces.

"English." Jehu smiled as if he found support in that. "And let me see those spurs again."

Old Godwin's rusty voice called out, "Don't you want to count his teeth?"

"Fair enough, men. Meeting called to order. Dress him when you're ready. I never saw him kick." The clipped mustache widened to another smile. "Likes to save himself."

"I'll saddle him myself," Lat said. The horse shrank from the blanket. The blanket, laid and smoothed, shook to his fine trembling.

"Goddam!" Jehu said. "Don't know why he hates a rider so. Just naturally, I guess."

87

"He's scared," Lat answered, knowing, and in that instant hated Jehu. "He's been abused." The trembling now was not so fine; it shook the horse. "Wait, Tom, on that bridle!" He eased the saddle up. At the very touch of it, Sugar humped his back and humped more as the cinch drew tight.

Lat stepped up to his head. "Gentle, Tom." He took the bridle. "Whoa, boy! Whoa, now!" Sugar tried to rear and couldn't against the short hold of the rope. The gatepost cracked but held. The bit went in. The headstall had to be let out.

Jehu's voice came loud. "You boys best get where you can dive for the fence. Old Sugar goes plumb blind."

Tom said, "More goddam scare talk, Lat."

They had the headstall long enough and, now, the throat latch buckled. The circle of watchers had edged out and still was edging. Only Carmichael, only Ram kept close.

Jehu's wave was waved to all. "Me, I'd hate to climb him with that saddle, gents." He spoke loud as he talked to Lat. " 'Scuse me, boy, but it ain't much more than a pancake and a string."

Ram saved an answer. "Any objections, suh?"

"No. No. Too late to reconsider anyhow. Rules is rules, and no one can change his mind. One thing, though. He's got to get on by himself. No holders. Hear?"

"Moses has let loose with another commandment," Carmichael said.

Jehu straightened to his full height. Slow as Moses and as solemn, he came back around to Lat. He put forth his hand. "Son, watch out, please, you don't get hurt. Shook loose, you leave him careful. What's money, stacked against your health?" The turned-down mouth said, "Luck!"

"I'll put up fifty more" — from the fringe of thought the sore words broke — "and you put up the horse."

Jehu bent his head. "Run home, chickens!" His eyes rose and narrowed to two sparks that swam and anchored beside the ridge of nose.

"You overreached yourself, makin' our boy mad," Carmichael told him.

"If he's rode," Jehu thought aloud while he counted on his fingers, "he maybe won't bring fifty, just depending. And if he isn't, like he won't be, come on more outside money!" His eyes came up again. "Put 'er up!"

"I'll just hold the fifty," Ram said. "Them long legs can easy catch me."

So now. Now, at last, the time. *Sink or swim, live or die, survive or perish*...Grandpa speaking, out of the years, across the miles. *Sir, before God, I believe the hour is come.*

Lat took the reins and pulled the horse around. The men about him melted farther back except for Ram there and Carmichael there and Tom. They sidled close. The walking wasn't taking out the hump in Sugar's back.

"Hey, you Ramrod!" It was Jehu. "You boys quit blocking that horse!"

"When Lat's aboa'd. And don't say you got a rule!"

"Easy. Easy, boy." Lat stroked the trembling neck and tightened up the reins and caught hold of the mane and with his right hand turned the stirrup for his boot. The horse wheeled, snorting, as he brought his foot up. "Easy, now." Ram had side-stepped to front the moving head. Another try, another snorting wheel, and Jehu's words as from a distance, "Can't even fork him, then the money's mine."

He let go of the mane and grabbed the cheek strap of the bridle and, by pulling hard, crooked the horse's head around. He kicked for the stirrup and swung on.

Nothing happened. He set himself. There was the head, held up like in surprise and fright. There, fading back, was Tom. There were the men retreating and, beyond them, rolling up, a carriage that the sun danced on.

Nothing happened except the trembling, felt quick in legs and seat, until Jehu raised a whoop and charged in and slapped out with his hat.

The horse bounced and fought the reins and tore them through the hold and bogged his head, and the earth sprang away and slammed back and sprang again. Like many a horse. Like horses ridden. Pile-driver. Rough as rock. Not rough enough. Sit soft to jolt! Watch out, that jump! Two pitches. Four. Five or six. Bets in the bag. This bronc to boot.

Not yet! Not pile-driver. Sunfisher! Live fish out of water. Head and rear beating. Switched out of joint. Earth and sky switching. Men and the carriage. Fort Benton flopping, back into the river. A voice crying, "Stick him!" Guts torn loose and gasping. No head on the horse. No eyes in the rider. Bets hung on a pants' thread. How long now? How long?

The ground appeared to level and begin streaking underneath. It seemed the horse was running. It seemed he answered to the spurs with speed instead of pitches. Earth and sky broke off and took their proper places.

Lat pulled him in and let him blow. "Good going, boy." The horse rolled back a big, still-frightened eye. Greenly, he let himself be guided.

Back at the gate men pushed in around them. Some were shouting, the Rebel cries of Ram and Stevens rising high. Tom was pounding old man Godwin. Carmichael threw his hat up. Moo Cow fired his pistol at the sky. In the front seat of the carriage sat a Negro driver. From behind him the red and white and purple of women's dresses showed.

Lat shook hands put out. Like the horse that stood winded by his side, he hadn't much run left. He caught hold of a piece of air as Jehu crowded through. "Satisfied?"

Jehu eyed the horse. "Sugar, as a business proposition you have put me belly up." He grasped Lat's hand. "Boy, leave me know when you want a job of breaking broncs."

"Let's celebrate." Tom took Lat by the arm.

"Fittin' thing, I'd say," Ram added from the side. "Oregon, here's Texas makin' a salute."

"I want to walk." Lat pulled in another breath of air.

"Of cou'se then. We'll see the hosses get led down. You and Tom just mosey on."

They had to pass the carriage. It stood close, hitched to a high-strung team. The colored man had on a uniform of sorts — a white, high-collared shirt, an old, too big dress shirt and a hat that rode him high. Lat looked off from the women's smiles. There was a girl there, though, nice of mouth and nostril, with yellow hair like good fall range. His eyes lifted and caught hers and held. She smiled a young and friendly smile, not so open as those of the other two.

Tom, his head turned too, gigged him in the ribs. "We ain't hardly got a start on fun, Lat."

6

Dark had drawn on fast, and with it a chill that riffled along the skin without getting to the bone. Inside the tent pitched on the fringe of town the candle, burning straight, played blocks of shadow on the sidewalks.

Tom Ping puffed a little with the cold and wished for Texas, where Ram and some were free to go. As long as he was wishing, he wished that Lat would hurry up. "Shake a leg, Albert Gallatin," he said. He'd had enough whiskey, he could tell, to make his tongue slow, but some more wouldn't hurt where they were going.

Lat squatted by the candle, those letters in his hands. "Just a minute."

Tom had to hop to keep his balance while he stuck a leg into his new pants. They were striped and nice but cost real dear in this man's town. "You've read 'em a dozen times already."

"Not quite."

"Everything's all right at home, you said."

"Uh-huh."

"You learnin' 'em by heart then?"

"Yeah."

Half the boys or more had gotten letters — news from home, from girls along the line, from pardners of old times — and had gone aside and read them and, by looks and talk, felt good.

Tom pulled the pants up. They fit fine. They'd catch somebody's eye. "In my whole life I never got a letter."

"Not even one?"

"From my old man or my old lady! Hell! If they're livin', they don't remember that they borned me or give a good goddam. Couldn't read or write, regardless, not as I'm much better."

Lat was looking up. "Friends?"

"A kid don't make no friends, Lat, not with men, and I was only ten when I shook loose from home. Oh, they used to get me drunk and take me to the whorehouse, and they had fun doin' that, but they was older and I was just a little freak, though tryin' man's work all the time."

What had they cared, what did they care now, any of them, Ma or Pap, the men once tickled to see in kid in bars and hook-shops,

95

the grown-up girls who'd giggled and forgotten? It didn't matter any more except, for a fact, he'd been lonesome, wanting someone to tie to. Even later, an honest-to-God friend somehow had been hard to come by. They'd josh around and drink with you, the men you rode with would, but goodbyes were goodbyes and left you by yourself again. But to hell with all that now!

"Pard," he said, "please get a hustle on!"

Lat folded the sheets and got up. One hand went to his head and felt his haircut. He didn't stir himself. He acted as if he had to think first.

"They mistake you for a bull calf at brandin' time some time?" Tom smiled as he spoke and clapped Lat on the shoulder.

Lat's smile seemed kind of weak. "Tom, what do we do?"

"Now?"

"Next week! Next month! This winter and all!"

"In time we got to die, but look close, Lat! We tend she-stuff tonight. Tomorrow that Shonkin outfit's pickin' up this tent and other plunder, so we find us a hotel and wait around for work. We got enough to last a while."

"Ever think of wolfing?"

"Nope."

"Moo Cow says with luck there's money in it."

"Lat, I'll ride with you, but now, for God's sake, ride with me!"

Lat started to take off his clothes. What he'd bought for dress was plain wool pants and a plain wool shirt, not striped pants and a collared shirt and a brown plush vest with darker braid and a red silk handkerchief and sash to set them off. Ol' Lat didn't appreciate full war paint yet.

There wasn't a good mirror in the tent or, for that matter, light enough to give a real look. Tom ran a comb through his hair. There would be a white swath where the barber's shears had worked. He angled on his hat. " 'Bout ready?"

"Just about." The words came out on a little sigh.

Tom moved over and took Lat by the elbow. "I been onthinkin'. You're kind of played out. That ride must've took some starch out."

"Some."

"A drink'll fix you up."

For himself Tom felt fine, felt smart in his clothes, felt ready. Any girl would take a second look, he guessed. But Lat? Lat in his plain clothes? Good face, still boyish if too sober. Lean body, medium tall. But no prize over all, not in this rigging, not with that borne-down look.

"Pard, you take first choice," Tom said.

Lat followed Tom outside and went on slow, as Tom did, while he waited for his night eyes. It was the stars that came out first, burning bright as fires, and then the high hills heaving for them. To the left a freighter's outfit grew out of the dark, sounding to the munch and stamp of work stock tied about. Down along the river the town sat dark and huddled, with here and there a glimmer that was a lamp inside a bar or shop or home. Or house.

Fort Benton, far from Oregon, away from old, respected ways, divided by the miles and mountains, linked only by frail air and trusting words on paper. About now, over there, Ma and Pa would be reading from the Bible.

"Let's step it up," Tom said.

In the distant darkness a squaw wailed for her dead, and dogs chimed in, joined by coyotes on the hills. They sent a shiver up the spine, of chill and lonesomeness and dread and hope of things to come. Step by step the town marched toward them, step by step the waiting lamps, one waiting lamp somewhere among them.

"Them girls we saw live this way, Fatty told me." Tom slipped his arm through Lat's. "It's a frame house, name of Miss Fran's." Tom's hand gave an eager squeeze. "Stylish place.

Regular parlor house, the man said. Even got a nigger to bring drinks."

They angled around a pole fence and a barn that smelled of cows and crossed an open, weedy lot. A dog all legs and backbone ran from beside a shack and growled, and the Indian woman keened again, and the dog rumped down and raised his nose and howled the bass.

The house sat low. It had a picket fence around it and a light inside, hidden by a curtain that glowed red.

Tom rapped on the door. From inside came the creak of steps. The door opened. The Negro driver stood there, still in his rusty coat. "Yes, suhs, come in, you all."

The Negro was maybe forty-five or maybe fifty. He had a long, sad face. The brass buttons on his coat gleamed as he turned and bowed them in.

In the hall, before an open doorway, Tom said like one at home, "Evenin'. This Miss Fran's?"

A fat, square woman in a purple dress with big bows at the shoulders sat on a sofa doing needlework. She put it aside and got up, easily for her heft, and stepped toward them on feet no bigger than a faun's. She had a bosom like a butt of hay, and too much of it bulged bare above her dress.

"Howdy, honey," she said in a voice as rough as a file. "Rest your hats, you and your friend." She cracked her paint and powder with a smile that didn't touch her eyes. "Fran's my name and fun's my failin'."

They entered. Lat put his hat on a steer-horn rack and then saw Tom had kept his on his head. The light played on the silver plates along its band. The woman turned back toward the sofa. Another butt of hay bulged out behind. Except for it she might have fallen on her face from the overload in front.

"The girls'll be in directly. Set." Before she eased herself back on her seat she sucked in a breath and sent it out in a bellow. "Company, girls!" Her eyes went to the Negro. "Happy?"

The Negro said, "Yassum," and scuffed to a door at the back and went out.

Lat watched Tom for what he'd do and sat down when he did. There was a big, gilt-bordered mirror on the wall and a couple of pictures, one of a horse and the other of a woman with a haze of light around her head.

Tom kept on his hat. "Nice place you got. puts a man in mind of them bigger Kansas towns."

The floor was bare except for small rugs, on one of which, with a show of petticoat, Miss Fran had crossed her tiny feet. A piano, ringed by the sweat of glasses, stood against a side wall. At one end a wood fire flickered in a stone fireplace. What other light there was came from a big, pot-bellied lamp covered with red roses.

Miss Fran was saying, "When I can't run a decent house, I won't run no house at all. And if a girl don't know how to play the lady, she don't belong in here." She raised her face from her needlework and bawled again, "Company. Hear?"

The Negro named Happy came back in the door he'd gone out of, balancing in one hand a tray of drinks. he served Miss Fran first, then Tom. He stood by, after Lat had taken his, and it struck Lat late that he was waiting to be paid. Happy took the ten-dollar gold piece to Miss Fran, who reached high under her skirts and brought out a purse and started making change, saying, "We'll take out for the girls, too, long as we're about it. They'll be dry. Happy, fetch some more after you've give the gentleman his money."

Happy said, "Yassum," and brought the change and lagged back out the door, looking as if sin was heavy on his conscience.

There was the sound of laughing then, and a door by the piano opened and two women entered. One had a mouse's dark, quick little air, the other a thin, fair face that her smile turned mostly into teeth.

"You kep' the gentlemen waitin'," Miss Fran said, not as if she really meant to scold. "Gents," she said, motioning, "this here's Jen, and this here's Amy Lou." Jen was the mouse and Amy Lou the set of teeth.

The door they'd come through swung to of itself.

Lat got up before he noticed that Tom didn't. Tom just hitched in his chair. "I'm Tom, and shake hands with my pardner, Lat."

The girls came over with a sway of hips. Their hands clung. They showed too much of bosom, too.

"You're cute," came through the crop of teeth. "Isn't he cute, Jen?"

"And not just on a horse," Jen said. She smiled smaller than the other and spoke softer.

"Doesn't anyone like me?" Tom asked. "Won't so much as shake my paw."

It was Amy Lou who answered. "Why, Sugar Tit!" They both went over, and Amy Lou took off Tom's hat and fiddled with his hair.

Miss Fran went on with her needlework.

The girls' dresses fit tight around the hips and came low to the shoes but in the back as in the front were cut away. Amy Lou had a ribbon around her neck that crossed her Adam's apple. The hair of both was drawn up and curled high in front.

Happy came in with more drinks.

"Don't let the gents get thirsty," Miss Fran told him, not looking from her work. "And see what's wrong with Callie."

"Yassum."

Tom had jackknifed Jen into his lap. "You put me in mind of a baby coon. Cunnin', I mean."

She smiled her held-in smile and sipped her drink and melted against him.

"We'll team all right," Tom said. "But wait!" Of a sudden he drew back and looked at Lat. "Your first pick, Pard. You rather have this baby coon?"

"You keep her."

"If that's the way you want it." Tom's hand went to her knees.

Amy Lou swayed over from them. "Are we leaving you all by your lonesome, Sugar Tit?"

He started to get up, but the side door opened, for the moment halting Amy Lou, and let in the girl remembered, the girl with hair like good fall range, or more like molded butter. She halted, standing young and slim. She smiled as if in hesitation. Between the parted lips her teeth showed white and even. Anywhere but here her mouth might be thought sweet. Somewhere else her eyes might be remindful of a clean noon sky.

Miss Fran kept busy with her needle. "That's Lat over there," she said. "Lat, this here's Callie. The other gentleman's named Tom, if Jen will let you see him."

Tom stopped his pawing long enough to let out, "Howdy."

The blue eyes barely touched Tom and came back. "I saw you ride," she said.

He had gotten up, and now he cast back for his chair, his gaze held by hers. "That's good. I mean — it took some starch out of me."

She half turned and went over and sat down by Miss Fran and looked again. While she moved, he saw that Amy Lou had ceased her stand on him and was seated and finishing her drink.

"Let's have a drink," he said. "I feel like drinking."

"Happy's fixin' you up, if he ever gets here." Miss Fran kept her face down-turned on her work while she let loose her bawl. "Happy! Make it all around."

The "Yassum" came muffled from the rear.

"And get your thumb out!"

"It was a dandy ride." After Miss Fran's bray the girl's voice sounded soft.

"Thank you."

Happy scuffed in with the tray.

Tom quit his nuzzling to accept a glass. "We'd have kilt him if he didn't stick." His dark face was darker yet with heat and whiskey. He raised his glass and grinned. "Here's to Albert Gallatin Evans! Hadn't been for him, you wouldn't've had the pleasure of knowin' us on account of us bein' broke."

"I'm glad you won," the girl said as a nice girl might have said it, meaning no more and no less than that.

"I got a good horse out of it. That Sugar will turn out a good horse. Won't he, Tom?"

"It's horses that my pard loves," Tom said against Jen's neck.

Happy had sidled over, Tom being too busy to be bothered about money. Lat put another gold piece on the tray. Miss Fran took it all this time.

Amy Lou got up, her mouth closed on her teeth. She walked to the door without a wiggle and went out.

Lat looked at the lamp, the pictures on the wall, the fire that Happy had just fed. He slid over Tom and Jen and caught the blue eyes on him. "You're lucky," Miss Fran told him.

"I guess I was."

"Hmm." Miss Fran bit her thread in two and began needling in another place. "It ain't that. Callie here's my niece and takes advantage of it.

Likes to pick and choose. And in this business!"

The girl just smiled. Her teeth, half showing, were white as alkali.

"Then, mister, here you come," Miss Fran went on as if somehow she'd seen and figured everything without glancing from her lap, "and right away, so help me, if you ain't the blue hen's chicken!"

Callie didn't protest. She kept smiling quietly, her blue gaze unembarrassed on his face as if, against Miss Fran, they had an inner secret, or as if Miss Fran spoke the simple and admitted truth. But she might have heard, she would have heard, these words before, put out as bait for backward men, and had answered to them, teasing, as she answered now.

Miss Fran held out her fancy work and squinted at it and brought it back and plied the needle. "Men's all alike, that's what I tell her. Got the same fixin's. Want the same thing. But no." She paused. "Picky," she told her piece of embroidery.

Jen got off Tom's lap and stood up, and Tom stood up, and both faced the door the girls had used on coming in.

Miss Fran smiled her approval. "Fun's our failin'."

Tom held the door for Jen and patted her behind as she went out. He looked at Lat and winked. "See you." The door closed after them.

Miss Fran took a stitch or two. "Well?" she said to Callie.

The girl rose to her feet. The look she gave him was a question, too.

The yellow head shimmered ahead of him, through the door, into a pitch-black hall. He heard her hand upon a latch and then the whine of hinges. A shaft of light cut through the dark. She held the door and made a little gesture, inviting him to go in first.

The room was small. A coal-oil lamp burned low upon a washstand which also held a basin and a pitcher and some towels. There was a bed. The far wall had a curtained window. He heard the door come to.

He went to the window and parted the curtains and made as if to look out, seeing only blackness and lamp shine reflected on the pane. Behind him clothing whispered. He caught the little intake of her breath. He turned around.

She stood there naked with her yellow hair let down, stood delicate and high-breasted as a bird. Her face expected something of him.

That much he took in before his eyes went down and saw fallen about her feet the dress that was the single piece she wore.

He felt blood in his neck and the hammer of his heart, and the rest of him was dead. He started around her, and she held out her arms, and he went past, catching from the corner of his eye her quick change of face. He put his hand behind the chimney and blew out the light.

He stood then with his back to her. Far off, it seemed, new voices sounded in the parlor and someone tried the keys of the piano. "You'll get cold." The words came strange, came hollow in this pen of darkness where no words had been said.

There was no answer, none but the rustle of her movements — the turning down perhaps of bedclothes, the slipping into bed and then the waiting for him to undress and join her.

He felt her brush him, heard the long scratch of a match and saw it sputter into life and give life to the lamp.

She had her dress back on and on her face, framed by the fallen, yellow hair, a look he couldn't read. She waited, her gaze open, mixed with his, raised because she was so small.

"It's not that it's you," he said.

Still she didn't speak.

He couldn't face her any longer. "You know, that — that ride took the starch out of me."

"Yes." The one word wasn't yes or no.

"But some other time—"

"If you want to."

She was too delicate, too small and fair for men to take to bed. "Honest, it wasn't that it's you, miss."

She only shook her head and motioned toward the door.

He reached back and pulled the latch, and the parlor sounds pushed in, the piano banging and a man's voice singing the last lines of "Shoo, Fly, Don't Bother Me" above a clack of tongues.

He looked in that direction and the other and at the rear end of the darkened hallway saw the gleam of glass. "Could I — the back?" he asked.

She stepped in front of him at once and led him down the hall, away from the parlor and the people there. From some room at the side came Tom's wordless tones and then Jen's wordless answer and then the giggles of them both.

She opened the door and stood aside, her face in shadow, her hair touched by the light. The voice of Carmichael carried to him from the parlor, and a laugh rang out, the rich, warm laugh that would be Ram's.

"Good night." His hand jerked out and offered itself. She took it tardily. "Good night," he said again, but she stood still and didn't speak.

He hadn't paid her! He pulled his hand away and dived it in his pocket. The pocket was the wrong one. It held the letters got from home. He reached again and with his fingers sorted coins inside the right one. Twenty? Too much. Twenty? He put the twenty in her hand.

He repeated, "Good night," and now she said, "Thanks and good night." He turned away and heard the door close after him.

The Indian woman was still crying and the dogs and coyotes joining in. He was almost back at the tent when he remembered that he had left his hat.

7

Ram mopped his forehead, where Lat could see the sweat kept beading. "It ain't the heat," he said. "It's woe."

"Bronco whiskey or them home-trained cards?" Carmichael asked.

"They double-teamed on me."

They were seated, just the three of them, on the porch of the Choteau House, which was in shade now that the sun had passed its peak. From a double-handled pump at the side a man was watering a couple of spindly trees that tried to grow just off the platform. They were about the only trees in town. Fuel shortage, someone said.

Ram turned his head to Lat. "So it's wolfin'?"

"Seems so, when the season comes. There's Tom and me and Moo Cow."

"And just maybe me," Carmichael said. "I ain't thought it out, but it would be a change." His lean face grinned as if in preparation for the answer Ram would make.

"Like a baby's pants, always wantin' change, Mike. Change to guts and stink! Moo Cow, now, his head is shrunk fo' it, and, not to mention it, but Tom he had a little trouble down in Texas, and them tin-star heel flies might get worrisome. But you two—"

"Trouble?" Lat asked.

"What's past don't signify," Ram said and waved the question down. "But you two pistols, hell! Lat, you ought to try them longhorns and the trail from Texas once."

"Montana for me."

"If you asked real nice, we'd maybe let you join the brotherhood," Carmichael said to Ram.

"To freeze! To go broke, meantime, playin' with these Yankee tinho'ns!"

"You'll go broke anyway."

"Wheah a man can get a sweat up at his luck."

Lat looked out to the river and the levee and the cargoes piled there. Except for them, this Front Street hardly had another side, the town was hunched so near the bank. A crew was working around a steamboat, shuttling back and forth with packs of hides and robes and sacks of ore or wool and barrels of some kinds of raw stuff for the east. Beyond the boat, in the bottom on the farther shore, a few tepees nippled up, and squaws moved in and out. Still farther, the river hills climbed high.

Ram rolled a cigarette and took a puff and spat. "A cob would be mo' fittin' to my mouth today."

Three men strolled up and looked at them and nodded and passed into the bar. Down the street a little piece a freighter cursed a mule train pulled up before a store. From underneath his wagon a dog ran out and sailed into a smaller one, and their racket snarled the air until the smaller one tore loose and raced away, yelp dying into whimper.

Watching, Carmichael spoke to Ram. "What you need is some hair of the dog."

"Nope. For now I've done my howlin'."

A smile seamed Carmichael's face. "No fools, no fun."

"Late as it is, I'm takin' off this ve'y day." Ram stirred but didn't rise. "Goose me, Mike, and get me goin'." He flipped his cigarette away. "Time and past that them southbound boys was showin' up."

"Can't count on Sally. Last night he was so drunk he asked me would I close his eyes for him so's he could sleep."

Ram barely smiled. "But Stevens, Oscar, Mexico and them?" He sighed. "Maybe waitin' at the ba'n."

Behind them a door creaked. From under the

LADIES ENTRANCE sign a lady without paint gave them one cool and glancing look and turned and started down the street. She wore a decent dress. Her hips she carried straight.

Ram gazed after her while he fiddled with his fingers. "Didn't see you around last night, Lat."

"I was, though." The answer might have come too fast. He slowed it down. "For a while."

"Uh-huh. A young lady was askin' 'bout you. A sma't towhead." Ram's eyes seemed sharp, his grin inquiring.

"I just stayed long enough."

"Long enough? Boy, she was one plumb daisy-do!"

"Glad you liked her."

"Now why you humpin' up?"

"I'm not. Why should I? Over her?"

Ram's eyes were like eyes on a page instead of on a face. His mouth went straight before he looked away, but when he spoke it was only to say, "Time to traipse. I'll look in at the ba'n." He got up then and put his hand out. "Mike?"

"So long, Ramrod."

"Meet you again in Texas or somewhere."

"Hope so."

"Lat?"

"I'll see you off."

"Good," Ram answered, but before he led away he said with just a touch of smile, "I don't guess the bed is to be trusted as a judge of all a woman is, Lat."

Lat watched them go, watched Ram head out, trailed by his pack horse, and the rest fall in, some red-eyed from last night and stinking with today's eye-openers. They had straggled up by ones and twos, and Mexico and Oscar had argued for another night in town and had been silenced by Ram's saying he was pulling stakes regardless.

The little train began ankling down the street, weaving by a wagon, silent but for the complainings of the gear and now and then a word spoken to a horse. These sounds faded with each step. They got lost in other sounds, in boatmen's voices and the thumps of loads let down, in the knocks of carpentry, in the how-de-dos and how-are-yous that people passed, in music from some hangout down the line, in the creaking of a wagon and the rustle of a breeze and the steady little murmur of the river. At the corner Ram would turn and lead the train from sight.

The hostler came out of the barn and said, "Long trip," and looked up and down the street and over to the river as if he ought to keep an eye on everything but didn't want to much. He went back in, leaving behind the not-bad smell of horses.

There were things to tend to — his bed and warbag to get out of the barn, his horses to make sure were cared for right, a room in some hotel to rent — but still he stood and watched. Ram had reached the corner. He and the others started round it without waving. The last of the string rode out of sight. In some Texas bunkhouse maybe they'd remember and describe this clutch of log and 'dobe houses and rare new brick and false fronts and Indians, mule-skinners, bullwhackers, soldiers, what-not, whores that were a daisy-do. Just in time, they'd say, they got out, before the town froze up, before it was deserted by the last steamboat and by the Indian traders who looked south to the Musselshell and Judith because the buffalo had left the country north. Wonder what has happened to that crazy Lat? Evans was his last name.

The stable man spoke from behind him. "Bunch quit you, huh, or other way round?"

"Some of them." Moo Cow somewhere. Sally drunk. Carmichael. Tom, who was at home in houses. All four busy in their ways.

The man moved closer, so close as to give off along with the smell of the stable the smell of

116

stale whiskey. He was a man of middle age with a stomach that rode low. He worked his jaw, tonguing home a chew. "Always, when the bunch quit me, I felt like a drink."

"Did you?" By and by if he watched close he'd catch a last glimpse of the train as it wound up the hill high above the town.

"A swipin' job don't pay enough to keep a man in whiskey."

"I guess not."

"I was a top hand once, and when I hit town I smoked 'er up and spent my money free. No poor bugger thirsted while I had a piece of change, you bet."

"Did you?"

"If you was to ask me, now, I'd say you need a drink, too. Ain't no medicine like a drink, whatever ails you." The voice stopped and went on with a kind of weary grievance. "But you ain't listenin'."

"I'm listening." Lat stepped out from the stable so as to have a wider view. There they were, halfway up and more, already shadowed by the evening shadow of the hill. Up on the flat the sun would still be bright, and they'd push on a while and build a fire against the dark and gather round and talk.

The hostler's voice was close. "Can't see things like I used to. Nothin's like it used to be with me." He went silent and stood watching, too.

The string trailed toward the top. It buckled into the last pitch, seeming small and slow with distance. It reached the brow and started over, the skyline climbing on the horses, on the riders, making half horses, half men, hats, and then nothing at all. There was just the trail there and the barren climb of hill and the deep sky arching over.

"Now, like I was about to say," the stable-keeper said, "I got a prime idea. Why don't you go and get a bottle?" He hurried on. "It ain't all one way. I'm invitin' you to sleep here in the barn. There's good hay for a bed. We'll be favorin' each other. Them hotels bite pretty deep, and your stuff's inside already?"

The voice ended with a shake. The man was trembling, sick, his sick eyes springing tears that wouldn't wipe away. "You'll be real cozy," he said. He waited for an answer and, getting none, abruptly stiffened. "Damn you to hell, then, and all your get! I don't want your idjit whiskey. I've drunk with men." He couldn't hold it. The shakes returned, the eyes leaked more, and it was as if he stood naked with his weakness, asking only what he would have given in his time. "I ain't myself. It's awful to be nothin' but a thirst."

"I'll get the bottle."

The promise acted like a drink itself. "I figured you for all right. Can't fool me on men. Fetch, and we'll have a jolt, and I'll get steadied up and give your nags an extra dose of oats."

Now, near late suppertime, the half-faced street was busy. It moved with people of all sorts — a Chinese with a basket, three laughing Negroes, straight-faced Indians, outdoor men and indoor, a big man with a star fixed to his vest, a priest in dusty black. By ones and groups they streamed on by. They entered doors and came out, their faces catching light from the lamps just being lit. And all were strangers. None knew. And nothing but the bottle would be expected at the barn, and nothing would be known. About last night or anything.

It was then that he spied Tom. He held up even before he saw that here, in public, out in open sight, Tom had Jen beside him. Tom acted proud. His forelock bobbed as if he bubbled. Jen's hand clutched his arm. They were laughing in each other's faces. They went into a restaurant, on the heels of a family man who had his wife and child along.

Lat bought a quart of whiskey at a store and, along with it, some cheese and crackers, which would save going out for supper.

The hostler waited at the stable door. "Come in! Come in! You'n me, we mix like mud." He led the way into an office and struck a match and held it, shaking, to the wick. "Now, boy."

The office was a pigeonhole. It had two stools in it, a coal stove, a narrow bunk, a table with the lamp and a tablet and a stub of pencil on it. On the dirty window ledge a big jar sat, holding something pickled.

"Set," the man said, eyeing the whiskey. "You can call me Whitey. I didn't get your name?" Lat held out the bottle.

"Lat."

"Lat, we'll take her easy." The trembling hands worked at the stopper. "I watered all the horses. Ain't nothin' left now but to feed 'em. Here!"

"You first."

Whitey kept both hands on the bottle and fixed his mouth to it and swallowed deep. "Ah-h-h." A splash trickled down his chin. "Drink hearty!"

Lat tried the whiskey on his tongue.

"Drink up! You ain't a bird, Lat."

The whiskey burned its way down and settled, burning, in the stomach.

"Yes, siree," Whitey said, reaching for the bottle. "This cures the miseries. What's yours?"

"My what?"

"Misery. Miseries. Hope you don't mind my askin'."

"Nothing."

"Huh, and ain't that dandy?" Whitey gulped another heavy shot. "When I was your age it was mostly girls, and now it's mostly that it mostly ain't." He smiled as if he spoke a grain of truth. "A misery is like an achin' tooth. Pull it out, and then the hole hurts." Still smiling, he shook his head. "Wisht I was young again, or more knowin' when I was. It ain't what you done that spoils your sleep but what you missed. But here, Lat! Have another." He passed the whiskey with a steadied hand. "That's right. Take a man-size snort."

"It's like doors closin' all around," Whitey went on, his face turned sober. "That's my misery. I drunk myself too fat and soft to ride much any more and, besides, the years done caught me, and so I dwindled off to jugglin' horse turds. But with a drink or two or three, all them closed doors open. Take a swig, please, and leave me have another go. I'm feelin' up to anything almost."

The whiskey came and went, and Whitey kept on talking. He held the bottle up and measured what was left. "Not bad for two greenhorns," he said. His face in the lamplight wouldn't stay quite fixed. It moved as if not tied tight to his neck. It was a good face, though, whiskey-loose but good. Couldn't trust booze, either, as a judge of all a man was.

A gleam of light kept dancing on the big jar on the window ledge. Whitey's face swayed toward it. "That's my prize," he said. "Can't tell from here, but there's a baby in that jar. yes, sir, a slunk baby someone ditched here in the barn. Awful small and born too soon, I guess, but perfect just the same. So, to make a showpiece, I bought some alcohol. Seems like a waste of drink sometimes, but mostly not."

"A baby?"

"Sure. Perfect. Dainty. Want to see her?"

"No!"

Out of the shadows, out of Whitey's "Suit yourself," out of a pickled, perfect baby girl, the bright head had to come now, the bright head and the breasts proud as a grouse's breast and the soft, suggested folds of groin. She stood and let him look, and her mouth smiled sweet and her teeth showed white and her eyes were kind and happy that she fired him.

Whitey got up and crossed over the the bunk, but still she had to stand here. "Now my nerves is settled, I just think I'll catch a nap," he said.

Lat left the stool. It clattered over. Whitey, swimming on the bunk, asked, "What?" and he answered, "Feed the horses." The door frame

122

bumped his hip bone going out.

A loft window let in a little light, enough to feel around and find the feed by. He spilled oats in the boxes and forked hay in the manger, falling to one knee once when the earth tipped.

He went out the stable door and started off. He had plenty of money, right here in the right-hand pocket, not in the left one. He turned around and went back in the barn and found his saddle and opened up a saddle pocket and put his letters in it and pulled the tie strap tight. Then he started off again.

The mind knew the way if the feet didn't. The mind could make the feet track. The mind had a mind of its own. The mind could do anything except, now, change its mind.

The red light shone out of the house. The door knocked to his hand. Happy swung it open. Inside, Miss Fran rode the sofa. Two men with hats on bobbed around. The piano beat a tune. The pictures on the wall kept time. A set of teeth was laughing.

And then he saw her, saw her sharp and steady, and she was there alone, she and his arching need of her, and he bumped someone and faced her. His head jerked toward the hall-way door.

She got up from her chair. A slow, inquiring smile came to her eyes and mouth, beneath the shining hair. She turned and led the way. In the dark hall her hand, child-small and warm, took hold of his. "I hoped you'd come," she said.

Part Two

8

Lat dumped his armload of wood and took off his mitts and rubbed his hands. In this weather even a few minutes outside made them tingle now they'd been frost-bitten once. He wiped the water from his eyes and waited for his sight to sharpen. After the glare of the snow the windowless cabin was dark, though an open fire blazed and a lantern burned on a cottonwood block.

The poker players still sat on the floor, fixed shadows in the flicker of shadows around them. "Raise you five," old man Godwin was saying. His hands came up. One by one he would be dropping the dried beans that did for chips on the dried hide that did for a table.

"Take it, hog." Carmichael lifted his head. "Want back in, Lat?"

"Guess not."

"That Lat can't play for wantin' to freeze his tail off," Tom said. "Leave it to him and we'd be huntin' hair while hell iced over. Ain't it so, pard?"

"Yep."

"It's yours," Moo Cow told Godwin, and Godwin clawed the pot in. "The weather ain't no colder'n me."

Indoors a man could keep fairly warm, though he had to turn himself now and then before the mud-and-stick fireplace like a bird on a spit. Or he could stay in bed. Or, like Tom, who sat farthest away, he could make out for a while with a blanket drawn over his coat. Out from the fire the cold showed white with the breath. It came in through sidewall and door and pushed at the half circle of heat.

Even with his clothes on, even with two blankets and a green buffalo hide and the help of the graying coals, Lat slept chill at night, wanting someone to snuggle against, dreaming sometimes she was there and moving closer and waking to the touch of the frost as he left the little heat his own body had made. Moo Cow and Carmichael bunked together, and Tom and old Godwin, leaving him to himself — which was just as well in view of the dreams. By morning the green cow skin was frozen, and he slid it off as he would have slid off a board and, if it was his turn, went shaking to build up the fire while the others waited, drawn tight in their beds like cold dogs.

"Might as well quit frettin', Lat, and take a hand," Carmichael said as he riffled the cards. "The Lord don't want us to work today." He kept talking as he dealt. "We got cards and a fire and a roof overhead. Home, sweet home. What else you want?"

"Women and whiskey for me and just pelts for my pardner," Tom answered.

Home, sweet home was a weather-rotten shack of a place, half dugout, half log, put up and used and deserted by earlier hunters of the upper Musselshell. With an axe and a shovel and bullhides for weatherboards they had tightened it up. It was good enough, though — for them and the field mice and the wild rats that sneaked in at night. It had spring water close by and wood enough down the draw.

"I wish we could move," Lat said.

"Today!" Carmichael grinned as he shook his head. "The way it is out, a polar bear would howl for them warm Ar'tic ranges."

"I know." Lat put more wood on the fire. Today would be, it had to be, another day of no work, no setting baits, no killing buffalo to use as bait, no skinning wolves already poisoned, no storing up a nickel. Another day, today, of cards and gab. And itch.

So long as they stayed here, even a turn in

129

the weather wouldn't mean much. They'd done poorly so far, for from within range of the cabin most of the buffalo had been chased off or killed off or had wandered away. The real buffalo, a trader had told them, pulling up as they rode alongside, were beyond the divide on the Yellowstone. A scad of 'em. The great northern herd. See him when they had cow hides or wolf pelts to sell, though it didn't look as if they'd do good where they were. Wolves followed the buffalo. Whiskey? Best in the business. Bottle for the price of a cow skin. Take it or leave it. Plenty dry bellies where he was bound. Tom took. The trader spat through his frozen whiskers and cursed at his mules and whined away, angled to southward.

"Raise you the limit." It was Godwin again. At his suggestion the limit had been set at two bits so no one could be hurt much. A big loser might be a big pain.

"Call."

Godwin lost the pot and got up and came over to warm his behind. The others held up the game. "Cold snap'll break, and we'll get more wolves," he told Lat.

"Not enough around here. That trader was right."

"It'll let up by and by, and we'll skin what we got and get out. But, boys, there ain't no

130

great northern herd." Godwin made the point by pecking his palm with a finger.

Tom said, "Seems we heard you say that before."

"What's left is leavin's," Godwin went on. "From talk and from seein' myself, I say there ain't but a handful of buffalo yon side the Missouri. In Canada nary a head. None west on the Tansy and Medicine rivers. None, you might say, where they once was thick as the grass. And, by God, no wonder! You take just one case like I seen and add a million to it and then, just to be safe, multiply a time or two. I know I ain't told you about that."

They were silent for that was the way of them, to play cards and talk and tell stories and listen and wear the day through to another day of the same. Tom climbed to his feet and came to the fire and fed it a log and backed up beside Godwin.

"It wasn't such a spell ago, 'sixty-seven or about then," Godwin said. "I had scratched up a little gold and decided to go to the States just to see if city people was as crazy as ever. It was a low-water time, and steamboats was havin' trouble gettin' to Benton, so I went to Cow Island where the old *Imperial* had had to tie up and was loadin' for the return trip down the Missouri.

131

"So we paddled down, and there, close to the mouth of the Yellowstone, they was makin' a crossin' – more buffalo than a man could count in all the time since old Adam, more'n there's a name for or a spyglass built strong enough to find the lead and drag of. The pilot he banged right into the middle of 'em and backed up the paddles so as to stay there, and everyone run to the rails and began blazin' away, with rifles and fusees and scatter guns and pistols and pea-shooters and whatever threw lead. Three hundred dead-game sports there was, allow a few one way or the other, all havin' the time of their lives while the buffalo swam crazy and wore themselves out, a big bunch just drowndin' and a bunch gettin' bullet-killed and the wounded and weak boggin' down in the shore mud and waitin' there helpless while a hell's slew of wolves danced on the bank."

Godwin got out his pipe and filled it. "We left 'em there, all except three cows that we hauled in to eat. Some of that meat spoiled before we got to it." He lighted a branch from the fire and brought it to his pipe. "Big doin's. A whole damn world full of God's best eatin', and we kill it off so's to make room for them sealion, swamp-angel, bull-tough, piss-poor cattle from Texas. And seems like that's how the government wants it, the government and the

132

railroads to boot. Kill 'em off and make tame beggars out of the Injuns."

"And still you're still killin'." Carmichael's words were half question.

"Yeah, for grub and for baits, and one gun don't make any difference much." The force had gone out of Godwin's voice. "It's the order of things, the teetotal end of the buffalo is, and where's the man that can change it?"

They had no answer, and it was a minute before anyone spoke. Then Moo Cow said from the floor, "You boys goin' to play or palaver? I can't get even on gas." He was always talking about getting even, always studying his hand, his little eyes squinched, his little mouth drawn at the corners.

"If you want to lose more," Tom answered and moved back to the hide.

"Wait on the cook," Godwin said. He picked up the coffee pot and moved to the water bucket. "Damn water's freezin' already." He broke the skim of ice and poured the pot full and set it against the fire and toed closer to the heat the stew kettle that sat at the side. "Wish some brave boy would go out and shoot some meat. Our mulligan is boiled to ravelin's. Now you can deal."

Lat sat down on his bed. Flour they had, and beans, brown sugar, coffee, salt, no meat but

133

what the kettle held. Twenty-five or so buffalo hides skinned from baits and worth about two dollars each. Maybe a hundred and thirty wolf pelts, some unskinned, just the best of which would bring five dollars. That much for weeks of work. That much against their outlay for horses and a wagon, for equipment and supplies. That much to be divided. One fifth for him to start a ranch with, one fifth plus five dollars each for breaking twenty broncs or a teetotal of a hundred dollars which Jehu hadn't paid but promised to in time.

They could have worked harder. Earlier they could have pushed on to the Yellowstone and not holed up here to live through the winter on poker and stories. But who cared but himself? Who skinned the buffalo, small though the return was unless, like professional hunters, you killed them by hundreds and had skinners who used teams of horses to yank the hides off? Usually who slashed the carcasses and kneaded strychnine in muscles and guts and posted a flag to keep the wolves off until the meat froze and so couldn't be gobbled, thus making the poison go farther?

Not that it made much difference here, for the harvest came small. Not fifty wolves at a clip, as there could be in places, but two or five and once fifteen, wolves lying dead and dying and heaving with cramps, gray wolves, white wolves, wolves like rich cream, but not enough of them. Coyotes, too, not worth the skinning. An eagle once, and magpies.

"Straight," Moo Cow said, and Godwin said, "Full house," and Moo Cow said, "By God, four aces wouldn't win for me!"

How would they be, these partners of his, when a thaw came and the skins that wouldn't come off when frozen flint-hard to flesh had either to come off or spoil?

He shook himself. He was being unreasonable. His fret made him unreasonable. Tom was all right, and Godwin and Moo Cow and Carmichael. As Tom said, except with one different word, he himself had a wild hair in his rear. Or you could call it ambition.

"My deal," Moo Cow was saying, "and I try to treat myself right." He always said that when the cards came to him.

Ambition, this fret peculiar to him? Or the wish to make up for money spent wrongly, a reaching from shame? Not one shame alone. Shame repeated. What was a head and a face and a body, no matter how good, as long as all were for sale? She lay sleeping in the early light, sleeping sweet as a child, her hair golden against the white of the pillow, golden above the smooth plane of her brow, soft under the clean lines of her face. Her eyelids fluttered and came open, and there was the caught blue of the sky, and for that caught moment he was fool enough to think he saw deep, to the bed of her being, and she wasn't embarrassed, drawn warm flesh to flesh. She put her hand to his head and stroked his hair back. "Lat," she said. "Lat." Like a fool, too, he had the feeling of having burst free.

He wrenched to his feet and went to the door and swung it half open, and the white cold bellowed in.

"Close it!" Tom shouted.

Outside, it was the same as before, but a north wind was blowing. The snow was knee-deep, knee-deep and powdery and glitter-white on days that were fair. It cried under heel like a crunched gopher crying. Hunting, a man saw it take shape and bound away, white moving on white, white with dark eyes and a dark tuft of tail, white that was jackrabbits dressed for the winter. The sky was an ache, and the snow was an ache, and the bounce of the light stabbed the eyes.

"Close it!"

Lat pushed the door to. Behind him Godwin said, "Limit."

9

When they fell silent, as now in the shack, Carmichael could hear the long cry of the wind and the sift-scratch of blown snow and the tick-tack of a tatter of hide on a sidewall outside. Wherever they were, the buffalo would be humped and grizzled with frost and the wolves chilled to silence and even the jackrabbits huddled and numb. He'd seen a day once so cold that a couple of buffalo bulls wouldn't move, choosing instead to be shot or to freeze on their feet.

But here, snug from weather, denned off from the whistling reaches of land, here was a fire and a skin full of food and the good smells of tobacco and coffee. In how many bunkhouses had he sat such storms through? Kansas. Colorado. Wyoming. Dakota. Good times, looking back, as this time would be, as it was now if you just let it be. A man learned to rest easy, to take things as they came and make the best of them, to swap yarns and think of still

137

others to tell, knowing that soon enough he'd be out rawhiding again.

That Lat was at the door, bundled thick against the cold. "Them horses are all right," Carmichael told him, but Lat went out without answering, and the crunch of his feet on the snow got lost in the wind.

Carmichael rolled up a smoke. He sat on a block by the fire. Godwin was messing with water and flour, making what passed for fair bread. Moo Cow and Tom, taking time off from cards, lay stomach-down on the bunks with the covers drawn up. "Blow! Damn you, blow!" Tom growled to the wind.

"Lat sure nurses them horses," Carmichael said. Nobody answered. "Wish I owned that Sugar, now he's got him dog-tame. Ain't a jackrabbit, hardly, can foot it with that horse."

"Yeah." Godwin let out the one word.

"Don't be so damn talkative, boys."

Tom spoke from the bed. "Wish I was in Fort Benton, instead of lettin' Lat toll me out here."

They had all been tolled in a way, even old Godwin, though his explanation was that he might as well wolf as loll around until spring. Tolled by the youngest of them. Tolled by a kid. And it was all right if kind of comical. Who gave a damn?

"Pard or not," Tom said, "why in hell did I

do it, not speakin' of you others?"

Carmichael had the answer. Fool around with reasons and you came to the right one and found the words for it and felt satisfied, as with a story that had to be shaped and, sure enough, at last was. "A man with a purpose don't lack for a party," he said and would have gone on, but Lat opened the door and came in, looking wind-blown and cold.

Moo Cow stirred to ask, "Well, how's it out?"

"Same."

"Always the goddam same." Sighing, Moo Cow put his head back down.

"This was your idea much as Lat's," Tom said. "Quit your cryin'!"

Godwin stirred the fire and added wood and put his dough in the Dutch oven.

Outside it would be growing dark. Almost as if he really saw, Carmichael could see the streaming, shortened shadow of the snow, the world shrunk close and shrinking closer, the fierce worry of the wind. Against the cabin the wind moaned and whined and whistled, and a piece of it squeezed in and blew the fire.

Tom and Moo Cow silent in the soogans. Lat pacing one step, then another. Godwin wordless as he fooled with grub. All glum. All ready to burst out at nothing.

"It just come to me," Carmichael said, hitching his seat on the block. "Two Plumes was that Injun's name. Two Plumes, a Piegan."

For all the heed they paid him he might as well have kept still. "It was real educational."

Tom raised his head and propped it in his hands.

"Ain't seen him since, and that was seven, eight, maybe ten years ago, but if he's alive he ain't wastin' words." He fished tobacco out and started on a cigarette. "When we eatin', Godwin? I'm ga'nted up."

"You mean bloated, but let's hear it."

Moo Cow had his face up now, his eyes waiting in their slits, and Lat moved over and sat down.

Carmichael lit the cigarette and took his time. Hurry spoiled a story. "It was at Fort Benton," he said then. "I showed up there from over in the Deer Lodge country, not expectin' such a jamboree. The place was lively as a hot carcass, for the nabobs from the fur companies had come up from St. Louis, like they did every year, to see how much they'd been cheated out of their legal and honorable earnin's. Steamboats on the levee. Other visitors aplenty in town — bullwhackers, muleskinners, prospectors like Godwin, traders, tinhorn gamblers, crews from the boats, new crop of girls, all bein' merry.

"And to boot, there was a big bunch of Injuns, mostly Piegans but Bloods, too, and other kinds I didn't savvy. A passel, I tell you. Their tepees was pitched out a ways, God knows why, for mornin', noon and night they hung around town.

"People was a little ticklish, seein' them Injuns was so many. Give them savages some little excuse, they said between hiccups and rumpuses, and they might forget their manners, which wasn't high-toned at the best.

"Then, from some tradin' post, a pack train showed up. Tied on one of the mules, with the muzzle pointin' the same way as the mule's, was a little brass cannon, or what they call a mountain howitzer.

"It took a little time to see that here was the big IT. The trouble with opportunity is that its name's wrote on its butt. But this time somebody seen it before it went over the hill. Fire that cannon, the smart somebody said. Make boom. Make goddam big hole in far bluff of river. Show Injuns real medicine. Scare devil out of red devils.

"There wasn't no argument on that motion. It had just to be put to get a unanimous vote. So the boys went out to round up the Injuns, tellin' 'em by tongue and by sign to come see the big show. Meantime some others said

141

they'd cut the mule from the string and plant him close to the river. Them with no special duties kept circulatin', makin' sure that all hands was informed.

"Everyone was, Injun and white. The Injuns came in a herd, in blankets and buckskins and bare skins, and so did the whites, all of 'em, includin' some ladies not so damn lady-like they couldn't enjoy theirselves. You never see such a crowd.

"Like now, of course, Front Street was half-faced, buildin's on one side, river on t'other. The mule men had led the mule to the shore. On yon side was a cut bank they figured would make a good target. The rest of us pushed around close, makin' a kind of half circle, the heathens composin' one horn of it and us re-deemers the other, though there was some mixin' up, it bein' hard to remember it was them that needed to see and get educated.

"Now in the front row of the Injuns I spotted this old chief, Two Plumes, that I had smoked with a time or two. He had his arms folded and the look on his face that a redskin can wear which says nothin' will ever surprise him, in particular white men and their doin's. The other bucks was wearin' it, too. You can't beat an Injun for lookin' like he wouldn't let on that you stink.

"The men with the mule got the cannon loaded, one standin' on a box so's to get at the muzzle and feed it a whole hatful of powder and then poke the ball home.

"So then all was ready save for the sightin'. Aimin' the piece meant aimin' the mule first and then seein' to the refinements. Wasn't no trouble. That sleepy old mule was agreeable. He led around and whoaed with his tail dead on the target and went back to sleep. With one man at his head, another climbed up and squinted over the barrel and fiddled with doo-dads and got down, claimin' the piece was trained finer than frog hair.

"The ramrod of this frolic, whoever he was, made a little speech then, tellin' the Injuns to look-see across the far water where the white man's terrible medicine iron would blow the dust tall. With that, he turned to his terrible crew. 'Ready?' he said.

"They sighted again and nodded for yes, and he told 'em, 'Fire away, men!'

"One of 'em touched a match to the fuse.

"The fuse fizzed and fizzed, and Mister Mule opened one eye and then both, and he flapped his ears back and let out a snort while the crew hollered whoa and hung hard to his head. Huh-uh! The mule hunched a hump in his back and began buck-jumpin' around in a wheel, the cannon bobbin' its big eye at one and another and all of us innocent bystanders while the fuse et down toward the charge.

"For a shake no one could move, but just for a shake. Me, I found myself lyin' behind a scatter of driftwood, and some feller was tryin' to scratch under me like a mole, prayin', 'No! Don't shoot! No!' to the mule.

"That feller tunneled me up over my fort. The mule was wheelin' and the fuse fusin' and the cannon pickin' up targets, and them innocent targets, I tell you, was wild on the wing or dead flat on the ground or neck-deep in the river, duckin' like hell-divers when the muzzle swung around. But the Injuns stood still, waitin' for the tall dust to blow.

"Then, like a close clap of thunder, the cannon went off!

"It didn't hurt anything. What with the mule's jumpin', it had slid back, down on the slope of his hump, so's the ball skimmed his tail and went into the ground.

"Men began comin' from cover and trailin' up in the dust and the powder smoke, smilin' pale and damn silly.

"I walked over to Two Plumes, who was standin' with his arms folded like before, with nothin' in his face that showed anything.

" 'How?' I said. 'How chief like 'im?'

"He answered, 'How?' and let the rest of it wait, but in that Injun eye was a gleam. Then he said, 'Paleface jackass poop.' "

They were laughing. They had been laughing. And it was good, for them and for him and for all. "Now leave us eat, Goddy," he said.

10

Slowly the thaw came. One morning the weather turned warmer and the next warmer still. By day the icicles on the edge of the roof glittered wet in the sun. By night Lat slept to the now-and-then drop of melted snow from the eaves. He could forget how he had suffered outside, with feet like dead stumps and the bone ache of cold in the hands and the body drawn in toward the spark of the heart. He could lie grateful in bed and let sleep wash him away, to Oregon and Pa and Ma and, in his drowsy weakness, to a girl named Callie Kash.

They worked these days, digging out wolf after wolf from the snow and the brush they'd heaped over the bodies in colder weather to keep varmints and birds from tearing the pelts. They skinned and pegged skins, making a raw carpet of skins round the shack. All of them worked, making belly cuts, leg cuts, flaying the carcasses, worked from daylight to dark as if glad of something to do or glad of the warmth and the root-whiff of soil in the air.

Working, they joked one another. "I loved you more, Tom" Carmichael said, holding his nose, "when your perfume was cow instead of corruption." Or they cursed with good nature when new wolves were found at old baits, for no longer were fresh baits being set: the job was to clean up and go. "Never get to the Yallerstone," they said, grinning, "not with that Lat wantin' to skin whatever wears fur."

They were close to the end, though. Just a little more time and they could pack up and trail south where the real buffalo ranged and the wolves followed thick on the drags. Now, at the close of day, with darkness already camped in the hollows, they were nearly done at this bait. Two or three cold-stiff cases to go and one more of these softer ones that got poisoned today or last night.

The world was silent, not a sound sounding but the snicks of their knives as the day went to sleep, not a sound but the small tears of skin off of flesh. The other men, like himself, were too tired and hungry to talk much as they knived and peeled pelts near a souring bull carcass that in time numbed the nose and so didn't stink as at first. Maybe, like him, they got satisfaction

147

out of making spent muscles move surer and faster than ever.

He pulled a skin free and pitched it aside and straightened up, slowly because of the cramp in his back. He felt too tired to feel, to move his eyes from the night-shaded, gray-and-pink, film-slick remains at his feet, too tired to be surprised any more at the poor, skinny surprise of a wolf without hair on.

"Next," he said under his breath and stepped on, closer to Tom, seeing the three others still working a little piece farther on and the horses standing patient and safe, and all of them hazed and misshapen by the incoming dark. "The fresh-dead ones sure are easier to skin out."

"Yep," Tom answered while he plied his knife, "and they don't gag your guts like these froze-up, part-thawed, bloat-belly articles, neither."

"Still warm, the one I just finished."

Tom glanced up. "You ain't goin' to tackle another!"

"Sure."

"Can't hardly tell front from back now. Christ!" Tom pulled in a deep breath. The whites of his eyes glimmered as he looked around. "A day like today, and a man ain't sure who he is. Might be somebody else killin' himself. Call me by name, and I'd wonder wherever I heerd it. Say I was skinnin' wolves, and I'd ask you where. And still you ain't had enough!"

"We're about through."

"And it ain't really dark, but light as a cave!"

"I know, Tom, but let's finish."

Tom set his mouth and returned to his work, and Lat turned a wolf over and went about skinning it, and the night settled thicker. Later the stars would come out and the world get some outline, but now, as he took an instant to look, the sky showed only one blink and the snow round about ran off into the darkness and the shapes that seemed to rise there and hover were the outlines of nothing. He could imagine them real, far off or close, while knowing they weren't, but still have to pinch himself. As with the shape close at hand, here almost at his side, the shape misting out from the night like a wild dream dreamed again. He blinked to clear it away.

"Christ sake, Lat!" The words hissed the dream off.

It stood white in the night. It had eyes, it had teeth, and both grinned. It shuddered. It moved, stick of a body, finger-bone tail, trembling on peeled stalks of legs. Its tongue licked its teeth. A whining cry came out of it.

"Shoot!"

A gun roared behind him. His own was in his hand. The flare of it flashed in the grinning eyes. The sick-white form jerked and went down, and the eyes faded out while the teeth kept on grinning.

"You ain't goin' to get him any deader." It was Godwin, speaking from behind. "Poison just stunned that feller, and the undressin' brung him to life."

"It's the wolf I just skinned!" The weight of the revolver bore down Lat's hand.

"Don't blame you for spookin'."

Tom looked away, out in the darkness where, Lat saw, the night shapes of nothing loomed thicker. His words came out on a small, breathy laugh. "Talk about hants!"

11

Sooner than expected, they found what they wanted. A short day's travel east and south from the breaks of the Musselshell brought them to buffalo. Buffalo in bunches and herds. Buffalo's banding hillsides and swales of high rolling prairie. Buffalo churning the wind-shriveled snow and the soil underneath, leaving dirt scars and dung scars and steam from their slop. Buffalo nosing for feed while lone bulls stood guard on the ridges around; or buffalo running, the galloping heave of them dark against the white of the land. Watching, Carmichael said, "The country's haired out."

And here were wolves to make a wolfer feel rich, white buffalo wolves and big timber wolves with yellowish sides shading off into gray, and both kinds dressed in pelts that would bring top offers from traders. They traveled in packs, ten or more to the pack. One lot, by Lat's count, totaled thirty, plus an old dog of a leader.

Buffalo. Wolves. Deer. Elk. Sometimes mountain sheep. Everywhere antelope, like extra sentinels for their buffalo friends.

There were hunters around, unseen or seen from afar. Godwin usually first spotted the signs of them — the two-day-old trail left by Indians, the far-off buffalo running from something or someone, the latticed skeletons and puffed carcasses of hide-hunters' kills strewn along coulee and slope. Now and then they heard, beyond sight, the repeated echoes of rifles.

Godwin would pull up to listen, his eyes thoughtful and sad above the mask of his beard, and, respecting his feelings, they would rein in and hear what he thought.

"Hemmed in. Plumb hemmed in," he said once. "Last stand of the buffalo, or close to it. Sure to be Rock Injun hunters and Sioux on the east and, to the right of them, Blackfeet and Crees and Red River breeds, and Crows and an almighty army of whites on the south."

"West?" Lat asked to prompt him.

"There's the mountains for a fence there, but closer up, though, you can bet, is them hungry slope tribes from over the divide."

A long way off a herd crested a hill and began

to pour down it, and Godwin pointed that way. "Take a good look, boys, at them and the others. Take a good look so's you can tell your children."

Wood was scarce in these parts and grass short, and they spent a day looking for a place to make camp and then, toward the end of it, came to a sag where a frozen wash wandered, edged by a straggle of brush. There was some graze here, under the snow, and, what was better, a stone-and-pole cone like a tepee, slanted and torn by the wind, which Godwin said was an old Indian war house, put up as a shelter and fort by some roving party of hunters. He didn't guess there was much chance they'd return, not with the war house so old, and, besides, it could have been built by Sitting Bull's Sioux, who knew better than to come back from Canada after wiping out Custer.

They shoveled the snow out and righted the poles and fixed hides on the outside to cover the cracks, making a den of a sort, and agreed it was anyhow as good as a tent, even if too low to stand straight in, and maybe less likely to catch others' notice. "Not that Injuns is so tough any more," Godwin told them. "Won't scalp you unless they can do it secret and safe, though they fudge some with wolfers, hatin' 'em extry because strychnine poisons their dogs. But they

153

sure-God will steal. Government and missionaries and all the angels in heaven can't cure 'em. That's something for them would-be ranchers to think on."

Into the thin screen of brush they rolled their wagon, which was still lightly loaded because they had cached the skins taken before, planning to pick them up on the way back. By day they looked sharp to the horses. At night they kept them short-tied and close by, and one night they took turns at guard, having cut the fresh trail of Indians that day.

It wasn't like riding watch on the trail over from Oregon. No herd. No songs for the herd. No friend to meet as they countercircled the bed ground. No smell of summer. Not a star even tonight. Just the black sky and the long shimmer of snow and the taste of more snow in the air and, near and far, all around, like the night itself howling, the howling of wolves.

Ma and Pa would be asleep or, if awake, thinking about him, maybe asking the Lord to lift His face on him, to lead him not into temptation. In his dreams Grandpa would be giving the British what-for. Nice to be Grandpa, to have outlived all appetites except for food and a pipe. Ram, down in Texas, was scratching his jaw, his eyes full of doubt, while he heard how a skinned wolf came to life.

Now and night and wolf howls and the hoof stamp of a horse and space like a long, dazing drain on the blood and no one alive at all except in the space of the mind; but beyond here, beyond this time and this place, over the bar of now, a ranch house and a helpmate and life sanctified. *A virtuous woman* – Pa read from Proverbs, his face stern as stone – *is a crown to her husband: but she that maketh ashamed is as rottenness in his bones.*

He had two horses toward that ranch, and one of them was fun to work with and a joy to own and fast as any he had ever seen and just maybe faster. Only two, though, and, in addition, a few skins, an interest in a team and wagon, a few dollars, no cows. But the land was here, the good land, the rich buffalo and bunch grass, the bluejoint, owned by nobody, free to all. Godwin was too gloomy. There would be ranches, Indian thieves or not. There were ranches already, and not a million miles from right here, like the one a big man named Granville Stuart was said to be setting up in the Flat Willow country. There'd be more, including his own. So much of prairie, of miles endless and vacant, allowed chances and choices beyond all reasonable hope. It did now, at this minute, as Oregon must have before crowds wore the trail to it deep. All that was needed was cattle or money for cattle. That was all.

A star lighted up through a crack in the clouds and went out again, and the breeze fingered around, keen as cold metal, trying to find a hole in the clothes, making a man move to keep warm, to tramp back and forth while he kept eyes and ears open.

They had strychnine enough to poison wolves enough to form a dozen ranches. For the biggest of carcasses, just three eighths of an ounce, and death then in each bite; and after working it into the flesh a man went around afraid of his hands. But most of the wolves were scared, too, or too wise, or they preferred their own kills, or they gorged themselves on the tons of good meat that hide-hunters had left to rot on the prairie, as in that one spot, not as big as a catch pasture, where sixty-one peeled buffalo lay. Wolfer to rancher! Plowboy to president.

Over east, day began knocking on the skyline, but north and west and south the dark lay thick and deep as if unwilling to clear out. Nobody would be up yet in Fort Benton, but here it was time to stir, to boil the pot and ride bait and skin skins and put out more poison and hope for a turn in the luck. Nothing ventured, nothing gained, thou good and faithful servant.

He put his head inside the war house. Moo Cow was snoring signals to Comanches. "Feel like getting up, you boys?"

12

Tom Ping reined in, puffing a little from riding hard after Sugar and Lat, who had stopped to let him catch up. "Just because you can fly, you don't have to leave me the hell out of sight," he told Lat.

Lat gave a grin that showed he was pleased. "I wasn't pushing him, even." He bent over the saddle and patted Sugar on the neck. He sure did love that horse. Hadn't ever suggested that another man try him, which was all right. Too many cooks spoiled the broth, or the other way round, maybe, with Sugar for broth. "Got plenty wind, too." Lat sat back in the saddle. "Let's go on."

Tom fell in alongside. "Git on. Git on. Git on." He let the words out on a sigh. "Live long enough and you won't be rich, Lat, but just wore to a frazzle. Remember them badgers."

"How else do you do it?"

"All I've ever knowed is work, seems like, and

where's it got me? Work for the nabobs. Work for the brass-ball gentlemen, and don't dast to slap your brandin' iron on anything because the nabobs done it first and called King's X. What's fair for one ain't fair for all no more."

Lat didn't answer right away. He looked over the long snow fields as if he was thinking and squinted toward the sun, which shed light. God knew! but no heat. "There ought to be a way, a rightful way," he said and paused. "And maybe our luck turns at the next bait. If we could only get enough pelts!"

"Sure, if we could, and didn't bust our backs bendin'."

"My father always preached that nothing good came easy."

"Huh! I don't allow that it's so, but my old man wouldn't know the right or the wrong of it, never havin' anything worth a damn unless you count his knack as a stud." He took a minute to get his thoughts lined up while he studied Lat. "You aim high, pard. Bein' better educated is part of it, I guess. You want things nice. Nice outfit somewheres. Nice range. Plenty money. A house with carpets on the floor and a lace cover on the table. Nice hired hands to do the work. Nice, pursy friends. Ain't it so?"

"Part of it." Lat wasn't ruffled, though his smile was small.

"Me, I don't ask much. Money for grub and a roof of my own, instead of ram-jammin' around just for beans, and I'd like to be necked to a woman that suited me. That's about all, but where in hell is it? You can have all your damn high society."

Lat answered soft. "You're just ringy today, partner."

"I s'pose so, Lat, but I hate this badger work, and I don't go for swelled-up men and high-toned, dear-me ladies and stuck-up manners and houses built to mortify a common man."

Lat said, "No," and they rode on.

The bait lay in a hollow and looked from above like a dab of meat in a saucer, dark against the cupped china of snow, a dab with four crumbs of wolves by it that would have to be skinned.

"Four's all," Tom said to Lat after they had halted and counted from the edge of the rim, "and that's plenty for me." Underneath, without reasons enough, he felt a little beat of uneasiness that he wouldn't mention to Lat. They'd be like ducks in a pothole down in that dip, blind to what went on up above.

He took a slow look around, on the open benches and the long flats, and saw the game quiet and nothing else moving. Yesterday, though, they had seen fresh signs of Indians, and In-

160

dians might be ornery here at the end of nowhere with just the pair of them to face. It had been Lat's idea that their party split up and ride bait in two directions and so get more work done. He himself had held his tongue. What the hell? He was as game as the next man.

Why feel spooky? Today was as safe as the days gone before. Who, any more, was afraid of Indians, of the gut-eating beggars that even the proud tribes had become? He wouldn't suggest to Lat that one of them watch on the rim while the other one worked.

"Those wolves won't skin themselves," Lat said.

"I wouldn't care if they're froze too hard already."

They rode down the slope, and Tom unforked his horse and tied it to the horns of what was left of the bait, wishing his knot-headed pony would stand ground-tied like Sugar. He tilted his rifle on the buffalo head beside Lat's.

"One's warm," Lat said and went on to poke the other carcasses. "These don't seem too cold to skin."

Tom slit the belly of a wolf and started on the legs and stopped and looked around again. The earth was quiet as a coffin save for Lat's busy knife. The wolves were bayed out and the buffalo too distant to be heard. Not even the wind whined in this dip, and nothing moved, not a bird, even, in the sky.

He went back to his job. If the saucer rim cut off his view, it hid him, too. The hunches that didn't pan out would fill a good-sized backhouse. Nothing to worry about but the burn of iced flesh on cold fingers. Quit peeking under the bed!

But for Lat, he could be riding stove in some snug bunkhouse, loafing time away until the spring roundup. He could have whiskey and a woman. He wouldn't stink. He wouldn't ache low in the back. He wouldn't call a boar's nest home. He wouldn't be feeling in his hands the creeping bite of frost. Damn Lat and his big notions! Damn Lat! His knife blade whispered that idea.

He wrenched at the pelt and gave it a last flick and tore it loose and stood up. Lat was almost done, too. His hand around the handle of the knife looked red and thick and clumsy.

"You take the warm one," Lat said.

"Goddam it!" Tom answered and hunted more to say. Not much came out. "Your hands is just as cold as mine, pard."

He grabbed the other wolf and went to work, his hands almost unfeeling, touched with frostbite, but still they moved the wolf around and managed the cuts and began the job of separation. Lat, on the softer carcass, was making faster time.

A shake or two, Tom told himself, and he'd be through, thank God; but all at once he felt them at his back, felt them through the lifted bristles of his neck, and he came slow around, and there they were — a line of Indian bucks on foot with loosened shoulder wraps and hands free on their guns.

He said, "Lat!" and, watching, straightened up. Too late for warning now, his pony caught the smell of them and sucked in a snort.

They stood there, six of them, no more than twenty feet away, and bored him with their eyes. On his thigh he felt the chancy help of his six-gun. Yonder, on the bull head, were his old Sharps and Lat's repeater.

From behind him Lat's voice sounded flat. "Easy!" It rose a little. "How, friends?"

An old and withered Indian with a face like a sick hawk's stood a pace in the lead. He grunted through closed lips, sending a small quiver through a sprout of feathers on his head. The others held up, waiting on him. Only their eyes stirred, sliding off to the bait, to the two horses and quickly back again. A young and squatty Indian in a white man's hat kept glancing off at Sugar, his braids swinging to his turns of face.

Now, above them on the hill, Tom saw their

horses, held by squaws and children, saw their dogs rumped down, checked by hand holds on their scruffs.

The old leader stepped ahead, talking in his chest, and the rest pushed forward, guns swung up short and ready. Tom felt Lat beside him.

"How?" Lat said.

"Smoke?" the chief asked. "Drink?" Between their narrowed banks of lids his eyes swam off to Lat.

"Tobacco, Tom?"

"No."

"Present, no, for Injun?" The eyes swam back.

"At camp," Lat said, pointing that direction, and stumbled for their way of talk. "Much smoke. You understand? You savvy? Much meat. Much things for empty belly." He patted his stomach. "Injun savvy?"

"Me savvy. No good."

A broad-faced buck, knife-scarred from eye to jaw, growled words behind the chief and stepped ahead and swung around on him and growled out more. Then all of them were arguing, crowding around the old one and yammering in Indian and swinging out from him to point with hands and musket barrels as if asking yes to murder. But hardly for a minute wasn't someone watching, ready with his gun.

At the side, beyond safe hope of reaching, rested the repeater and the Sharps.

Tom sneaked his hand toward his revolver. Before his fingers touched the butt the chief waved down the hubbub and spoke up. He pointed north and east and south and west, his face lined and solemn, while he talked Indian talk. A man with the pinch of fear in his guts could grab for the idea. White man there. White man there. White man there and there. Injun best walk careful or white man rub him out.

The chief dropped his hand and closed his mouth and waited, his eyes going from buck to buck as though tallying the vote.

They didn't like to simmer down. They grunted, sore, and paced around and swung their muskets, their eyes still mean, but now it was if they just goddamned the luck.

The young buck in the white man's hat held still of a sudden, looking, and passed his gun over to another and quit the bunch and made for Sugar. One by one the rest fell silent, watching him. He picked up the reins and turned and smiled and called back as if laying claim. Sugar put out his nose and snorted at the smell but didn't pull away.

"Whoa, Sugar!" Tom said soft to Lat and didn't get an answer. Lat only stood and watched.

But Sugar let the buck climb on, let him bring the reins snug and put moccasin to stirrup and heave up, let him do it, even, from the right or Indian side.

The Indian waved and dug his heels in and lashed back with the rein ends. For a blink or two it looked as if things would be all right. The Indian lashed again. Then Sugar bogged his head and boiled. Out of that almighty pitch he came lock-legged and went sideways in a spin before the Indian's gutty grunt was done. The buck flew off. Like crack-the-whip. Like the end man in the game. He hit hard and slid and tumbled over and lay spraddled in the shallow snow, and the old chief started for him, hand out as if to ward off hurt.

The young buck moved. He got his hands and knees under him and then his feet and found his bearings and began to lag back to the bunch. Seeing he wasn't harmed, the other Indians started laughting, soft at first, then louder, and louder yet as they made out the black storm in his face. They whooped and hollered and clapped their mouths and pointed at him, adding to the storm.

His step steadied and quickened. He came at them as if to whip them all but, instead, he grabbed his gun back. He wheeled around and leveled for an aim on Sugar.

A blur of movement at the corner of the eye. Lat lunging for the man, lunging open-handed, forgetful of the six-gun on his hip. A shout from somewhere, and the young buck heeling round and seeing and jerking up his musket, and Lat lunging dead on to the eye of it. His own revolver leaping from its keeper and going off, too late. Two blasts, and his the second. Lat staggering backwards, the young buck going down, and then hands on him from behind, hands from everywhere, muscles, a mess of bodies, weighting him to earth, tearing the six-gun from his twisted arm, and him spitting snow and crying to the snow, "You sons-of-bitches! You dirty sons-of-bitches!"

The chief's voice, cracked and commanding, rose above him. Some of the hands left him, but still he couldn't wrestle up. The chief spoke more, and other hands left him and the feet that belonged to them screeched in the snow, and the hands still on him yanked him upright.

He fought his dizziness. He saw Lat standing pale with the burn of powder on his chest, and the young buck standing, too, but gimpy-legged, while the chief bent at his side and fingered for the bullet hole.

Hands still held him. Guns still pointed. He asked, "How bad you hurt, Lat?", and Lat answered thin, "It took me high."

Bending, the chief jerked up his head and held still with the look of listening. Tom heard it then, the sound of rifle shots, one and another and three together, fired out of sight beyond the rim.

The chief snapped straight. His words were shots. He wheeled and beckoned to the squaws and young ones. They set up a clatter as they started down the hill, and he wheeled back, anger in his face, and hushed them with his arms.

One buck ran and gathered up the repeater and the Sharps. One elbowed Lat to Sugar and let him try to get on by himself and then shoved him in the saddle and stepped back for an instant to see would Sugar buck.

The hands left Tom. Something poked him in the back. It was a musket barrel, jabbed by the scar-faced buck. The buck pointed to Tom's horse and made a shoving motion toward the west.

Tom got on and hitched around. Some of the Indian men were mounting. Two squaws fought dogs off from the poisoned bait. Close by, Lat sat sagging in his saddle. The scar-cheeked buck shoved toward the west again and made out as if about to fire.

"Hang on, Lat, and tell me if you can't. He

means us to rattle hocks." Tom wheeled his horse. "You up to it? Lat, tell me! You up to it?" Behind him he heard Sugar stepping out.

"Now what's the head and tail of this?" he asked himself, hardly knowing that he spoke out loud until he saw his horse's ears bent back.

A quick look gave him the answer, and for an instant, which instantly shamed him, he had a notion to light out, for the Indians were falling in behind. Alone, he might have got away.

13

Bullet ache and cold ache were one, and night and day and snow and sky and climb and fall. They mixed in the mind, in the eye, in this torment of flesh that was his and not his. One Indian was another, and Tom Ping one of them, his black forelock whipped by the breeze like their braids. A horse wasn't a horse, not even Sugar. They were all parts of a dream that wouldn't shake loose to let a man find himself well and warm and snug in his bed.

Now it was day, and now it was dusk, and there in dusk after dusk were the night camps, the tatters of blankets and hides and the tiny fire under tiny meat that the stomach dreamed made it sick. Night moved into sunup, and the sun fired the snow and the snow fired the skull, and in the white blindness level and ridge and shallow and drift were the same. Or the bright day gave way to gray, with the snow weeping thick and the bitter wind mourning, driving into the clothes and back out, letting other winds have their turns at the pinched life inside.

No Oregon, except in other dreams. No Fort Benton. No Pa or Ma or Callie Kash. No God even. Thou shalt set no god above no-god. No nothing, then or now. Ghosts of night and day. Ghost-ache of cold and wound. Ghosts of other riders, heads crooked against the wind.

He went on in pride, in the hard dream of pride, among hank-haired shadows of men, now alongside a shadow who went on in pride, his Indian mouth shut and his body unflinching and his leg swelling up in its legging, while around was the snow and the soft death waiting there.

"Country's changed some, Lat. See them mountains north? Where's that take us, you reckon? And what's these redskins up to, pard? But don't make talk unless you feel strong enough."

Buttes floated. Mountains waved. They swam ahead, keeping their distance, no nearer ever. Nothing was nearer. Nothing changed. Step by step, he and the shadows stayed fixed where they were, in light and dark and cold and blow and ache.

"You better, Lat? Feelin' perkier, boy? We'll make out, you bet. Can't whip us, these tatter-assed Injuns."

The face against the gloom of night was like a dark moon over him, a close and ragged moon. "I swear it looks some healed. Leave me swab it now with this hot rag."

The rag was wet and warm and wasn't real and didn't touch the pain.

He thought he heard himself say, "Thanks." He thought he tried a piece of meat that Tom held to his mouth.

"Plenty grit in your gizzard, boy."

Asleep, maybe he could shake the dream.

As if the devil or someone had sworn to wipe out all life, the storm whistled out of the north. Tom felt it like fire, like a blown flame that shriveled the flesh and withered all but the little knot of the guts which itself hurt with dying. Or he felt it like knives — this licking wind, this sharp, driven snow, this thrusting frost. It cut through the clothes, through the flesh, and stabbed at the bones. It froze the breath on a man's collar, froze the hair in his nose, froze the eye-water that kept crying down in his beard. It iced the snoots of the horses, building milk moss from the leak of their nostrils and the ooze of their spit. It slashed them to southward against bit and rein held tight to the west.

It had been cold before but not close to this.

This was as cold as cold ever could be. Even the camp fire at night was only a whisper of warmth, a promise of heat somewhere in the world, maybe far off in Texas; but here in itself was the whole world, lapped white from skyline to skyline, with no end to be seen and none to be hoped for.

But except for one goddam blind-streaming, blind-screaming, goddam ground-blizzard day when a man had to feel his way back from taking a leak, the Indians kept going, the older ones hunched deep in their loose fittings of blankets and skins and two little ones riding in a skin hammock hung between skid poles hitched to a poor-as-dirt pony. Now and then the two nits that would make lice if they lived long enough poked their heads from under their buffalo robes, silent and round-eyed, and ducked back under cover at the slash of the wind.

The devil was after these Indians, or so they must think. Or other red devils like the Sioux or the Crows. Which didn't make sense, or why would they hold him and Lat prisoner? Maybe, cut off from some main band, they just wanted to sneak safe to their reservation where they could scatter and lose themselves, or maybe they aimed to go on into Canada like Sitting Bull. Meantime they'd hold him and Lat with them so's word of their doings wouldn't get out till too late. What proved something or other was they kept going.

West, always west, and now north of west. A little draggle-tail column of bucks, squaws, cayuses and curs, each puffing clouds with his breath, and the snow squealing under hoof and the wind for once stopping to catch its wind so it could blow more, and the air so still that the cold itself was a sound and the white lifting of buttes far ahead was as lifeless and fixed as a glassed-in picture of buttes.

When he tried to think how long, the days since the shooting ran into each other. It could be Tuesday or Sunday, or the fourteenth or the twentieth or whatever. Time as unknown as the lost country they traveled. Time blurred always by worry. Lat so weak and sick! And the two of them like brothers, better than the real brothers he used to know.

He heard a grunt behind him. It came from the scar-cheeked buck, who was telling him to catch up with the bunch. All right. All right. But another day would come. No one could ever say that Tom Ping turned the other cheek, which Lat once said was in the Bible. Fool advice if it was there, like other pious bull he'd heard.

On and on and on to Jesus. Through this unending snow. In this forever land. Under this cruel-hearted sky. On to everloving Jesus.

"How's it go, Lat? Just get through today, and you'll make the rest, boy. Warmin' a little, ain't it? And you got some blood in your face."

But what was the good of it with Lat mostly unanswering, his whole, little strength spent in keeping himself in the saddle?

Night, and the squaws setting lodge poles with hands stiff as clubs, the squaws wrangling firewood and boiling a pot if they had something to boil, and the proud palefaces getting the leavings and one of them being grateful for that much. The ground for a bedstead and a saddle cloth and an old robe for a bed and frost breathing up out of the ground, frost breathing sideways and down from the sky, the froze hands of frost raching into the tepee that four of them shared, and, unseen on the hills, the wolves rumped and crying. The wounded buck, Hole-in-the-Leg, twisting and moaning, and Lat moaning, too, in sleep both of them loosed from their holds on themselves.

Spread Lat with your robe, boy! You haven't got a wound in your chest. You've got blood in your system and muscles to exercise to keep it stirred up. Lay it on gentle, and to hell with the old chief and his watching eye. Sleep's what he needs, sleep and a warm bed and something

175

to eat besides an old piece of elk gut. Bad off, he is, but still not too bad to sleep with his bridle so the bit'll be warm for his Sugar. Lay it on gentle.

A man lay and thought, or just thought he thought, things dodging in and out of his head while the cold stayed there. Moo Cow and Godwin and Carmichael, and were they alive any more? Here, roundabout if half-froze, were Hawk Face, the chief, and Cut Cheek and Hole-in-the-Leg who used to be White Hat. Names came for all of them, like Jug Butt for one of the squaws. Lat was Hole-in-the-Chest, not Lat any more or in any way, not in speech or in looks, for he hardly spoke and looked older and thin, and the muscles ridged tight on his jaw points.

Come morning, they'd break camp and push on with not one Indian complaining, though Christ knew how they lived in what passed for clothes with them when even the dogs trailed along whimpering and the horses, starved down to ribs, wouldn't try for a nibble of brush. He and Lat were better-fitted, warmer-dressed, but nearer froze to death, Lat natur-ally. But Hole-in-the-Leg naturally, too, then. Not Hole-in-the-Leg but Swole Leg, Swole-Big-as-Hell Leg, Swoll-to-the-Grave Leg. And there would be one good Indian.

176

A fed man, like a fed steer, could stand cold, but where was the meat? No buffalo here. None now at all. Only an antelope once in a long time, or an elk or a deer, and these next to impossible to hunters who used bows and arrows because arrows were quiet.

But let it go. Let it all go. Don't think at all, not even of Lat, not even of Jen and what she has waiting there in some other world. Catch some sleep if you can. Go to sleep with the cold.

Along toward the white-dark of night they came to some brush where a summer stream must have flowed once, and the bucks slid off their horses, saying without word that here was the place to make camp.

Tom staggered for balance as his feet hit the ground, staggered and steadied and hobbled ahead, his voice crying, "Lat! I'll help you up, pard."

He bent over Lat. "Can't sleep in the snow, boy. Can't give up now," he said, but as he spoke he thought it was no use, and more words came trembling from his throat. "The dirty sons-of-bitches!"

Lat moved. With the help of an arm he got up. But still, by God!

14

There was a whisper in the night, a distant
stirring, a sort of blowing music that the ear
kept reaching for. It could be no more than
dream or fever, or the murmur of tired blood
inside the head, for all was quiet here — no
flutter of tepee, no shrill of wind or rasp of
snow, no click of brush. And yet, and yet, at the
edge of hearing, the singing rustle, like a low
chant from the land or like the flurry of far
wings.

Lat could feel the slow tap of his heart, tapping blood toward hands and feet and parts
that blood would never reach. Slow pulse on
pulse, and blood enough to feed the mind,
which sharpened as the body failed, as if God
let a man have one last look before blowing
out the lamp. He needed to turn over, to huddle closer in his covers, and by and by, when
he found the will and strength, he'd do so.
After a while. Everything in time. Easier to

lie cold than to move.

Was it angels on the wing, that far-off rustle? The dark angel soon to take him to the Light? Or the devil riding? It was nothing. It was whatever crazy thing the mind made up. And it didn't matter. Angel or devil, up or down, let it come, harps and golden streets or fire and brimstone.

A dog barked outside, and the young buck here in the tent spoke out in his sleep and breathed short and shallow afterwards, as if the one word had worn him out. Two for the Light then. Two for hell's heat. A pair for the happy hunting grounds. The music blew closer, faded out.

Tom was trying to rub himself warm again, his hands in the dark sounding harsh against clothing and skin. Better to be so near dead as no longer to care. But thanks, Tom, for sticking. Thanks for not making a break when you might have. Thanks for it all. Will you see the grave's covered with rocks so the wolves won't get to it? God restoreth the soul, but the body still likes to be kept in one piece, not gnawed on and chewed up and left scattered as filth. You can understand that, Tom?

A little gust of wind worried the tepee and cried away, and another came in its place, and another, running ahead of the breeze that began to blow steady.

So that was the music. That was the rustle of wings. The warning of wind where winds always blew and after the warning the wind. That was all there was to it.

Nothing looked so big at the last. What were women then, or a girl that he could see just as a flash of yellow hair? What did it matter that Tom could be so coarse, or that he himself had felt guilty thinking so? What was sin, or punishment if it did come? What was home and the drawn-off memories of it? What was life or death, and where was the mortal dread? The little things counted, like deciding whether to move, like feeling the cold as something close and far off at the same time and letting it have its way, like struggling against a cough because a cough hurt. A person just waited.

He felt he could turn now, and he eased over and brought his knees to his middle, and slowly it came to seem that he was warm at last, warm and comfortable and drowsy as it was said a freezing man came to be. A good way to die then, with nothing hurting and the mind swimming out into sleep.

Tom wakened him with a tap on the cheek. "Hey, boy! Hey?"

"What?"

The smudge of Tom's face in the dawn light

180

of the tepee broke wide in a smile. "Lat, by God she came! The chinook came! Warm as spring outside!"

The warm wind kept blowing, the dry wind out of the southwest where a cloud bank sat low and dark on the skyline. In a day it lapped up most of the snow, baring patches of earth furred with last season's grass which the gaunt horses snatched at under saddle and cropped into the mud on night picket. In two days it made next to nothing of drifts once head high and higher. And still it kept blowing, until the whole body of earth lay brown and breathing except for the topknots of buttes and, away and away, the high float of mountains.

Out of somewhere came magpies and snow-birds by dozens. The Indian children wiggled out from under their robes. The bucks loosened their wraps. The squaws dared to chatter. The horses walked with new life. Under a wide-sailing sun small bunches of antelope stood and watched and took alarm and circled away, their rumps shining whiter than the remembered white of the land.

Riding and resting, Lat tried on his tongue the words for this wind. Chinook. Promise of spring. Breath of the dark cloud, the long, singing breath. Life-saver. Soul-saver.

One soul, not two. By a miracle Hole-in-the-Leg rode his horse still, but his leg bloated his pants leg and bulged through the slits cut to allow for the swell. Not even pride could keep him these days from riding one-sided. His face was as old as the face of suffering, as young-old as the face of a sure-to-die child. His eyes stared ahead as if opened on things beyond this earth and this sky and this close wind-riffle of grass. But the hard present will of him showed, chiseled in cheeks and chin.

The sight of him soured the rest of the band. The bucks would be going along, glad for the wind and the warmth, and one or another of them would happen to look, and the face he turned would have turned ugly and he'd pat his gun. Around camp they poked orders. They growled at giving up scraps of meat. They encouraged the squaws to point and make dirty motions like those of dehorning a man.

Only the old chief kept apart. Like a father he rode along silent and set-faced, his gaze going often to Hole-in-the-Leg, and at the fire stayed close by his side. There he burned grass he had gathered and into the blaze sprinkled pinches of stuff from a pouch, saying medicine words as he did so and making a clack with some kind of rattle. Afterwards he stared at Hole-in-the-Leg as if through his eyes he could lend him his strength.

Once, seemingly, he argued to pitch camp and stay there for the sake of his son, and the rest of the bucks gathered round and talked back, and the next day they went on, though Hole-in-the-Leg had to be dragged along in a travois like the children.

"You watch them two like you was sorry," Tom said to Lat. It was early night, and they sat cross-legged at a little distance from the others. A squaw passing them stooped and reached toward Tom with one hand and made believe to get a handful and to cut it off with the other. "Louse-bound sow!" Tom said as she left. "Lat, sure as Hole-in-the-Leg cashes in, they aim to scalp us or worse."

The camp fire had died to a blown spark. The mother of the two children, in the darkness looking more than ever like a walking sack, was herding the two little walking sacks to their tepee. One buck grunted to another, and the other grunted back, and both fell silent, having said in two grunts all there was to be said.

"Listen, Lat! You ain't even listenin'."

The chief sat silent and unmoving by his son's side, his head bent and his hawk's nose catching a little of the firelight against the shadow of his face. After a while he would help

Hole-in-the-Leg to the tepee, but now, right after supper, he let him rest under a buffalo robe spread near the fire.

"I thought you was crazy back there, talkin' in your sleep about comin' out the best man, but this is sure-enough crazy, feelin' sorry for 'em."

It was enough to sit quiet with the warm wind blowing, to sit dog-tired after another day in the saddle, and slow and deep inside to feel the body knitting. As another body wasn't. He didn't want to talk, but still he said, "They don't know the first thing about doctoring."

"It ain't no skin off'n you that they burn smoke and shake rattles, thinkin' to cure him."

"No," Lat said. In his mind's eye were those waiting-to-die eyes. Grandpa could tell the chief how to work on a fester. A horse sneezed in the darkness and went back to ripping the grass roots, and a couple of night birds cried back and forth, asking each other, please, would things be all right, and somewhere a dog growled out no, not if left up to him.

"We ain't doctors, either, and if we set up to be and still he died, there'd right away be three to bury."

"You just said we'd die anyhow."

"That's what I'm comin' to. We got to make a break." Tom's head turned toward the scar-cheeked buck who was keeping an eye on them, his gun close at hand. "They're watchin' us closer'n ever, thinkin' you might be well enough to skedaddle."

"Not yet, Tom."

"Got to be soon. That son-of-a-bitch might croak any time." Tom waited for an answer. "You ain't even got the gumption to be scared!"

Fear was a thing remembered. The leap in the chest, the suck of breath, the knot in the stomach — these belonged to strength and full blood. Weakness and tiredness just made a man wonder. "When the time's right," he said. "I'm dead for sleep now."

The next day they came to a river, to a sheet of tree-bordered ice so broad that it had to be the Missouri. The chief made them line out, so as not to put too much weight in one place, and led them across fast, the horses sinking hoof-deep in the top slush and snorting at the growl of live water beneath.

Although it was no later than mid-afternoon and two of the men seemed to want to go on, the chief ordered camp pitched in a broad gully leading down to the stream. While the squaws rustled wood and one buck went hunting for meat, the chief helped his son from the hammock and put him down on a robe and sat there and sat there; and Hole-in-the-Leg was no better but worse, his eyes like drying potholes in the dried plains of his face.

As the sun edged the westward bluffs and dusk began to smoke the river valley, the chief rose and faced around to the north where a bald hill lifted close. He took a breath and set out for it, his feet working slow in the mud. Lat watched him climb, watched the tired pull and hoist of his moccasins and the upward creep of his figure. High up, the slanting sun touched him, glowing like firelight on his buckskins. He stopped at the top and sat down, facing this last light, and the trunk of his body moved back and forth as if saying, "Please, if it be thy will," to the gods of the sun and the sky and the empty land. For a long time he sat there, his figure bronze and then black against the great arch of sky, and then he got up and lagged down, his face set, and went to the boy and saw that the potholes had closed over.

A cry wrenched out of him, a half cry choked off at the instant of sound as if crying wasn't for men. It left nothing but silence and un-spoken ache, left nothing to do but the one thing.

Lat got up and went to them, and the way of Grandpa's treatment stood clear in his mind. "Me doctor."

"Lat!" The word came from behind him. He

bent over. Hands grabbed him from the side. They belonged to two bucks who yanked him up. He twisted free, feeling the tear of his own wound. "Lat! Goddam it!" The hands grabbed him again, and the chief spoke throaty from the ground, and the bucks loosened their holds. The chief had his own hand up. He spoke some more. The bucks backed away. The chief's eyes were waiting questions.

"Medicine," Lat said. "Cure him, could be."

The questions stood sharp, stood doubtful and wondering, and then the chief bowed as he had on the hill, lowering both body and head.

Bucks and squaws and young ones and even the camp dogs formed a ring around Lat. He pointed to a kettle and then down the slope to the river. "Water. Get water." At grunted words from the chief the fat-rumped squaw waddled to the kettle and started for the stream. The fire was too small, and he set about to make it bigger himself, but the chief spoke again, and another squaw began piling on wood.

"Need knife," Lat said. "Knife." A buck touched his arm. He was holding one out.

Hole-in-the-Leg lay under a blanket, still breathing, still hot with live fever. Like an overstuffed casing his legging peeled away at the push of the knife, and the released flesh bloated out. At the rim of firelight two feet trudged and halted close. It was the squaw with the water. A point to the fire took her away. Up and down from the scabbed ends of the wound the poison was cooking, sending red streamers into the thigh from the purpled swell of the knee and the calf. The toes, even, were fat, like the toes of some monster baby.

The leg was laid bare. The kettle was heating. Needed now were some cloths and a forked stick, one with a long shaft. "Blanket," he told the chief, touching the one the chief had drawn over his neck. "Soogan for medicine." The chief took his own off and handed it over and watched without movement or speech while Lat cut it in pieces and dropped one piece in the kettle and the others close by.

Now for the forked stick. He would have to find it himself. Not through his words or his signs could they understand. He moved to the edge of the circle, and the edge opened for him. "Get stick," he told the chief before going on. They let him go, all of them silent, the bucks, the squaws, the old chief, but not Tom, who stood back, for the moment forgotten, and blocked the way.

"What in hell, Lat!"

"Got to."

"Why?"

"I don't know."

"Turn the other cheek, and we both lose our ass!"

"Call it crazy, but I couldn't just let him die, Tom."

"I got a notion to make a run for it, that's what! Plenty of chances with them so interested in you makin' medicine."

"I couldn't keep up with you anyhow, and no other partner would have stuck half as long. Do what you think best and be awful careful and don't be sore at me, Tom. I'm forever obliged as it is."

Tom's face went soft and uncertain. He bent it from sight and scuffed at the ground. "You'd've done the same," he said, "and you know goddam well I'm not takin' off now."

Lat touched his arm and walked on to a willow bush where in the darkness he found a crotched stem. He cut it and trimmed it and sharpened the end of the shaft.

The water was hot when he got back. He fished out the piece of blanket and dropped in another and took the first over and swathed the sick leg.

Later he used the second piece and later a third and a fourth and later the first one reheated; and the late stars came on to shine like other eyes watching, joining those of the chief and the bucks and the squaws and the fire-glinted eyes of the dogs, all taking cold note of how he had to drag slower and slower from kettle to leg and to kettle again.

But the time had come anyhow, if it ever was coming. He signaled to build up the fire so's to have light and skinned down the last swathe, baring the top scab, and with his knife worked at its softened crust. He had thought when it came off that the pus would well out as if a cork had been pulled; instead, it leaked up in slow beads, too slow and too small to drain out the corruption. He lifted the leg and flaked off the underneath scab and again got only an ooze.

So there was just one thing to do, according to Grandpa. He lowered the leg and lifted his knife and took careful sight and drove the blade in, hearing the quick mutter of the Indians around him. Hole-in-the-Leg didn't murmur or move. He might have been dead, except that up from the pull of the knife sprang a sick stream. A jab underneath let out another.

Lat forced his forked stick in the ground and lifted the leg and set the heel in the crotch for good drainage and raised his eyes to the watchers. They had gathered close. They showed no anger, no thanks, nothing that a white man could read.

Let them spare him or kill him. All he wanted

was rest. He rose and by motions attempted to tell them to keep hot packs on the leg. As he started away, Hole-in-the-Leg let out a long, groaning sigh, of pain or relief.

15

The chief led the way, riding easy on his knot-head of a pony while the wind played with his braids. The others strung back from him, going along easy, too, as if now and at last they could almost afford to relax, though twice they had veered away from their set course, once to avoid meeting up with a freight train and again a little party of horsemen. Behind Lat the squaws kept up a chatter, maybe telling that here was their brother, their white brother, maker of the big medicine.

To the west was a lake, shored white with alkali, and ahead to the north two side-by-side buttes with a gap in between, and all floated tiny, rocked by the wind, in the billows of space. Space had no beginning and no end, or the wind, either, and so neither was real, and a man pinched himself but still dreamed.

Lat looked back at Tom, whose eyes were like eggs in the black nest of his whiskers, and farther back at the squaws, at the fat squaw; and it was night again in the riverside gully, and Hole-in-the-Leg had come to his senses and his leg slendered down. And the scarred Indian was saying, while he waved toward his wife, "My squaw, you squaw. You take 'im." The fat squaw was smiling and nodding. She still nodded, and the buck, too, as if both understood, after he stuttered, "Bad medicine. Poison he come back to Injun. Spirit say no."

The chief pointed his horse toward the gap between the two waving buttes.

Or it was later, and Tom Ping was saying, "You should have took on that old hay bag. I would have, even if I don't like 'em so hefty. The closer the bone the sweeter the meat." But it was old Colly speaking, his words windborne across miles and time, old Colly at last making sense: the closer the mountains the sweeter the chinook, the sweeter the chinook the better the range. That's it, eh, Colly?

The buttes reared and steadied as they rode through, and ahead a broad valley slept in the blown sunlight, and a stream slept, and trees.

The better the range the better the beef they butchered by night, above a distant scatter of lights which Lat could hear Ram Butler saying was Sun River, not so far, boy, from the trail over from Oregon. Stolen beef, but they were hungry. To cover up, one of the bucks had skinned out the figure 4 brand and cut off the cropped ears and buried them all in an old badger hole.

"Lat?" Tom rode alongside, his face turned and the nest of his whiskers flattening out with the wind. "Thought you said we'd cut loose today, now we know pretty well where we are?"

They could have cut loose before, could have struck out as they pleased, in any direction, after Hole-in-the-Leg began to get well. The bucks had quit riding herd on them then and with ceremony had turned back their guns, and the squaws smiled instead of making out to unman them. But for want of a better choice they had stuck, being out of danger and, till last night, hazy about their location.

"What do you say?" The wind took the words from Tom's mouth, leaving just their echo in the eyes squinched against it.

"Pretty soon. From what I can make out, the chief's got a spot picked."

"He don't have to show us."

"Wait."

They didn't wait long. A little farther on the chief pulled his horse in and looked back, telling them without words to come up. The rest of the bunch straggled up, too, but, except for Hole-in-the-Leg, kept a few feet apart, giving them council room.

The chief pointed east, to the valley and stream that curved east from the north and lost themselves in the folding reaches of plain. he raised his hand without changing direction, pointing still farther, to the end of the earth, to the wash-up of land against sky. "Benton," he said. "Go all same river."

For a while he kept pointing, then swung his arm to the north which the valley sloped down from before bending east. To the left, to the west, over the benches, stood the snow-white and rock-blue of the mountains. "Tansy," he said. He had trouble with the word. "Tansy-town."

Lat answered, "Me see," but the chief jabbed with his finger as if to dispute him. Looking closer, he saw what the chief's sharper eyes saw — a building, a cabin, two cabins or more in the bed of the valley.

The chief's hand came down and moved in front of him, the back of it turning under and the thumb sprouting out. "No!" he said. "Go Benton better." His eyes fixed on Lat.

Lat bowed low over the horn of his saddle. If the chief feared Tom and he might ride to the cabins and recruit a war party, let him rest easy.

The chief bobbed his head and heeled his

horse without saying goodbye and then, as the rest were about to set out, swung around and came back. "Rising Moon, me."

Lat tapped his own chest. "Lat Evans."

The chief had a try at the sounds and made a poor out. "Medicine, you. Heap Medicine." He gestured toward Hole-in-the-Leg. "Little Runner."

Hole-in-the-Leg smiled, his teeth showing strong in his still peaked face, and went grave again.

"What do you call me?" Tom asked, reining closer.

The chief answered, "Injuns go now."

He heeled his horse again and stopped it before it could start and, as if not enough had been said or done, held out his hand. When they had shaken. Hole-in-the-Leg pulled over. "Brother," he said as their hands met.

They rode away at a walk, and after them went the others, the bucks, the squaws, the little papooses, all of them making little signs of good luck and good-bye.

"By God, the ball's over," Tom said, watching them go, maybe feeling himself the close emptiness left in the emptiness everywhere.

There were the Indians, step by step drawing off. There was the valley, close and sweet to the west wind, and the river and trees sleeping winter away. "Which way?" he asked Tom, knowing the answer.

"You got one guess." Tom's smile moved his whiskers. "I been around, pard, too much, I s'pose." The smile had faded and Tom's voice gone soft. "I don't know why, but damn if that Jen don't rub 'em all out."

The sweeter the meat.

"Benton," Lat said, and together they aimed for the far wall of sky.

Part Three

16

"You awake, Lat?"

He was lying out on the plains again, and it was Tom's voice speaking, sounding curiously soft and light, and then the words lifted him from his dream and opened his eyes. Callie stood at the bed holding a breakfast tray, her mouth smiling a little asking smile, as if she were eager to feed him or go away, whichever was his pleasure.

He hitched himself up on one elbow and saw through the window that it was snowing outside, and yet, when he looked back at her, her hair seemed to shine even in this dull light. The little wood stove by the sidewall was crackling cheerfully, sending out a pleasant warmth, and for an instant he could see her firing it, trembling in the chill dawn while he lay asleep, working with quiet, careful movements so as not to rouse him before the room was comfortable.

For nothing he had things so nice. The wages of sin were a warm nest and breakfast in bed. A no-good's delight!

He said, "Wide awake."

"Hungry?"

"Uh-huh. Thanks."

She looked with open curiosity at his bare arm and bare chest. "You're getting back some weight. I swear, you were the thinnest thing!" She set the tray on the stand by the bed and then sat down in the straight-backed chair close to him. As usual, she would watch him eat, insisting that he consume the last crumb. "Now go to it," she said, "and don't start fussing because I bring you breakfast."

He took a bite, wondering how much she was out of pocket for bacon and eggs and other good fare. "I'm leaving here today."

"Not yet, Lat! Please!"

"Why not? You want me to sponge on you forever? Tom went out and got a job."

"But you were hurt. You didn't know how weak you were." She reached out and put a hand on the covers, over his foot. "I like to take care of you."

He sipped the coffee and savored the taste of it before answering. "I'm strong enough now."

She waited until his eyes came to her and then moved in the chair, lithe as a kitten, maybe purposely tempting, as if, where all was understood, all was open and innocent. "Here you had what you wanted, you said once."

It had been what he wanted, not just to have her but to lie in bed, in a good bed, and be warm, and warmer for the warmth of the small body alongside, to eat and to rest and to sleep and to love in the warm, lingering mist of sleep, lost to all wishes but these, lost in the good of them to the right and wrong. What did guilt matter then or what people could say? And it was true he hadn't known his own weakness on reaching Fort Benton, half frozen and famished from bucking a storm that howled down from the north after he and Tom had said goodbye to the Indians. They had managed to get clean clothes, mostly on credit, and had tidied up at the barber's and come straight to Miss Fran's, and Callie somehow seemed to be waiting, and he had given himself to her comforts.

She raised her hand from the bed and spread the small palm in a gesture of asking. "Isn't this good enough?" Her voice was wistful. "Aren't I?"

"Better than I deserve, but don't you see?" While he studied what more to say, footsteps sounded in the hallway outside. The door opened without a knock and let in Miss Fran.

She eyed them as if she had caught them in sin, in the sin of not being together in bed, or in the sin of being in bed without money to pay, which was more to the mark. She hadn't put her hair up yet or changed to her company dress. She looked like a ruffled goose — big breast, big tail, tilted on sparrow feet.

Her tone was more fussy than harsh. "I just thought I'd tell you again, Callie, that it's about time to hustle," she said, her eyes on Lat. "More of them traders and such is driftin' back."

Under her gaze Lat asked, "More?"

"Buffalo's peterin' out, like you know, which means we got to shake our tails not to peter out, too."

Callie said, "All right, Aunt Fran. Now please leave us alone."

Miss Fran looked from Callie to Lat and to Callie again, saying more with her eyes than she could say with her tongue. "Sometimes I wisht you wasn't my niece, Callie. It's a bad example for the house." To Lat she explained, "We got to have money."

Callie gave her a hard stare, which the soft cap of hair made harder yet. "Please go!"

"Oh, I ain't faultin' you, dearie. You're a good earner, I know." Aunt Fran half turned with an air of discouragement. Her head went down, and her eyes studied the floor, over the outthrust of bosom. One hand came up, asking for understanding. It was a teensy hand, crowded with flesh at the wrist. Her voice held the note of soft grievance. "I'm just tryin' to look out for you, like I promised." She sighed as if the job had been almost too much for her. Her gaze lifted to Lat and held on him while she spoke to Callie. "I don't know what your folks would say to this, was they around."

"I'll make it up, every cent," Lat said.

"Please leave us alone," Callie asked.

Miss Fran kept on looking at Lat. "Yes," she said finally. "Leastwise I hope so."

She pivoted herself clear around and pegged to the door on her tiny feet. She opened it and went out and drew it to and opened it again. Half of her came back in. "It's a high price to pay for lally-gaggin'," she told Callie, as if she could have this little triumph and seal the door upon it. "And it won't get you anywheres. Never, anywheres." The latch clicked sharply after her.

Lat listened to the tap of her heels, tapping down the hall like overloaded canes on the march, to money and business and the responsibilities of a going and respectable house where the likes of him was too low, being broke, and lower yet, being so high-minded about virtue and sin. One working hive and he the drone, damning the work while swimming in honey; the drone listening to the now-and-then day-time visitors, to the male voices at night and the shrill come-ons of Amy Lou or Jen and the scuff of feet down the hall and the re-scuff as someone ankled out, satisfied; and here he stayed, a guest of the house, keeping a good earner from her honest business.

"Don't mind Aunt Fran," Callie said.

"Mind her? She's right. I'm no better than a tinhorn P.I."

"Eat your breakfast," she said and, as the words struck her: "Not you, Lat! Not us!"

"Not a dime to my name. Nothing in sight but a bill that Jehu won't pay."

"It doesn't matter. We'll get along."

"You want me to be known as a pimp?"

She spoke in a small voice. "Don't call yourself that. It's dirty words that make things dirty, like — like whore. Don't call me that, either, Lat, ever."

He was half of a mind to ask her what she was then, but he held back the question in the face of another. "What have I got that you waste your time and your money?"

She got up without answering and pulled down the shade, darkening the room to all but the shadow of light and the flicker of fire through the damper. She came back and moved the tray to the side of the table and sat on the edge of the bed and laid her hand on his face. "You're just upset with yourself, Lat. I know. I know you."

"What do you see?"

"Someone that's kind," she answered, low-voiced, her head turned away while her hand stroked his forehead. "You don't know how hungry a girl gets for someone that's kind."

There flashed into his mind a picture of her, small and forlorn, knowing only the rough and heartless embraces of rough men and the heartless concern of Aunt Fran. Because he was kind, she loved him, because he never spoke sharply, like now, and never wanted to hurt her, being sore himself, like now. His hand closed over the hand on his face.

The low voice went on. "You're a gentleman, Lat. That's why you're mad at yourself, thinking you're not being one. But you are. You always will be."

She turned to him and slipped her hand out of his and cradled it under his head and leaned slowly forward, with the torn look of hurt, and caressed his face with her lips. Against his chest one of her breasts arched and moved.

This was what she knew to give, the great and pitiful little. This was the natural relief, the final comfort, the first and last of woman's services, for money or for love. As a man believeth in his heart, so was she — warm, all-giving, bound and blind to wrong, through use useful. The drawn shade, the lips on his face, the breast on his chest, all were of one piece, all done with the one wish to soothe and restore him, to make him forget in the flooding act of forgetfulness.

All done to bind him closer perhaps, all binding him closer at any rate — but he lifted his face and found her mouth.

"Lat," she said, her lips moving on his, "just be happy! Be happy for now!"

He brought her down by his side, under the covers, and fumbled at her dress, and her hands joined his and unbuttoned it and slipped it off. Another time, an earlier time, and she would have undressed out of bed and let him warm to the sight of her, as she just now would have done had he asked her to. Somehow she seemed to know that immodesty by itself bothered him.

She stretched out beside him, awaiting his wishes, and he pushed his hand under her neck and cushioned her head on his shoulder and lay flat on his back while one thing and another took turns in his mind, putting off for the time the time that was bound to be. This place. This stage in his life, and what did it mean for the rest? This wheat-yellow head against his and thigh against thigh. This accepting of charity. This almost pimping. This branding himself, if decent men knew. This branding himself, anyhow, before God. The way of the transgressor was hard, and the sins of the father passed on. Then be gelded, like Sugar. Sugar, the good horse, the fast horse, being kept on the cuff by old Whitey, who liked his whiskey, while Jehu dodged honest debts. Where were Moo Cow and Godwin and Carmichael? Dead yonder on the shrill plains, worse treated than another transgressor whose wages were a girl at his side? Worse treated than Tom, who was happy with Jen and by day did rough work so as not to be on charity, too? Transgressor Tom, who took little stock in the Book, asking who made such rules and where was the why of them. Let Pa answer that one. he could lay down the law. Don't question! Don't doubt, son! Only fear God, Who loves one and all, and keep your hands out from under the covers!

Callie kissed him behind the ear and said, almost whispering, "I save myself for you, Lat. When you're gone, I will."

She might have been a good wife swearing faithfulness, and for a moment he didn't know what she meant. Then it came to him. By keeping cold with others, by just pretending warmth, she kept love pure for him in her sight. He saw them, the lines of grinning men, obliged and billed, who thought they'd had her but within herself left her untouched. Public body, public vessel, pure and secret heart!

He answered with a little flex of the muscles under her head and lay still, feeling her breath light and warm on his neck. She pressed closer to him so that he felt her all along his side, from her feet to her knees to the warm triangle of groin to her breasts and back to the triangle. The proud and shameful strength was ready in him, but Pa stood in his mind's eye with the whip in his hand and the wrought-up righteousness in his face.

"Don't you want me to?" she asked.

"I'm glad," he said and nodded his head against hers while the words drifted out into the edge of things, away from him and the hay shed in Oregon and the small neighbor girl and the unbuttoned trousers and the raised yellow dress and the young curiosity. They were only looking. They knew nothing but that. But there stood Pa in the door of the shed, his eyes squinting and hardening, his face like the tool of God's, his face God's itself. The girl cried out faintly and dodged around and ran off, and the will of the Lord came on.

Callie's voice breathed in his ear, "Tell me what's in your head, Lat," and he answered, "Nothing much," and was silent, for the whip was whistling justice, was visiting the divine wrath on the trespasser. There were the sing and the hard cut of it and the blow of Pa's breath and the sing and the cut and the blow. They stopped, and Pa stood, breathing deep, and slowly his face changed, from the set of wrath to the twist of some torment. From what was left of the wrath his mouth got out, "Now take care! Pretty soon you'll be old enough to ruin a girl. I'd rather see you dead!"

Pa looked up then, as if to find word he'd done right, and afterwards down at the ground. His shoulders sagged, and the eyes he turned on Lat seemed deserted and beaten. He wasn't God any longer or God's tool or Pa himself, but a stranger on whom God's hand lay too heavy. At last he said, "I'm sorry, son," and stood there, unsure and lonely; and this was the worst, worse than the shame and the wrath, to see Pa undone, lost somewhere between the Lord and himself. This was the end of things. Lat cried out, "Oh, Pa!" and ran to him and felt the whip hand kind and sad on his shoulder.

Lat moved in bed, hardly knowing he had until Callie spoke. "You think too much, Lat."

She was inside him somehow, partner to the

beat of his heart and the tick of his mind. Her hand trailed down gently, from his face to his chest. It lay warm on his stomach.

He reached over and put his other arm around her and turned her to him and kissed her, and the strength reared in him again, and Pa backed off into shadow. Whatever this was, it couldn't be ruination for her.

But before they went on, she drew her face away from his and smiled a small, half-joking smile and said, "I know how to handle you, mister. I'll always know how to handle you."

Her face sobered then. "Will I, Lat?"

17

Lat opened the door and stole a look around before letting himself out. No one was watching, and he stepped ahead and eased the door shut, hearing behind him Happy's soft Negro voice. "Come back, Mist' Lat. Jes' feel at home any time."

Yesterday's light snow was thawing under a sky in which one cotton cloud sailed. The footpath was slippery and the road at its end raw with half-melted clods. Down from the house the Missouri lay frozen, slush-white but dark-patched with the promise of reviving life underneath. Ahead, a couple of birds dared the footing, stepping dainty but hopeful, their heads cocked as if they expected a bug to pop up any minute or a ripe berry to push through the frost. The slanting roofs of houses and stores dripped melted snow and, where the snow had withered away, shone moist and sunny. A man could imagine spring was just around the corner.

It was a day for decision, a day to take a new hold, to put plans in action. But how? Get a job as a puncher at forty or fifty a month, saving bit by bit over the years so as to set up for yourself in old age? Ask for work with I. G. Baker and Company or the T. C. Power outfit or others who bought and sold and freighted goods by steamboat and wagon? A slow way to work up to rancher. Badger work, Tom would say, though he was doing it now.

A bull train, its wagons half up to the hubs in the mud, lurched along Front Street, held to the churn of earlier wheels by the river on one hand and the close-facing stores on the other. The whacker would pull up by and by and quit cursing and whipping and, with his chores done, would look for women and liquor and so waste what he'd slaved for and, like a slave, go back to work, hard up and sore-headed and wiser for maybe one day.

It was a quiet time, Miss Fran and her returning traders regardless. Along the whole street there were maybe a half-dozen men, idling in and out of stores or saloons with the mud squeezing out from under their boots. The river shore was dead, emptied of the hogsheads and kegs and lumber and packing cases that the steamers brought up and of the rough

214

cargoes they carried down. One hammer pounded somewhere, rapping shame on loafers. A team stood hip-shot at a rack, both horses half asleep — dumb muscle waiting for a ruler who maybe couldn't rule himself. Across the river a clutch of tepees rose, tan-white in the sun, with smoke lazing from two smoke holes and a dog sniffing for a scrap that wouldn't be there. Here at the side of a store an old, blanket squaw stood still and unwinking as if counting time until at last it came to its end.

Lat looked in at two saloons and saw no one he knew. Lilly's Billiard Hall didn't have a customer. He turned back from the door and poked on, to nowhere in particular. He could go and see Tom at Kleinschmidt's if Tom wasn't busy, which likely he was, or he could go and see Sugar if it wasn't that Whitey might ask him for money, or he could look up Jehu and brace him if he knew where to find Jehu. A broke stranger didn't have many choices.

Only the fat bartender, unsmiling as ever, was in the Here's Luck saloon. He bobbed his head for hello. "Back, huh? What'll it be, bronc-fighter?" With a towel he made a swipe at the bar.

"Broke."

"Sorry case, all right, but more's been broke

than flush. Don't take on about it. A young feller thinks what happens to him never happened before." He poured a glass of whiskey and pushed it out. "Drink hearty and say a prayer for the house."

"Thanks." Lat raised the glass. "Seen Jehu around?"

"Now and then."

"Today?"

The bartender shook his head. "He gave up the stage job as unfittin' his talents. Say, though, tell you who I did see!" He paused for the question.

"Who?"

"That feisty old bastard, him with the poke o' dust that went wolfin' with you."

"Godwin!"

"If that's his handle. Had that other man with him, that grinny feller but still salty-lookin', shorter'n you."

"Just the two?"

"One, he got himself kilt, so they said. Wasn't that him with the squinch face?"

Godwin and Carmichael had made it, out of the snow and the long wind, but Moo Cow—

"Wasn't that Squinch Face?"

Lat nodded. Somewhere out there Moo Cow lay, frozen and maybe chewed up by wolves, maybe untouched with his slitted eyes staring to heaven from the mismatch of his face. Moo Cow, steady loser, loser of the last pot of all. Losers weepers, they said, and the winners went on, one winner cheered by the promise of company. "Where are they?"

"Where are they? Where you been? In a hole with the hole pulled in? Or playin' house steady with a calico queen?"

"I asked where are they!"

"Please to close the damper. I didn't mean to start no fire. Where are they? They're at the race, I would bet."

"Race?"

"Bunch of Piegans pulled in with their bellies rubbin' their backbones, but they had a dapple-assed pony with wings on his feet. Or so I hear. A bartender, he don't get to see nothin'. You know how it is — pourin' whiskey, rasslin' barrels, settin' plugs, buryin' dead soldiers and all that. All I've had a chance to see is that them Piegans is eatin' high up on the hog."

Lat got up and faced the door.

"Ain't a mite of use you settin' out," Fatty said. "They had to take them ponies way up on the flat where the snow's blowed off. Time you got there you would meet 'em comin' back. Set!" He refilled the glass. "You can pay when and if. I know an honest face, which them with money sometimes don't."

217

After a third drink they began to drift in — cowmen by looks, traders, trappers or hunters, two soldiers, out-of-job idlers, businessmen. The Indian horse had won again, far as you could throw a rock. Yes, sir, there's a racehorse, and, mister, don't bet against him unless you got money to burn. Owned by a damn Injun, too, or more likely stolen, but that cayuse can fly.

Lat listened, watching the door for Godwin and Carmichael while he fooled with the idea of money to burn. It took him an instant to recognize Jehu, standing tall on the threshold, his face indistinct against the sunlight outside.

Jehu came in, walking slow, showy with his shaped hat and fringed jacket and dress pants and the revolver peeking pearly from his side. Outfit, mustache, high, curving nose, all suggested he might own the territory or have an option on it at least. Into the racket of voices he said, "Howdy, gents."

Lat tackled him before he could get to the bar. "I've got business with you." With a hand on his elbow he urged Jehu to one side.

Jehu let himself be led. He held out his hand for a shake. "Howdy, boy. Glad to see you again." The mustache tilted at the corners.

"What about my money?"

"Now that's been on my mind, I tell you.

Heavy on my mind."

"Mine, too."

Jehu nodded gravely. "I'm glad to hear that because, you know, you didn't more than rough-break those horses." His eyes lifted in a question.

"You been working them?"

"No, but just the other day I got some of them rounded up there where you was supposed to be taming them, and I tell you glue wouldn't stick 'em."

"What could you expect without working them?"

"I was expecting to sell them for something. The way they are, I bet I couldn't get twenty-five dollars a head."

"At that price I'll take my pay in horses."

Jehu put a hand on Lat's shoulder. His smile as much as admitted he'd been caught short. "Smart boy, but I'll gamble with them. There's suckers left somewhere."

"I'm broke."

"That's a shame, and it's a shame we can't settle somehow, but it's no use to dicker now. I'm in on a deal that takes capital, all I can rake up."

"The debt comes first."

Jehu put his hand back on Lat's shoulder. "Boy, I'll be gone for a while, two weeks or so, to Butte City and places. See me when I get back. We'll come to a figure, all right."

The hand dropped. The curved nose and the mustache turned away. The dress pants scissored the owner of the territory to the bar.

It was no use to wait for Godwin and Carmichael. They were wetting their whistles at some other saloon, if they had any money. He could look for them, shaking his head to bartenders' what'll-it-be. He could go home — so Miss Fran's was home now! — and hear that things would turn out all right, Lat. Now don't you worry.

He lagged from the Here's Luck and lagged on the street and stopped at a corner. Straight ahead or to westward the roads wrenched out to the straggled edges of town and the winterworn country beyond. A buckboard went by, leaking coal from a sack, its driver hunched up against the new-blowing chill from the north. Over the river ridge the sun was drawing away, giving up as a bad job the business of warming the world. A tinkle of music blew along Front Street, thin as a tune long lost to mind. A man in townsman's clothing hurried out from under a sign that said FIRST NATIONAL BANK, his hand patting his pocket as if all he wanted was to be alone with his money. The building was brick and three-storied. The sign said the bank was upstairs. With a gun a man bold enough might pry some cash from it. Or a man with any prospects at all. One could dare hell and the other shoot for the moon and both arrive some place at least.

Yells came from behind. "Hey, you! Lat!" "Evans! Whoa!"

It was Godwin and Carmichael, whiskered and still dressed in their foul wolfing clothes and both, it appeared, a little boozed up. They pumped his hand and pounded him on the back and invited Lat, you old bastard, you, to come have a drink. Come tell us about you, and whereabout's Tom?

"Tom's fine," Lat said. "Working at Kleinschmidt's — but Moo Cow?"

The whiskey cheer left their faces. "Poor devil," Godwin answered. "Shot with an arrer right through the lights while he went to look to the horses, and the horses was snuck away then, and all the time me and Mike waitin' unknowin' until we had waited too long." He spit a stream of tobacco as if to show what he thought of himself and Carmichael.

"They raised that cache we left," Carmichael broke in. "Easy come, easy go," he added, not as a joke.

"So there was nothin' to do but start hoofin'." Godwin looked at his feet. "Wasn't till we

221

tramped a million miles more or less that we found some horses to borry."

Lat asked, "Who was it?"

"You think if we knew 'em that we'd be draggin' butt here. Injuns, of course, but God knows which ones. Come have a drink."

"On what?"

"Hell," Godwin said, "we got money. I come back with a few pinches of dust and just doubled it bettin' on an Injun cayuse. Only horse I seen lately that might beat your Sugar." His hand tugged at Lat's sleeve. "You ain't told us about yourself. Come and ile up your chords."

A drink or two more, and he'd ease off his edge — till tomorrow. "I can't right now," he said and saw the lie discovered in Carmichael's eyes.

Godwin turned and spit again and fingered in his pocket. He held out a ten-dollar gold piece. "Medicine," he said.

"Much obliged."

"Now you're well enough to stand a round yourself, come on!"

"Not now," Lat answered.

Godwin stepped back as if to get a better view of him. It was a minute before he spoke. "What the hell ails you?"

"Nothing."

"Nothin' wrong but nothin', huh?" Godwin

studied him some more. "Pitiful, ain't he, Mike?"

"Lay off, Goddy." Carmichael's half-smiling eyes held a glint of understanding. "A constipated toad don't like to jump."

Godwin turned as if to leave. "When your bowels get circulatin', let us know."

Carmichael held up long enough to say, still with the half smile wrinkled around his eyes and mouth, "We'll be lookin' for you, Lat, and meantime take 'er easy."

They faded down the street. There was the chill breeze left, and the discouraged sun and the roads to nowhere and Sugar and the dappled pony and the bank.

He pushed inside and went upstairs before more thought could keep him out. A man sat busy and unheeding at a desk, like a prisoner told to push a pencil on pain of death, but an open-faced office stared from the side, and in it a man in a wide, white collar sat grooming a mustache that horned down over his chin. His eyes, lifted up from his desk, asked what now. He didn't rise or speak but only sat and smoothed his horns and looked.

Lat went to him. "You have the say-so here?"

"I do."

"I need money."

The man weighed that a while. "A common complaint."

"My name's Evans, Lat Evans."

"Conrad," the man answered and put out an unwilling hand. "Will you sit?" He stacked some papers neatly on the corner of the desk. "And what do you do?"

"I been wolfing."

"Hmm. Not to be personal, but that work isn't a very high recommendation."

"I know how to double a loan."

From under the mustache came one word. "How?"

"The Indians have a racehorse here, and I own one that can beat him."

No answer showed in Conrad's face, but his hand came away from his mouth and stopped in mid-air and settled slowly and drummed on the desk. "There's work for those who want it," he said. "The town's shy on fuel. They're looking for men now to bring in coal from Whoop-Up and to cut wood that will be floated down Shonkin Creek when it breaks up." He waited to see how the suggestion sat.

"I can find work like that, but now if you'll just loan me a stake—"

"You couldn't pick a chancier thing, not even Montana weather. We're not in business, Evans, to back gamblers."

"You gamble all the time, on weather and grass and the price of cattle and whether steam-

224

boats get through or get wrecked. Please listen, Mr. Conrad!"

Conrad got up slowly. He put one hand flat and solid on the desk. "We're both wasting time." His eyes lifted, the "No" showing hard in them. "One thing recommends you as a businessman, Evans — your nerve."

Lat was on his feet. "One thing recommends you as a banker. That's your want of it." He heeled around and made for the door, feeling Conrad's gaze and the gaze of the condemned pencil pusher on his back.

He found himself hurrying down the street as if to something urgent, as if to leave behind the fool he'd been. To think a bank would back him! One foolish try, one foregone failure — but still the chance was knocking. He slowed down and dragged on.

Murphy, Neel & Co. Tobacco. Exchange Saloon. General Merchandise. River Market. Overland Hotel. The street stirring with strange freighters, strange Indians, strange drifters, strange drunks, strange men going home to supper with time to have a quick one on the way. The early lamps being lighted. The rimed slush crying under foot. The smell of wood smoke in the air from homes unknown. The good, the well-known smell of horses. Whitey's livery stable.

He turned back and bought a bottle and went on.

Whitey wasn't in, though fire flickered in the smoky lamp in what he called his office. Outside it in the darkened barn Sugar whickered low, wanting hay or oats or both and a hand to scratch his head.

Lat spoke and came up easy and felt the leaned-down muscles. "Got any money to burn, boy? Could you fly?" There was only a wisp of hay in the manger, and he forked it full and spilled a can of oats in the feed box and found a curry comb and, working in the darkness, brushed Sugar up.

Whitey had returned to the office meantime. He looked up from the bench that would do as a bed, his shoulders slouched over his low pot of a belly, his eyes big in their pouches. "Bring anything?" he asked, meaning maybe money, maybe liquor.

"It's under your nose," Lat answered and lifted the overlooked flask from the table.

"Ah-h." He took the bottle and twisted the stopper. "Ain't had a drink in a whole day or two. Short of funds, short of fun." He drank and passed the bottle over. "Must've found yourself work?"

"Not yet. You're protected as long as you have the horse."

"Pertection ain't wampum. Won't buy beans

or booze." He got up and went to the stove and put in a stick of wood and reached for the bottle on the way back. Before he drank, he said, "It's poor thanks I'm givin' you, Lat. The poor, all they got is poor thanks."

"And a bed?"

"And a bed. Anyone brings me a bottle gets a bed, such as it is. That's my rule." Whitey's eyes moved off into space. "It's hell to be poor, drawin' just flunky's wages, and double hell if your appetite's handsome." He waved toward the window ledge and the dusty jug with its pickled baby. "I even been tempted to see if I couldn't sell my little girl there. But sit down, dammit! Have a drink with me on you!"

Lat perched himself on the stool.

Whitey's eyes swam away again and swam back. A twist of a smile touched his mouth. "On'y thing is, she keeps me company." His face asked if Lat could understand.

"Yes."

"She don't cry or get sassy, and she listens when I talk." Whitey took a slow drink and wiped his mouth slowly and sighed. His gaze came away from the jar as he brought one hand up and stuck out the thumb. "See that, too?" The thumb was missing a knuckle. That's a dally-welter for you. You savvy dally-welter?"

"Sure."

"He throws his rope and makes a ketch and anchors to it then by takin' hitches on his saddle horn, so quick he sometimes hangs a finger in the turns. A Texan ties his lasso to the horn and keeps his meat-hooks. Not as I go for them Rebel ways, either." Whitey kept studying the thumb. "But why am I tellin' you that knows already? Scours of the mouth, I got. There ain't no one much for me to talk to any more."

"Go on."

"When there ain't, damn if I don't find myself palaverin' with that stub thumb and with my little girl there yonder." He rubbed his jaw with the stub-thumbed hand. "Fool thing, but it kind of helps, 'specially when I feel low."

"Same goes for everybody."

Whitey hitched himself up. "Well, goddam you, Lat! You're young and strong and got spirits independent of a goddam bottle. Jesus J. Christ! What I'd give for that!"

"You're not so old, but what would you do?"

"Let's have a drink while I think on it." But Whitey only sipped at the bottle this time, sipped and held it in his hand, seemingly forgetful that there were two of them. His words came slowly, as if from far back in his mind and life. "I was somethin' at your age, Lat. I was really somethin', there in Nebraska and surroundin' parts. Yes, sir, made a pile of money and spent it open-handed, and the bar-keeps they liked me and girls from all the top-notch houses. Bought many a round in my time and wived up with many a calico. Yep."

"How?"

"Movin' horses mostly and movin' others back." Now Whitey passed the bottle. His eyes were sharp. One of them seemed about to wink. "All branded stock, o' course. All legal."

"All branded? All legal?"

"Don't go nibblin' into my past!"

"You think I care?"

Whitey smiled, easily. "Well, now it's brung up, time was I could change a brand as quick as scat. Slow brands, but long enough. Just give me a jackknife or a hot iron and wet buck-skin. Bars to boxes, circles into figure 8's, one letter to another. I was a artist then."

Lat popped the thought that popped into his mind. "Could you do it now? Could you change Jehu's brand?"

18

Work was slow in the mornings, or missing entirely, and slow in winter afternoons, too, the dullness unbroken then by the summer parades around town that teased men to the house and so made for more work at night. A girl passed time by sleeping, by tidying her room and tidying herself and dressing her hair and, off and on, talking with the other girls and Aunt Fran about the company they'd had and the ones they liked best while Happy dusted and swept and sometimes put in a word like, "Yes, ma'am! That Mist' Lat, he's a shuah-enough gennelman, on'y wheah at is he, Miss Callie?"

She tucked fresh blankets on her bed, wishing she knew, or, better yet, that he would come back. He would have his hat off as he stood at the door and would speak like a gentleman in the presence of ladies and never openly refer to his wishes, or need to with her. Too many men seemed to think a girl in a house had no feelings at all and so could be whooped at and hazed around like a heifer. Why didn't he come? He didn't have to have money.

She punched and smoothed a fresh pillow. Why not take, since she wanted him to? It was hers. People so close to each other didn't count tit for tat and would lose the best part if they did, for the giving was good. Let him come out ahead, if he did. That was good, too.

The room was spic enough now, ever for Lat. It wasn't his manners entirely that were the thing. It was the look of him, the lean, honest look and show of the boy in the man. "Weanlin'!" Aunt Fran had said once, though she couldn't know, and "Handsome is as handsome does," and "Ambition's fine, but cash is trumps in this game, dearie." It was his need of her and his spells yet of backwardness. It was that there was no meanness in him. It was that he would lie spent with his arm under her head, and then they would talk, through words or through silence. Bad business, according to Aunt Fran, who liked men who got the act done and pulled up their pants and made way for others, as unheeding toward the girl, almost, as toward a chamber used. Most men were that kind. Payment, maybe thanks, good-bye — and they were gone, except sometimes one asked how was it that so nice a girl fell to such work.

From the kitchen came the knock of a spoon in a pan, and she knew that Aunt Fran or Happy was scraping up lunch. She ought to help, and she would by and by, after she had put wood in the stove and stood close to it warming her bottom, which the wind through the loose-fitting window had chilled. You had a pitiful story for the men who made out to pity you, always after they were satisfied. You were an orphan, or you were starving, or the man you had trusted had got you in trouble, and what was a poor girl to do? Never speak for the life! Never act amused or put out by the question! Never ask where or whose was the wrong! Make up a story! Some girls did every time, and often it paid off in cash. Sometimes, feeling so sorry, a man had to have another turn in the bed.

To Lat she had told a part of the truth when he edged up to the question. She would always remember that first boy if only because he was first, but his face and his manner had dimmed with the years. What had drawn them together, she could see now, was her need of company. Her father had brought her down from the hill farm in West Virginia and had gone to work in the coal mines; and there she was, in a strange town, without a mother or brothers or sisters or anyone. A person wanted someone more than a father who was home only for breakfast and supper and just grunted then no matter how tasty the victuals she cooked. So what happened happened. She didn't blame the boy, not even for skipping town. She hadn't wanted to marry him. But her father had gone on the rampage, him that had been so uncaring before, and had stormed around, hunting, and finally had taken her, crying, to the home of a granny who knew just the trick of fixing girls up, good as new. She had been sick for what seemed a long time and for a longer time sad. Then her father had shipped her off to Aunt Fran, who was doing well in the west, in a boarding house or in land or in business of some kind, he wasn't sure what since she hadn't named it exactly. What no one had understood, what no man could understand now, what she hadn't told Lat, was that she had wanted the baby.

In her way Aunt Fran had taken to her, and she had learned a few things. Being with men left you the same as before, just so you took care. Maybe you didn't always feel like it, maybe it made you a little sick to your stomach at times, at first especially, but when you got up, you were still you, with money to put in the sock. It was no more than exercise except in particular cases. So why the cloud that never quite left the mind? And why the to-do by the proper? Sometimes even now Lat himself seemed held back and almost afraid — and somehow she loved him more for it and found extra pleasure in bringing him on.

"What you doin', Callie?"

Amy Lou stood at the opened door, her thin, fair face in the daylight showing tired lines and the beginnings of puckerings. She wore an old dressing gown, over which her hair tangled down. Her eyes wandered over the room. "Cleaned up already, huh?" Through the push-out of teeth her breath smelled of stale whiskey.

"All through. You look tired. Want me to help you?"

"Aw, it can wait." Amy Lou's gaze came around uncertainly. "But you wouldn't happen to have just a little drop, would you? Fran's gettin' tighter than alum."

"Not here."

"I s'posed not." Amy Lou lowered her head. "Christ!" Standing there with her shoulders slumped and her face loose and spiritless in the dangles of her, she reminded Callie somehow of the end of too big a night, with the visitors gone and the house messed up and silent and another day dawning gray through the windows.

"You don't need more, Amy Lou. Really you don't."

"Don't need it!" Amy Lou laughed a high, shivering laugh. It uncovered teeth like a horse's, like the yawn of a horse did a horse's. "All I've had today you could put in your eye. And after last night!"

"Why don't you rest?"

Amy Lou's mouth straightened but didn't quite close. Her eyes wavered from Callie's and fixed on the window. The bare branches of a cottonwood were bending to the breeze outside. "Johnny threw me over. Said I wasn't worth keeping, and after me working my tail off for him!"

"Now you'll have some money of your own then. You gave it all to him." She disliked to say pimp, which was what Johnny was, and she didn't want to lower Amy Lou's feelings.

"You know how it is? With Lat?"

"I do not! Lat isn't Johnny!"

"Pardon," Amy Lou said, dismissing the point. "My resting days are coming," she went on in the way of someone saying something often thought. "Know how old I am? Twenty-seven. Can't even hold a cheap P.I. like Johnny. I never called him that before. No money and nothing much to sell much longer, Callie. It's turned stale already." She looked away from the window, to the floor, to the stove, to the walls, to Callie. Suddenly there were tears in her eyes, big tears that welled up and spilled over and ran down to the corners of the mouth that couldn't keep closed on the teeth. "And you say I don't need any more!"

It was only part of the truth. Amy Lou would have last days before her resting days, outcast days with soldiers, hide hunters and their like until at last she wasn't good enough for them. A worn-out old hay bag, all would say as they had said of others.

"Don't, Amy Lou!" Callie told her. "You're just upset." She went to the bed stand and picked up her purse and took out a dollar, feeling both guilty and strong because she had a stocking hidden away with savings in it to save her. "Here."

Amy Lou wiped her eyes and took the dollar in her wet hand. "Thanks, Callie. You're a real sugar tit." She turned and, in her heeled-over slippers, lisped off.

Callie waited a minute, for nothing, and followed her out. Happy was showing a man into the parlor. The man told her, "Hello," and cocked his head toward the back and asked, "Yes'm?"

She should ask him first if he'd have a drink. She answered, "All right."

She took him back and took care of him and afterwards of herself and then drew the bed smooth. The fresh pillow and blankets, put on just for Lat, wouldn't be fresh if he happened to come by today.

She went back to the parlor, just in time to hear a knock at the door. The knock was Tom Ping, dressed in his work clothes. The dark front lock of hair fanning down from under his hat would have made him look sporty if his face had been smiling. "Come in," she said. "I think Jen's still in bed."

His voice was low-pitched. "It's you I wanted to see."

"Me!"

He put up a hand as if to ward off the thought. "It's business."

"What?"

He looked around, as if making sure that no one else was in earshot. "That Lat, he's headin' for trouble, and me, I can't turn him."

"Lat in trouble!"

Tom still spoke low. "Just three or four knows it, and you keep your mouth shut."

"Yes." Her voice was hushed, too.

"He's doctorin' Jehu's horse brand so as to have a stake for a race."

"He wouldn't do anything wrong. Jehu owes him money."

"It ain't the right or the wrong. It's gettin' jailed or maybe strung up." He waved his arm out, questioning. "What if Sugar loses? That Injun pony's no clubfoot."

She didn't understand all of it yet, but now that she understood something she couldn't quite match Tom's uneasiness.

"He'd have to pay off in slow-branded horses, and them slow brands don't stick forever. 'Course, he's got sales bills to back him, but who drawed them bogus bills up but that fine-fingered Carmichael, who seen one maybe once and so's gone to practicin' law?"

At her silence he went on, using both hands to help with his talk. "Look, Callie, I ain't above takin' a trick if the odds ain't too long, but this is plumb crazy. You got to do something."

Maybe Lat was taking this chance just for her, out of the proud and overblown sense of his debt. She felt him out there like a hurt part of herself, penniless and cut off and driven, sworn not to see her until he could come with the money that made him a man.

"What can I do, Tom?"

"Talk him out of it. If anyone can, it's you."

"Do you really think so?" She hadn't meant to sound so eager.

"I know it."

"He — he hasn't been around for a while."

"Too damn busy, wranglin' and brandin' and gettin' set. But he's at the livery barn, or just was."

"I'll send a note."

"Why don't you go see him yourself?"

"He might not like it."

"Why not, for Christ sake? You're his girl."

"He's never asked me to go out with him, Tom." Now she sounded self-pitying. "It's the money, you know," she said quickly. "I'll send a note."

"I better not take it, for he might savvy I put you wise. I'm due at work anyhow. But you toll him in! You change his mind!" Tom signaled out a goodbye and let himself out.

She hunted out a pencil and a scrap of paper and sat down on the piano stool. It had been a long time since she'd written even one word. It had been a long time since she'd sat in a mountain school and learned her letters, bullied on by a man teacher who loved books and hated his pupils. But now she had a reason to write, and to Lat. She could ask that he see her for his sake alone. She could say it was urgent. She could say it was strictly business but mighty important. She could say anything so long as it brought him. She wanted to say that she loved him. What she wrote at last was just,

"I am lonesome," and this she left unsigned.

The words stared at her from the sheet.

Company, girls! How-de-do. Pleased to make your acquaintance, ma'am. Yep, a drink, but saloons they sell them. Get your thumb out, Happy. Yes, ma'am, let's go. That's what I come for. Uh-hh, Baby! Here you are, and see you again.

Men. Men blunt and all business. Men making believe other feelings till the one got its answer. Men rough and cruel. Natural men. Unnatural men. They came and they went, faceless in memory. Which of them cared except for the act and the moment? Who wanted more than the one thing? Everybody's girl, nobody's girl, barring some rare stroke of luck. A girl's only friends, if they were that, were the other girls in the house – Jen, Amy Lou, Aunt Fran for whom money was company. So entered the Johnnies, the love sharks, to ease the lonesomeness, to give hope that someone at least cared. This was the price.

She called out to Happy and heard him shuffling from the kitchen. He came in with his coat off and stood waiting, his black face saying whatever she wished he would do. One friend. One against emptiness. And Lat.

"I'll find him, Miss Callie," Happy said to her words. "Now don't you worry yourself."

She ate with the girls in the kitchen. Jen was dressed for the day. Amy Lou, still looking sick, had given herself a lick and a promise. Aunt Fran didn't usually fix up until night. They talked about nothing, about clothes and callers and the night coming up. "Everybody is boomin' Fort Benton," Aunt Fran said, "but I swear I don't know. Hide business is shot, and to me that damn comin' railroad seems likely to screw us as a port. Thing now is to make hay while we can. Callie, you hear? We got to fight for our share. There's some pretty fair girls, I can tell you, even in them one-towel shebangs." She sniffed. "Competition!"

Callie listened without really listening and watched without watching. Lat might rap at the door any time. He might come or not come. Could he keep away? Or did she have the power? Women always had the last power, with one man or many, each according to her nature, each pleased to prove it. Which was one reason, maybe, for houses. She kept telling herself he would come.

He didn't until midafternoon. She knew his step on the stoop and his knock at the door and hurried to greet him. He gave her just the trace of a smile, and she scolded out in a joke, "You stay-away! What's the idea?"

"I got your message," he said. He came in

and stood near the threshold with the door closed behind him as if not to go farther. "I haven't much time."

It was a poor way to greet a girl, but with the thought she forgave him. He was here. From wrangling or branding or bets he was drawn here — and men under strain were likely to be fretful with women. She said, "You ninny!" and took hold of his arm. "Time enough to talk, or you wouldn't have come."

He let himself be led into the bedroom but there held to his hat and didn't move to take off his jacket.

She stood apart from him and smiled to give the right turn to her words. "I didn't aim to add to what you think of as your debt."

She was sorry then, for he answered, "I've got a deal on," as if holding out the promise of payment.

"I know. I'm scared for you."

"No need to be," he said and didn't go on to ask how she'd learned.

"But if you lose, Lat?"

"I don't think of that, but it's swim or sink anyhow." He put his hands in his pockets and took them out and shifted his weight. A frown narrowed his eyes. "What I think about is a stake and a ranch on the Tansy. That's where Tom and I will set up if we can, somewhere out of Tansytown."

She was out of place in his thoughts, crowded aside, poor second to cattle and grass. He would leave her if he could, would follow his interests to parts far away and forever be lost to her except that at night now and then perhaps he'd remember and hitch over in bed, wishing he could have her or forget her in sleep.

"Would it be a good place for me?" She spoke before she thought. The rest came to her mouth in a rush. "Everyone says this town's bound down hill and the railroad will finish it."

"Too small," he said quickly, and then his face softened, as if at last he was seeing her and was moved. He put out his hand and raised hers and held it. "Callie," he said, understanding. His smile was like the smile of a man with too much to say.

He dropped her hand and half-turned away, and the thought-wrinkles of cattle and ranching grooved themselves again in his forehead. "I'm going through with it, Callie, so it's no use to argue, and I don't want you to worry."

She tried to be light. "Can I see you when you're locked up?"

His face didn't change. "All I'm sorry about is that I've got so little to bet." He paused and watched his toe scuff the floor. "I tried the bank."

"How much have you?"

"Few head of horses."

"The bank said no?"

He might not have heard her. He might not even realize she was there. He was running the race or putting beef on the range while he toed the floor and frowned at his boot. She saw the great miles of this country stretching between them, the lost and impossible miles, and the miles of his interests reaching farther and farther, beyond sight, beyond all but the whisper of memory.

She had her savings! The thought left her unsupported, cast loose. But she could loan them and so perhaps keep him, could tie the tie tighter — which was scheming and mean, as unfair to him and her heart as her fear. It was herself that must hold him, not favors that he would repay and remember.

He had taken a turn in the room and stood with his front to her, hands deep in his pockets, eyes still cast down; and she wished only good for him, only the best, even if wanting to be part of the best.

She said, "Lat," and walked to the bed and stooped and dragged out the trunk and opened the lid and took out the stocking. At the last count it held upwards of one thousand dollars. She held it out to him, in doubt what to say.

"Make a bet for me — for you."

He drew back, his face puzzled, and she added, "Here's almost a thousand. I'm playing bank."

He took another step back and raised a hand, palm out. He looked almost angry. "Never! Not me! You keep it."

"Be sensible!"

"I'm not that low."

"You'll pay it back."

"When, if I lose?"

She moved to him and with both hands pressed the stocking on his chest. "Being you're you, it's just like money in the bank."

"No."

"If you won't let me help you, then you don't trust me," she told him, feeling that somewhere that answer made sense.

"But, Callie!"

"Take it!"

The look of the boy came to him then, the look of young wonder and awe and open thanksgiving. "Callie," he said, again as if by name alone he was saying all that he could.

She stuffed the stocking into his pocket while she blinked against her tears. "There now."

"I'll never forget it," he said and kissed her gently on the forehead, and words and kiss together were return enough.

But still she had something to prove. She pressed against him and raised her mouth for his. His arms went around her, soft and hard and harder, and she could hear his breath and feel his body answering to hers. He urged her toward the bed.

She put her hands on his chest and pushed back. "Not now," she whispered, knowing she was using a tool, a rightful tool, of her power.

"Yes."

"You haven't much time."

"Callie!"

"Tonight?"

He didn't like it – which was good – but finally he said, "Tonight then."

She led the way to the door and, when he was gone, stepped back to see Amy Lou, who sat alone in the parlor wiping her eyes.

19

Lat told himself they were here, they were real — these people, these few friends, these strangers and Indians, some afoot, some in the saddle, some in buggies and wagons. They appeared and made sounds and so must be real, like the sky and the hills and this flat under foot where without fail two horses would race. Sugar stood real or followed along, led by real reins that felt unreal to the hand.

" 'Bout ready?" It was Whitey at his side.

To him he could say, "This me, Whitey?"

"What's your name, huh? Puddin-an-Tame, like it says in the pome." Whitey took his arm. His over-size eyes showed understanding. From Lat they went to the men who kept circling around. "Don't let 'em fever you."

One of the men dug a chew of tobacco out of his whiskers. He called out, "Can that big bronc untrack himself?"

"And don't let 'em stampede you," Whitey

went on. "It's your money ridin'."

Beyond the man who had spoken, beyond a farther scattering of people where a couple of dogs smelled the ground, another bunch, mostly Indians, formed a ring. Through the screen they made came glimpses of the dappled horse. A horse to knock a man's eye out, seen close. An Appaloosie they would call him in Oregon, one of the strain bred for bottom and foot by the Nez Perces.

"Them brands ain't been questioned so far, though it's just as well we bet Jehu's ponies with Injuns," Whitey said under his breath.

Lat nodded. Horses, men and outfits seemed to dance and mix and voices high and low to be one flowing voice. "You did a fine job."

"Not up to my old self."

The secret days and nights of work came back, of hunting, chasing and corralling horses and of throwing them when dusk or dark provided cover. Then Whitey, sobered up and eager, would get busy with his knife. "Can't risk a fire," he'd said, "so irons is out. Knife's nigh as good, but this night work strains my peepers. Lucky for that moon. Remember, just in case, Lat, to cut always with the hair. Won't do to go against it. Leaves blood beadin' out."

The circle of men had drawn closer. Out of their talk a voice rose. "Let's get on with the race, boy! That horse'll putrefy."

Whitey moved back and stroked Sugar and looked him over with an old horseman's eye. He would be wondering if Sugar was conditioned enough. A few days of good oats and good hay, which hadn't filled out all the wrinkles. A few days of exercise with Jehu's ten broncs. That was all. That was everything possible. No time for more. No use to wonder. No use to worry that the false brands would be found false.

Back there in his office, before the branding, Whitey had figured. "Jehu's brand's a Lazy F," he'd said and with his stub of pencil branded a piece of paper F. "Now the way I see it, don't take no horses with prior brands, no matter if they're vented and Jehu's later brand put on. Just Lazy F, that's what we want. You get it? As for changin', look here." He worked again with the pencil. The F became ⊟. "That's Double Box, I guess. Too simply, maybe. We could put wings on it and call it Flyin' Double Box, but that's a little hard to swallow." He lengthened the line between the boxes and now had ⊟. "Yeah. Yeah. I told you I used to be a artist. Basket, we'll call her, the Basket brand. Can't bring to mind any such before."

Now Whitey stepped back from Sugar. "Looks pretty good, considerin'."

"Whitey," Lat said, keeping his tone low, "I don't know why you let yourself in for this. It's not your funeral. I was crazy to ask you."

"Quit thinkin' blue!" Whitey said, almost too loud. "Hell, Lat, I like a stir. Beats whiskey, even, or why am I playin' camel?"

Lat breathed deep. The air came out in a sigh. The circle was less a circle now than a press, loud-mouthed and curious. Into it the banker man, Conrad, was edging, one hand on the horn of his mustache. Lat caught the cool flit of his eyes. A man in a plug hat put his palm on Sugar's rump. "A hundred this bag of bones loses, that is, if ever he starts." Conrad answered, "Not me."

Whitey asked, "Feel like warmin' him up?"

"Yeah."

"Don't worry, now. Remember Tom'll be at the start and Carmichael and me at the finish and Godwin one place or another."

Out in the open to the west, watched by the crowd over there, an Indian was limbering up the Appaloosie. The horse galloped short and frisky, fighting the hold that held him in.

Lat said, "I just wish it was longer."

"Six hundred yards is pretty long in this here country," Whitey answered as if he had not said the same before. "Line to line, we diddled 'em out of maybe more'n that." His head turned. "Here's Tom now."

Tom strode up from the side. The six-shooter hung big on his hip. "What's the matter?"

"Nothing."

"Let's get on with the ball then. Godwin's got the stakeholders under herd, and Carmichael's set, and I'm beggin' time off from work."

Hearing him, the men close around chimed in. "Come on!" "Fork him!" "You stuck on a sandbar?" "Race or get off the pot!"

Tom pulled Lat close and spoke in his ear. "The rider they're pittin' against you won't weigh eighty pounds with his tepee throwed in." His eyes, showing trouble, asked what about that.

"Can't be helped." Over the brow of the hill that led down to the town a carriage was coming, drawn by two horses, the black top of it climbing the swell of the earth, lifting to view the dark face of Happy up front at the reins.

Lat mounted. "Someone ought to see the track's clear." He wound through the watchers and, in the open, let Sugar lope. Ahead rolled the quiet plain. Ahead lifted the quiet hills. There, where headland and sky touched, a man could watch the slow, white-against-blue drift of a cloud.

For late winter, fine weather, it seemed —

springtime in Oregon. Almost no wind. Ground bare, it seemed, and turf good. Sugar eager. A fair race coming up, or so it seemed.

Yonder now the course was opening, lined by rigs and people. The red and blue of blankets, the brown and black of white men's clothes, now and then the gleam of metal, of buckles, rings and plated spurs, brown faces, white faces, swinging braids, ribbons, feathers, colored quills, weathered wagons, weathered buggies, the black shine of a carriage, horses sorrel and bay and black and pintoed – all nothing against the giant nothing of the land. Light and dark in polka dots, the Appaloosie was prancing near the start. And Sugar was warmed up.

They moved aside as he came up, their tongues quieting while their eyes worked. Tom stood at the starting line. It was a couple of sticks with a mark scratched between. The Indian rider was cutting didos with his horse, bidding for attention. He had a face like a skull and a bob-tail of a body that wind and sun had sucked dry. He wore leggings and moccasins and a blanket, fallen now to his waist, that he'd likely discard. For a saddle he straddled a cloth surcingled with a ribbon of rawhide.

"Bring 'em up when you're ready." It was Tom, taking charge.

Lat swung to the ground. "Not yet. I'm shucking this saddle."

While he worked at the latigo, a hand poked his shoulder. The Indian rider had reined close and leaned over. "Me bet," he said out of his almost bare bone of a face. He pointed to Sugar. "Him." The finger changed aim to the Appaloosie. "Him."

"You own him?"

Tom put in, "No, Lat!"

Someone said, "Put up or take low," and someone else added, "Ante or crawl."

"You don't want to risk Sugar!"

"I'm gone if I lose anyhow."

"All or nothin'," another voice called. "Can't let a damn Injun out-gizzard us."

The Indian repeated, "Me bet."

It wasn't the voices. It wasn't gizzards. It was a case of up or down, one way or the other. "It's a bet then," Lat said. The tone wasn't his own. He looked at the faces around him, dark and light faces, faces haired out and smooth, the faces of three squaws on the fringe, the eyes of an Indian remembered from somewhere, all of them pointed with interest. "You heard," he told them. "My horse against his." Like bobbers to a fish bite some of the faces bobbed.

He turned back to the saddle and without

253

looking knew that Tom had pushed close. "Jesus Christ, Lat!"

"It's done. Now stop!"

"Yeah, pard." Tom breathed in a deep breath and let it out in a whisper. "With the Injuns maybe we got a hole card, worst come to worst. That old son-of-a-bitch of a chief — what's his name? Rising Moon — he's here playin' hard to see." The whisper stopped for an answer and went on. "We could make it hard for them Piegans. We could make the tribe ante up or some of 'em go through a frolic, our way?"

Those were the eyes remembered, the eyes of Rising Moon, father of Little Runner, who had prayed for his son in a time realer than this one and had seen the prayer answered and gone on his way, friend out of enemy. For an instant Lat jabbed the knife again, and the poison flowed out. For an instant there was their parting again.

"After the race, I mean. Hear me, Lat?"

Lat peeled off the saddle. The ring of watchers cracked to let him through. Rising Moon had his blanket drawn up on his face and his chin tucked down in it, and it was only his betraying eyes that asked if here was friend or foe. Lat put out his hand. "Rising Moon, how?"

The blanket fell away. The face was even leaner than before, as if from longer hunger.

From the starved flats of his cheeks his nose hooked starved but proud. "Heap Medicine!" His mouth spread in a smile that furrowed mouth and eyes. "Me you, all same."

Lat wheeled around and made his way through the ring and climbed aboard Sugar. A voice said, "All right, you two. Ease up there! We want a fair start." Tom was still taking charge.

From the tail of his eye as he brought Sugar up, Lat saw the Appaloosie spinning and mincing, scattering people aside while the rider pretended he couldn't help it.

Ahead stretched the course, here lined with people fanning out for the start, there ragged with a rig and a wagon and nothing and a wagon and watchers on foot inched in too far, and yonder, dizzier than distance accounted for, the finishing clutter with the gleam of a carriage top in it.

The Appaloosie spun close. Sweat lathered his neck. The Indian still wore his blanket. Sugar stood steady enough. Tongues quieted, except for one. "Bring him up. Easy! Not on the run!"

Wind drowned the "Go!", the surge of wind at the hard surge of flesh, and hoofs beat it out on the turf. Quick in the lead, too quick to believe, there went the dappled horse, the rider bent low, a corner of blanket aflutter behind.

Let him run! Let him tire! But try to keep close! These two lengths! Not more! Then fast for the finish! Then drive for the line!

A wagon flashed by, the wave of a hat, a man and a scared team, blankets with heads on, lines and bunches of men. They charged and swept past, now ahead, now behind, pieces of things, winks of movements, parts of men open-mouthed and unheard.

Sugar was steadying. He was leveling out. In the seat of his pants, in the grip of his legs, Lat felt the bunch and thrust of his muscles and the faster and evener stride. Three lengths to the spotted rump, three lengths, still three lengths, no loss but no gain, the lead fixed for-ever, riveted into the earth. And here came the finish!

Lat bent ahead and said, "Now!", and kicked Sugar, and the blood began to run in him, up from this final and utmost straining of flesh. A foot gained. A yard. And another. The gap closing, stride by brave stride. Here was the tail of the spotted horse, here the end of the rump, just there the rider, and still Sugar rolled the earth under hoof and the other horse with it.

The Indian's head screwed around. His mouth made a quick hole in his face. He turned back, and his arm moved, and the blanket, torn from his waist, flashed out in a blinding flutter.

Falling, Lat grabbed for the mane, the pinch of the knees lost and the hold of the seat as Sugar bolted aside. With the sliding heel of his boot he dug for a catch on the spine. Face up, cheek hard against hide, he willed his hand to hold on and his heel to stay anchored on bone while Sugar steadied and went on. He willed all of himself to hang on, to hang on, through the bounce of his head against muscle and the wild jerkings of sky.

By a hair and a hair his heel gave, and then all gave at once. And so it was no use in the end. He hit the ground and fell and was rolling...

He was in bed with a headache. He had his head in a lap. Fingers touched soft on the ache, and a soft voice was saying, "Be all right, Lat! You have to be all right."

A rougher voice said, "He better be! Lie still, you Piegan peewee, or I'll grind your face off in this gravel!"

The soft voice went on, "You won! Can't you hear me? You won!"

20

He had a headache and a knot on his temple where Sugar had clipped him by accident, but he had eleven horses, too, and almost a thousand dollars in cash, not counting what Callie had loaned him, and he'd settle with her, for everything, and settle with Whitey and still have enough left for some kind of a start as a rancher.

What Tom said went in and out of his ears as they lazed down to the town, himself leading Sugar to walk the heat out and Tom with the Appaloosie in tow. Godwin and Carmichael and Whitey would haze in the other horses he'd won, to the stable corral where all but maybe a couple would go up for sale. Most of the crowd had faded away, toward home or saloon or office or store, the tag-enders spread out but in sight ahead, led by the black carriage that was rocking from view round a corner. Here there were just Tom and himself and his luck.

"That Carmichael sure surprised me." Tom

couldn't keep from talking. "Easygoin', but, quick as scat, he snatched that little Injun off his horse and rubbed him in the dirt. Don't know what he'd done if you'd lost or been hurt bad." Tom grinned as he added, "It couldn't be that he likes you, Lat."

"Without you and the others I couldn't have done it."

"Aw, we didn't do nothin' much. But I wish I could have been in at the finish. How you hung on, nobody knows."

"Luck."

"Huh-uh. I was talkin' to a man that seen it all, and he said it was gumption glued you on. Hey, that reminds me. He said maybe you'd like to talk to him. Conrad, his name was, with a dust-catcher on his lip."

"He did!"

"What would it be about, do you reckon?"

"I don't know." About money, now it was too late? About a job better than cutting wood or skinning a team? About bidding for Sugar so he could race him himself?

"That Callie, Lat! She came bustin' out of that rig like a shot."

"What else did Conrad say?"

"You know, Lat, we're lucky." Tom's tone had turned thoughtful. "Y'ever stop to think? We ain't no special prizes in the grab bag, but still there's Jen and Callie?"

"What about Conrad?"

"Oh. That was all. Just said maybe you'd want to see him. Just asked me to tell you." Tom's voice trailed off.

In silence they reached and entered the town. At the bank Lat held up and put Sugar's reins in Tom's hand. "Hold him," he asked.

"What for?"

"For me to see Conrad."

"For God's sake! Mean to say he's a banker?"

"Supposed to be, anyhow." Lat turned and went in. A man with money in his pocket didn't think of a bank as a jail, of the pencil pusher there as condemned. He could say how do you do, or the weather was fine and ask what was in mind and go out of the place, yes or no, as big as before.

Conrad's voice came from the side of the place. "Come in, Evans." He got up and stood waiting, a smile spreading the horns of his dust-catcher. He put out his hand, saying, "Sit down," and, when they had shaken, reached to his coat and pulled a cigar from a raft of them that nosed up from his pocket. "Smoke?"

"No thanks."

"Don't smoke, huh? Good. Never touch them myself." He put the cigar back in his pocket as he took his seat. "Needless extravagance." His eyes studied Lat. Under its horns his mouth let out, "I keep them for clients."

"I'm not a client. You turned me down."

"So I did. So I did." Conrad looked away. "I saw you today. I know the whole story."

"All of it?"

"Enough to have formed certain suspicions. Two of those horses you wagered I happened to recognize. Call it a coincidence. Bankers do get around."

"Jehu wouldn't pay what he owed me."

"So? You're not alone."

"And I turned his horses loose, so where's the crime?"

Conrad's hand waved as if to throw something away. "Crime? I might mention your nerve, but I wouldn't say crime."

Lat kept silent.

"But, above all, it was the way you stuck to that horse. I like stickers, Evans. Wish we had more of them in our organization."

"I don't want a job, Mr. Conrad, not after today. I know I'll have to start on a shoestring, but I'm not after a job."

Conrad's hands came to his desk. His eyes were direct. "Did I say you were?" His fingers tapped on the wood. "How much did you win?"

"Eleven cayuses, counting the race horse, and about a thousand dollars in cash."

"What are your plans?"

"Ranching."

"Cattle or sheep?"

"Cattle."

"They call sheep the golden hoof."

"I like cattle."

Conrad nodded slowly as if he allowed a choice. "Texas stuff?"

"No, sir. Take away the horn and bone, and what have you got? Give me Durham strain."

The head bobbed in stronger agreement. "You have a range in mind — or do you yet?"

"Somewhere along the Tansy, close to the mountains."

"Tansy?" Conrad said as if trying the word on his tongue and not finding it quite to his taste. "There are outfits already there. That section's older, you know, than some others. What's more, it presses the reservation. Hungry Indians don't honor brands. Have you thought about that?" He went on with hardly a pause. "The big men of the territory are locating east, for instance along the Flat Willow and Musselshell. There's new range that direction, now that the buffalo are being cleared away, and it's practically empty and at the same time big enough for all the cattle in Texas." His eyes lifted, asking how this advice sounded. "I'm talking about people like Kohrs and

262

Hauser and Stuart and Davis. You know them?"

"I've heard of them." Who hadn't?

"They know what they're doing."

"Maybe so."

Conrad leaned forward. "Say it, Evans! You don't have to stand back. What about the Tansy?"

"It's pretty high, and high grass is fat grass, everyone knows."

"Thinner, though."

"Some places. Some seasons."

"And that's all, just that grass at higher elevations is fatter?"

"No, sir. It's the chinook. As an old man said to me, the closer the bone the sweeter the meat, only he didn't mean it in the way you might think."

One horn of the mustache crooked up, as if Conrad was thinking what you would think. "I don't get the connection."

"The chinook's warmer close to the mountains. It blows more. It's sweeter."

"Uh-huh." Conrad was tapping with one finger like a man tapping to thought. While he tapped, looking up at the ceiling, footsteps sounded behind Lat, and a voice said, "W.G.?"

The visitor had on a smart overcoat and a hat straight and business-like and a high, white collar with a gap at the neck filled by a

263

black bow. "Could I see you?"

"I'm busy right now. Can you come back?"

Lat said, "It's all right."

"Sit still, please," Conrad answered.

The man smiled and said, "Later," and made for the door.

"Be at ease, Evans, for heavens sake!"

"I don't mean to keep you from business."

Conrad's thumb wagged toward the doorway. "Borrowers always come back." He looked away, his eyes maybe seeing long lines of borrowers, each with a story of hope or hard luck. It was a minute before he spoke again. "The chinook, you were saying?"

"It clears off the snow cover and lets cows down to grass."

"Of course. Of course."

"I sound simple, I guess."

"But?"

"But, all right, you want the chinook to blow often and warm. That's the Tansy."

"Let's suppose it is best. What's your thought, long range, I mean?"

"About what?"

"Cattle. The territory. The future."

Out of the chance, unconnected bits of his thought he was asked now, all at once, to sum up and come out with answers. He got a pinch-hold of one. "First of all, Mr. Conrad, I see the time when grasslands will have to be owned or anyhow leased."

"You see a long way. There'll be free graze in Montana for longer than you'll ever live. Uncrowded graze."

"That's your notion!" With the words out he almost wished he hadn't spoken so strongly. Conrad was an older man and a banker besides. But he still could be wrong. "They said the same thing in eastern Oregon not so far back."

"Yes?"

"And now ranges are so crowded that cattle half-starve and some ranchers think heifers and cows should be spayed. Smart men are putting land under fence, owned land and leased land. Costs money, but it pays off. The cattle get feed. And the cows don't mix with scrub bulls."

Conrad said, "Hmm."

"You'll see more cows in Montana than you ever dreamed of, from Texas, Oregon, Washington, from all over the country, and all of them rustling for grass already chewed off. Then what about a bad winter?"

He had hold of another idea now, pulled whole from the pieces of thought. He'd say it and then take his leave. "They claim cattle do fine here without feeding. They claim natural pasture is all that you need, even in winter. It isn't. Cows get poor in the winter. Too many die. Calves come out spindly. Beef weighs less and brings less than it should, even after good summer graze. Who knows but some day we'll have a cold stretch like you can't remember? Come spring, the cows you loaned money on will be dead in the coulees."

Conrad said, "Go on."

"We'll have to make hay and feed hay. Just tallow is one reason, and risk is another. Knocking around in this country, a man sees hay growing wild wherever there's water. I bet with a good ditch a gravel bar would come up in redtop."

"Hay? Fences? Homesteads?"

"That's the way I see it."

Conrad didn't move except to bring up a finger and feel his mustache. His eyes swam out at nothing. Under the feeling finger he asked, "How much can you get for your horses?"

"Fifty dollars, I hope. I'll take the rough off the worst ones."

"That and your thousand won't buy many cows."

"I'll pick up what I can as close by as I can."

"Too bad your winnings weren't more," Conrad said. He'd forgotten, it seemed, that he could be blamed.

"If I had more, I'd go over west and buy cows and calves because they throw the calves in."

"You'd trail cows and young calves?"

"Anything to get started."

"Cows and calves from where?"

"Oregon likely. Last year, I know, you could get a cow and a calf for around fourteen dollars. Steers cost more."

"Uh-huh," Conrad said and was silent.

Lat got up from his chair. "I guess a man could go down to the Emigrant Trail and try to pick up some sore-footed oxen cheap."

"That's been done," Conrad answered, still sitting quiet. "Who was the first?" He frowned, trying to remember. "Grant. Captain Richard Grant, in maybe 'fifty or 'fifty-one."

"I wouldn't know."

"It doesn't matter." Conrad swung around. "Sit down! We can't talk if you keep a burr under your tail."

Lat sat.

"Where'd you get these ideas of yours?"

"Partly in Oregon. Partly here. I've had plenty of time to think. We were snowed in, wolfing, and then, in slow and mean weather, two of us trailed back here from the Musselshell."

"Held to a cabin, most men play cards."

"Yes, sir."

Conrad tapped with his fingers again. "I don't agree with all you've said."

267

"I don't ask you to. You wanted me to tell you."

"They're ideas, though, worth considering. But the ride raised the curtain. I like stickers. By the way, if you trail cattle from Oregon, you'll need some or all of those horses you won."

"I'm not doing it. Haven't money enough."

"You haven't, huh?" Conrad hunched forward, his elbows propped on his desk. "Get your money together, Evans. Find a range to your liking."

"That's first, of course."

Conrad put one hand flat on his desk. "Come back when you're ready. We'll match your money or even do better. I like stickers."

"What!"

"Just that."

"That — that's wonderful!" Lat answered in place of shouting or jigging.

"Straight business proposition. The money will cost you one per cent a month." Conrad smiled. "That rate makes figuring easy."

Lat got up as Conrad did. He put out his hand. "You won't regret it, I swear."

The mouth brought the whiskers into solemn position. "One point, Evans, if I may make it as an older man. Too many men seem to think that the business of ranching can be tended

268

to in bars and hookshops."

Conrad had seen. Of course he had seen. Lat felt the blood climbing his neck. "I know better than that, Mr. Conrad. Evans — not to brag, but Evans is a good name in Oregon."

Conrad said, "Fine," and tomorrow was a new day and a new chance, and a new man could float out of the door of the bank and down the stairs, out into the clean dusk and clean chill, out to Sugar and the Appaloosie and Tom.

"Tom!"

"What? Took you long enough."

Lat grabbed Sugar's reins and Tom's arm. "Come on! We're in business!"

"Meanin' what?"

"Meaning we're matched and more."

"Matched?"

"By the bank, you old muttonhead! Our money against theirs. A loan."

"I'll be damned!" Tom pulled back against the push on his arm. "But look, Lat, I ain't got anything. The chips is all yours."

"I thought we were partners."

"Jesus Christ, Lat!" For the rest of his answer Tom gave a quick clutch to the hand holding his arm. After a while he added, almost in a whisper, "Seems like no one ever gave me a second thought till I met you and Jen."

Ahead was the livery stable, where they'd put up the horses and, on Whitey's arrival, settle the score he kept. That would leave Callie. Callie? Just the name was a call. All of her was a call. Together, how they could rejoice! Once more then, since he wished it and she would? Once more, out of some due and upside-down decency? A poor start for a new man. Evans is a good name, Mr. Conrad. But damn it!

Tom slowed to a stop and faced around, head bent with some thought, and slowly lifted a face that his eyes and the shadows of darkness made serious in spite of his small turn of a smile. "I was workin' up to tell you, Lat, comin' in. Bein' we're so close—"

"What's on your mind, Tom?"

"Well, you see — hell—" Tom never was embarrassed. "We want you should stand up with us."

"What!"

"You'n Callie, that is."

"Stand up?"

"Me'n Jen, we're gettin' hitched."

"You? To her?"

"She says I'm good enough."

"Tom!"

"We'll make it proper, Lat. If that good preacher Brother Van's in town, we'll have him tie the knot."

"Think about it!"

"I've thought enough. Oh, I know, Lat, I got nothin' savin' pardnership with you, and she's got nothin', but between us we got each other, or will have, and that beats a cipher to hell."

"And her trade?"

A shadow came over Tom's face, deeper than the shadows of dusk. "I ain't so pure myself, no more'n you are. I asked you a question. You goin' to stand up with us?" His tone softened. "We'd like it the best in the world."

Stand up and be counted. Let everyone know. Read it in the paper, in the Benton Record, which Mr. Conrad would read. Send home a clipping. Mr. Tom Ping – Miss Jen – what was her last name? Mr. Albert Gallatin Evans and Miss Callie Kash of Miss Fran's well-known establishment, attendants.

With no choice left, Lat spoke bluntly then. "Tom, she's a whore. Wife or not, always she'll be known as that."

Tom threw down the Appaloosie's reins. He might be going to swing. "You! You that are so pious and so pussy-struck! I'm a mutton-head, but I know who you're thinking of." His face twisted. "Goodbye!" He wheeled around and started off.

Lat took one step after him, to say he'd stand

up after all, but Tom turned back. "I wouldn't let you take a piss with me!"

Then Tom swung around and went away, walking hunched and fast as if to leave something behind forever.

Part Four

21

"I've got to ride over south," Lat told Whitey. From the window of the cabin the prospect didn't look pleasing. Last night's snow lay a foot deep and, in the first sunlight, the air danced with cold. He leaned forward in his chair and drew a pair of Dutch socks over the two regular pairs he'd put on. "Those cows might have hit the drift fence."

"It's a wonder how a cow ever lived till you come along." Whitey took the water bucket and filled the teakettle that fretted on the stove.

"A lot didn't."

"Want me to help or anything?"

"I guess not."

Whitey began gathering up the breakfast dishes. "I'll swamp out the shack then and take off for town."

"You're welcome to stay."

"Manners!" Whitey said. "You'll never live down your trainin'. 'Course I'm welcome to stay. You told me enough times. But Carmichael's due in town today or tomorrow, the note said, and this is a dry camp to boot."

"Tap it careful."

"You forget I got a dose of your trainin', too. Hell, I've turned into a temperance shouter, pret' near. I keep hearin' your old man at prayers, and strong drink is a mocker and that stuff. Every time now I take a snort, I look to see is God watchin'. Hallelujah!"

"You'll get me thinking you're cured, and for good. It's quite a while since you heard those prayers."

"Once in grace always in grace, don't it go?" Whitey pointed with a fork. "And it's just young squirts that think three years is a coon's age."

Lat put on his moccasins. Two suits of underwear, three pairs of socks, moccasins, overshoes, pants, overalls, chaps, heavy shirt, sour-dough coat, wolf-skin cap, wool gloves inside heavy mittens — with these a man could make out though they burdened and slowed him. Just the same, from the look of the weather, he'd better take along some pine splinters soaked in coal oil so's to have a night fire if he needed it.

Whitey had the dishes in the pan. "Not to bait you, but I figger your old man must wear

God out, always chewin' His ear," he went on in the manner of one just wanting to talk. "Or maybe he's got an idea the Old Gent is deef."

He had said the same before, but Lat kept still and let him ramble.

"Or maybe he just naturally needs more help than we do. S'pose so? S'pose he's got a hid weakness like drink or women?"

Lat got up. "You're way off the track."

"Maybe so." Whitey stepped to the stove. "Here, you set down, and we'll have some more coffee. Your butt'll be cold enough by the time you get back." He poured the cups full and set the coffeepot back on the stove. "But that prayin' and Bible readin'!" he said, taking a chair. "I can't get it out of my head."

"Now you know there wasn't so much."

Whitey pursed his mouth. "Like the goose said when he emptied out nine miles up, a little of that goes a long way. That blessin' the food, when me and Mike and old Goddy would've rather took her unblessed and et in the barn!"

"Yes. I know."

"More'n your father and them prayers and all, it was your mother. A good woman she scares a man that's spent his time rawhidin' around in rough country. He can't face her for thinkin' that maybe, onthinkin', he'll break wind or something. Seems like every time I set down to that table of yours my belly was growlin', or I had an itch where it weren't nice to scratch, and I was afraid of forgettin' that, too. And talk! What's there to say without a cuss word for seasonin'?"

"You did well enough," Lat answered, but he saw them again, the three of them three years ago, all ill at ease and spare-spoken in a good home, before a good woman, in the general odor of goodness.

"Want your coffee het up?"

"No thanks." There was that last time, when they were about to start out with the cattle he'd scratched up in Oregon. They stood on the porch, he and his crew and Ma and Pa; and Pa had to choose this time and this company to make him a gift of a new leather-bound Bible while he said for a joke not meant much as a joke, "You can carry the Word to the heathen, son." For a minute all stood stiff and speechless, and it would have helped to have Grandpa on hand for a saying, out of the grave to which he'd gone a few weeks before. Whitey and Carmichael fingered their hats, and, seeing them, Godwin uncovered. There was thanks to say while they watched him, their eyes solemn and guarded. Afterwards, Godwin looked at the Book and got out, "Handsome," and Carmichael said, "Real handsome," and Whitey,

"Uh-huh!"; and they were happy to clatter down the steps and win free, not knowing, not being of kin.

"The way I see it," Whitey was saying now as he sipped at his coffee, "that's why cowpunchers and such mix with chippies, feelin' on what you might call common footin'." He added with a grin, "Another reason, o'course, is they're women."

"You said once you'd got beyond that."

"Not so much beyond as be-damned. It just ain't worth the effort." His eyes, as he went on, were half sly, half accusing. "It strikes me, Lat, that everyone excuses, for themselves, what they like best."

"So be it." Lat got to his feet.

"Don't snort at me, boy! You know damn well I'm like one of them Roman confessions. Hear all and blab nothin'."

"I'll see you in town tomorrow."

"Me?" Whitey asked, grinning.

The cows were all right, Lat told himself, but he'd be easier in mind if he made sure before going to Tansytown tomorrow. He heeled the Appaloosie and felt the faster amble of him through the powdered, knee-deep snow. Now, in March, with spring by rights around the corner, it was like Montana for winter to strike back.

Not that he had any right to complain, not last year or this one or that first year when the cattle from Oregon were new to the range and softer than now. The weather had been mild and open, the cows and calves had wintered well, and people had laughed at the little fenced-in stacks of hay put up against hard seasons. Losses had been small, from cold and hunger and wolves and boggings-down and rustlers white and red – none from diseases like the Texas fever and pleuro-pneumonia that Montana ranchers feared.

"Dearest Son" – the opening words stood clear – "We thank you, and God bless you! You bought a new carpet with the money." It was real pretty, and the first they'd had in almost forty years. But still they couldn't get used to his living in a wild land like Montana where even the names were strange to other ears.

The Tansy. The Sun. The Missouri, better called the Smoky Water, as the Indians called it. The Goose Neck. The Knees. The Judith. The Musselshell. The Dry Forks. The Marias. The Crocondunez near Fort Benton. The Freezeout. The Two Medicine. Names strange to Ma but wild and sweet on the tongue. Far-ranging names that acquaintance with the country made better. A hundred miles behind him, when he turned to look, he could see the mantled nipples of the Sweet Grass Hills.

Names and places, and things no words could tell. Spring in Montana. Summer. Fall. The look of ranges, bench on bench. The month of the wild rose. The time that cactus flowered. Everywhere the grasses straight or blowing. Cows and calves, and all the fat earth for a pasture. The chinook, out of its mother cloud over the mountains. The feel of winds. Winter, even, and the tonic feel of cold. The sky. Always the sky.

He pulled a hand out of his mitt and rubbed his face. Sunburn, they called it, but snowburn was closer, the burn from the sun that bounced from the snow. Better now and here, though, than later on the bags of his cows. Not even mother love would let a calf suck a sore tit.

Nothing was in sight, nothing but white seen through the tear-shimmer of cold and bright snow, nothing but the mountains to westward chiseled from frost and the Tansy hard by, smothered under its blanket, fringed by willow and cottonwood standing poor as a Chinaman's beard. No rabbits were out, and no birds but for one chickadee dee-deeing to nothing. The cattle would be somewhere in the brush, if they hadn't gone farther.

"Well, how's it coming?" Conrad had asked just last spring.

"Still shoestring but good."

Conrad smiled under his mustache there at Fort Benton. "Note's due, and you're prompt. How many head do you tally now?"

"Counting calves, right at eight hundred head."

"Good." Conrad smiled again. "And that plan of yours, how's it panning out?"

"There's the count."

"And the land?"

"There's my desert-land claim and the ditch, which I told you about. I aim to make the ditch bigger."

"Yes?"

"Two friends of mine, Godwin and White — you might have met them — have filed on claims for me."

"How much an acre?"

"Fifty cents to a dollar, depending. I'd like to be able to give them a dollar, but they won't raise a row."

"Don't be too open-handed."

"And another friend, Carmichael, will do the same thing."

Conrad had nodded, as if at last he recognized that ranges were crowded and more cows were coming in every season. "Fenced?"

"Part of it." Dollars? Dollars? Who had the dollars? Dollars for grub, for entry fees of two bits an acre, for barbed wire, for interest, for payment on principal, for a few tools and stuff like a window for the cabin he'd built mostly himself?

Conrad's face had gone serious. "Owe anyone but our bank?"

"A little. To Mr. Bob Ford at Sun River, who loaned me money for a mower and rake."

Conrad made a humming noise in his throat. "Who else?"

"A little to Marshall Strain, which is the same as the Tansytown Mercantile Company."

"How much, altogether?"

"Just a couple of hundred."

Conrad hummed again.

"That's it, except for those land entries made for me, and they're not due yet."

"How about our interest?"

"I've got it."

"Payment on principal?"

"I can pay some this fall by selling my three-year-olds. Mr. Ford will be combing the country, wanting to buy. He's got a big Canadian contract. He'll trail to Fort Mcleod, where the beef will be rationed to Indians."

"I know." Conrad spread his mustache with his thumb and forefinger. "Where did your money come from?"

"From wages. I've sold a few head when I had

to, but mostly it's money from others, earned in the time I could spare. I hire out when I can. To keep going, I have to."

"Nose to the grindstone, tail to the blizzard?"

"Pretty much."

"Work never hurt anyone." Conrad picked a fleck from his broadcloth. "What you say jibes with reports that have come to me. Play isn't your failing, they say."

"Thanks."

It was over then, or better than over. "Don't sell the three-year-olds," Conrad had said with a smile. "Let the principal ride, and the interest, too, if you wish. Actually, Evans, in view of your record we're prepared to advance you more money."

The snow was running with a breeze from the north, sifting now straight ahead, now in windings and twirls; and a man could lose himself in it, imagining it was white water and his pony a boat until he looked farther and saw a butte lifting, fixed to the solid earth, stock-still in the sky, and even it was an iceberg, or could be, moving too slow for sight. The storm had come on last night, borne by a Hudson's Bay chinook, and the night had been a raw one for cows but good for a man if he shut out the thought of them and lay snug in the soogans, hearing the wind crying wild and the sleet rasping outside and the cabin complaining but standing brave to the night. Whitey's snores had become one with these sounds, had become proof that someone else was alive in the world if dead to its doings.

He had his cabin and his claim and the rest. More than his holdings, he had free range for his cows, though it was grazed close – which accounted for the trouble he'd had with that Whey Belly Hector. The man stood in his mind, big-jawed, big-eyed, big-mouthed like a frog, with the look in his body of someone whose height had pounded down in the saddle. "Why, goddam you," he was saying, "you're inside my line! Ask anybody! Look in the *Rocky Mountain Husbandman,* where I paid for a notice! And you figure to squat here? Now get out!"

For himself he was saying, "It's owned by the government. It's open to all, to file on or graze."

Hector leaned forward in his saddle. For an answer he patted the butt of a rifle slung underneath.

"I'll be here," Lat said, and Hector wheeled around and galloped away. There hadn't been any more trouble. There wouldn't be any. Hector was running a bluff, or attempting to.

The wind had swept out any footprints.

There was nothing to go by but the fact that the cattle would have drifted south or southwest, down from the long river flat where in winter he tried to hold them by close herding and occasional dribbles of hay. A nursemaid, they called him. In every direction the snow to the skylines stretched empty and clean, without movement on it or the smudge of a fur.

To the right, though, like a hump in a blanket, rose one of the Indian wolf traps he'd built. Probably it would be empty, wolves having grown fewer, but more than once it had given him pin money for town, and at no cost but the sweat of putting it up. He reined the Appaloosie that way, again seeing himself and Little Runner wrestling the poles, pole by pole builing a pen so sloped at the sides that wolves could climb up and drop in, so high they couldn't leap out. Beat strychnine for costs.

He rode around it, peering over and down. There was nothing inside but the snow mounds of jackrabbit carcasses he'd thrown in for bait.

No pin money, no side money here. What he spent tomorrow in town would have to come out of his regular pocket.

"No, Lat!" He was hearing Callie again. "But why do you always make me take money?"

Miss Fran would turn in her coffin at that, or would screech in the place she'd been sent to.

Wherever it was, it would be hell if she couldn't yell, "Company, girls!"

He sat looking at the mounded carcasses. Miss Fran dead — the big bust, the big bottom, the little feet and fat wrists, the hunger for money all gone away. Fort Benton near dead, with no cargo blood in the vein of the river.

"What shall I do, Lat?" Callie had asked. "I don't want to stay here. I don't need so much money. Aunt Fran left me some. We could operate smaller." She waited. "And wouldn't it be easier for you if I moved to Tansytown?"

It was easier.

He found the cows along about four o'clock, not against the drift fence and not in the river brush but in a coulee to the west that gouged down from the benchlands. A spring seeped there, crowded by snow, and clumps of sarvice and chokeberry fretted its course, clicking to a touch of the overhead breeze. The cows stood dumb and unmoving, their coats glinting with hoarfrost, their snoots puffing vapor. Their slow eyes, circled with ice crumbs, asked what they had done to be punished this way. But they were all right. Only a rancher maybe too keen for tallow would worry about them or think to haze them to grass.

Nevertheless he pushed them out on a slope that the wind had brushed thin of snow.

They'd get a few mouthfuls before they came back.

The straightest line home lay up the ridge to the north, over the pitches and into the gullies that lower down flattened off to the Tansy. Not in weeks had he ridden that way. He just might find a stray.

At the top he reined in and looked back. The herd was grazing halfheartedly, making a ragged patch on the blanket of snow. Now that the sun was low, the reds and roans of the bunch were dimmed with dove-gray. Up here was no wind at all, no least movement of air unless the creep of the cold could be called that. Up here was no sound but the silence of cold. The wrinkled country ahead seemed frozen tight, locked up forever, dead and preserved like a fish frozen-in in the frozen ocean of air.

Farther on, with night closing down, he spotted a blotch on the hazed sheet of the earth and reined in to look. The blotch moved, setting in movement smaller blotches around it. He kicked the Appaloosie.

Wolves and a stray cow, or a bull, three wolves circling round, dashing in and back out. The stray wheeled to meet them. Lat blinked and looked again.

He had come out of nowhere, this ancient

288

buffalo bull, out of hidden hills or lost plains or the great hole in the ground that the Indians invented to account for the disappearance of the herds they once knew. A lone bull, the last bull, hooking at the places the wolves had just left.

At Lat's shout the wolves raised their heads. They loped off as he came on. At a little distance they slowed and faced around and rumped down. They knew when a man wasn't armed. They grinned at him, their teeth showing white against the dark of their muzzles.

The bull didn't move except to front the new danger. Starved to bones, rimed with frost, he stood with his head down, daring anyone to come on, daring the world and everything in it. Above his stubborn eyes his forelock dangled, still fuzzed with last season's burrs, still sandy from remembered wallows, from watering places he wouldn't see any more. The blizzard had driven him, the wind and the cutting snow, out of some echoing solitude down here to ranges made strange since he grazed as a calf.

If he could be driven on toward the cabin, to safety and hay?

Lat pulled off a mitten and untied his rope, feeling the quick bite of the cold. He maneuvered closer and flicked the bull on the side and got a sweep of the horns in return. He tried again, and again, too close for comfort.

The three wolves were still laughing. Before help could arrive, they'd have the bull down and the soft parts, the guts and the bag, eaten out.

There was nothing to do but ride on.

22

It was midafternoon, and here was the town, and he had no worries now that the west wind had sprung up, making mush of yesterday's snow. He could idle with Godwin and Whitey and Carmichael, if he had arrived, and see Callie afterwards and spend the night there and ride home in the morning, made free and easy by knowing the cows were all right. It was seldom enough he had nothing to do and so could find pleasure in doing it.

He put Sugar up at McCabe's corral and started down the street for the Tansytown Merc., stepping careful so as not to ruin entirely the shine on his boots. He could buy a bottle at the Gilt Edge or the Lally Cooler or the bar at the Jackson Hotel, where the ranchers held out when in town, but because Marshall Strain trusted him he'd pick it up there.

Take away the saloons and there wasn't much

left, just the mercantile company with the post office in it, the hotel, McCabe's barn, the blacksmith shop, a meat market of sorts, Bob Reed Saddles and Harness, a couple of shacks that did for offices — all pressed against the board walks that the townspeople had pitched in to build along the main track. Back of these, now in sight and now out, sat the homes, built mostly of log. Callie's house, put up by an overblown booster who'd been forced to sell it, looked big by comparison. Not much of a town, even counting the bars. It was the ranchers that kept the place going. But a town was a town.

The snow squished under foot. The ring of steel against steel came from the blacksmith shop and, between blows, a word and an answer and the clicking of chips from the Gilt Edge. Two boys were throwing snowballs in the street, and a man in a work wagon yelled, "Hey, you!" as he ducked a throw. A woodpecker splashed with red hammered at a cottonwood in front of the Jackson Hotel. Whey Belly Hector came out the door and gave a grunt and passed on, his legs bowed from weight and riding. One saddle horse stood at the hitch rack in front of the Lally Cooler. A team slept alongside the Tansytown Merc.

No one was inside, though, except Marshall Strain. He came up smiling, a spectacled, grayish man who looked out of place in a store. He held out his hand. "Been wanting to see you, Lat." Out of his ears, under the pencil he kept slanted behind one of them, little tufts of hair sprouted. "Where you been keeping yourself?"

"Out of mischief."

The place smelled of coal oil and potatoes and smoked meat and new shoes. It had a counter and shelves and stacks and sacks and barrels of stuff, all arranged to be handy, and in the rear, close by the whiskey barrel, a little grilled box of a post office.

"There's a letter here for you," Mr. Strain said. He stepped to the box and sorted it out and brought it back. It was from home.

"Much obliged. And I'll take a quart of whiskey. For cash."

"Your credit's good."

"Thanks. Not for whiskey."

Mr. Strain nodded. "Still your rule, huh? Except for necessities, pay as you go or don't go." His smile said he understood. "But what whiskey you buy isn't much." His gaze turned to the door, which had whined as it opened. "Come in."

"Evenin'." It was Happy, standing solemn with his hand on the latch, his eyes like dark moons in the lighter moon of his face. He closed the door softly.

"I'll be with you as soon as I wait on this gentleman."

"Yassuh."

Lat bobbed his head for hello.

Happy gave a bare "Howdy." Outside the house he never named names learned there.

"Poor soul!" Mr. Strain said under his breath. He shook his head slowly and raised it and went on as if to justify himself, "But they have to eat, Lat." He took a bottle from under the counter and went to the barrel and filled it and came back, twisting a cork in its mouth. "You'll want it wrapped up, of course," he said and proceeded to wrap it.

Lat put two dollars out, but before making change Mr. Strain put his palms flat on the counter and leaned over. "Would it be possible for you to have supper with us tonight?"

It was the first invitation to come from anyone like Mr. Strain.

"I told my wife I was sure you'd enjoy a good family meal. Nothing fancy, just home fixings."

"I appreciate that."

"What's more, I've got something I want to say to you, something to suggest and talk over. Can't you come?"

"Why – uh – of course. I'd be happy to."

Mr. Strain straightened and said while he returned fifty cents, "About six o'clock then."

"Fine." Lat went toward the door, passing Happy on his slow way to the counter. He stopped before going out and stuck his bottle in an overshoe displayed on a bench and opened the letter from home.

DEAREST SON,

It has been a long time since we heard from you, and I thought I would write to say that we are both well and hope that you are.

Your pa and I keep wondering why you stay in Montana when you could be right here in Oregon, but that is your business now you've grown into a man. Maybe you will change your mind later. I know whatever you do, anywhere, will be a credit to you, and that is the greatest comfort of all. You were always a good son, and it isn't for old folks to interfere when their children grow up but just to pray that their rearing was wise. That was always first in your pa's mind, to make you a find and successful man. He wished it so hard that it hurt him sometimes and made him seem cross, wishing you better things than he ever had. He has taken life hard, so I could put it the other way round, which is one reason why he's so anxious for you. It may take you a while yet to understand, until you have your own children.

A family named Newton took over the Graves place a couple of months ago, and I wish you could meet them. They have a daughter, Mary Moore, who is just as sweet and good as can be.

Your pa has had a touch of rheumatism lately and isn't too frisky. In other ways he's fine, and there's nothing to worry about. He said Sunday he wished you were home to eat my chicken and dumplings with him. Remember how you two used to gobble them up?

I hate to tell you that old Shorty is dead. Pa found him in his stall where I guess he died in his sleep. He was a colt when you were a baby, and just to tease me your pa used to say it looked like the blue ribbon for mothers went to the mare.

Thank you for that money, son, but you had already bought us a carpet, and we don't like to think you're going without. Don't send any more, dear. We can make out.

Please, please take care of yourself. We think about you, and our prayers are with you every day.

All love,
MA

P.S. Write to us when you can. Pa gets as lonesome as I do.

Lat stuffed the letter in his pocket and picked up the bottle and went out, hearing Happy's voice with the back of his ears as he brought the door to. "Yassuh, an' some whiskey. A gallon, she say."

Ma wanted him to come home. She wanted him to meet a girl as sweet and good as could be. She wanted him to understand Pa. Old Shorty was dead and please write. Their prayers were with him, and their thanks for the money.

Yes. Yes. But no web-foot, close-herded, pot-poor life there while here the sky sailed high. Tonight with a good family he'd have a good supper, complete with grace. And then?

From blessing to bed, and for what we are about to receive!

It was good to be with old friends again, Carmichael thought, good to be shooting the breeze in this Tansytown shack that Godwin and Whitey were baching the winter in, good to be told that Lat would show up by and by. Lat was still Lat, they were saying.

"For a man that watches his money —" Whitey began.

"It ain't that he's tight," Godwin was quick to

297

put in. "It's just he wants to get where he don't have to be tight."

"For a man that watches his money, he's open-handed with friends." Whitey spread out his palms. "Know what? Don't matter how pushed he might be, I never appealed to him yet that he didn't fork over. When that damn McCabe lays me off at the livery stable, Lat's got a chore for me or a few bucks to loan. He ain't forgittin' his friends."

Godwin said, "Hope."

The shack held a table and two stools and a cookstove and a couple of tarp-covered bunks on the sidewalls and two wooden crates for a cupboard. To a man who had ridden all the way from old Jim Fergus's place north of the Judiths and arrived stiff with cold, it was skookum. Good enough for any old bunkhouse rooster for that matter.

"And with him you're always plumb welcome to bed and board for long as you please," Whitey was adding as if this item was the clincher. "Not as I abuse it. And I don't forget my debts."

"You don't have to stand up for him with me," Carmichael said. Of them all maybe he understood Lat best. Looking back in his life to the young years, to the years that had left him almost middle-aged, he saw in Lat some lost part of himself. He'd had a rearing, too, though no one would know it now, and he had had hopes, but always to be acted on later, until it was too late. The difference between them was itchy feet and a funnybone. But a man had to make choices, and he had made his and didn't regret it. It was just that he felt close to Lat underneath and so took a close pleasure in his advance.

A little center of things pretty sure to grow bigger. That was Lat. A man that men tended to follow. Godwin. Whitey. Even himself. He was reminded of what he had thought out before. "A man with a purpose don't lack for a party," he said. "I hear that little hooker followed him here."

"It ain't what you'd call an open subject," Whitey answered.

"Who says?" Carmichael asked, already knowing.

"Lat."

This, too, he understood, thinking back to his first times with women, to the green fears and the shame and the longer concern with what good people would say. They didn't matter to him now, none of them, the talk as little as the rest. They didn't need to. But they mattered to the Lat in him. He could understand.

Tom Ping didn't. Tom couldn't. There in Fort Benton, where Carmichael had broken his ride from the Judith country, Tom had leaned across a bar table. "The son-of-a-bitch!" he said. "The high-toned son-of-a-bitch!"

Carmichael had taken it quietly. "What's the real trouble between you and Lat? No one ever told me."

"Just say he's too good for the likes of us. That's all. A high-toned son-of-a-bitch."

It was all that Tom would say, but it was enough to give a general idea, enough to show how unlike one was to the other. Unlike in situation, too. Tom was freighting coal and seemed hard put to support a wife and child.

Now Godwin was saying, " 'Course, Lat knows we know about that towhead chippie. Not as his little secret can be kep' forever, but we try to hold our tongues, for it's the public that he's touchy on, for reasons all his own." Godwin shook his head slowly. His finger made a small circle on the bunk where he sat. "Oh, I s'pose I understand, but it wasn't until white wives and picket fences began comin' in that a man got damned for actin' the man." He thought about the question some more. "No one hates a whore like a cold wife unless it's the husband she won't let out of sight. So we got vice for a word."

"I'd be proud to show that Callie around," Whitey said.

Carmichael smiled. "Not if Lat's pa had broke you to harness."

"Don't even mention it! No!"

The door opened almost too soon on their words, and Lat came in with a bottle under his arm. "Hi, Mike! Glad to see you! When'd you get in?" He came over to shake hands.

"Yesterday. Your ears burnin'?"

"Should they?" With what Carmichael could tell was real welcome and not mere politeness. Lat shook with Whitey and Godwin.

"We were wonderin' about you. No bull."

"No bull, huh?" Lat's smile disappeared. He gestured with the bottle. "I saw a bull yesterday! A buffalo bull!"

"Where in hell's the circus?" Godwin asked.

"On the range, for a fact!" Lat pointed the bottle at Godwin.

Listening, they grinned at him, not quite believing. But Carmichael believed.

"So he reminded you of me?" Godwin asked. "Don't match him with me. I ain't the last nor on my last legs."

"I am," Whitey said, "unless you open that bottle." He didn't look so far gone. He had lost some of the whiskey bloat of stomach and face, due maybe to Lat.

Lat peeled off the paper and set the bottle on the table; and here, Carmichael thought, was cowpunchers' ease, with friends at his side, with nothing to do but lie around and sip whiskey and trade lies and maybe have a go at the pasteboards, letting happen whatever happened outside. The stuff in print made it out that a man couldn't have any fun on account of Indians and stampedes and weather and rackets with bad men, whereas a rider alone on a drift line could polish up stories and try them out on his horse and get tickled by looking ahead. Here, now, even Lat appeared free of his fret and ready for lazy fun.

"Alongside me," Whitey said, moving up to the table, "a desert is flooded. I'm witherin' like a burnt vine."

Lat handed over the bottle and drew on his training. "The last shall be first."

"Sounds holy." Whitey took the cork out and sniffed and lowered the bottle. "But don't Christ me or I'll Christ you back. You're too young to hear, Lat, but I call to mind the elder that prayed for rain and got a cloudburst and, seein' his chickens floatin' away and his outhouse torn down to the roots, you might say, he says to the Lord, 'I wanted a root-wetter, not a gulley-washer, just a gentle sizzle-sozzle. Cravin' Your grace, but this here is plumb idiotic!' " Whitey measured the bottle. "Not as this drop will give us the squizzles."

He drank and started the bottle around.

Lat took off his coat and hung it on a wall spike, and, watching him from the bunk, old Godwin asked, "Dressed for a buryin', are you?"

Lat was dressed to lay corpses, all right, or whatever — white Stetson, white shirt, red silk neckerchief, horsehair chain looped from his neck to his watch pocket, California pants, boots that looked made to order. He ought to have added a six-gun.

Godwin went on, looking at the ceiling. "A funeral is final, and thank God! But a weddin' is everlastin' unless the good Lord cuts the rope. It means wipe your feet good before you come in the door. Take your hat off inside the house. Don't set on the bed, it messes it. Eat like you wasn't hungry. Sleep without snorin'. Hang up your duds. Go to bed in a night bib and freeze your bare tail in the mornin'. The idee, sleepin' in what you've wore so's not to get cold by changin'! Don't matter if it is, don't call it shit!"

"You been married?" Carmichael said.

"Wherever she is, she's got the place tidy."

Whitey walked over and took the bottle from Lat, who had perched himself on a stool. "We make out without women," he said, wiping his mouth. "Godwin, he burns the mulligans when

I'm workin', and I take a hand when I ain't, and let us get r'iled at each other, and we don't either one weep. If I want a drink, he don't holler, and if somethin' I et disagrees with me, he don't pertend that it's whiskey."

"Not when you're cookin'," Godwin put in.

Tom Ping came again to Carmichael's mind as he glanced at Lat, but a story pushed ahead. "I been halfway weaned from the bottle," he said. "Not that tellin' the how of it will make you booze-fighters swear off."

Lat said, "Go ahead."

"It's thanks to a friend of mine that I'm so temp'rate."

"Who?" Whitey asked.

"Acey Duncan was his name, a good man drunk or sober, though I'm guessin' at that last. The two of us set out one time to drink Ogallaly dry. Five or ten days we were at it. The count is mixed up in my mind. Anyhow, in tryin' to drain the supply, we got separated, which didn't matter. By that time we'd forgot we started in harness together. Then come a night of such terrible cold that spit froze on a stove, and old Acey, whose heart was touched easy, ran into a sheepherder with whiskers enough for a hair blanket but nothin' else that stacked up as assets. Acey asked him was he thirsty, which was a fool question. He asked him did he have a bed, which he didn't. So Acey saw to his thirst and by and by bedded him and his whiskers alongside himself in the spot I forgot to come back to. Next morning when he woke up, Acey had come to himself, more or less. He turned his head careful, like a soft-shelled egg, and spotted those whiskers spread long on the covers, and he reared up and tooted, 'In the name of God, Mike! Carmichael, how long we been here?' "

When the laughs had died out, Carmichael said, watching Lat just with the tail of his eye, "I forgot to tell you. Tom Ping's liable to move out this way. Got a job promised from the TS outfit, and he's thinkin', besides, of stakin' a land claim hereabouts."

Lat answered up. "There's good land still open to entry, and the TS is all right. I hope he does fine."

The thing was, the point was, Carmichael thought, that Lat meant it.

23

Happy came in the back door, carrying what he called his tote sack, and set it on the floor and began taking the things out.

"Mist' Lat's in town," he said, lifting the jug to the work table.

Callie swung away from the dishpan and the little stack of soiled dishes. "Lat's in town!"

"Sho' is."

"Then he'll he here tonight!"

"He di'n' say, but he sho' will."

"Tonight!" she said again, more to herself than to Happy, and looked out the window where the sun dawdled on the snow. "Happy, I'm sorry, but you'll have to go back. Get some peaches or berries in airtights, something good for a pie."

"It ain't no bothah, Miss Callie."

"You know how it is living alone. Men crave something sweet."

"Yas'm." Happy took the last article out of

the sack and made for the door, slow as molasses, slow as the long afternoon.

When he had gone, she finished the dishes and then got out flour and lard and a dough board and rolling pin. It was good to have something to fill in the minutes and better yet to be doing something for Lat. Later tonight they'd slip down the back stairs from her room, she in her wrapper and he just half dressed, and they'd talk and eat pie and afterwards, without any need of suggestion by either, go back to bed.

The girls were upstairs. She had this time all to herself, if some man just didn't knock at the door. She found herself humming a half-remembered song. "Fair, fair, with golden hair..." Lat liked her hair. "...sang a fond mother while weeping..." She laughed. "Fair, fair..." Did a wife feel like this?

She fed the wood range and turned up the draft and rinsed off her hands and mixed the pie dough and rolled it out and was about ready when Happy came back. "Man don' have nothin' but· peaches," he said, "but I brung along a scrimption of cheese."

"That's fine. And, Happy, you can kind of pick up in the parlor and answer the door if anyone comes."

He answered, "Miss Callie, shuah," and moved out.

She mixed sugar and flour, using plenty of sugar, and opened the peaches and stirred in the mixture and filled the pan. For a surprise, then, she cut LAT in the top crust. She laid the crust on and crimped it and looked at the oven. It was hot enough. She put the pie in.

By and by it would be cooked. By and by the sun would go down. In time, darkness would come. After supper she'd part her hair in the middle and draw it back snug and tie it at the beck with a bow and let it fall in a tail, the way that Lat liked it. And she'd put on the new dress with the shawl collar and the skirt with two rows of ruffles. On the kitchen wall the banjo clock that had belonged to Aunt Fran said 4 o'clock. After a long time it said 4:01.

It was past 7 o'clock when the first knock came at the front door. It wouldn't be Lat, though. He always came to the back. Happy showed in two men, one tall and one medium. In the manner of so many men they stood with their hats on and grinned with uncertainty while they sized up the girls and the place. It was a good-enough place, clean, orderly, furnished with Aunt Fran's piano and sofa and mirrors and chairs and pictures and lamps, and a carpet she'd paid for herself. It was better than the bunkhouses they knew, she thought without faulting them.

Amy Lou walked to the tall one and said, "How, Sugar Tit?"

His eyes slid away from her. It was mostly the drunks that Amy Lou got nowadays and the men who'd rather take her than wait. Aunt Fran, already grumbling before her heart quit, would have put her out of the house long ago, huffing off the idea that Amy Lou was more than age, teeth and a thirst.

Callie said, "Happy, see if the gentlemen don't want a drink. Won't you boys sit?"

"Yas'm." Happy looked nice in his white coat.

"Whiskey for us." The medium man took a seat on the sofa by Daisy. Daisy smiled the smile that struck men as shy. A new girl, she was gypsy-dark and smooth-skinned and knew the trick of making her eyes wide and inquiring like the eyes of a rabbit.

The tall man maneuvered around Amy Lou and sat down.

They had come from work, these two, and had the marks of work on them. Their collars were ringed darker than the rest of their shirts. Their pants showed wear and stain. On their boots were corral flecks. Young, unknowing, so awkward as to be rude, they were like many another. There was nothing bad in them, nothing at any rate to be seen. A house took such boys, for a price small compared to their hunger, and sent them out eased, ready again for line camp or ranch.

Happy brought in the drinks, and Callie collected. Over his glass the tall man let himself look at her. "Now you're real pretty," he said and caught himself and turned quickly to Amy Lou. "No offense, ma'am."

Callie smiled. "Not tonight."

The man moved his eyes to Amy Lou by degrees, as if hoping she'd changed since he examined her last.

Amy Lou came over and sat on his knee. Her hand went up and pushed back his hat and fingered his hair. "I'm a good girl, Sugar Tit."

Something Daisy said made the medium man laugh. "You're a daisy, all right," he told her, "a plumb daisy-do." His young eyes drank her in. His hand touched her leg as if he couldn't quite believe a touch was allowed.

The tall one didn't look happy at the way they had happened to pair off. He swallowed his drink and swallowed a sigh. "Come on, then." Amy Lou got off his knee quickly and led the way to the stairs. Daisy and her man were slower, but they followed after a minute.

They had just gone from sight, just clicked their doors shut, when another knock came at the front. Callie started up before she remembered it wouldn't be Lat. "See who it is," she asked Happy.

The door swung open before Happy could get there, and Whey Belly Hector came in. "Howdy," he said. "How's the boss of the roost?"

"I — wasn't expecting you, Heck."

He didn't notice her tone. "No business being here. You play hell with the ranch." He walked over and let himself down in a chair and told Happy, "Bring me a drink!" It wouldn't, Callie thought, be the first.

Happy went out without speaking and would take his time coming back.

Under her lashes she looked at Hector, at the big bulb of his stomach, at the powerful shoulders and arms, at the broad set of his jaw and the head that narrowed up from it. A rude, demanding man but natural to himself, honest as cactus was honest, or animals. A steady customer. There was a time, she thought, looking back to her green and notionable days, when she would never have taken him on, but a girl naturally got over being so picky. It was just that she wished he hadn't shown up tonight, though sooner or later it was certain to happen.

"You can dock off the other boys," he said. "I'm staying the night. Where's that nigger?"

"He's coming."

"So's Christ."

"It can't be tonight, Heck."

"Can't? How come can't?" Little veins ran in the eyes he lifted to hers.

"But one of the other girls —"

"I've paid for an interest in you."

"You should have let me know."

His big eyes slitted. "So now I got to sign up in advance!"

"It's just tonight, Heck."

He came to his feet and stepped to her, slowly. "A goddam way to act with me!"

She hadn't thought of him as mean. She teetered up from the chair, crowded by the thrust of his stomach, her breath quick in her throat.

Happy came in with the drink.

"Set it down and get out!" Hector said.

Happy's wide gaze came to Callie.

"Get out, you nigger pimp!" Hector took half a step around, his shoulders hunched beyond the bulge of his stomach. Happy looked frail beside him.

"It's all right, Happy. You can go." Her voice came clear and firm and wasn't hers.

Hector took another step. It put him between Happy and the kitchen. "Get, I said."

Happy sidled to the front door and turned

the knob and sidled out, his face turned backwards on them.

She didn't see it coming. She stood dizzy and confused and spun about while the blow came to life on her cheek as the leavings of his open hand.

"There, sister!"

She braced herself and turned and stood straight and met his eyes. "Good night!" She gave her back to him and started to the rear, walking slowly with her head up.

She heard his boots then, clumping after her, and caught herself hurrying, almost running. She slowed down to the inner whisper that the show of fear would make him worse. Step by step, to the kitchen, to the butcher knife, the heavy pots and pans.

There was the butcher knife! The simple, rightful self-protection! She might have reached it, but she swung around and met him coming in. "It's my time, Heck! Don't you understand? It's my time!"

He stopped. He gazed around. His large eyes steadied, fixed — and understood. She knew why before she looked. On the table the pie, with the LAT baked ragged in the crust. "So!" he said.

She felt herself reeling, falling to the hoof of his hand, heard herself yelling from the floor,

"You can't! Not tonight! You can't make me!"

"Go to hell!"

The belly swung away, and the back marched from sight while inside her she cried, "You bastard! You dirty bastard! You'll have to come back!"

She didn't know Happy had entered the back door until his voice sounded. "Callie! Miss Callie!" She felt his hands on her arms and the lift of his old-nigger strength and the steadying hold of him after she had got to her feet. "You all right, Miss Callie?"

She was solider now. She pulled away from his hand and breathed deep. "I'm fine. It was nothing much."

Over her voice came the goodbyes of the tall and medium visitors and the made-cheery goodbyes of the girls and the clunk of the closing front door.

When she looked at Happy again, she saw the butcher knife in his hand and his head bowed over it. He was trying the edge with his thumb.

She said, "Put it up, Happy! Don't be crazy!"

He said, "Yas'm," and laid it away.

She went into the parlor where the girls waited customers, carrying her head high. She dug out the work book and steadied her hand for the entries.

Daisy $3.00
Amy Lou $3.00

"I'll be in my room," she said and mounted the steps without hurry.

In the bedroom mirror one cheek appeared thickened, though hardly enough to be noticed. She washed her face with cold water and smoothed her hair and lay down to wait.

She closed her eyes and, keeping them closed, opened them on a ranch where there was a garden to tend and a calf orphan to mother and Lat first of all to take care of, and she could step out of the house and let the wind blow her — the wind that would whisper of the old Saturday-night parties, the old talk of men, the old live news, the old power over men!

A madam had no business crying.

24

It was 6 o'clock sharp by his Waltham when Lat knocked at Marshall Strain's door. A fine home, he thought while he waited, white clapboard, green trim, enclosed by a white picket fence.

The knob turned. "Welcome, Lat." Mr. Strain put out his hand as if they hadn't seen each other today. Behind him Lat caught a glimpse of a man and a woman. "Let me have your hat and coat." Mr. Strain hung them up. "Come on in. I want you to meet Mr. Gorham, A. L. Gorham, attorney-at-law."

The man got up, six feet two or three of him, and shook with a firm hand, saying, "It's a pleasure. I didn't get your name?"

"Evans. I'm sorry," Mr. Strain said.

"Evans." Gorham had a manner. He was maybe thirty or thirty-five but already a little ˙ at the temples.

Strain went on, "And here, Lat, is my

316

niece, Joyce Sheridan. She just arrived from the east, from Indiana."

She couldn't be more than nineteen or twenty. She had almost black hair and almost black eyes and a complexion almost milk-white. She said, "How do you do, Mr. Evans."

"It's a pleasure," he said and remembered that Gorham had said the same thing. He needed a black broadcloth frock coat and a black tie like Gorham's, not this cowpuncher outfit that must seem showy and outlandish to her. He extended his hand, knowing too late that he shouldn't, and she put out her own, quickly as if to cover the blunder. Her smile put life in her face, sudden and unexpected.

"Evans," she said. "Sometimes in Indiana they pronounce the name Iv-ans." Her eyes were fluid. Somewhere else, in someone else, they could be teasing. She drew her hand away. It had felt small but strong.

"We're hoping Joyce will stay here a while," Mr. Strain was saying. His gaze went smiling to the girl. "People manage to live outside Hoosierland. But take a chair, Lat! Sit down, Mr. Gorham! It will be a few minutes till supper."

Lat took a chair side-lined to Miss Sheridan's. He noticed now that an old dog lay stretched on the carpet beyond her. The dog blinked a sleepy eye and raised his head and, seeing nothing worth his attention, laid it back down.

Mr. Strain went on, "I hope Mr. Gorham will settle here, too. There's a place for him now, and there'll be a bigger one. I see statehood for Montana. I see Chouteau County – which must be about the size of all Indiana, Joyce – I see it split up. Tansytown will be a county seat." Mr. Strain waved his hand. "We could use some law here."

The girl said, "It all seems so bare, so lonely." She had a nice profile – high forehead, straight nose, upper lip tipping out to the lower, chin just firm enough. It was her eyes, though, that struck a man, against her pale skin the dark eyes that turned to him now as if she had felt his gaze on her.

"Pshaw!" Mr. Strain told her. "In time you'll be glad you can see beyond the end of your nose without climbing a sycamore. Eh, Lat?"

"It suits me. It always has."

"When we first moved to Helena from Ohio, my wife felt as you do," Gorham said to the girl.

He wasn't a suitor, then.

"You'd be surprised," Mr. Strain went on. "The ladies aren't as lonesome as you think. et together to visit and sew. If plans pan

318

out, we'll have the Eastern Star here before long. There's already the Ladies' Industrial, connected, of course, with the Methodist Church. The Methodists organized more than a year ago. No church hours yet and no regular preacher, but a church just the same."

"Wesley in the wilderness," Gorham said pleasantly.

Mr. Strain nodded, smiling. "That brings up a surprise. Brother Van Orsdel rode in today, up from Sun River, and would like to hold a service tonight. I don't want to push you into attending, but, if not, I'm afraid you will have to excuse us a little early." He looked at his watch. "No hurry, though. We had to get word to the members, and some of them live out a piece."

"It's worth it alone as a lesson in the art of persuasion," Gorham said. "I wish I could talk to a jury as Brother Van talks to us sinners."

The girl's dark gaze came to Lat. "Why not?" he said and saw a smile touch her lips.

"Good." Mr. Strain raised his eyes as Mrs. Strain bustled in from the kitchen. He got to his feet. "Mother, you know Lat Evans."

She came over and shook hands like a man. A big, full-breasted, motherly woman, flushed now by the stove's heat, she was one of a kind that seemed always to carry along the good

319

smells of the kitchen. She might have dropped in on Ma to talk chickens and children and to trade recipes. She said, "Welcome! I've been hearing about you."

"Thanks, Mrs. Strain. I'm glad to be here." He had remembered to get up.

"It's ready, folks."

They went into the dining room and sat down at the table, set with white linen and napkins, and Mr. Strain cleared his throat. "Blessed Lord, make us truly thankful for these, Thy bounties! Bless this food to our use and us to Thy service! Amen."

The girl, seated beside Lat, gave an "Amen," and he lapped the end of it with his own. How long since he'd listened to grace! How long since he'd sat at a gentle table, with the Lord's blessing on the chicken and dumplings Pa and he used to gobble up? He was home again, close to home, home from the rough, outside years.

The girl's eyes offered a penny for his thoughts.

He felt enough at ease to say, "Two bits in this country."

"What?"

"No pennies. No nickels or dimes. Two bits minimum, even for a thought."

"Two bits?"

"uarter."

Again the brief smile lighted her face. "Are your thoughts worth a whole quarter?"

"More than that, Joyce," Mr. Strain broke in. "Men like Lat will make this country, they and their sons after them." He paused and went on with a grin, "But it's a little early to talk to you about sons, isn't it, Lat?"

Mrs. Strain said, "Marshall!"

"I just remarked it was early, Mother," he made believe to protest.

Lat looked away. The old dog had padded in and sat close to Mr. Strain, his whole face asking if he couldn't have just one bite.

"Oysters!" Gorham said as he plied his fork. "A feast in themselves in Montana, Mrs. Strain." Speaking for a mulligan bachelor, Lat thought, he could have mentioned the fresh pork, the dressing and gravy and light rolls and butter and apple butter and even the peach pie served for dessert.

Afterwards Mr. Strain asked, "Shall the men excuse themselves now?"

"Please do," Mrs. Strain said. "We'll clear the table and join you." She came to her feet and spoke to the dog. "You, Roamer, come on!"

Mr. Strain led the way back to the parlor and offered cigars. He and Gorham lighted up.

"To get to the point, Lat," Mr. Strain said when he'd got himself comfortable, "we're overdue for a school."

"I see," Lat answered, not seeing.

"To have a school, you have to have a board."

"Yes?"

"I want you on the board."

"Me!"

"You, my boy."

"I'm not a family man."

"Ah-h." With his cigar Mr. Strain brushed the objection away. "What matters is the make-up of the board."

"I would guess," Gorham said, "that there'd be no question of your election, not with Mr. Strain's backing."

"But I'm not much educated."

"No?" Mr. Strain took a deep puff and blew it out in a gust. "Look around you. Who do you see?"

"I haven't looked," Lat said. He looked now, with Mr. Strain's words warm in his ears.

"Sleep on it." Mr. Strain drew on his cigar and studied the ash and carefully tipped it off. "But, Lat, I can tell you it's a starting point. From there the right man — meaning you — could go on if he wished, to county office, to the territorial legislature and even further. Right, Gorham?"

"So long as he's a Republican," Gorham ed with a little smile.

"Gorham's initials stand for Abraham Lincoln," Mr. Strain said. "Without knowing I'd still know you're Republican, Lat. Most solid men are."

"That leaves me out," Lat answered. Mr. Strain's words made him feel among solid men. "But my family, though from Missouri, stood solid for Union."

Mr. Strain nodded. "I want you to know that my niece may apply for the teachership, but don't think you have to support her. No strings at all, Lat. But I can say with complete honesty that she has all the qualifications except experience. Honor graduate of Earlham College in Indiana. Took a lot of elocution." He pulled out his watch. "If they'd get done with those dishes, she'd have time to recite something for us." He yelled toward the kitchen. "Mother, Joyce, get a move on!"

He needn't have shouted. They were just coming in, followed close by the old dog.

"Joyce, how about speaking a piece?" Mr. Strain asked.

"Uncle Marsh!"

The dog was letting himself down in the middle of the room.

" 'The Wreck of the Hesperus' maybe. I've been bragging. You can't go back on me."

"Don't insist, Marshall," Mrs. Strain said.

But Gorham, without thought of the girl's feelings, insisted, "It would be much appreciated."

Her liquid gaze went from one to another.

"Please, Joyce," Mr. Strain asked.

As if she had noted Lat's silence she said, "If Mr. Iv-ans agrees, I'd rather give something newer. It's by a western poet named Joaquin Miller."

Gorham alone nodded to the name.

With no show of embarrassment then, with an opening gesture both delicate and sure, the girl started speaking.

Once, morn by morn, when snowy mountains
 flamed
With sudden shafts of light that shot a flood
Into the vale like fiery arrows aim'd
At night from mighty battlements, there stood
Upon a cliff high-limn'd against Mount
 Hood,
A matchless stag, fresh forth from sable
 wold . . .

Except for an instant's hesitation at the word "stag," the words came flowing, came almost singing. She had a clear voice, a little deep for a " and she stood slim and poised, seeming le lines speak themselves, even though the old dog began barking softly in his sleep, chasing stags he'd never seen.

I ofttimes wonder'd much; and ofttime
* thought*
The beast betray'd a royal monarch's mind
To lift above the low herd's common lot
And made them hear him still when they had
* fain forgot.*

Lat had lost himself in the words until close to the end. Then he took a careful breath, making sure. The old dog, lying gassy, slipping wind no nose could miss!

They all clapped, not just to be polite, and she sat down. On her pale face was a glow from inward.

"That was splendid," Gorham said. "Now I have two people to envy, you and Brother Van. Knowing Miller's works, I suppose you know that introduction to the poem on Byron?"

The girl shook her head. Lat thought he saw the slender nostrils barely widen. The dog had done it again.

"Go on, Gorham." Mr. Strain got up. "Make way there, Roamer! Don't you know an attorney needs leg room?" He took the dog by the neck and put him outside.

"Let's see now." Gorham came to his feet

and coughed and cleared his throat. He took a few steps while he tried to remember.

In men whom men condemn as ill
I find so much of goodness still,
In men whom men pronounce divine
I find so much of sin and blot,
I do not dare to draw a line
Between the two, where God has not.

He sat down, smiling, and said to the girl, "Something of a contrast with that line about the low herd's common lot?"

The common lot was improving now that the dog was gone.

"What's your favorite poem, Lat?" Mr. Strain asked.

It was like asking him to draw a card from the air, to reach out into nothing and come back with a bower. What did he know? Trail songs. Pieces of Mother Goose. Snatches of rhymes read and heard. Even if once he knew, a cowman forgot. "My grandfather didn't like England," he said, "and so he was strong for the patriotic stuff." He shouldn't have called it stuff. "That one about Concord?"

"Sure! 'By the rude bridge that arched the ͡ ͡ ͡ their flags to April's breeze unfurled...'"

͡ e Mr. Strain had gone any farther, Gorham and Mrs. Strain began helping out and then the girl and then Lat himself, for most of the words came back to him now; and they went on to the end, their voices warmer with each line.

There was a silent moment afterwards, and then Mr. Strain was saying while he held his watch, "Time to go, folks."

The meeting place was a building that had been a saloon. Faded across the false front of it was a sign: THE FAMILY LIQUOR STORE. Maybe twenty people were inside, children included. They were standing and moving around and shaking hands, their talk making a low clatter above which now and then rose the cry of a child.

Mr. Strain pushed in and began introducing his party. From his manner Lat might have known nobody. "Mrs. Cooper, I want you to meet Mr. Evans," or, "Brother McLean, meet Mr. Evans, if you haven't already." A man who hadn't made much of a point of getting acquainted felt as if he was standing for office already.

Brother Van was a long, black preacher's coat around a thick chest. Above the coat was a heavy, pleasant face topped by thinning hair. Mr. Strain shook hands with him. "I'm sorry you couldn't get around for dinner, but we'l wait for the fried chicken and green corn. Here, Brother Van, is my niece, Joyce Sheridan."

Brother Van swallowed her hand in his. "God bless you, Sister!"

"She's a Hoosier Methodist."

"Methodism is not metes and bounds." Brother Van shook with Gorham then.

"And I've brought you a real live sinner to work on," Mr. Strain said. "Lat Evans, here."

"You can do more with a live sinner than a dead saint." Brother Van's hand was warm and large. On second look his face was less heavy than merely oval. It smiled good will.

The people got seated, and Brother Van opened with prayer, asking the Lord in His love to be merciful, to lead sinners to righteousness and unbelievers to the truth and the light, to comfort the afflicted, to make His children worthy of His unceasing love and their hearts ever humble to His will, for His ways were mysterious and beyond understanding.

The strong voice went on and on. In the back a baby whimpered. An old voice kept saying, "Amen." From the corner of his eye Lat saw the girl's head bowed, her hands still and folded in her lap.

the Territory of Montana, we pray O Lord! Bless the good people here!

Bless the mothers and the fathers and the lame and the halt and let the little children come unto Thee! Make us strong in our faith! Make us strong in Thy works..." Underneath the long coat and the stout trunk it enclosed, Brother Van's legs appeared thin.

"Amen," the people said. "Amen." "Amen."

"Let us sing!" Brother Van started in a strong voice, and others joined in, stronger for him.

> *I love to tell the sto-hor-ee*
> *Of unseen th-hings above,*
> *Of Jesus and His glory,*
> *O-of Jesus a-and His love.*

Tunes remembered. Times remembered, high expressions. Mercy. Faith. Eternal love. Eternal life. The old, and sure simplicities. The Father and His sheep. The wind and the shorn lamb. Oregon and boyhood and a just God overhead – Who had to have His ear chewed on, the deaf Old Gent. Wives and picket fences and a word called vice. Words called grace, called glory, called salvation.

> *It satisfies my longings...*

"Sing!" the girl told him with that quick, surprising smile, between breaths holding the tones that had struck him as so true and so different.

Back in the Oregon of long ago he found the lines and sang them out, and in the rear a nosey tenor lifted just as in the days remembered, just like the voice of old Clem Bowers.

"We will read from the Scriptures," Brother Van said without opening his Bible.

He that dwelleth in the secret place of the most High shall abide under the shadow of the Almighty.

I will say of the Lord, He is my refuge and my fortress: my God, in Him will I trust.

Surely He shall deliver me from the snare of the fowler, and from the noisome pestilence.

The Almighty. The secret place. Trust. Refuge. Fortress. Deliverance.

They were singing again.

There's a land that is fairer than day,
And by faith we can see it afar;
For the Father waits over the way,
To prepare us a dwelling place there.

Over the girl's felt nearness, over the cough-
~~1~~ amens, the old phrases echoing, the
nises sounding, the call to righteousness

330

calling again. Carmichael would smile, not in ridicule, if he knew. Whitey or Godwin would snort. Callie? Louder, he sang with the rest:

In the sweet by and by . . .

Brother Van rolled out, "Brethren and sistren . . ."

God loved the world, and the girl listened. God mourned at the evils of men, and a baby cried out and was hushed. God hated sin and the Devil. "Amen." But God awaited the return of the sinner as the father awaited the prodigal son. God was love. God was mercy and justice, but woe unto them who observed not His commandments and repented not. "Amen." "Amen."

In the love of the Father Brother Van was uplifted. His voice swelled and broke. His eyes streamed with joy. In the crowd as he paused was a silence like the whisper of good, like the straining for grace.

Brother Van straightened his face and wiped his eyes and went on more calmly. "Under God, blessed people, we shall have a church house in Tansytown. We have put our hands to the plow, and we shall not falter, and then shall we be more than ever delivered from the snare of the fowler and the noisome pestilence."

Mr. Strain passed the plate. Lat dropped in

331

a five-dollar bill. The girl lifted her eyes from his hand and leaned to him and whispered, "I peeked. It's too much."

"Not considering." In a way she was right, though.

"Now for a concluding hymn what shall we have?" Brother Van asked.

A man's voice answered, "Sing 'Diamonds in the Rough,' you alone, Brother Van."

" 'Diamonds in the Rough.' " Brother Van rubbed his hands.

The girl leaned over. "Do you know it?"

"I don't think so." He didn't, it turned out. He let the unfamiliar words flow past his ears until he heard the beginning quiver of the hearty voice, the overflowing thankfulness, and saw the shine of tears again.

The day will soon be over,
And diggings will be done;
A few more gems to gather,
So let us now press on.
When Jesus comes to claim you
And says you've done enough,
The diamonds will be shining,
No longer in the rough.

service ended with the Lord's Prayer, many of the congregation were quite ready to go home. They began to shake hands some more, talking about the weather and the new church and what a fine message they'd heard. It wasn't too often that some of them got out in company. The ranch people here would go back to their cabins and put a night light in a window as always, saying, without saying it would be someone to talk to, that someone might get lost and need shelter.

Brother Van and Gorham stood at the door as Lat and the girl came up. "Sister, come again, and God bless you!" Brother Van said. His warm hand overflowed Lat's. "New faces delight the Lord."

"I was reared in the church, Brother Van."

"THE church?"

"Methodist."

"Praise be! Praise be!" Brother Van released his grip to shake another hand.

"I'll wait for Mr. and Mrs. Strain," Gorham said. He asked in lowered tones, "Can't he wrestle the devil, though?"

The girl looked at the question and let it pass. Behind them others were trying to see Brother Van. "We're blocking the way," she said to Lat. "Why don't we stroll on? They'll catch up."

The outside air tasted sharp and clean, and the Big Dipper stood frosty, and all over th~

sky the stars flashed — the heavenly lamps set in windows, Brethren, for the help of the lost.

"Could any night beat a night like tonight?" he asked as the church voices faded.

"Such stars!" She had flung out her hands and lifted her face. The still air breathed of wood smoke. "Someone said if the stars came out just once every hundred years all men would bow down."

"It took him a minute to frame his thought. "Wouldn't they bow even more if there was just one star? Or, say, the moon?"

"Moon star!" she told the sky. Then she looked at him quickly. A smile came. "Swains would grow weary waiting."

He wasn't sure how to answer. "It's good enough as it is in Montana."

"But here it's like standing on top of the world," she said, her eyes fixed on the far shadows of land. "There's just distance, so much that there's no place to go. Don't you ever feel crowded by distance?"

"Crowded? I feel free."

"Free?" she said and fell silent as if she had to let the word find its place. Suddenly she went on, "In spite of the stars even God seems lost here."

Methodist?" He didn't know why he .ted to say that.

334

If she noticed his tone, she dismissed it. "The sky is so high, and the mountains so cruel, and all the land is so bare."

"If you ask me," he answered, "it's the best thing that God ever did."

"You don't pass judgment on God. But why do you feel that way? Because of freedom?"

"What's better?" He sounded harsh to himself.

"Trees," she said quietly. "The sense of protection. The feeling that God is right overhead."

"God on a quarter section!"

"A mountain might tumble, or the sky disappear, or the earth fall from under your feet."

"None of them has so far." Of a sudden it struck him that, underneath, she was really uneasy, made timid by the great shape and scope of this land. He added, "I'm sorry. It's just that you're new here."

Night had brought an end to the afternoon thaw, and, from the board walk of the main street, they stepped off on a path cobbled with frozen footprints. She walked along sturdily, keeping a few inches between them, and then slipped and was falling. He caught her before she went down.

"Maybe I'd better hang on," she said and slipped her hand into the crook of his elbow.

They went on, until he heard the quick in-take of her breath and felt her fingers clinch on his arm.

It was only Little Runner, arrived out of the night without warning. He stood just a few feet away, unmoving, not speaking, while the eyes in his high-boned face took them in. His hair hung braided and ribboned. He had an old blanket over his shoulders. "White squaw heap scare," he said.

Lat felt the fingers still tight on his elbow. To her he said, "He's a friend," and then, "How?"

"Heap Medicine, no meat in brother's lodge. Papoose cry."

It was true on the face of it. Little Runner was thin and peaked with hunger. He could have gone on to say game gone away, white agent to Injun damn thief, no care Injun starve, no care papoose cry, where rations? where Great White Father? what Blackfoot do without meat? What a lot of them did was to make meat of white beef when they could.

Lat pointed straight overhead, meaning noon. "Sun up, come my lodge. Papoose no cry."

Little Runner put out his hand. "Brother."

"Brother."

Little Runner slipped into the shadows.

"What was it?" The girl's breath still had the small whisper of fright.

"He's hungry. His family, too. I'll give him a cow."

"A whole cow!"

"He's my friend. He keeps his brothers from making off with my beef."

"I would call this an expensive evening." She might be taking into account the five dollars put in the plate.

"The cow's got lump jaw. All right to eat, though."

They reached the Strain home and stopped at the door. "I'm sorry to be a fraidy-cat," she said, letting go of his elbow, "but thanks for a nice evening."

"What's the show to see you again?" He would have to speak like a common cowpuncher.

In the glow of the light through the curtained pane her face was a mist in which, unexpectedly, a small glint of mischief appeared. "My family would want to know whether you play cards."

"All the time, tell them."

"Do you use the Lord's name in vain?"

"What's talk without seasoning?"

"Do you break the Sabbath?"

"Cows don't know Sunday."

She laughed lightly. "Fibber. Yes, It would be nice to see you again." The door closed behind her.

He stood there for a second. He would meet the Strains on the way back. He could tell them he'd had a good time, an unusual time sure enough. Only he wished he'd been able, he wished he was able now, to put Callie out of his mind.

Inside, Joyce took off her wraps. It was unreasoning, she told herself, to feel safer here where walls shut off the far land and far heavens. Boards and plaster weren't protection. It was unreasoning anyhow to be awed, to feel empty, to know the small beat of fear just because this strange land lay so vast. Still, she felt relieved.

The dog limped up to her, wearily wagging his tail. "You scoundrel!" she said and stooped to pet him.

Maybe she shouldn't have teased the man, she thought. Calling him Iv-ans? Watching him in his overdone modesty as he gave away that five-dollar bill and, more than that, commenting on his extravagance? Asking him lightly about the rules of behavior she believed in? Western men were said to be impulsive, even violent. But he had been a complete gentleman, counting even the times she couldn't explain when he seemed almost curt. He was nice.

The dog brushed against her. The smell he had made, and the holy, the unsmelling, the never-say-die look on Lat Evans's face! It was indecent, but she had to giggle, remembering.

25

Lat met the Strains and thanked them and spoke to Gorham and went on. He ought to get his horse, he told himself, and travel home. But Happy would have told her, and she would be waiting, sure that he would call. The thing must end; but now he pictured her, small, patient, hopeful, and then wounded when he didn't come. He'd kept her waiting as it was, had tried to lose the thought of her while he enjoyed himself. Right or wrong, weak or strong, he thought, he didn't have the heart to hurt her. As if that was all! As if he was just being kind and lofty and empty of real fondness! Or knew no urge of body at this mind's-eye view of her! Once more, then? Once more, and on to righteousness and public office! He cleared his mouth and spat.

He halted across the street from the house. From there he could see the light in her window. He could watch it and think, or let the

340

stray thoughts run. The low herd's common lot. The school board and the legislature and maybe higher places. The land that was fairer than day. The dark eyes in the pale, the virtuous face. Do you play cards? Use profanity? Break the Sabbath? The hint of mischief in the face. Tom Ping and Tansytown. The noisome pestilence, which a man could catch. The light waiting yonder and the bright head. The flesh. The present flesh. But in the sweet by and by?

He pulled in a lungful of air and let it out in a sigh. Where was the decent way out, if he could make himself take it? The decent way out of indecency? And why did he feel he must find it at once? Because of a sermon and songs? Because of grace and a meal? Because of a girl? Because of politics? There were those reasons, worthy or cheap, he had to admit, and one in addition — and that was his own nature, excited tonight. He wanted to be good. He wanted his life open and solid and respectable. He had always wanted to be good, to be a good boy, a good man, eventually a good husband and father, and to be known as such. He was a Methodist.

But to cut off, hard and unheeding, from Callie? Good or bad? Right or wrong? The thought struck him that it wasn't right and wrong that wrung men; it was the choice of rights.

A shadow moved on the drawn blind up-stairs, moved and stood still as if, standing, she willed the minutes to pass.

He went to the back door and knocked softly. Happy let him in. "She expectin' you, Mist' Lat. She always tickled when yo' in town." He gestured toward the rear stairs. "People in the settin' room."

She ran to answer his knock and pressed herself into his arms and held tight, breathing, "Lat! Lat!"

"What's the matter?"

She flung back her head and smiled through a glistening of tears. "Can't I be happy to see you?"

"Not so happy you cry." He took the head back to his shoulder. "Sorry I'm late. I've been to church."

"Oh?" There was a large question in the word.

"It was like being home again."

She drew in a slow breath. "You liked that, didn't you, Lat?"

"I guess so. Yes, I did."

"You had a home."

"It wasn't all sunshine, though." Thinking, he added without thinking enough, "I hate a lot of things, Callie."

She drew her head back and lifted her face,

the "What?" standing big and blue in her eyes.

"Not you!" He gave her a little shake. "I mean the way of things."

"Like?"

"Like the way of me, for one thing."

She bent her forehead against him. "For coming here?"

They were too far and too soon and too crudely into the question. "I wanted to see you, or I wouldn't have come."

"But to come from church?"

"What do you know about the Methodist church?"

"I know a lot about you."

"Too much and still not enough!"

"Everything," she whispered against him. "Oh, Lat, be happy! Let's both be happy to-night!" Her voice sounded at once hopeful and sad. She pressed her thighs against his as if hope answered sadness there. He felt the wet of her tears on his shirt.

He said, "Yes," and lifted her and said, "Yes," and put her gently in bed.

So they went through with it, and it was hasty and spoiled by the naggings of thought.

She kissed him lightly in the hollow of his shoulder afterwards. "You've got the fidgets."

"Yes."

"Want something to eat to settle you down?

A piece of pie maybe? I'll run down and get it."

"I'm not hungry. Thanks."

Her fingers were light on his temple, on his cheek, over his mouth. Downstairs someone was playing the piano and two men were singing, cowpunchers probably, for the song was "Hell Among the Yearlings." Diamonds in the rough, he thought while a piece of Brother Van's solo echoed in his ears, diamonds in the rough, finally to be called to Jesus, no longer in the rough.

"You're nearly always keyed up, Lat. You're not even here now." Her words barely reached him. "We're different. With you I can forget everything."

"Callie?"

"Yes."

"They want me to stand for the new school board and maybe higher office later."

Her hand stroked his shoulder. She was slow to speak. "You'll be a good one."

"I don't know about that, but I just thought I'd tell you."

"You're one that's on the way up, Lat."

"I owe my start to you."

Her hand withdrew, as if her thought lay in it, and her body moved away, and she might have been lying alone, remote from him. Her voice held the note of change. "But you have to

344

finish by yourself." It was not a question. "That's what you want to tell me."

He wrenched up in bed. "I cared, Callie. I care now. Call me names, but I care. If I could only do something for you—"

"Lie down!" She'd never used that tone before. It raised as she went on. "Your name is Mr. Albert Gallatin Evans, and you want a starched wife and a starched home and importance and a starched reputation, and there's not a damn thing you can ever do for me."

She flung his reaching hand away.

"Don't mind me, Mr. Evans! Just keep climbing! You'll get there. Remember I'm only a madam. For three dollars I'm any man's woman. I'm a common whore. The only place I can get is to bed, and proud of it."

"Don't, Callie!"

"Oh, I know how it bothers you, you care so much! But just leave me poor and honest, without any put-on!"

"For God's sake, Callie!"

"And don't feel sorry for me!" she answered shrilly. "I wouldn't marry you if you asked me. Think I'd give up the parties and the drinking and the fun and the different men just to live dull with one? Not on your life, Mr. Evans!"

He felt weighed down and wordless. "I'll go," he said. "You want me to go."

"I'd miss all that fun." She took a breath and let most of it out and just with the end of it breathed, "A girl gets that way." She turned her head to him and cried out, her voice breaking, "Oh, Lat!"

"Callie. Callie," he said, in his breast such a fullness that the name came out choking. "Please don't cry!"

"But I'm sorry! I'm sorry! You're you. I'm me. That's all."

He brought her close in his arms. "I wish—" he didn't know what all he wished.

"It's no use to wish. Lat, I'm so unstarched."

Of a sudden she was on him, her mouth open and broken on his, her body tight and trembling against him. A sad, strong eagerness came to him, and no unmanning thoughts. Sorrow must be close to love; this time was the tenderest and best.

Later, much later, she asked, "Want a piece of pie now?"

"I'd love it."

"You don't have to dress. I'll slip something on and go down and get it, and we'll have our little party right here."

The all-forgiveness, he thought when she had gone, the full forgiveness of mind and heart, of mouth and breast and groin, of all of her.

He couldn't forgive himself, though. It would take God Almighty in His wisdom to do that.

Part Five

26

Lat Evans headed for town early, driving a light wagon to which he had hitched his best buggy team. It lay in his mind that the day ahead of him was cut out – provisions to buy and a night meeting to go to, but with full hours left over to spend with Joyce and the baby. It had been a week since he'd seen them.

An inch of snow lay on the flats. What breeze there was still breathed of winter. Spring was slow to come, he reflected; it was as if it stood timid before the violent months just passed. At the best this was the barren time in Montana, the time of not a leaf or blade, of dead colors, raw gales and squally storms and dismals in the mind. But still, as the team spanked along, he felt good.

In a draw a bunch of magpies were flapping around a bunch of dead cows, cheering at the generosity of nature. In every draw and gully, nearly, other bunches would be doing the same.

The magpies and the coyotes and the quick carrion bugs and the maggots yet to hatch were the only ones that the winter's ill wind had blown good. Evans sniffed. Already the air carried a taint. Come summer, it would stink to high heaven with half the territory's cattle dead. Where was the rancher now to say that feeding hay was foolishness?

He'd just squeaked by himself. Storms in November, December, January, February. Twenty-two below zero, twenty-seven, thirty, forty-six, sixty. He'd almost had to count each straw of hay.

"It's a crime against nature, Lat!" Carmichael came to mind, fresh and half frozen from a range inspection that Evans had loaned him out for. His face for once was bleak. "Dead cows from hell to breakfast! Others dyin', their bellies drawed tight to their bent backbones! Cows with tails froze off and legs froze and horns exploded open with the cold! Cows forever bawlin', driftin', pilin' up, goin' down air holes in the river ice! Don't say you feel sorry for the ranchers! Feel sorry for them cows! No man has any right to brutes he can't take care of."

Owned and leased land, irrigation, hay, closer herding — though these meant smaller herds, they had at last paid off, Evans thought as he jolted along. It had taken a long time to cinch the point with Conrad, but the proof was overwhelming. It had taken a long time to show the territory, but from now on things would never be the same.

To the east where the west wind cooled, it had been even worse than here, according to the talk. "Why, hell," one drifting puncher had reported, "there ain't enough beef left in them parts to stoke a shirttail crew. Can't tell till after roundup, but more'n one man will tally up a by-God cypher."

The winter of 'eighty-six–'eighty-seven, which people would talk about as long as minds remembered! It was no wonder men were bitter.

He let the horses spend their ginger. The sky was clear today and the snow thin, and his cows could forage. He'd have this afternoon with Joyce and Little Lat and tonight with Joyce.

Right after roundup a smart man would go out and buy cows from men bent and broken, Evans thought with a distaste felt before. Capital out of catastrophe! Profit from need! But they'd be glad to sell; they'd be begging him to buy. The hard fact was they'd have to sell. He could do them this bleak favor; he couldn't undo their misfortunes. For most of them he wished he could.

Once, given the means, he would have thought less about taking advantage of the chance now offered. A man's ambitions changed, he reflected as he topped a rise and sighted the town. They widened, to include not only money-making but work and worth apart from that, in the service of his place and people. Inflated talk, some might say, the mouthing of a politician, but it was true, allowing still, though, for the wish of self-importance.

A man saw the country growing up around him, saw settlers moving in, wild acres fenced, families coming into being; and he saw unsolved and multiplying problems, like the wretched, immediate problem of the thefts of livestock, which had no right or lawful answer. There were others in plenty, more important ones. Education. Law. Law enforcement. Courts of justice. Progress toward statehood. There would be still others. The territory would continue to increase, if differently, after last winter.

Grandfather Evans' old words came to memory. "A man likes to grow up with the country. And when he gets growed up, he likes the country growed up, too." Now Evans understood what was meant. A country didn't grow up alone. It grew up through men, who, if they were worthy, wanted to feel that something of themselves, some strength and hope and work and vision, went permanently to public benefit.

He reached town and slowed the team. He'd done some things already, he told himself. He'd been active in the church. He'd served the school board as well as he knew how, though marrying the schoolteacher, approved though the wedding was in a section short of women, hardly could be called assistance. He'd lived honestly and honorably. He was, he thought he could say, generally respected. He wanted to do more.

So much of everything he owed to Joyce! He drove straight to the house and tied up at the fence.

Joyce turned from her work table as he opened the back door. Her eyes widened and lighted in welcome. She put a floured finger over her lips. "Sh-h! I wasn't expecting you."

"Baby asleep?" He walked softly over and kissed her. "You don't have to hold your hands out like a bird stretching."

"I'll get flour on you, silly. And yes, Little Lat is asleep." Her eyes laughed into his. "Have you forgotten he takes naps?"

"How is he?"

"Oh, Lat, he's just fine. Still getting stronger every day. The doctor came through yesterday. He says when spring really comes there's no reason we shouldn't move back to the ranch."

"Hallelujah!"

"What brought you to town?"

"Things, including you."

She rinsed her hands. "There's fresh coffee. Let's sit down."

He did. "I feel fine today."

"Because this is one day you're not killing yourself?" She poured the cups and set the pot back on the stove and took a chair across the kitchen table from him.

"Naw! Because I'm here."

She looked him over, a shade of worry on her face. "You work too hard, Lat. Roundup, branding, trailing, feeding, making hay, breaking horses, one thing after another. You haven't an ounce of flesh on your bones."

For the fun of it he sang a piece of hymn they'd just learned. " 'Work, for the night is coming...' "

She joined him in the next words, softly so as not to awaken the baby. " 'Rest comes sure and soon.' " It was like her, he thought, to shift moods, to turn quick from the light to the serious and back again, and often to laugh at the way things appeared and to make him laugh, too. A man couldn't tell what she might say.

Her smile went away. "I don't want that kind

of rest to be sure and soon for you, Lat."

"It won't. I'm even thinking of buying some more cows."

"Oh?"

"After this winter a lot of men will have to sell, if they can."

"It doesn't seem fair." Her hair, drawn back from her brow and wound in a pug, made her look girlish. Actually she was girlish, girlish in appearance, in the play of her thoughts, in her quick, brimming pity for those in distress. She was unseasoned yet, unhardened, resentful of the harsh facts and the hard necessities. Not that he was so reconciled himself. He pushed away the shadow of tonight's meeting.

"I didn't make the weather, sweetheart," he said. "And don't hold it against me that I was prepared."

"Lat, I don't hold anything against you!"

"Maybe we have a right to sit pretty."

"You don't sit long enough to be pretty." Now she was smiling.

"So I'm ugly?"

"As a mud fence." She put her hand across the table and laid it on his. "I love mud fences."

"I'll just go on being one, then. You can explain to people that tastes have a right to diffeh, as a Texas man once told me."

"He's the man that kissed a cow. Are you

comparing me to a cow?"

"Now where did you get that? Out of the crazy box? But all right. Now a cow, though. A prime heifer."

"With calf."

It took an instant to understand. "No! Not really!"

"I mean Little Lat, of course."

"Oh." He hadn't understood after all. He said, "You're blushing."

She put her hands over her cheeks. "You make me."

"I love you for it."

"Let's get back to the subject."

"What was it?"

She took her hands away. The flush was fading. "Being a man of highly unusual taste, you had just kissed a cow."

He got up and gave her a kiss on the forehead and sat down and drank the rest of his coffee. "Now that the cow's taken care of, any mail?"

"Saw, boss!" she said. Then, "No mail for you. I got a letter. Things are all right at home."

"None for me?"

"Lat?" Her face was suddenly sober again. "How long since you're written your folks?"

"I sent them a check."

"In lieu of a letter?"

"In lieu of them being hard up."

"They'd rather know about you, about us. As long as we can afford it, it's so easy, just to make out a check. But I keep seeing them, those two lonely old people, waiting and waiting to hear."

He saw them, too, saw them earlier, saw them at the time of the wedding trip there to the old home in Oregon. His mother was flushed and smiling with pride, and her worn hand was warm and tight on his arm. "Why, Lat, she's just lovely! So good-looking and so refined! She's already like a daughter." She pushed him away to look in his face. "I always knew you'd choose a girl to be proud of."

Joyce asked, "Why don't you write now, Lat?"

But Pa was pushing into the room, on his mouth a strange little twist. "You're a picker all right, son. Yup, some boy, you!" The twist moved uncertainly. Pa might be speaking of other things besides a bride, of land and cattle maybe as against a stingy farm. Age was in his face and some hint of pleading; and Evans felt a sudden loss, an emptiness, as if time had dwarfed a giant. Pa put his hand on Ma's shoulder. The smile left his mouth. He wasn't known for his praise, but these words came like sworn words, "If she makes as good a wife as your mother, God has blessed you."

Joyce's voice sounded over the old conversation. "Right now, Lat?"

"Today," he answered, seeing her and himself and the pair of them before and since. He had been bursting proud then and was just as proud now, proud to be seen with her, proud to hear her recite, proud to claim her as wife. Pride? It was pride and still more. She was Joyce, and she was his. It was as simple and great as that.

"I'll get you a pencil and paper."

"Not now, dear." He came to his feet. "This afternoon. While I've got the team hitched, I'll load up what I need for the ranch so as to get a good start in the morning."

"You'll be here tonight then?"

"Sure thing."

"There's choir practice."

"Can't make it. Got a meeting."

"What kind?"

"Range business." He chucked the uplifted chin and turned away. "General ranch matters. I'll be back before long."

Reverend Bradford was passing the Tansytown Merc., as Evans tied up. He stepped over to shake. "How are you, Brother Evans?" He had a hand as big as two, with something left over for seed. It crossed Evans' mind that God's men all seemed to be large men, the Methodists anyway.

"Fine, Reverend. I hope that you are."

"By the grace of the Lord. You'll be in for services Sunday, of course?"

"If I can. There's lots of work to be done."

"In the vineyard." The eyes in the square face were mildly reproachful.

"Sometimes I think I might as well get out of the choir. I have to miss practice again tonight."

"Go on with you!" Reverend Bradford gave Evans a playful little push. "I know what you've been up against. You wouldn't play hooky."

"The winter's been a fright, I don't need to tell you."

"The lean years." Reverend Bradford thought about them. "With the Lord's help we'll make out."

"Yes."

Reverend Bradford put his heavy hand on Evans' arm. "God bless you and your good wife!" He walked off slowly.

Before Evans reached the store door, someone hailed him. Flannery, Pete Flannery, it turned out to be. For a wisp of a man he shook hands hard. "And how is it?" he asked.

"Fair enough. You?"

"Niver a cow left, I'm thinkin'," he answered brightly. "Free as a damn bird in the hivens."

"Not that bad?"

"So good I can be thinkin' of politics and what thievin' friend gits into high office."

"Oh?"

The lively eyes cocked at Evans. "And me of the true faith, meanin' Dimocrat! May my old man and old woman forgive me, not to mention the saints!"

"Don't strain yourself, Pete."

"Sure enough, the divil's got in me." He gave Evans' arm a last pump.

No customer was in the store except for Mrs. Murdock, who sang alto in the choir and now was screwing a potato stopper in the spout of a can that Marshall Strain had just filled. She shook hands, too, leaving on Evans' fingers the smell of coal oil.

Strain was a man who honestly liked to shake, not that the others didn't. "How are things, Lat?"

"Missing mostly. I need barbed wire, grub, tobacco, Lord knows what all. I've got a list."

Strain took him by the arm and led him back toward the post-office grill where Clarence, the young clerk, wouldn't hear. "Well?" His eyes and the sprouts of hair in his ears waited an answer. "I hear the meeting's tonight?"

"I'll go along with them, but I don't like it."

Evans could see them riding, the Vigilantes, the Avengers, as they called themselves, in secret joined in a war against rustlers that appeared to them, or some of them, holy. "What do you do without law? Take it into your own hands, I guess."

Strain nodded soberly. "It will just be the one time."

"One time and over. One time and never again." Evans wondered if he believed what he said. "Anyhow, this will be my first and last."

"If it gets out, it could hurt you politically," Strain said, not in argument.

"Then it will have to."

"And there's Joyce." Again Strain wasn't arguing.

"If I must, I'll try to explain," Evans said, seeing her catching sight of the shapes, the falling, the swinging, the dying shapes that were taking shape in his head. Even in himself he found the scene hard to justify.

"She's so gentle." Strain let out a sigh. "I could talk to her, Lat, in general terms. Let me talk to her!"

"In general terms then. My answer has to be yes."

Strain repeated, "It has to be yes," and reset the pencil that rode behind his ear. "Now where's that list?"

27

Whey Belly Hector leaned forward in his chair, his thick hands on his knees. The eyes in his frog's face were wide. They caught a glitter from the lighted lamp. "Well, Evans?"

Antelope Rax sat on the hotel bed, lacing and unlacing his fingers. His gaze held the question, too.

"I thought this was supposed to be a meeting," Evans said, looking from one to the other. Behind Rax the wall at the side of the bed was smeared with the mashed leavings of Jackson House bedbugs.

"McLean and Chenault left word they'd go whichever way you did — which they told you a full week ago. What you want? A vote of the Bible class?"

"Unanimous," Evans answered and closed his mouth on the rest.

"Not so loud," Rax told Hector. Except to tone Hector down, he had hardly spoken. He was a small, hard nut of a man, almost Indian in appearance, who kept pretty much to himself at his ranch over east on the Muddy. People said he'd rather live on straight antelope meat than butcher one of his cattle. Now, being looked at, he barely parted his lips. "We've stood enough."

"The winter was enough," Evans said quietly.

"Hah!" Hector broke in. "Sure, the winter busted everyone but you, Evans, or damn near did. You and your goddam hay! But what's the weather got to do with rustlers?"

"You can take it out on the rustlers."

"Look! You came through in fine shape. You wintered fat by comparison."

Rax lifted a finger. "Not so loud!"

"It's enough to make a man yell," Hector told him in lowered tones. He turned back to Evans. "Maybe you can afford to feed thieves. But what about us? We're scrapin' bottom, us that ain't scraped it already clean."

He had a point, and Evans nodded to it.

"All right, then," Hector said and began counting on his fingers. "There's Whitlock and Johnson and Howie, besides me and Rax, all feelin' the same way, and there's you and McLean and Chenault maybe, dependin' on you. You talked to Marshall Strain, of course?"

"Yes."

"He's too pretty-pious for me, but he cuts a quiet swath in this section. There was reasons we let him in on it, and him alone besides us.

"For the influence he might have on me," Evans said.

"Well, sure. Why not? For Christ or customers, I'll say, he saw things straight. But that isn't all. We wanted to know would he stick up for us if it came down to that. There's just a chance the law might try to move in if our names get whispered around. Then we'd need him."

"The law that you say doesn't exist?"

"Good God! You think you can get it to chase down these jacklegs and get the evidence and throw 'em in the crowbar house? Strain regardless, it just might tackle us if there's talk enough, so we got to be secret like the old Vigilantes, but no law dogs will ever tree them." Hector's mouth curled. "Or do you think so?"

This time Rax hissed out, "Sh-h!"

Evans had to answer, "No. Not soon, anyhow."

"And we can't wait. Kohrs and Ford and Fergus and Stuart and that bunch didn't wait over east three years ago. They couldn't, no more'n we can. They shot 'em up and hung 'em high, and some they only scattered. It's part of that scatterin' that's plaguin' us now."

"Stuart's Stranglers," Evans said. "Next, Hector's Stranglers?"

"Names don't count," Hector answered. A smile put the corners of his mouth almost in line with his ears. "They don't, that is, unless it's a name like Senator."

Evans grinned, for no real reason. "I wasn't counting much on the outlaw vote. Friends like you will put me in."

Rax said, "We sure will, won't we, Whey Belly?"

"Senator Evans."

"Thanks," Evans said and waved that talk away, though he imagined that Rax, for one, spoke honestly. "What have your losses from rustling been running?"

"It's a guess, but with cows not less than four or five per cent. They'll for sure run way higher now we got so few head. Ain't it so, Rax?"

"All of that."

"God knows about horses, but I can tell you one thing. They're bein' stole right now, the rustlers thinkin' we're too busy cryin' at winter kills to notice the broncs. That's why we ought to hit 'em quick."

"I'm missin' two horses since the other night," Rax put in.

Hector pointed at Evans. "You asked about

our losses. What about yours?"

"Smaller."

"So I heard. So I heard."

"Keep listening to Tom Ping! Some day he might tell you why the Blackfeet call me their brother."

"Hold on now! I didn't mean anything, and I don't take much stock in Ping. Who does?"

"And you might remember I watch my cows closer."

"Sure. Sure."

"Let it go."

Hector got out a cigar and moved over and puffed as he held it over the lamp. He sank back then and crossed his legs and squinted at Evans through a spiral of smoke. "If Injuns are still on your mind, I already told you this won't be a scalp hunt. We'll leave your red brothers alone. Sure, the rest of us lose beef to 'em, but we ain't askin' for trouble from Injuns and government both. It's the whites and some breeds that we're after."

"Who in particular?"

"All rustlers in particular."

"By name?"

"Hell, I don't know all their names. Who does but themselves? But there's Casteen and French Joe and Hartwig that don't look so clean. At the head of 'em, it's my guess, is

Bigsbee." The name brought blood to Hector's face. "He's a damn troublemaker besides bein' a horse thief. I'll smile when I see him laid out. For a fact, though, there's no real he-elephants in the crowd, but just little bastards. Ten men, ten good men, could handle the kit and caboodle."

Evans said, "Maybe."

"They won't be expectin' us unless some fool unties his tongue. Why should they? We never tried to lay a hand on 'em yet, and all the time they been cabined up north there in the breaks snug as a bug. We can jump 'em."

Evans threw out, "And because they're there, they'll all be guilty?"

"There ain't any innocent men in them breaks, like no angels in hell." Hector took a tatter of cigar from his thick lip and flicked it away. "Evans, you got a reputation as a man slow to make his mind up, so take a look ahead. With pickin's scarce as snake tits, what's left for the buzzard boys? Lat Evans and his hand-nursed cattle naturally. Oh, it'll be riskier and harder, but wires'll cut and critters drive. You'll take sides then, my friend."

Rax kept twiddling his fingers, his eyes on them. "You're a key log in this jam."

Hector motioned toward Evans with his thumb while he looked at Rax. "And I can remember, just six or seven years ago, he was too small to keep, almost."

"Big enough to hold my claim," Evans reminded him.

"Yup," Hector answered agreeably. "But you ain't big enough, alone, to keep your stock."

Rax lifted his swarthy face. "Whey Belly's right as rain."

"Hector," Evans said, "you and your boys will be drilling everything in sight."

Hector chewed on his cigar. He took the cigar out and pecked at the air with it. "That's in your craw?"

"It is."

"Tell you what, then," Hector said, still pecking. "A promise. No shootin' 'less we have to. No hangin' till we're sure."

"You can speak for the rest?"

"Do my best."

From the first there had been just one answer, but at least this much had come out of his stalling, Evans thought, this much out of his questions, this pledge for what it was worth. No blind blood-letting — maybe. He got up abruptly. "All right. I'm in. Good night," he said and made for the door, hearing Hector say, "Good!" hearing Rax say, "Fine! Whey Belly, we'd best wait and get out of here one at a time."

Evans walked the little hall and went down

the closed staircase. Outside, where the air was fresh, he stopped and lit his own cigar. The night was a little chill for comfort, but he stood quiet at the edge of the walk, puffing on his smoke and letting the tags of thought drift through his mind. Even if Hector kept his promise, it would be a dirty business, a dirty, bloody, necessary business. In imagination he could hear the suck of Joyce's breath, could see her look of blank disbelief. Hector? Whey Belly? Frog Face? What was his promise worth? Thieves were thieves, though, and other men already had had to make the rough choice. Rough on them, too, it had come about, especially if any wanted to go to the Senate. This time might be different. In any case his course was fixed.

Evans looked up and down and across the street. Here and there lamplight shafted from saloons, but elsewhere the town was buttoned up – shops closed, kids put to bed and honest folks asleep. Only a couple of teams stood at hitch racks. A tied-up saddle horse shifted position in front of the hotel bar. In the night quiet the creak of saddle leather sounded sharp. out in the darkened street the snow was ground to a dirty gray. A blanket Indian came padding down the walk. He passed by, noiseless in his moccasins, homeless in this white man's claim

371

to hunting grounds. Homeless, but more at home with open land and wild, uneven weather than any paleface could be.

Little Runner, for example, Evans thought, Little Runner saying last fall, "Goose vamoose heap quick. Duck vamoose. Cayuse him hair like bear. Brother, keep plenty wood in lodge." And then the white owls came like shapes of snow, the Arctic owls unseen here before, and Little Runner drew his blanket close. "Ugh! Much cold! War, coldmaker say."

Evans heard the hotel door swing open. Rax came out and glanced around. From up the street, out of the new dance hall which inside was a few rough boards thrown together for floor and bar, there came the sudden whine and tinkle of a fiddle and piano and the thin laugh of some girl who got commissions on the drinks her partners bought, not to mention other earnings. Rax watched and listened and came on and passed close, barely nodding. He went to his team and untied them from the rack and pointed home. If it was day instead of night he'd see more than a few dead cows before he got there. Tally one for town: it smelled clean.

The cigar was dead. Though it wasn't half smoked yet, Evans pitched it in the street. He ought to go home. He wanted to go home, but, after tonight, he wanted a drink first. One drink.

He was temperate. He walked to the door of the hotel saloon and opened it and saw Tom Ping at the bar. He was about to back out, but Ping's eyes found him, and he couldn't. He should have looked to see whose saddle horse was tied up at the rack.

He stepped to the bar and ordered whiskey. The bartender said, "Sure thing, Mr. Evans." He was a new man, seen before no doubt but not remembered.

Ping's eyes slid over, and Evans met them, and they slid away. Ping was whiskered and unclean, and he had a wife and two children who lived in a breed shack.

"You ever see a one-horse rancher, Herb?" Ping asked the bartender. Sugar, he meant, and a day and a race in Fort Benton. It wasn't the first time he'd put the question to third parties in Evans' presence.

Herb didn't answer. He put out a bottle and glass. Evans poured his shot. Ping had a fresh one in front of him. For a minute no one spoke. Then, so suddenly as to spill most of it, Ping pushed his glass to the back of the bar. "Pour it in the swill bucket!" He turned and legged it to the door and slammed it behind him.

Joyce was still up. She raised her eyes from her mending as he came through the door.

Smiling, she asked, "Guess what?"

"You're pretty."

"Wrong. You just missed seeing him. Little Lat took three steps, not holding to anything." Her face sobered and softened. "He's really getting sturdy. And he's so bright!"

"Chip off the old block." He stooped to kiss her.

"Whew!" she said as his lips touched her forehead. "You smell like an old cigar soaked in whiskey."

"Half a cigar. One drink. Big day for the candidate." He let himself down in a chair.

"I'll have to talk to our minister." Her smile held a trace of reproach, not because of his smoking. "It's a bad example." She lowered her head and took a stitch. "Think of Whitey!"

"I promise to sober up before I go back to the ranch."

"He's been behaving?"

"Like a lamb. Now, Joyce, he's worth his salt."

"How's Mike?"

"Carmichael? Drunk again."

Her eyes lifted, knowing better, and she bit off a thread. "You're so funny. How is he really?"

"Just fine."

She said what she'd said before, "I like Mike."

In memory Evans saw Carmichael. Carmichael, his chest mashed by a bronc, lay here in the house, a lean, not-big man of smiling words and tall tales — and pain that showed itself only when he thought no one would see. He had been apologetic and gentle and refined beyond all expectation. "Wolf bait is wolf bait, Lat," he had said. "You ought just to dump me out on the prairie." A small grin tried to cover his suffering. "Baby, you little bronc-stomper," he had said. "Mother," he had called Joyce after a week. "Please don't fret about me. You have your hands full with Little Lat." In less than two months he was ready, he swore, to go back to the ranch.

Now Evans answered, "Mike's one of the family." He wondered what Joyce would say if she knew the other side of Carmichael, the side that took him to a woman sometimes even yet and left him without regrets. No, he thought, he didn't wonder; he knew.

Joyce dropped a sock into the basket at her side and picked up another one and snugged her china egg into its toe. "How was your meeting?"

"All right. Fine. Nothing important." In Indiana men didn't go hunting men. In Indiana the law, impersonal and remote, took care of things, leaving people in peace, in the gentle peace that was almost like a mist around her. "I love to look at you," he said.

She gave him a quick smile. It faded as she went back to her work. When she spoke, it was as if a part of what he thought had reached her. "Lat, I hate to think of Little Lat growing up in this town. All saloons and gamblers and dirty Indians and, you know, vice."

"What's wrong with the ranch?"

"Not a thing," she said at once. "Not a thing for us. But he's born to be a doctor or a lawyer or maybe a professor. You can tell it by looking at is head."

"You mean his tail's not for the saddle?"

"Now, Lat!"

"I'm sorry. We'll give him all we can. But to me there are worse lives than a Montana rancher's."

She didn't speak.

"Well, I'm tired," he said. "I'm going to bed." he watched her, waiting for her answer.

Her eyes kept on the work in her lap. "Why don't you go on, then? I'll mend a while."

It wasn't yes, and it wasn't no, neither one, because she was of gentle birth, out of Indiana, out of Earlham College, because she was herself. With her it never had been yes or no in words, nor, after one time, was his asking ever open. Better that way, too, he told himself, mostly better.

He got up and walked through the kitchen where a night light burned. Outside, the privy stood naked. Later the hopvines would gentle and shield it. Coming back, he saw that the water bucket was empty. He carried it out and pumped it full and brought it in. Joyce wasn't too strong. She wasn't meant to be strong like a squaw, like the squaws of the squawmen. He didn't want her to be the beast of burden that so many wives in the territory were.

He put the bucket on the kitchen stand and went into the parlor and made for the bedroom. In that curiously timbred voice that always stirred him she said, "Sleep tight, dear."

"Don't be too long."

"I'd like to finish."

The opened door to the parlor let light enough in the bedroom to show Little Lat, asleep on his stomach, his finely fuzzed head turned and his raised baby hands resting limp at each side. No troubles here. Just peace and trust and sleep and nature still unmolded. It was already late, Joyce said, for the christening.

Evans bent and touched his lips to the soft curve between head and neck, holding his tainted out-breath. Breathing in, he smelled the good baby smell.

He undressed and put on his nightshirt and kissed Little Lat again and lay down. He didn't want to go to sleep yet. Neither did he want to lie awake and see rustlers swinging from trees.

The late knock startled Joyce, until she remembered that Lat was at home. She turned the knob and looked out and then swung the door wide. "Why, Uncle Marsh! Quiet! The two Lats are in bed."

He entered, explained he'd been working after hours at the store and had seen the light in her window.

She eased shut the door to the bedroom and asked him into the kitchen. "I can give you a piece of cake and a glass of milk? Or coffee?"

He chose milk and sat down at the table, waiting quietly for her to lay out the snack. When she had done so, he asked, "How did your visitor strike you? Did he get to see Lat?"

"Who?"

"Methuselah in the flesh."

"Oh, I forgot to tell Lat. You mean that old man with the dirt and the whiskers?"

"I forgot, too. Friend of the family from way back, he told me."

"I imagine!"

Uncle Marsh nibbled at his cake and sipped at his milk. It was a little while before he asked, with what seemed to her, somehow, more than usual concern, "How's the baby?"

"Wonderful. He's almost learned to walk."

He swallowed and wiped his mouth. "Fine boy. Fine man you've got, too, Joyce." She always liked his smile. "Fine wife he's got. Fine family."

"Did you come just to compliment us?"

"To remind you it never hurts to remember our blessings. Count yours if you're ever in doubt."

"I count them every day, Solomon."

"Solomon," he said after her. "Solomon on a low inventory." He ate more cake.

She asked, "Did Lat tell you we can go back to the ranch pretty soon?"

"Fine."

But there were the wind and the cold there and the punishing sun and the wind and the great loneliness and the wind, and Lat coming out of them and desiring her beyond her desire. She had tried to keep her crying to herself, to cry alone, and the wind would cry, and outside was desolation, not the friendly hills and trees and peopled acres that she knew but raw and aching distances, space that was a fear with nameless fears inside her, that crowded in and suffocated, that ran out and dispelled and took her soul and body and the body in her womb to nothing. To the bedroom and the slop jar that she threw up in. And she would splash her face with water and rub color in it and meet Lat at the door, chanting, " 'Home is the sailor, home from the sea, and the hunter home from the hill.' " It was part of an otherwise sad little poem she had just learned, and he loved to hear her recite.

"Now that he's on his feet the ranch will be just the place for Little Lat," Uncle Marsh said.

"I hope so." It hadn't been, though, for Little Lat. He had been croupy and upset and wan, so much that their hearts were torn. The doctor's prescription of boiled cow's milk and oatmeal water had brought him around, but still she wished they'd leave the ranch sometime and leave this shabby town and give Little Lat his rightful chance. The weeks at Helena, rude as that city was, would be relief. There would be other senators there, representatives, men of affairs, the new governor – Leslie was his name – and with them their wives and families. After Helena? There was no harm in thinking maybe Washington, D.C. Lat would make his mark in any place.

Uncle Marsh pushed back his chair and stood up. "I must be going." At the door he kissed her on the forehead.

She listened to his footsteps on the porch and heard them crunch off. He had told her to count her blessings. As if she needed to be told!

She went into the bedroom then and, working very quietly, changed the baby's diaper, thinking, as she pinned a fresh one on, how soon the man-child showed his hard and ready sex.

A black shape flapped in the timber and by and by grew wings and climbed, and another joined it and another, springing up over the rim of the world, springing now by hundreds, by thousands. He perceived all at once that they were crows or ravens or buzzards, not many of them any more, the many swelling back into one with a wing span that crowded the sky. It hovered up, shadowing all the land underneath, and its great eyes fixed on him and the great beak swung his way.

He was dreaming, he told himself, and for an instant knew comfort; but the bird came on, flapping with a slow, sure eagerness, the grind of its beak sounding over the wind of its wings. He stumbled away, knocking Tom Ping aside. To the south the sky was still clear.

To the south then, of all things, he saw her, far off but still close and distinct as if through a glass. High on a hill she was smiling and waving, and the horse underneath her grew into Sugar as he sharpened the focus. With both hands he waved her his way, yelling, "All right!

381

That's enough! Come on home!" for over the hill was the dreadful drop-off. "Come back, I said!"

She kept smiling and waving and riding on toward the lip, and Sugar came to a stop and let out a shrill peal and went on to her urging.

She was lost, most of her, in the blinding blue of the sky. It was her eyes that he saw, the dark, gentle eyes and the pale flicker of face and the mouth shaping, "Goodbye." He cried out, "No! No! Don't you know! Sugar, whoa!" But she had her back to him now and Sugar kept going.

He had to catch up with them. He had to run. He put his mind to running. He put his toes, his feet, his knees, his thighs to running. He put his straining will to it and fell down paralyzed and aching with his need. "Callie!" he called into the dirt. "Callie!"

It was wrong. It was some enormous and ruinous mistake. Around him sprouted ears like cactus, tilted to his error. Her name! Her name! What was her name? His crazy mouth yelled, "Callie!"

Now she was gone from sight, and now he could run, now maybe catch hold of goodbye. Fast as the wind, to the hill, up the hill, to the crest and beyond! She wasn't there, nor the horse, but only the falling white tail of goodbye. He lunged grasping for it, shouting, "Callie!", and the cactus lifted their ears, and just ahead suddenly, too close to escape, dropped the awful abyss.

He was falling, swift in the wind-shafts of nothing, falling to the sound of torn air, to the silence of the bottom rushing to meet him, falling in a sudden darkness cast by wings overhead.

"Lat, you've been trembling and jumping all over the bed."

"Joyce," he said. "Joyce."

"You're still asleep."

"Last jump woke me up."

"Is something troubling you?"

"Just a dream."

Outside, the sky was growing gray. It was time for a one-horse rancher to get up.

28

They were to rendezvous at Rax's Bar O ranch, arriving separately and at different times so as not to risk suspicion. The Bar O was closest to the breaks but yet a long night's ride removed.

Evans took it easy, letting old Sugar set his pace and saying little. Carmichael rode beside him, mostly silent, too, around his mouth and eyes the traces of some inner humor despite the work ahead.

It had snowed again, enough to coat all except the windswept ridges, and a chill breeze played under a cold though cloudless sky. Now, when it was almost time for ranges to be greening, only the white of winter met the eye, it and the hopeless gray of brush and graveled rises where by rights the carpet flowers should soon be spreading. Westward the mountains piled an iceberg shore against the sea-blue of the sky. A late spring and high water, Evans thought, but, with this moisture, good grass later on.

Carmichael said, "Be a little late, time we haul up."

"Early enough."

"When a man wants to get away, seems like someone always holds him up." It wasn't quite a question.

"Yeah."

"He sure looked hell for active for his age." Half smiling, Carmichael looked at Evans.

"Yeah."

One trouble after another, Evans reflected. Note one named Mr. Hank McBee. He had come walking to the ranch at noon, a lively fossil with moss whiskers, and had drawn Evans aside. Apparently the exercise had warmed him, for the mangy fur coat that he wore was opened. His body through the unbuttoned gap looked spiderish. " 'Y God, I been lookin' all over hell for you," he said. He put out his hand. It felt like a claw.

"What can I do for you?"

" 'Y God, I got a surprise for you." The whiff of him was surprise enough. "I'm your grandpa."

"Sure. Sure."

"I ain't lost my wits, like it 'pears like you think."

"Then what's your game?"

"No game. I ain't jobbin' you. I come from

your ma's side naturally. McBee's the name. Yes, sir, traveled with your folks to Oregon, except I slanted down to Californy 'fore I got there."

"What year?"

" 'Forty-five, o' course. Seen your ma get hitched up on the way, her that was my daughter."

"Who?"

"Name's Mercy." One bony finger stabbed at Evans' chest. "Hell, you know it, if you own up to your name. It's Evans, ain't it?"

"Evans."

"My Mercy married George Brown Evans." The man's smile was a smooth, red cave in whiskers that soap might wash out white. "We called him Brownie. That's your father. It's just like yesterday."

There was no doubt. This was Grandpa McBee, come out of nowhere, broken big as life, or as small, through the curtain that the family had kept closed. This was his mother's father!

The red cave reopened, the tongue like a spit-slick clapper in it. "Tol'able glad to see you, boy, and I don't wonder you're struck dumb, never settin' eyes on me before and maybe thinkin' I'd done gone to my reward. You wouldn't want to guess the good luck that brought us two together?"

"No."

"When my woman died — typhoid it was, and a meaner damn sickness don't look to see. Worse'n broke-out syph. When I planted her, I went huntin' gold, bein' so low in my mind. By and by I got wind of the strike in the Sweet Grass Hills."

He expected some answer, but Evans kept still.

"Be-damned if I didn't run up against a friend of yours there. Godwin's his name, and by soundin' him out I found out you was here." With hardly a pause he went on, " 'Course, I never let on to him or to a Christ's soul that you and me was connected. Best to make sure how we struck it off. Relatives can puke you, like I know."

Again Evans held his tongue.

"I knowed already you was somewhere in Montana. Your folks wasn't sure just where."

"You saw them?"

"For a minute. I couldn't stay. But, like with your other grandpa, your pa and me was bosom friends." The clawed hand took hold of Evans' arm. "I helped raise him up, you might say. Son, you ought to let your folks know whereabouts you are."

It wasn't any use to tell him that they knew.

"Anyhow I found you."

"I see you did."

"I call it luck, the nick of time, you might say. You see, son, I was raisin' plenty color there nigh to Gold Butte, but then my spondulix played out, and I was pawin' air until I thought, why, Lat Evans ain't so far away, and he'll be glad to put me up till I get on my feet. Blood runs strong in us McBees." He raised a leg and broke wind heartily and said as if this were an incidental, "Nothin' but gas in me."

"There's grub inside."

"No hurry. Now that wife of yours, if she ain't a purty thing, and good, I bet, whichever way you figger." The inturned lips made a little smack. "Free-hearted, too, I'll bet to boot, or you would fan her little backside."

"Never mind about that! Where'd you see her?"

"Just inquirin' after you. Oh, I didn't tell her. Hell, no, not till I seen how you and me made out." Now, bright as a moulting hen's, the eyes came up and put a question.

Evans looked away, catching a glimpse of Carmichael watching and waiting out of earshot at the kitchen door, his face lined to a half smile.

"Son, I thank Christ Jesus we got years yet to enj'y each other, and it ain't as if you had the sorry job of layin' me away soon. Look!" McBee faced half around and bent his knees and jumped. It was a good jump, allowing for the coat. Straightening, he raised his hands and brought them down and touched his knuckles to the ground. "Notice my knees ain't crooked a mite. How's that for pressin' eighty?"

At the kitchen door Carmichael was grinning over the hands that rolled a cigarette.

Evans sighed. "How much to put you on your feet?"

A gleam flicked in the old-bird eyes, but the mouth said, "Oh, no, son. I didn't have my mind on that." With one scaly hand he pushed the very thought away. "I just figgered I'd stay a spell with you and maybe find a job of work and afterwards climb in my hole."

"How much?"

"You see, stickin' around, I could help you to the Senate where I hear you're headed. Be glad to. Hell, I know politics." He threw an arm out and addressed the prairie. "We got to have a good, honest, savin' administration, and who can do it better than Albert Gallatin Evans? I ought to know, folks. The good Lord made me his grandpa."

Evans said, "Fifty dollars and a horse."

"That's open-handed, real open-handed, but you know, not to little you, fifty ain't so much

389

with grub so high. I don't s'pose I could cut 'er on that, thankin' you all the same."

"Fifty and a horse."

"That little boy of yourn ought to know his great-grandpa. And your woman, ain't she curious where you come from?"

"Make it a hundred."

The dirty claws of hands came up and clawed each other. "That's closer to the mark, but God cuss me if I don't want to be real kinfolks to your woman. I want to see her skitterin' around, neat as a pin, and good, waitin' on the old man. Me'n her, I could tell, would team like tumblebugs."

"A hundred dollars and a horse. And goodbye."

McBee's sharp old eyes looked at the offer and decided. "All right, but I can't help wonderin' what your ma would think, blood of my blood, as the sayin' is." He drew himself up and buttoned his coat. "I didn't know you was so cramped for room." The note of injury changed fast. "A good horse, though!"

That was that, Evans thought as he and Carmichael topped the ridge of the Tansy valley and came to flatter footing for the horses. Or he could tell himself that was that.

Ahead the benchlands flowed away, their drops and pitches quivering in the dazzle of the snow, their wind-bare patches floating unsupported like loose rafts of earth. There was no brush here, no road, no fences, nothing but little snow mounds that would be carcasses in a swale and, not far away, one ribby cow with a bag that had been frozen. There were no landmarks even, no sure and bold ones, but a man went sure, ground kin to the V of wild geese that cried the sure north overhead. Like shouts of lonely reassurance their voices drifted down.

They reached the Bar O as night began to dull the snow. Already the others were on hand, plus Hector's hired hand, Gunderson. Ten men altogether, ten mostly silent men. Rax, the quietest by nature, had the most to say, 'We hit the right time maybe," he told Evans and Carmichael on arrival. "Howie had two horses took from under his nose last night, and Johnson says he's shy. Damn rustlers prob'ly figured on the snow to cover up their tracks. You missin' any?"

"Haven't noticed."

"Just so our thievin' friends ain't got the horses off their hands yet, or into Canada. Put your broncs in the barn. There's oats in the bin. Then come in and eat a bait."

They ate in haste, waited on by Rax's fat squaw wife, who paddled back and forth, unintroduced and speechless. Even her eyes, crowded between the thrust of her brow and the high flesh of her cheeks, seemed speechless. After she had poured coffee, she went into another room. Evans imagined Rax was a demanding man. In the fits of silence he could hear the slow squeak of her rocking chair.

"You boys think we'd better take along some grub?" Rax asked.

"Naw," Hector answered. He looked around at the rest. "We'll have a man or two for breakfast."

Soon after nightfall they were ready – bellies filled, guns and ammunition talked over and examined, horses fed and saddled, three extras put on lead ropes for emergencies. They moved out quietly, Rax at the front because he knew this country best.

Riding, Evans wondered what was in their minds. Carmichael he knew. Mike had come out of friendship and loyalty and perhaps something of the rider's feelings against a man who'd leave another man afoot. But the others? Which ones eager? Which maybe daunted? Which ones, like himself and McLean and Chenault, were reluctant but committed by the ugly need?

A horse sneezed and a mouth let out a word. Leather creaked, and the snow squeaked under hoof. From somewhere coyotes quavered, and from the blind night sky more geese cried north. Ten men, Evans thought, and each rode by himself. On that strong bay horse he'd been presented, Grandpa McBee could put a lot of miles between himself and Tansytown. Grandpa! Mother's father!

The moon came up like a Christmas orange and climbed the sky and changed into a silver dollar, bright on the land, bright on rifles and revolvers, on the taffy coils of new rope held by saddle straps; and they rode on through the night, up slopes, down slopes, across the flats, with minds alive and forward-cast, if they were like his own, and bodies tired and loose with tiredness.

As they struck the rougher country the moon squeezed out among the westward mountains, and darkness closed in like a hand, shutting out the mountains and the skyline and the stretching snow and all except a star and the half-imagined glimmer of a circle underfoot. All of them, as members of the Tansy roundup pool, knew something of this section, but in this darkness, on this uncertain footing, they strung out Indian file, leaving Rax to pick the way.

By and by, like a wound, the east showed a spatter of red. Not like a wound, though, Evans thought, letting his mind picture what it would. Like the fight of day against the night. Like the bloody birth of morning. The glimmer underfoot inched out, and the men ahead took shapes of black. An unseen owl asked who went there, and a horse shook himself, clattering his gear, and the coyotes sang again.

The file slowed down and stopped and grouped. "One cabin lays ahead and to the right," Rax said, low-voiced. "Second is down the crick a mile or two, but here's the biggest. Just yonder is a patch of brush where we can tie the horses. We best sneak up on foot. Ride closer, and a horse'll whinny." He waited for their approval and led away again.

They reached the brush and got off and tied up and drew rifles from their boots and untied the two new coils of rope and regathered around Rax. "There's a corral just left of the cabin, not more'n ten-twelve jumps away," he said. "That's all, it and the cabin, except an old shit-house."

McLean's voice was almost a whisper. "How does the cabin set?"

"Facin' us. South, that is. One window and one door in front and no place else for them to make a break."

"I'll leave Gunderson with the horses just to play safe," Hector said. "Gunderson, if you hear me whistle, fog one up."

Gunderson was Scandinavian. He answered,

"But ay shoot goot."

"Stay goot! Stay!"

"Yah, sure."

"Let's get posted." Hector started moving off.

Evans stopped him. "What's the plan?"

"Crawl up and take cover and wait for light to open the ball."

"Then?"

"Call 'em out."

"And shoot to kill?"

"If anyone resists."

"I don't like it."

Hector hitched his rifle impatiently. "What do you like?"

"Evidence. And kept promises."

"Christ, Evans, be reasonable!" Hector had raised his voice. He lowered it as he went on. "We'll listen to 'em if they come out peaceful. Where you goin' to get your evidence?"

"The corral's a chance."

Chenault said, "Why not?" and McLean chimed in, "That suits me, too."

"All right." Hector overdid his sigh. "Who scouts it then? One man's enough and two's too many. You?"

Evans said, "I will."

"But an empty corral won't prove they're innocent." Hector had to have this last word.

They set off slowly, led again, by Rax, careful

not to kick a stone or thrash a bush, though the cabin, it developed, was too far to call for such a cautious start. For a quarter of a mile or more they walked this way, their arms snugged close, their eyes hard on the next step. Rax halted at a gap between two knolls. "Through there," he whispered down the line.

Downhill and ahead the corral was a stripe of shadow that held a pool of darkness. Farther on the cabin made a blur.

Rax beckoned for a huddle. "We can circle round this rise, keepin' it between us and the house," he said just loud enough to hear. "Farther, but they might spot us movin' in plain sight. Yon side of the rise there's some brush and boulders in close range." Again he waited for their judgment.

Someone whispered, "Good enough."

Rax turned to Evans. "Looks like this is the spot for you to angle off."

Evans left the bunch, hearing Carmichael's parting "Careful, Lat!" behind him. He walked light-footed as he went down the slope, light-footed and hunched low, for from here the window looked on him. A rock rolled under his foot, nearly throwing him, and slid softly in the snow and came to rest. He held up, watching The little grind of boots above him faded into nothing. He reached the bottom of the slope and cut left and now was out of the window's eye.

The smell and sight of horses came together. They stood high-headed, minus bodies, like stuffed heads hanging, awake already to the scent or sound of him and ready to take fright. He went up slowly, keeping the corral between him and the house and, closer, spoke low to keep them quiet. They moved around, snorting softly, checked by the words he pitched to reach no farther.

They had bodies. They had brands, made almost readable by the rising blood-smoke of the eastern sky. He waited, looking through the poles of the corral. Thought waited. Time waited. The world and all had reached a stop, was deadlocked at this dead hour of morning.

A scar came out — Rax's Bar O on a buckskin. Then, as the horses shuffled nervously, Howie's Round Top T. Then Johnson's iron. They were sufficient, but still Evans moved around to see if there were more.

It was then that he heard the door open and close. He froze against a post, hands ready on his rifle; and a man passed almost close enough to spit on, close enough to show a crow's-wing forelock that was a brand itself, and went on toward the privy.

Evans sidled around the corral. He began running, as quietly as he could.

397

29

Carmichael lay behind a boulder the size of a bucket, his rifle pushed ahead beside it. Waiting, he wished he'd gone with Evans, who was too fair for his own safety. Brave enough, for sure, but measured in his judgments. A man quick on the trigger could perforate him while he gave the benefit of doubt.

Left and right, each behind a boulder or a bush, the other men lay spread out, their bodies black against the snow, their rifle barrels faintly lined with light. Nobody whispered much. Nobody would until Evans showed up.

Carmichael squirmed, inside himself reaching ahead for that time. A lot it would matter to Hector and Rax if anything happened to Lat! Yeah, a man lost, Evans it was, Lat Evans, the candidate of the Senate. Yeah, a pretty good man but upright as all hell. Didn't seem to want much to dirty his hands, either, in cleaning out that nest in the breaks. And was he one to pamper his help! Damn fool paid Carmichael in full for all that time he was laid up. Too bad about his woman. Too bad about the boy. For an instant Carmichael was back in the sickbed and Lat's eyes were on him, anxious and well-wishing, and Joyce's hands were clever and her voice gentle. For an instant the baby held out his arms, wanting to come. Until at last their feet quit itching, some men couldn't appreciate a family.

He raised his head and looked over the boulder. Things came dark-sharp to his eye in the slowly lifting light — the black cabin front with its window barely spotted by a sack or rag stuffed in a broken pane, a twisted cottonwood nearby with a limb made for a rope, a stream behind the house that ran inky except for one reflection of the morning sky, a fret of brush along the stream and, still farther on, the saw-tooth outlines of the breaks. From here the backhouse didn't show. A bird was cheeping somewhere.

By degrees the higher faces of the hills turned to a gray that straggling bushes left dark wrinkles in. The cloud bank to the east turned redder, but still the cabin held on to its patch of night. There was movement in the corral, though, a suggestion of movement. Down there close a man might read a brand by now.

Carmichael blinked and looked away. He told himself that this was what came of staying too long in one place — this nagging worry instead of carefree fun, this felt responsibility, this concern with Joyce and Little Lat and Lat himself, this riding after rustlers for that matter, though it wouldn't bother him too much to give a guilty man his due. He had changed, he thought, or been changed, for he had no regrets. Lat was a man to fasten to. So was his family. And at the last even a drifter had to fasten on to something, and was lucky to. A strange thing, as to himself and Lat, was that he should feel the older and the younger both, both needed by Lat and somehow needful of him. Age had got the best of him, and not age, either, for he wasn't fifty yet. It was a case of borrowed ambition, of things he might have had and now could have at one remove. It was maybe the direction that he couldn't find himself. It was maybe, to lean on, the fixed strength he'd never had. But Lat might profit by the kind of strength he did have, and by his old savvy, too.

"Can't see hardly a damn thing down there," Whitlock muttered fretfully.

But now sounds came from the left. Carmichael cocked his head around. It was Evans, humping up the slope, too fast for quiet. He breathed hard as he stopped and squatted down.

Hector let out, "What in hell! Something spook you?"

"No."

The others had crawled up to hear.

"Noisy enough! What then?"

Evans was still panting. "Stolen horses all right. Rax's, Howie's, Johnson's, maybe others."

Hector hissed at him, "Satisfied?"

"Must be they aimed to slip them horses out this morning," Whitlock put in. "What say we blow the bugle?" He was a nervous man, Carmichael figured, the kind without the mettle to bear waiting.

Hector said, "Too early yet. Too dark. Get back to place!"

They started crawling off. Carmichael beckoned to Evans. "Another rock by me." They lay down side by side.

Then, to Carmichael's surprise, to the surprise he felt like a breath up and down the line, Evans shouted out, "All right, down there! Come out! Hands up!"

The men made murmurs in the snow as they flattened flatter and brought their rifles up. Above the murmurs Hector's voice growled, "Of all the loco capers!"

"Come out!"

They waited.

The sack swept from the window. Fire flashed where it had been. Carmichael heard the ground thump of the bullet and the beginning echoes of the shot and saw the dawn light shaken on the peaks. Then around him guns were answering. He lined his sights and answered with them. Glass shattered in the window, flashing as it fell. Wood splintered in the flimsy door A bullet chipped the rock Carmichael lay behind.

"All right, Mike?"

"All right."

As he levered in another cartridge Carmichael saw smoke wisping from the muzzle of Lat's gun. In that split second before he shot again he wondered if Lat was really aiming. Foolish question. Of course he was. The window spurted fire, and the fire around him put it out.

Silence then, a waiting, listening silence. A white cloth poked from the window and began to wave. A blur of face appeared above it and cried out, "No more! *Mon dieu!* We come!"

"Come or croak!" Hector was taking charge again.

The door swung open and hung sagging behind two figures with upraised hands.

The bunch followed Hector down the slant,

402

their rifles ready, and halted maybe twenty feet away.

One man was small, and one was big. The little one was in his underwear. The other had pulled on a pair of pants. The little man fell on his knees. He had a breed's face. He lifted it. *"Mon dieu!* Pitee! Pitee!"* Barefoot and unclothed, he trembled in the snow but not, Carmichael knew, from cold.

The big man's right arm showed the stain and growing seep of blood. It came down slowly.

Hector told him, "Keep 'em up!"

"You sons-of-bitches winged me. Can't work my fingers, or I'd be firin' yet."

"Pitee! Pitee!"

Somehow the big man had found time to draw his boots on. He swung one of them, so fiercely as to send the small man sprawling. "You can pray in hell, you war whoop!"

Hector said, "That's Bigsbee."

Carmichael already knew it was. He thrust aside the softness for him that Hector, being Hector, was the cause of. To his knowledge Bigsbee had a noisy thirst and touchy temper and, by reputation, a light regard for ownership. As such men did, he had a toady following, in his case breeds and shady whites. Not that it mattered, but he also had peepholes for eyes and a nose like a potato and a mouth cut on the bias.

"Goddam your guts, too!" Bigsbee told Hector. "You're a land hog and a water hog and a natural-born hog and by rights belong on a rope, what with the stock you've mavericked."

"Pitee!" The little man was on his belly, his face raised like an otter's. "I have papoose."

Hector said to Bigsbee, "Talk's cheap."

"You mean dear — but worth it just to get you told." His good hand went to his wounded arm. "Ambushin's just your size."

"Wag your damn tongue while you can! Talk big or go to beggin' like your friend! We got a cure for both." Hector pointed to the cabin. "Anyone with you? Any more of you thieves?"

Bigsbee was slow to answer. When he did, it was to say simply, "Dead man inside. French Joe, shot through the face."

"Have a look! McLean! Howie!"

Before they could move, the little man gathered himself. He scrambled for the corner of the cabin, running half bent over. From the tail of his eye Carmichael saw Hector swing his rifle and for a wink thought of a hunter sure of his bag and cheered. The little man was squeaking. The rifle seemed a long time in exploding. Short by two yards of the corner he'd tried to put behind him, the man pitched forward and flopped around and lay still. From the corral came the snorts of horses. Hector opened the breach and blew into the barrel. He motioned to the others to keep an eye on Bigsbee and went forward and jerked his target over. "Saves hangin'," he said, straightening. "Now look inside, you two."

Carmichael heard, beside him, the hard pull of Lat's breath, the one hard pull that brought in air and locked it there.

McLean and Howie walked to the door and stepped inside and came out nodding.

Hector moved on Bigsbee, drawing the rest along. His hands were busy with a rope now.

"Make it right, Hector," Bigsbee said. "I wouldn't want to hang on the wrong knot." He stood, small-eyed, big-nosed, slash-mouthed, pale and ugly in the morning light. Drop by drop, blood was falling from his hand. But what Carmichael noticed more than all was the fine, the almost unnoticeable trembling of one pants leg. Bigsbee hitched himself abruptly, planting both legs.

"Tie his hands!" Hector said to anyone who would.

"We'll hear him out." It was Evans, speaking quietly.

"Hear him out? Good God!"

Chenault said, "We'll hear him out."

"We know he's guilty!"

"Shut up!" Evans answered, still quietly, too quietly, it occurred to Carmichael. "Bigsbee, what about those horses in the corral?"

"What about them?"

"They're stolen."

"Too bad about you nabobs."

"You have a hand in rustling them?"

"None of your goddam business."

"We're giving you your chance."

"Chance?" The down end of the big mouth pulled down even farther. "Jesus Christ wouldn't have a chance."

"You do if you're innocent."

"Sure, I'm innocent." The pants leg trembled again, and again Bigsbee hitched. "I'm as goddam innocent as Hector."

Hector put in, "Let's get on with it," maybe thinking of the calves he'd mavericked before the territory got some kind of order.

"Guilty or not guilty, then?"

Bigsbee would never break, Carmichael thought even before the answer came. He wouldn't beg or try to make a case. He'd die proud and defiant, and guilty, fighting the quiver of his muscles.

Bigsbee said, "Go to hell!"

Lat lowered his head and shook it slowly and then nodded slowly. "I guess that's it."

Hector dropped his rope and put two fat

fingers in his mouth and whistled, calling Gunderson. He and Rax and Whitlock marched up, surrounding Bigsbee. With his good hand Bigsbee swung on Hector. He missed and went down, felled by the pistol barrel that Whitlock laid eagerly along his skull.

Hector said to Rax, "Give me that piggin' string!" He tied Bigsbee's hands behind him and got the hanging rope and looped it over Bigsbee's head and, for a blindfold, used a used bandanna. Everything was very businesslike.

Carmichael heard the gallop of a horse. Gunderson rode up, a six-gun in his hand. Waving it, he said, "Svede ready. Yust show me."

"Never mind. Get off!" Hector told him.

Bigsbee couldn't hold his head up, quite. They dragged him under the cottonwood limb. "Handy," Hector said while he coiled the loose end of the rope. He cast it up and over the limb and made a hitch around the trunk. "Bring that horse up, Gunderson!"

They boosted Bigsbee on the horse and took up slack. "You plumb and pious satisfied?" Hector turned to ask of Lat.

Lat only nodded.

Hector looked at Bigsbee. "Savin' last words, we're ready."

Bigsbee didn't answer.

Hector picked up a stick. "Leave go the

reins," he said to Gunderson and smacked the horse's rump.

The horse lunged. Bigsbee bounced against the cantle of the saddle and jerked against the rope. It swung him up to 4 o'clock. He swung back and thrashed, his breath screeching in his twisted neck. In time the thrashing and the screeching stopped. The body swung slower and slower. It turned on the rope, front, back, front, and from the crooked mouth beneath the blindfold the tongue oozed out.

It was Hector who spoke first. "There's a good man now." The deed had left no shadow on his face. "We'll leave him hang just as a warning." He nodded to his own decision as he looked around. "Where you goin', Evans?"

Lat had turned and started off. Over his shoulder he said, "Backhouse."

"Have a look inside the cabin on your way. Might be clues there. Hey, I'll look with you." Hector strode ahead and took Lat by the arm and shook him playfully. "Backhouse, huh? You'll catch the crabs."

It was different when Carmichael reached them just outside the cabin door. They had halted there, and Hector's eyes were busy on the snow.

Lat said, "Let's go in!"

Hector looked up at him and down again.

With a glance Carmichael picked up what Hector saw, what none of them had noticed earlier — one-way footprints that slanted from the others and curved from sight around the corner.

"Come on!" Lat said.

"Now just a minute, you!" Hector stalked the tracks. Lat cast a glance at Carmichael and moved on after Hector. From the corner, Carmichael saw, the tracks led to the privy, not returning. The little breed close by had bled a red slush in the snow. It flitted in and out of Carmichael's mind that he looked cold. Behind them some of the other men were pushing up. Two stood at the corral, looking through the poles. Hector kept on stalking, his rifle cradled in his arm.

Longer-spaced and slurred, the tracks came leaping from the privy and veered west, up the thickets of the stream. Hector kicked the door in, uselessly. "One man got away!" His eyes were fixed on Evans.

"Looks like it. If you hadn't been so keen for blood, the breed would have told us who."

There was something here Carmichael couldn't understand. The men were gathered round now, all of them and all listening, while Lat and Hector stared each other in the face.

"You wouldn't say you spotted anyone?" Hector said.

"Don't be a fool!"

Carmichael saw thought working in Hector's eyes. "You were damn quick to hail the house." Whatever he was, Hector wasn't stupid.

Carmichael put in, "It worked, didn't it?" They might not have heard him.

"You've said enough." Again Lat spoke too quietly.

"Enough! You ain't raised a hand yet, except to block the work."

Chenault addressed them from behind. "Cut it out, you two!"

Lat turned. "Mike, we'll chase him down."

"You!" Hector said. "The hell you will!"

McLean had come up close. "Sure, let 'em go. Cinch to run a man on foot down. Two's enough."

Hector swung his eyes from Lat. "I don't trust him." One taste of blood, Carmichael thought as he watched them both, had turned his head. "He ain't got the stummick for it."

Now Lat spoke to the rest. "Hector would shoot the first man he saw, no questions asked. That's why he doesn't go. Some of you others could, except that Whey Belly's made the thing a case of trust."

Chenault muttered, "Hell, we trust you."

"How'll you have it, Hector?" It wasn't Lat to bull the game. Lat Evans? Carmichael cheered inside himself.

McLean said, "This is crazy."

"Keep out, Mac," Lat answered. "It's personal."

"Rough and ready." Hector was drunk on blood all right. Or was he? A bigger man all round. Strong and ornery as an ornery mule. A born brawler. Carmichael made a mental bet on Evans. A bad bet maybe. Alongside Hector, Lat looked almost frail. The bet was on what didn't show.

Hector handed his Winchester to Gunderson and peeled off his coat. Carmichael took Lat's rifle and watched him unwrap. The men were drawing back, making a circle around the two. "The belly," Carmichael found time to say to Lat alone.

Too fast to expect, far too fast for his swollen paunch, Hector crouched and charged. His fist caught Evans on the jaw and knocked him down. His boot kicked at the face that swung away not quite in time. Lat rolled to his feet, the boot mark showing on his cheek. Hector was crowding him. As if receiving them himself, Carmichael could feel the jolting, blind light of those heavy fists. He cried silently, "The belly! The belly!" Lat went down again. He got up, barely ahead of Hector's kick.

"Ah!" The half grunt came out of Carmichael

on its own, for Lat's left hand had found the target. Hector sucked for breath. He drew away and charged again. Lat took a blow high on his head and staggered back and steadied and got underneath. Two licks, left and right, deep in the bulge of belly. Hector didn't go down. He folded up, and his throat croaked for air, and his face when he raised it was gray. His hand slid toward the hip where his revolver had been left to hang.

"I wouldn't," Carmichael said. Hector's eyes came to him and saw the rifle ready. "Tell your Swede to take care, too."

"Watch it, Swede!" The voice was Chenault's.

Hector's gaze went around. His hand fell away. "You men think I'm crazy!" he strained out.

"It's open to debate." It was Chenault again.

"You been whupped," Rax said in his spare way.

That was the end of it.

Evans reached out for his rifle. "Come on, Mike." He led out toward the brush where the horses were tied.

Behind him Carmichael heard Whitlock. "Let's burn this robbers' roost."

He heard Rax answering, "And warn the cabin down the crick!"

Evans kept silent while they walked to the

brush and untied and got on. Then he said merely, "Straight ahead. He'll stick to the cover along the stream."

Carmichael knew his feeling or thought he knew some of it — the let-down after winning, even over such a man as Hector. The killings would be heavy on his mind, too. Not pretty, not in any part, but the men who died had asked for what they got. "Good fight, Lat." He tried a smile without results. "And your face ain't bruised too much. Won't have to say you run into a door."

Lat kept quiet, and Carmichael went to wondering. The footprints, the sudden hail, the other things?

The sun had climbed the cloud bank, half of it had, shining long-bright across the land. It would be a good day, a melting day, and cows would find grass greening underneath the thinning skim of snow. Calves would do well, up on their shaky legs, their snoots outstretched for all they cared of ma. Before too long now the white of the mountains would leak away to blue. Even Lat ought to feel good.

They wound through the willows and cut the boot tracks at the creek bed. Lat held up. His turned face looked abused and old. "It's Ping, Tom Ping," he said.

Carmichael held back his first surprise. "I

figured some such." Everything fell into place, even to the footprints that Lat had wanted to scuff out before the others saw. Carmichael sighed. He didn't ask Lat about the justice of it. A straight row could be too hard to hoe, and the men who hoed it too hard to travel with. All he said was, "Armed?"

"I don't know."

"He'll shoot you sure as hell. You let me take the lead!"

Carmichael knew beforehand what Lat would say. "Thanks, Mike, but no go."

"What you aim to do?"

"Run him down."

"Then what?"

Lat tapped his knee with the end of one rein while he looked off into space. "He saved my life once."

"I know. And since then overdrawed the debt."

Lat kept tapping his knee, his face sober and yet softened as a man's was by old thoughts. He was lost somewhere out there, somewhere in space and time with the Tom he knew once.

"You can't want to kill him?"

No answer came.

"Then why chase him down?"

Lat pulled himself out of the past as if he had to pass it point by point, stopping here and there to live some things again. "If he knows we know, Mike—?"

"Then he'll reform?"

"I keep thinking." Lat had slid into the years again.

Carmichael had a bite on something. He chewed it in his mind. "He's got to know we know — but you got to know he knows?"

Lat considered, his eyes far away. "Maybe, Mike. Don't ask me. I guess I do want him to see we're square." A long breath blew out of him. He started Sugar on the trail. "Anyhow, we're wasting time."

The footprints followed a game path that wound west through tangles of brush. Now and then they could trot, now and then even gallop, but mostly they had to go slow while they fended off branches — slow, that was, for mounted men. Ping's long stride in the snow began to shorten. Here he had stopped to blow and let off water. Here he'd sat down, probably to squeeze the feet squeezed sore by high-heeled boots. He could be hidden anywhere ahead, his finger on the trigger, his eye lined on the sights. First he'd take Lat, who rode steady in the lead, hardly watching as a man should. Carmichael pressed him close.

The brush ended. Ahead for half a mile was open country, and in the open, bound for the farther cover, a man was hobbling. Even from a distance it was Ping.

They put their horses to a run. Ping stopped and wheeled around. His hand was empty, his waist not circled by a cartridge belt. His chest swelled and went flat with his breath. His face was too dark for the teeth his panting showed.

Nothing was said. There was nothing to say, Carmichael thought while he waited. He turned the other cheek in the saddle.

Then at last Lat spoke. "The two of us know, Tom. No more." A man almost had to strain his ears to hear. "You can go on."

Ping said, "You bastard!"

Lat didn't flare up. For himself Carmichael wished he had, and for himself he said, "You're even, Ping! He done you quite a favor." At once he wished he hadn't spoken.

Ping said, "He can keep his goddam favors!"

Lat just waved his rifle. "Go on!"

Ping faced away. It was a dozen steps or two before he limped.

Lat's words were slow in making sense. "We'll have to have a story for the others."

Carmichael felt as much depressed as Lat had shown himself to be. He said, "I s'pose you'd ought to kilt him."

30

Evans and Carmichael reached the ranch by early morning, having forked off from the others in the extra darkness just ahead of dawn. From the slope that led down to it the place lay restful, the roofs of house and bunkhouse and barn steaming faintly in the slanting sunlight, the chimney feathered with the smoke of quaking asp.

Westward by twenty miles the sun fingered at the main range of the Rockies, picking peaks and faces for its touch. For a moment, during which he hold himself he was flighty with fatigue, Evans wished he could be lifted there. High in that all-whiteness, above the shadowed canyons, a man might look untroubled on the world, seeing each thing in its place.

He brought his eyes back to the buildings. They made a good berth, a berth made for a home. Inside the kitchen was a pump fed by a well he'd dug. Inside were a sink he'd soldered out of coal-oil cans and a hanging tank to which he could force water by pumping with the pump snout plugged. Tables, benches, chests, a good part of the house itself – these somehow he'd built himself. It was as if those days of waiting for the wedding day gave rise to special skills. The days of waiting and the thought of Joyce, who was not to wear her life away as other ranch wives did. The house even had a fixed bathtub, though the copper of it sometimes left corrosion marks on the skin.

And Joyce and Little Lat were coming back. He kept reminding himself of that. All night, while they rode, he had summoned it to mind. It was a matter for rejoicing.

Against his own silence Carmichael had kept speaking, drawing on old stories, on things seen and heard and stored in memory for happy times. "Ever tell you about old Doc Longeway down there in Ioway?" he'd asked. "Got in a fight, the doc did, and knocked the man down and straddled him and went to givin' him whatfor, paying no attention that the man was shoutin' out he'd had enough. So someone watchin' says to Doc, 'Quit it! He called enough.' Doc lets up just long enough to answer, 'I know he did, but he's such a goddam liar you can't believe a word he says.' "

Or Carmichael had been telling, "A feller got

418

arrested in Nebraska for callin' names, and they took him afore a justice of the peace. A unprejudiced witness took the stand. The j.p. asks him, 'Did you hear the plaintiff, Ole Beaner, called a son-of-a-bitch?' Says the witness, 'Your honor, I never knew Ole Beaner to go by any other name.' "

Now, as they neared the house, Carmichael said, "My belly's rubbin' my backbone, and I can't keep more'n one eye open."

Nothing to eat since Rax's, and how long ago was that? Night before last by the calendar. No sleep since then except for cold catnaps taken while they waited for darkness to cover the return.

The explanation he and Mike made up had seemed to work. No one questioned that they had had to shoot a man whose name they couldn't learn. A breed, they said, who wouldn't stand and talk but let go with an ancient musket not worth the trouble of collecting. The men had merely nodded. Already most of them had had enough of bloodshed. At the second cabin two more rustlers had been found and put to death.

They reached the barn and dismounted. "Lat."

Evans turned, to see Carmichael speaking over his saddle.

"Take my advice! Go armed from now on! In town or out!"

"Not my style, Mike."

"Damn it, rustlers got relatives, rustlers got friends, and word'll leak out. You want to be pot-shot?" It seemed to Evans that some extra thought flicked in the eyes that the years had turned more gray than blue. "You can't tell who might draw down on you."

Evans said, "Well?" Mike was probably right. Now what they needed was food and sleep. Mike looked as played out as Evans felt. The wrinkles around his eyes and mouth were drawn too deep for humor. "You take a couple of days off, Mike. You've more than earned it."

"Providin' you do, too — and providin' you go armed!"

"Just in time, boys," Whitey said as they came in after graining the horses. He stood at the wood stove, a soiled towel over his middle and his hat on his head. "Cook calls the turn, and sowbelly and hen fruit's the special today. Over easy costs you extry." They gave him hello, and he began breaking more eggs in the pan. "And I can remember when eggs was dessert, before Albert Gallatin Evans lassoed himself some hens. First thing you know, Mike, he'll buy a Jersey cow and be askin' us to milk. And what I'll answer is I would except

420

I'm too shy to take them open liberties."

"Please to center on cookin'," Carmichael said.

Whitey looked away from the pan. "You two don't look like you'd fared too handsome." That, Evans knew, was as close as he would come to asking what he could and would be told after food and rest.

"How's the calving?"

Whitey sang to a Sunday-school tune, "Dropping, dropping, dropping, dropping, hear the calvies fall..."

"Bein' alone sure overstocks your mouth." Carmichael spoke with tired good nature.

"Not alone!" Whitey motioned with his cook spoon. "Who in hell was that old rooster, Lat?"

"Who?"

"That smooth-mouth, cross between cricket and whiskers, touched up with skunk?"

"Didn't he go?"

"Not till this mornin'. Hung around and asked me more goddam questions, not as I answered. Then I tied a can to his tail."

"Good."

"He lit out in the direction of town."

Evans drew a breath. Out of the window the sun still lay bright on the mountains.

31

To pass the time, Carmichael went into the Lally Cooler. He had had sleep enough, God knew, since that sashay into the breaks. Almost round the clock. Lat's cattle — he couldn't help but think of them as his, too, in a way — were doing fine. Nothing to worry about, but still he worried some.

Three men sat at a table, ready to play cards. Two of them he knew. Then as his eyesight sharpened to the inside murk, he recognized the third one. A cross between cricket and whiskers, Whitey had called him.

Butch Schmidt waved Carmichael over. "Just waitin' for a sucker. Take a hand?"

"A few, maybe." Carmichael sat down. He motioned to the bar. "Bring us a drink, huh?"

" 'Y God, that's a pious idea." Whitey had been right, too, in saying the cross was touched with skunk.

They dealt and dealt. Carmichael wasn't

interested enough, he knew without caring, to pay attention to the game. Win or lose, he could kill an hour or three.

Between deals the musty whiskers opened and the gums inside them asked, "Where's the chief?"

"Who?"

"Your boss, then?"

"If you mean Evans, he's in town, at home."

"Is he goin' to be around?"

"Why don't you ask him?" Here again was something Carmichael couldn't tally. He asked himself why even Lat, tolerant though he was, didn't boot this scummy scarecrow to Dakota or over the divide.

Howie came in and barely nodded and ordered up one drink and went back out. Solo. Solo was the game. A man ought to keep his mind on it.

Carmichael said, "I'll try one," and went set.

"If you'd led out different now?" The gums showed moist. "Maybe solo ain't your fit, boy. Me, I'm a monte man. Hey, my deal!"

Whitlock entered and then Rax. They might be strangers from their manners. They drank and left.

Natural, Carmichael figured, natural for all of them to come to town after the big doings. They'd make the rounds, listening sharp for any talk, and act cold to each other while in secret bound together. He sluffed a ten-spot.

The man they called Nevada Jim got a bid and made it.

There wasn't any talk yet, none that he had heard. Things were quiet, men going peaceable about their little businesses. Today was just like any other sleepy, small-town day — palaver, cards, a drink or two unless, like Lat, a man stayed home to appreciate his family.

Carmichael said, "To hell with this game!" He kicked his chair back and rose and paid off standing up.

"Like a little stud, or freeze-out?" the old man asked.

"No."

Outside, a sheepherder by looks was coming up the walk, trailed by his dog. The dog was sober. Both of them managed to enter the Lally Cooler, the dog just squeezing through the closing door. Across the street the preacher's wife was giving a wide berth to the Jackson Hotel Bar, her head turned away as if to say that things not seen weren't there. "Whoa, now!" The blacksmith's hoarse voice grated on the air. Soo Son, the Chinese café keeper, must be frying onions.

Carmichael backed up beside the window of the Lally Cooler and rested his behind on the frame. He'd lost his taste for town, he thought, or was it just that he had scratched into a sore his senseless little itch of worry? More like a woman than a man, he was, hunting boogers underneath the bed. What was like to happen!

Woman? Bed? Think one way and you thought another. That new girl at Callie's, or Miss Callie's as most people called the place now, the girl nick-named Gus for Gertrude, with whom he'd lain before? Long after he had figured, the wild oats in a man kept springing up, if not so green or thick as once. Blood and bed, it seemed to him now, somehow went together, or one behind the other. All that time up in the breaks the hunger had grown on him. Maybe, more than all, a man wanted the tenderness that life was shy of. Maybe he wanted to go home.

Before he went home, Carmichael told himself while saying goodbye to such crack-pot ideas, he'd see that Lat was home. Then, for himself, he'd find home enough, all the home he could. He rolled a cigarette.

In an hour or so it would be dark. Across, the west side of the street lay in shadow. Overhead a bullbat sounded like a quivered shingle. He couldn't see Callie's place from here even if he tried. It lay behind him, shut from sight by the line of buildings at his back. His mind idled away to Whitey and the thumb he'd dal-

425

lied off against the saddle horn. "A greenhorn asked me how I done it," Whitey was repeating, "and I told him I'd plain wore it down by thumbin' ignorant pilgrims to the cathouse."

The Evanses would be eating now or in a little while. He'd go down to the Chink's and take a bait himself. He straightened from against the wall and gave his belt a hitch and then stood still and waited.

Tom Ping was coming, walking with his hands loose, his eyes busy in a face that a week's beard didn't help. He went by with his head up, not speaking, not showing that he saw at all.

"Dried-apple pie," Joyce said, opening the over door. "I wish we had fresh apples, even Ben Davis." She could almost taste the rich fruits of Indiana, russet apples, for example, strawberries, grapes, green corn. There were the wild crops, too, the pawpaws and persimmons to contrast with the chokecherries and serviceberries that were the meager riches of this western land. Here, even canned tomatoes were a treat.

She looked at Lat and Little Lat and had to smile. "I'm not complaining really."

Lat was bouncing the baby on his instep. "Me neither."

"I, either." She ought not to correct him even fondly, she thought. It wasn't as if he didn't know better. And even if he didn't? Count your blessings!

"Here we go, boy! Ride 'em high!"

Little Lat laughed a bubbling laugh and sobered in surprise at it.

Count your blessings, name them one by one...

It had been a good day, a warm, gently flowing, family day, one of those days in which a person, instant by instant, felt the touch of the All-Purpose and almost understood. Except that Lat had been a little restrained, a little aloof somehow. She thought she knew the reason for that, too, and she knew its cure. Later, soon, tonight! The air was different afterwards, like air rained fresh and clean of dust. For Lat's sake — and her own — she wished she oftener felt this way. Tonight!

"You can put Little Lat into the high chair," she said. "It's getting late, and we're almost ready."

A couplet — she couldn't remember whose — ran through her head.

> *A subtle chain of countless rings*
> *The next unto the farthest brings...*

Lat lifted the baby to his lap, on his face such

a look of proud affection that she was almost sorry to be hurrying things. "Patty-cake, patty-cake," Lat said, working the chubby hands.

The ranch would be better now, she told herself while she dished up the food. She could stand it. With the two Lats she could stand anything. And maybe, after Little Lat? There was tonight, and there was God in His wisdom. She ought to feel guilty, she supposed, connecting carnality and God, but carnality was His will, and surely He would understand.

Lat put the baby in his high chair and sat down and waited for her and then asked the blessing. Little Lat sang, "Mum-um-um," as food was spooned to him. She felt like singing herself, proper or improper at the table.

Lat smiled at her, and she knew he knew. Words weren't necessary, or seemly.

They had just finished supper when a knock sounded. Carmichael came in. "Hello, Mother. Hi, you little bronc-buster. I've et, so don't be lookin' in the kettle."

She asked, "Coffee, then?" and served him.

He sat sipping it, not telling stories as he often did. His expression, it seemed to her, was more serious than usual, but what little he said was light enough. After a while he asked, "When you goin' back to the ranch, chief?"

Lat looked at him. "Chief?"

428

"Boss," Carmichael said with an easy smile.

Carmichael never addressed Lat in these terms. She spoke the old declamatory lines he brought to mind. " 'Ye call me chief...' "

"How's that?"

"That's 'Spartacus to the Gladiators.' "

"Turn him loose!"

For the fun of his reaction she lowered her voice and went on. " '...and ye do well to call him chief who, for twelve long years, has met upon the arena every shape of man or beast the broad Empire of Rome could furnish...' " Her memory failed her.

"Don't camp there!" Carmichael said. "Got to get to grass and water."

It was Lat who remembered lines he'd learned from her. " 'If there be one among you who can say that ever, in public fight or private brawl, my actions did belie my words, let him stand forth and say it.' "

She and Lat regarded each other, trying to summon up some of the rest. Into the silence Carmichael said, "Not that you don't tell it nice, but that Spartacus was a mouthy man. Mighty high-toned talk."

It hadn't really struck her before how overblown the language was. As if he understood, too, the baby had started to complain. She took him into her lap. "You're right,

Mike." It took a cowpuncher, she thought, to set her right. No. It took Carmichael.

Lat had recalled more of the speech. " 'If there be three in all your company dare face me on the bloody sands, let them come forth.' "

She laughed. "Those words don't fit you at all."

Carmichael said, "No'm." His gaze went to Lat. "Except they're too fancy for him, they're more fittin' to a man, oh, say, just for example since I just seen him, Like Tom Ping."

His eyes met Lat's, and for a silly moment she imagined they shared some piece of knowledge outside hers. Looking at Lat, it occurred to her that it wasn't really Carmichael who had set her right about Spartacus and his bombast; it was the fact of Lat. She studied him, renewing for herself the shapes of brow and nose and mouth and jaw that went together to make a quiet strength, to make — she hunted for the word — rectitude. She wished Carmichael would go.

"I asked you when you're goin' back?" Carmichael asked Lat.

"Tomorrow sometime."

Carmichael refused more coffee. "Aim to be downtown tonight?"

"Hadn't figured on it."

Carmichael gave one nod of his head. "Don't

430

forget the winter has drove them wolves down from the north. Like me, you better take some hardware goin' back." He pushed his chair out and got up and made for the door. Lat let him out.

She put the baby to bed. In a few minutes he would be asleep.

Long after Joyce was asleep, Evans lay awake, her head on his shoulder, hearing her even, peaceful breathing, feeling her breath on his throat. Here, he thought, was the joined flow of quieted blood. Here was tranquility pooled.

He saw her again as she had sat brushing her hair, doing this last chore before bedtime. He halted at the doorway to watch her, for she had opened the door after getting into her night-gown. Her hair remained lustrous in a climate too dry for luster. The years in every way had been good to her. Even her pale and delicate skin hadn't weathered, like most, to Montana winds.

Then she had asked as thought the question were casual, "Don't you think girls are nice?"

"Sure I do. I've got the nicest of all."

The brush stopped its movement and hung arrested over her head, wanting something to start it again.

He stepped inside. "Why do you ask that?"

She got up from her chair, not looking him in the face, and came to him and bent her head to his chest, and his arms were welcome, and he breathed her clean fragrance. She dared to whisper, "I mean a baby girl."

Afterwards they had talked — about a still larger family, perhaps, about worthy, fine lives for all, about the ranch, about the Senate and maybe higher places. "Oh, Lat!" she said, close in his arms. "We can do it. Respecting each other, loving each other, we can do anything."

Anything, he said to himself, lying awake. Anything.

Quieted blood. Tranquility. The rustlers were a dream to be told in time and understood. She would understand. Being Joyce, she would make herself understand, strange and wrong though violence was to her. She would understand the accident of Grandpa McBee, if he had to be acknowledged. It wasn't her inability to adjust to circumstance, he thought; it was his own wish to shield and protect her, to save her from trial and hurt. Also, for his own part, he had to admit, he wanted always to stand high with her. So, for one reason and another, he had denied McBee when she had said, "A dirty old man, very old and very dirty, with whiskers, was inquiring for you."

"Hmm. Could be anyone, I guess."

He felt sleep drifting on him, felt his muscles loosen and flow into the sheets and his mind ease off and put him, swimming, in the air. One stroke of his hand would lift or raise him, like the easy tilting of a hawk. Below him lay the lovely land and the birds of the field and the beasts of the forest that were His, and the earth and the fullness thereof and the cattle on a thousand hills.

It was Joyce's voice or the measured knocking that dragged him out of dreams. Waking, it seemed he'd heard them both at once.

"Lat!" she kept on saying. "Someone's at the back door, Lat!"

Again he heard the knocking.

"Not in your nightshirt!" Her voice was a whisper.

He found his pants and pulled them on and felt for matches and, in the kitchen, lit a wick. He went to the door and opened it and looked out.

No one was to be seen. He looked hard, night-blind from the flash of match. "Hello, there!" The moon was lipping at the mountains. The time was midnight, maybe later. "Hello, there!" From yesterday, Carmichael: *Rustlers got relatives*...He stepped outside.

Then he saw.

"Mist' Lat?" From the side Happy came up, his face like an egg of darkness with twin spots of white.

Evans closed the door behind him. "What?"

"Please, Mist' Lat! Please!" Happy held out his hat like a cup to be filled.

"Quiet! What?"

The black hand came out almost invisibly, the white slip in it showing clear.

Evans took the slip and unfolded it and backed up to the gleam of light out of the window.

The note, unsigned, said, "I am lonesome."

32

Walking in the night, Evans tried not to think. He told himself: wait and see; no use to cross bridges that might not be there. The Callie he had known wouldn't undo him, that was sure. She wouldn't ask the impossible. Nor would she think to tease him back to her, now that his way was cut out. Maybe she needed a loan.

It was too late for anyone to be out. Even the saloons were dark. With the moon down, the stars had come out of hiding, pinholes of stars that shone distant and cold. A stray dog lay curled by a door. The town was silent except for the march of his feet.

Happy's words turned and turned again in his head. "Please, only come, Mist' Lat! Dey tell you why."

So he was coming, leaving Joyce warm and trusting in bed and the baby asleep in his cradle.

"It's Whitey," he had told Joyce after he had sent Happy on.

"At the door?"

"No."

"Drunk?"

"Sick, too. Needs help. Can't take it any more," he answered while he dressed. Whitey would forgive him, he knew. Whitey wouldn't care much, unfair as the words were.

"And he'd been doing so well, you said."

"Yeah."

"What will you do?"

"I'll see. Get him in bed at the hotel probably."

He was within a block of the house now and could see a light from it. He felt divided and disloyal and caught. He had put Callie out of his life and nearly out of his mind, had hardly even glimpsed her for years, for not often did she come out in public. Happy himself was a stranger — a jog in the memory quickly smoothed out. Of a sudden all had come back. He saw again the sunflower hair and the apricot skin and the small, high-breasted body. She was bringing in breakfast and saying he ought not to fret but only get well. Openly, naturally, somehow purely, she was teaching him the ways of woman and man. She was pressing a loan in his hand. "Lat, don't you see? Being

436

you're you, it's as good as cash in the bank."
Other days, old love, old sin. Old obligation.
Today was never a new day. Within himself he
cried out, "Don't you see, Joyce! Don't you
see!"

He went on.

Summer was coming, and grass, and the wild
aster would bloom in the mountains and the
cactus flower on the plains. A man on a horse
could watch the white drift of a cloud.

A breeze sprang up and found a tag of paper
and whisked it by him. He had torn up the
note. To his right he could see the wall of the
mountains. Slopers, they called those who lived
across the divide. The breeze strengthened. A
gust of it took his breath. In Montana a man
had to get accustomed to wind.

"If ever I can do anything for you —" The old
words, past into present, promise into perfor-
mance. "Don't you see, Joyce!" He was crossing
bridges again. He walked on.

Happy opened the back door, his eyes like
sad moons in the glow of the lamp that he held.
"Come in, Mist' Lat. Dey's in theah."

One light burned in the parlor. In the circle
of its shine Evans counted Callie, Jen, Carmichael, a girl he didn't know and, last of all,
his friend and supporter, Linc Gorham,
attorney-at-law. They sat quiet and still as if in

a picture, only their heads hinging around as he entered. Callie's hair still could catch the light.

He said, "Hello. Hello there, Callie."

"Hello, Lat."

Gorham got up. His head was silver. He held out his hand. "We've been waiting. Have a chair."

Evans sat down.

Gorham cleared his throat but waited for a minute before speaking. "Lat, we have trouble here."

"Trouble?"

"You haven't noticed." Gorham's thumb thumbed toward the shadowed stairway.

At the side of the stairs a bulging blanket lay. Two feet, toes up, pushed out from the end.

"Whey Belly Hector," Gorham said. "Knifed to death."

33

About all that Carmichael knew was that Hector was dead. Late at night Callie had come to the room he was in — Gussie's room, it was — and tapped on the door and led him downstairs to the body. Her upset showed mostly in a sort of tight quietness.

He was quiet himself until, stepping careful because Hector had bled so much, he made sure of death. "How'd it happen?" he asked.

"I don't know." Her hand was steady with the lamp but her face paler under the paint that she wore, pale and, he saw then, swollen, too.

"Anyone here?"

"I was upstairs."

"Where's Happy?"

"I gave him the night off. Mike, what do I do?"

He gave up on his own questions. For an answer to hers he couldn't think of anything better than to rout out Linc Gorham. He'd done that himself. When the two of them got back, Happy and Ping's wife were in the house, and Gussie was downstairs. All had gone into the kitchen so as to leave the parlor to Gorham and Callie, who talked for what seemed a long time.

That was all Carmichael knew, except that Happy had been sent to get Lat.

Now he said as Lat seated himself, "Us others will leave you three to yourselves."

Gorham motioned him down. "It won't hurt to hear." He turned to Lat. "This is purely exploratory, but a good advocate can't overlook any angles, and we may be able to profit by this moment of grace." He explained to them all, "No coroner here, and the deputy sheriff, I understand, is on business up north in the breaks." His eyes seemed to Carmichael to hold a bare glint. "A fruitless errand, I'll warrant."

No one answered.

Gorham's fingers played on the arm of his chair. "Do you want to tell him, Miss Callie?"

"You, please," she said through lips that hardly opened.

Gorham cleared his throat. "Correct me, Miss Callie, if I misstate the case. These are the facts, Lat, as given to me. Besides Hector, who was Miss Callie's — shall we say? — client, three people, three known people, were in the

440

house at the time of the killing. The three were Miss Gussie and Carmichael, who were in Miss Gussie's room, and Miss Callie herself. Another girl, normally here, left yesterday for a few days' vacation in Butte City." His hand waved toward Happy, who stood bent and listening a little apart from the group. "Happy had been given the night off and was visiting — with a half-breed family, I believe?"

Happy nodded to the question.

"All this can be verified, Miss Callie?"

"Yes."

Gorham cleared his throat again but didn't go on at once. In the silence Carmichael wondered what he was driving at. Why was Lat called? It was one hell of a fine place for him to be! In Lat's expression Carmichael couldn't read anything.

Gorham got up and began walking the floor as if it was a jury he talked to. "At about midnight, then, Hector left Miss Callie upstairs and came down for a drink, telling her to wait. She did wait, for perhaps a half hour. Then, curious as to the why of his absence, she herself came downstairs. Knowing the house so well, she didn't bother with a light."

Gorham took another turn and abruptly faced around. "Where was Hector's lamp, Miss Callie?"

The tip of her tongue came out and wet her tight lips. "He said he could find the bottle without one."

"I see. All right." Gorham put on his jury manner again. "As Miss Callie reached the first floor someone unknown assaulted her, as you can see."

They all looked at Callie. Her face would be discolored by morning.

"The assailant fled, we must assume. When she could, Miss Callie lit a lamp and found Hector there with a knife in him." Gorham paused. "It happens to be her own butcher knife."

Carmichael hadn't known that.

"You heard no noise, Miss Callie, no sounds of a scuffle?"

"If I did, I just thought Hector had bumped into something."

"Yes. Knives are quiet instruments. It could very well be that the only noise was the thud of the body."

Carmichael had heard noises, though, but had paid them no heed. Footsteps, movements, voices without words, all muffled by distance, none standing out. You expected sounds in a whorehouse. Thinking back, he couldn't figure just when he had heard them, whether right before Miss Callie called him or long before.

He had been occupied or asleep or half asleep.

Lat was looking at Jen, and Gorham caught him looking and said, "A friend in need. Happy got word to her."

Gorham sat down. "Can you tell us, Lat, whether Hector had any enemies?"

"I suppose you could say I was one."

"You don't count."

"Nobody liked him much."

"That hardly helps."

Gorham got out a cigar and nipped off its end and sat without lighting it. They were like dummies, Carmichael thought, a ring of dummies moving and speaking only to the strings Gorham pulled. Jen with her small, pointed face. Callie who'd look comical with a black eye. Gussie the hussy. Happy the solemncholy nigger. Himself. A funny bunch, putting on a wake in a hookshop. But Lat didn't belong in the cast. Looking at him, Carmichael asked himself again why they had called him. Lat sat bent forward, maybe wondering, too, his eyes going from Callie to Gorham and back, not shiftily but openly as was his way. The hands locked in his lap showed spots of white at the knuckles. It occurred to Carmichael to ask then why Lat had answered the call.

Gorham leaned forward as if his thoughts had come to a head. "Lat, do you believe Miss

Callie capable of murder?"

"Of course not."

"She's peaceful?"

"Yes."

"And law-abiding?"

"Yes."

"What would you say about her reputation for truth, honesty, integrity?"

Lat answered, "None better."

"How long have you known Miss Callie? How well?"

It was a wrong question to ask a solid married man and a candidate for the Senate.

"Since the summer of 1880."

"How well?"

Lat lowered his head and raised it and looked Callie full in the face. It was as if he had to look her full in the face before answering. "Once we were close," he said quietly.

"Intimate?"

In Lat's place Carmichael would have told Gorham off. Lat's gaze went to Callie again and then off into space. It seemed to Carmichael that he could see in his face those old days with her, the nights of rutting and heat that was dead now — the time of a closeness, it struck him, closer than flesh alone.

"Intimate?"

"That's enough, Linc."

"Hold on!" Gorham waved with his unlighted cigar and took another tack. "You just said she was law-abiding, or enjoyed that reputation."

"Yes."

"Yet her profession is outlawed by the statutes."

"Maybe it is."

"But you just said she was law-abiding?"

"She is, just the same."

"Did she ever loan you money, as it has been whispered, and, if so, does that influence you to speak in her favor?"

"I resent that."

"I'm sorry, but be patient. You don't know much about law and the criminal courts, do you, Lat?"

"Very little."

Gorham nodded. "Few do in this country." He lit the cigar at last and blew out a long plume of smoke.

Something was coming now, something was about here, Carmichael thought. He found himself edging forward in his chair.

Gorham took the cigar from his mouth and let it dangle. "Lat, I'm your backer and friend, as you know. But I'm also Miss Callie's attorney, and the obligation of an attorney to his client comes first. Still, I want you to understand fully. The questions I've asked are prosecution questions. There's a strong possibility, I think, that the territory will charge Miss Callie with murder."

Lat said, "That's ridiculous."

Gorham nodded again and got up and paced a half circle. The light wavered on his white head. "From the right sources a word in court to that effect would help sway a jury. If worst comes to worst, Lat, would you, as an influential citizen, testify as a character witness for Miss Callie?"

For a long instant, it seemed to Carmichael, they were all as dead as Hector, no movement, no sound, no breath, Lat with his head down like a steer stunned by a butcher's maul. Only the mind was alive, his own mind reaching for Lat's.

Lat got out of his chair slowly and by degrees straightened up and stood like a man daring the weather. He made the answer that Carmichael knew he would.

"I'll testify," he said.

34

Carmichael walked home with Evans. He kept wanting to say something, to discuss the case, to give advice, but Lat's silence checked him. Yet he felt that Lat welcomed his company. It was almost as if, from their wordless churnings of mind, thought still passed between them, or pieces of thought, anyway. It was no use to wish he could speak the other pieces; Lat had made up his mind.

The night was all right at least, silent and deep and undisturbed, sleeping through to the sun. When he looked up, he saw that even the stars were drowsing off. It was only men that worried, seeing God with white whiskers riding up there, a rod in His hand. He guessed it was men who made things tough on themselves, on the claim that God had so willed. The sky didn't give a damn.

Still speechless, they stopped in front of Lat's place. The house was dark; but Joyce would be inside, and the baby, both snug and safe-dreaming, and Spartacus would go in with his burden. " 'Ye call me chief. . .' " The deep-timbre voice. The fond glance at Lat. The face quick and virtuous and serene. Little Lat smiling a smile as if he hadn't learned quite how to fix it.

A queer spot, Carmichael thought, queer for him to be in. It wasn't his household, or his wife and child.

Lat stood stooped. He sighed, not speaking, not moving, like a man nerving himself. Carmichael felt that quick touch of sympathy felt often before. Here he himself was, younger and greener and, all right, better, but needing the callus that the years put on blisters. But Lat had made up his mind. Few fathers pulled weight with their sons. Everyone had to learn fresh for himself, and maybe the learning amounted to shrink.

Of a sudden it occurred to him there was still Callie.

Lat said, "Good night."

There was still Callie, and Carmichael answered, "Like as not it'll never come out, Lat. I wouldn't be openin' any gates before-hand."

"Thanks, Mike." That was all Lat had to say, and he said it as if more out of appreciation

448

than agreement. He started up the path to the door, walking slow.

For a few paces Carmichael watched him, thinking how lonely the right was, or what men took for right. Then he faced around and strode off, for he had work to do.

Walking up to the porch, he could see a low light in Callie's window on the second floor, but no one answered his knock. A drunk, they would think him, or a late customer who couldn't be let in if the corpse was still there. He tried the latch. It was locked. He beat at the door without result. He stepped back from the porch and yelled at the lighted window, "Callie! Callie! It's Mike. Mike Carmichael." He didn't have to care if good people heard.

He went back to the door and hammered again. At last through the curtained pane he saw a glow floating toward him. The latch clicked. Happy stood there. He asked, "What, Mist' Mike?"

"I want to see Miss Callie."

Happy didn't step aside to admit him. "She all wo' out."

"Doesn't matter. Call her!" Carmichael realized he was being harsh, out of dislike for his task, harsh enough to put Happy on guard. He pushed inside. The blanket still covered Hector. A pool of blood was drying at the side.

No one apparently had thought to get the body out of the house. Stalling for time, maybe, while they left the girls to sleep in a morgue.

"You ain't goin' trouble her mo', Mist' Mike?"

"No more than I have to. Go get her!"

Happy didn't move. He looked sad and reproachful like a broken-down hound. In his big eyes the lamp in his hand lit two little reflections. He said, "Please, Mist' Mike!"

"Call her, I said!"

"Whey Belly no good. Jes' common trash." Without his kind's fear of the dead, Happy flung a hand toward the body. "Needed killin', he did. But dey blame Miss Callie, and he not fittin' to lick her big toe." Carmichael had to fight the sudden, humble misery that showed in the eyes along with the tiny lamps. "She jes' all right, Mist' Mike, always all right. Please leave her be!"

"Get her or I'll get her myself!"

Happy turned and made for the stairs, almost stepping on the body as he passed.

Carmichael went into the parlor. He found a match in his pocket and struck flame to a lamp and adjusted the wick. Perhaps it was better, he thought, not to have a set plan. He'd start reasonably and then see. Not planning, he rolled a careful cigarette and lit it over the chimney.

Callie came down in a wrapper and slippers and took a seat close to him. Her loose hair fell down her back, yellow and shining but tangled, as if by a wind. He wondered, as she seated herself, if she'd had to start dyeing it. Her face was unpainted and looked almost sickly. Under one eye the bruise had commenced to turn blue.

She didn't speak until she'd sat down, and then she said one tired word. "Yes?"

He scuffed through his pile of thoughts, telling himself to start soft and sensible, to forget for the time the strong speech he felt spurred to. "Callie," he said, "I'd like to talk to you about Lat."

Again one word. "What?"

"You're a good girl, Callie. Always have been."

"Oh, sure."

"So I figured you wouldn't want Lat to testify if you thought twice about it."

"Do I have to think twice?"

"It's asking a lot, you know."

She didn't answer.

He went on, "Both of us like Lat. Wouldn't either one of us want to see him get ruined. That's how I see it."

It was, he thought, like talking to a battered china doll. No reaction. No response. Just the

451

glass eyes of a doll unwinking on him, the banged-up face, the lips that couldn't move.

"The territory needs men like him," he said, knowing the words to be feeble. "He could go a long ways."

For all that she showed, she might not have heard him.

"He's got a fine family, Callie, a fine boy, a fine wife. You wouldn't bust 'em up?"

Now her face with its comical mouse under one eye pulled down at the mouth. "Wouldn't I?"

"No, you wouldn't."

"I helped him."

"That's why he'll testify, damn it!"

He had known this Callie for years, Carmichael thought as he looked at her, known her ever since the end of the trail at Fort Benton. Then she'd been young and giving and beautiful. Now the skin remembered as fair and smooth had begun to show tarnish and grain. The blue eyes were popped. The face looked hard, looked professional. This was the price of the life she had led — and been helped to lead by the order of men.

"He paid back the loan?" he said.

Her head bobbed a yes.

"He paid you for everything?"

Again her head bobbed.

Carmichael drove himself on. "You had it to sell?"

She only looked at him out of her doll eyes.

"You had it to sell. No one made you a whore. You made yourself one. Everything's even between you and Lat."

"Even!" she said through closed teeth.

But still it seemed to Carmichael she had begun to shrink, to fall back. In the dull light of the lamp it was as if her face rode apart from her body, small and discolored and bitter-mouthed and maybe defeated. His old man came into his mind to state that this hurt him more than anyone.

"You ought to know the rules, too," he made himself say. "A good whore keeps things inside the whorehouse. No fair, going outside!"

Her face and body came together as she jumped to her feet. One had swung out. "It's always the men !" she cried. "No one else counts. It's always the goddam men!" Her whole face seemed one twist. "Shut up and go home, you goddam man!"

Carmichael got up. There was nothing else for it. He told her, "I'll change my story if need be. I'll say you killed Hector."

He found his hat and went out the door. Even in the right a man could feel wrong.

35

Evans told Joyce after breakfast, after the baby had eaten and been put back to bed for his morning nap. He told her all of it, making the words come to mind and his mouth force them out though each of them showed like a blow on her face.

"Now let me hear about Whitey," she had said brightly after she had tucked in Little Lat.

So the time had come.

He had asked her to sit down at the kitchen table and had poured more coffee and lighted a cigar to give his hands something further to do. He began with the old days in Fort Benton and carried through to last night, trying to speak the whole truth, no more and no less. She hadn't helped him, with protests or questions or nods or shakes of the head. Her face, soft and wide open with disbelief as he started, had flattened and stiffened as he went on. Her lips paled, pressing together. Only her eyes spoke, the dark of them liquid, stirred by his words.

Now, while he hesitated before the facts of last night, she said, her mouth hardly moving, "I supposed you knew something of women. Men always seem to."

"And you forgave that."

"But this wasn't just passing," the tight mouth answered. "It wasn't just a moment of weakness, one transgression."

"No. It was more than that."

"Did you carry it on after meeting me?"

"Once. That was goodbye."

"You never told me."

"There is such a thing as a good sinner." The thought hadn't struck him before, but he knew it for truth. "The bad one wants to unload."

"She was, I hope — adequate."

"Please, Joyce!"

"You loved her? You could love such a woman?"

"I could, and I couldn't. I don't know. It seems a long time ago." He put his hand out, wanting to touch her arm, to establish a contact their words couldn't manage.

She pulled away and sat tight and shrunken against the back of her chair, beyond any reach, distant, it seemed to him, as someone seen for the first time, driven years apart by the years he'd had to summon from memory. The distant mouth said, "You love her yet."

"You know I don't. You must know I don't. Look at me, Joyce!" She was looking at him. "I love you, only you."

"If you're such a good sinner, why are you telling me now?"

He took a breath and let it out and took another. He got up and put a stick in the kitchen stove and threw his cigar along with it and came back and let himself down. "Joyce, a man was killed in her place last night."

Neither surprise nor curiosity showed on her face. Nothing showed but the abuse that had stiffened it.

"It was Whey Belly Hector," he said.

"He was another good friend, I assume."

He could hear the loud tick of the kitchen clock, like time beating them farther apart. A little breeze sang outside. He wanted to get up and stride over the minutes, over the years, and kiss her back home to him. He said, "She is a suspect. She will probably be charged with the murder." The clock and the breeze kept on sounding. "Whatever she is, Joyce, she never could kill anyone."

She put her hands to her eyes though no tears were there. "You ought to know," she said as if he should.

"I do." He braced himself. "That's the thing.

If she is accused, they want me to testify as a character witness, in court, in public."

Her face sprang open to the thought and slowly closed. It was a long minute before she spoke. Then her voice barely reached him. "You'll have to appear then."

This girl, he thought, this wife whom he'd always tried to protect! Faced with the stern necessity, she measured up, out of the open honesty, the sturdy fiber in her. Bottom, they would call it in a horse. She could stand all strains. "I know," he said. "I knew you'd realize."

The mouth broke that he'd thought so strong. It jerked down at the corners and trembled in the middle, and she closed it with one hand while open tears welled in her eyes and started down her cheeks. "Lat!"

"Sweetheart!" He got up and put a hand on her shoulder. It flinched under his touch. "What's past is past and doesn't matter when we love each other."

She jerked away from him and rose, clattering the chair. She circled the floor, her head bent in her palms. Her voice cried at him. "After everything! After all we've tried to do and be! How can we face people? How can Little Lat and I?"

He heard the suck of her breath and felt the

hard hold that she put on it. He saw her straighten, saw her drop her hands and turn her stiff back to him and move away as if he'd been removed. The bedroom door clicked shut.

What occurred to him as he stood watching the torn space she had left was a piece from the Bible: *So teach us to number our days, that we may apply our hearts unto wisdom . . .*

Evans walked downtown. He had no place to go but no place to stay, not with the bedroom door at home closed against him and Joyce crying behind it, "Nothing can hurt us, baby. No evil. Nothing." He pictured her, holding Little Lat hard in her arms or kneeling at the side of the cradle while the tears fell.

She needed to be by herself, he thought dully. More talk wouldn't help. All had been said. If by a miracle anything served him, it would be time. Beyond her hurt and the hurt yet to be she had seen that he had to testify. Maybe, at last, she would see him as he had been, young and bursting with sap and enthralled with his first woman because, all right, first, she was Callie. It wasn't likely, though. Things fell between people, never to be removed, at best to be reached around awkwardly.

He lagged up the street. Over the benchlands beyond the creek the sun was rolling high and heatless, its rays bright and clean on the town. In all the sky not a cloud showed. On a side road a milk cow ankled away, her emptied bag flopping. A rooster crowed from somebody's backyard, and another replied from far off. Southward the open land swept away and climbed into buttes just starting to green. He couldn't see the Sweetgrass Hills, but they would be north there, across a hundred miles of grass and stream. Back of him, beyond the upland reaches, he could feel the great wall of the Rockies, each lift and canyon fixed in memory.

Here was his land, he thought. Here he was the land's. Miles, mountains, sky, waters, grass — they freed and claimed him. Here he'd hoped to work and build and rear his family and deserve a name for service to people, to a territory that was sure to be a great state. Given any choice, here he'd choose to live and die.

His ranch didn't figure to bring much with money so shy, and his cattle might want for a buyer. It brought him up short to remember that Joyce hadn't said she'd live with him elsewhere.

The town was quiet. The few people he saw didn't stop to talk about Hector and so hadn't heard. He found himself outside the Tansy-town Mercantile Company and went in, for nothing. Marshall Strain sat figuring at his high desk, and eyeshade low on his forehead. He peered from under it. "Welcome, Lat." He clmbed from his stool and held out his hand. "What's the news?"

"None."

Strain glanced around as if maybe an ear might be cocked round a barrel. "Joyce hasn't heard?"

"What?"

"What! About you and those rustlers?"

"No."

Strain looked down. "Glad to see you aren't unprepared."

Evans couldn't remember strapping on his revolver. Even what he'd told Joyce was mixed now in his mind. "Carmichael's doings," he said.

Strain nodded and cut back to his first words. "As I told you, I tried indirectly to smooth the way."

"Yes."

"With her training, her background — You don't seem as concerned as you were."

Here they were, Evans thought, talking of something no longer important, something as good as forgotten, dusted over, withered up by worse troubles.

Strain wasn't through. "Oh, I know she'll be

all right, too, given a little time." He scratched his head with the blunt end of his pencil. "Such things aren't likely to happen again, either. We're changing fast, Lat. The whole country is. More and more, Joyce will come to feel at home here."

"Sure."

"It takes a little time to civilize a new place, but we're almost there." Strain looked off into the future. "We'll have better courts, better law enforcement, more churches and schools, a more general respect and support for the finer things." He stood gazing as if these things had come to pass and he could see them — the sunny schools, the Methodist churches, the happy law and order, the good life under God. He turned with a smile and tapped Evans on the chest. "And you, my boy, will play a big part in the process."

"That egg hasn't hatched."

"It's hatching." Strain went on with assurances.

Listening while he shifted from one foot to the other, Evans had to remind himself that here was a kind man, a friend and kinsman, a steady well-wisher. It was his own disturbance of mind that branded him now as over-talkative, overgood, too blind by nice choice to what went on in sporting houses and who went in, or had gone. He put down the wild impulse to wise the man up.

"Now that I've practically got you elected," Strain was saying while his smile apologized, "I'd like to mention a favor."

"All right, Marsh."

"How about heading up the church finance committee this year? The preacher will ask you, but I wanted to put in my oar. It's needless to warn you that the committee comes down to one man. I've been that one man for too long. We need younger blood."

As Evans hesitated, Strain said, "Don't give me an answer now. Think it over. There's no hurry. You'll have to take your own affairs into account, I know."

"Yes."

"Fine." Strain's glance was both kindly and sharp. "You're a man of few words today, Lat," he said without criticism.

Evans made himself grin. "Must be a relief. Go back to your pencil-pushing, Marsh." He went out, sensing that Strain's eyes followed him.

Carmichael was loafing alone in front of the Gilt Edge. They gave each other hello and stood silent as men did, Evans thought, with too much on their minds. Finally, after a last drag at his cigarette, Carmichael said, "There's that damn body, Lat."

"Didn't Gorham see to that?"

"Not that I know of. No one was thinkin' practical last night." His face questioned Evans. "Can't speak for you, but it bothers me, them girls cooped up with a corpse."

"Gorham will know what to do."

Carmichael pursed his lips and looked away and after a little while answered, "Yeah — but I was just down to his place. He ain't there. Won't be today, a note on the door said."

"Maybe he wants Hector left for the time being."

"Maybe. But them poor girls!"

Evans could see them, too, could see Callie, locked in the still house with the great, still body of Hector and the dried lake of blood at the side. But what could or should he and Car-michael do, except at the most to serve for a moment as company? A thought touched and left the edge of his mind. As it went he said for something to say, "I didn't know you were concerned about them."

"I was stunned-like last night. Then I got to thinkin' about Gussie and all." Carmichael's hand took Evans' elbow and urged him to move. "We can see. That's the least we can do." He added, "Not as I'll ever arguefy for much more."

Evans let himself be led. Why not? No harm could come of it; the harm had been done. A man reached a stage in which tiny kindnesses counted, and they not for much.

They walked in silence until, as if the silence had spoken, Carmichael asked, "You didn't open no gates, Lat? Don't tell me!"

"Everything in the corral." It occurred to Evans that everything in fact was there, everything, in such a corral as Carmichael didn't imagine.

Carmichael went to the front door as if a man never gave thought to the back. He knocked and knocked again, making his fingers into a fist.

The door opened at last. It was Jen with her rodent's face who held to the knob.

"Mornin'," Carmichael said. He turned like a man introducing another. "Lat here wants to see Callie."

"He does, does he?"

Evans told her, "We want to be of help if we can. There's the body for one thing."

"Everything's took care of, Mr. Evans." She made a point of the title.

"What do you mean?"

"Just what I said."

"Where's Callie?"

"Now wouldn't you like to know?"

464

"Where's Happy, then?"

"Wouldn't you like to know?" Hers wasn't the face of a rabbit or mouse, it seemed to Evans; it was the face of a weasel.

"Yes," he said, "I'd like to know."

"They're gone, both of them, Callie and Happy."

"Where?"

"Away." She strung the one word out.

"Away where?"

"Away."

"For good, Jen?"

"You'll have to ask them, Mr. Evans."

On sudden impulse Evans asked, "Where's Tom?"

From her silence he clinched some of the answers. Tom would have taken Callie and Happy, probably to catch the stage at Sun River. Beforehand, Tom somehow had disposed of the body. But a big question remained. "Why, Jen? Why did they go, and both of them, too?"

Carmichael spoke up quickly. "She ain't puttin' out, Lat, and maybe don't know. And it's their own business besides."

Jen said, "Askin' why, for God's sake!"

Carmichael pulled at Evans' sleeve. "This winds it up, Lat. They ain't likely to be chased, much less to be caught, so there's no trial, no nothin'. Come on!"

"But why did they both go?" With the question Evans caught the spreading glimmer of the truth. "Whey Belly mistreated her, Jen?"

For once he got an answer. "The dirty puss-gut!"

It was all there to see now. Evans said to Carmichael, "Happy killed Hector."

36

As they walked away from the house Carmichael said, "You missed your callin', Lat, not bein' a detective, but just what was it that gave you the clue?"

Evans didn't feel like talking.

"I was way behind, not even in sight of what you seen quick. Wish you'd smart me up."

"Callie couldn't be guilty."

"That didn't for sure elect Happy, though?" Carmichael waited for a reply. "What did?"

"Whey Belly."

"Don't be so damn teasy!" From Carmichael's smile Evans couldn't tell how much he'd already figured out. "It's like you had put a price on your talk."

"Whey Belly was the kind to abuse a woman. Change Callie's story a little, and you had the answer." It struck Evans and weighed on him that if he hadn't whipped Hector up there in the breaks, Hector might not have taken his rage out on Callie.

"I reckon Happy would have tried to protect her all right," Carmichael said.

"He would."

"So she covered his tracks?"

"Yes."

"Figurin' he was some guilty, and him bein' a black man might work against him?"

"Yes."

"He could have fessed up, but likely she told him not to." Carmichael spoke in the tone of conclusion.

There they were, Evans thought, a white woman and a black man, held together in innocence by the one true attachment either had ever found. There somewhere they fled, without funds enough maybe, with only what cash had been ready to hand, without friends by the way, without a place to go or one to call home. That was how it was at the last. Out of the many, the friendly, the high and unreckoning times — this!

Before they reached the boardwalk of the main street Carmichael halted Evans to say, "You noticed how Jen acted?"

"What does it matter?"

"I ain't sure it does. But some things you're a detective on. Some things you ain't." Carmichael spoke earnestly. "She didn't get that way by herself, Lat."

"Let it go."

Carmichael wouldn't. "A favor to some people works out like an insult."

"You mean Tom."

"How I see it, he'll think he's one up on you. You were even, but not now. Who took Hector from the house? Tom Ping. Who helped Callie get away, not to mention Happy? Not you, Lat. Tom Ping again."

"He's not so loco as to figure that way."

"Maybe not. But people's got their quirks."

"For the Lord's sake, Mike!" Evans hadn't meant to sound so impatient. "I don't care. Let him be one up. Come on!"

As they began walking again, Carmichael asked mildly, "Changin' the subject, then, are you travelin' back to the ranch today or tonight?"

Evans wished he was there now, shut of his load of thought. "We'll go tomorrow, I guess."

The street was almost empty, for the sun shone at high noon and the men who had homes to go to had gone home to eat. Those who didn't would be a Soo Son's café. Carmichael came to a halt in front of the Lally Cooler. "Might as well have a drink?"

"Not for me. Thanks."

"Wouldn't hurt you, I figure." Carmichael's

eyes showed concern. "Look, Lat, it didn't turn out so bad. It turned out good for what it was. Of course there's Callie, and that's sorry but still better to my mind than you bustin' yourself over a damned old wild oat. It's a bet they'll never catch Callie. You won't have to testify. You can go home knowin' that."

Home is the sailor, home from the sea . . . The lines, deep-throated, ran in Evans' head. Home went the sailor, home with the flabby, insufficient, crawling plea that he wouldn't have to testify after all. "Get your drink, Mike," he said abruptly. "I'll be seeing you." He walked away without looking back.

He had no place to go and no wish to go any place except to the ranch, which was too far from Joyce. He idled on the streets and in the saloons, now and then talking of nothing with men who had nothing to talk of. He saw Carmichael again and signaled in passing, knowing Carmichael's gaze traveled with him.

The sun tipped and sank toward the west, and he idled some more. At one place or another a ranch hand complained, "The damn house is closed. Miss Callie must be takin' time off." A cloud bank sat over the mountains, yellow at the crest, then fiery, then purple, then black. Higher, one wisp of vapor was burning up. At this hour of no wind a breeze fiddled in the town's trash.

He hadn't eaten since early morning, after Little Lat, bright as a button, had awakened to the new day. He wasn't hungry now. He went to Soo Son's and spent time over what was said to be pot roast and rice pudding. It was dusk by the time he got out. Maybe, just maybe, by this time? Maybe she waited.

He walked up the street to the hotel bar. No one was there but the bartender, Herb. Good men and true had their feet under the family board. He asked for a beer that he didn't want and took it to a table. A man's mind got exhausted. There was nothing in his, it seemed to him, but the passing of time, but the float of half-thoughts, nothing but another beer, a cigar, a third beer, nothing but men coming in and trying to make talk. The clock, when he looked at it, had wiped out two hours.

The door squeaked open and shut. A voice said, " 'Y God, Lat, you're a hard man to find." The smooth cave of the mouth was wide in a smile. "Even your woman didn't know, so I been to the ranch by shank's mare and all the way back the same way."

Grandpa McBee took a chair. The pat of his hand was too friendly.

Evans didn't speak.

"Oh, I had a horse once all right, and it's a sad story."

"Tell a funny one."

McBee lowered his voice. "Not faultin' you, for you're generous, but that grubstake was a mite skimpy. Still I wouldn't dream then of askin' for more. Only thing I could do to piece out my funds was to come to town and have a go at the pasteboards. Monte's my game." The mouth closed and drew down, riffling the whiskers. "You know, 'y God, you ought to do something about these crooks."

Evans held his tongue.

"For a minute I had a notion to tell them sports we was connected and watch 'em take cover," McBee went on, too softly for others to hear. "Then I says to myself, nope, Hank, it ain't for you to claim kin but the other way round. Right, huh?"

Evans looked into the sly old eyes, by his silence making McBee continue.

"Now, son, I hate to ask for more, but it's just a loan till I get on my feet, comin' to only two hundred in all besides a couple of horses."

Here again, Evans thought, was a problem shriveled to nothing. Here now he held the upper hand, here alone. He said, "Not a cent."

"Now think it over, Lat. It ain't fittin' to treat your old grandpappy like that. Me without money to get out of town or buy even a bait, and what would people think, knowin' you're rich-like and me pot-poor and the same blood in both of us?"

"Not a cent."

McBee shook his head. "I'll be mortified to tell folks we're kin."

"Tell them!"

"That's final?"

"Absolutely."

McBee quit play-acting. "I'll say to you," he said while a new glint came to his eyes, "your mother birthed a bastard."

"Names are safe at your age."

"Not you." The wizened, whiskered face was one mean blur. "Not you, but your older brother, him that's dead. Easy now! I ain't a fightin' man! But what I know I know, from back there on the Oregon Trail. The good Lord gave me eyes to see with and a mind to figger, and your ma was my own daughter and got herself knocked up, and not by Brownie, either."

Evans had the beard in his fist, had the head yanked up and then the body upright. He backed it to the door and with one hand reached ahead and found the knob. He spun the body around and kicked it out.

Only then did it come to him that the deed had been automatic, without thought — muscle

473

anticipating mind. He stiffened himself against a bare nudge of doubt. A man stood so much, then no more. He stepped back to the bar, ignoring the eyes cast his way. Some of the beard was in his hand. He snapped it off and wiped his fingers on his pants. "Whiskey," he said.

"Served him right." The bartender was nodding. "I know him. Stinkin', exasperatin' old bag o' bones. Everyone's a crook but—"

"My grandfather," Evans said. The shot glass felt cool.

Herb wiped the bar.

Eighteen forty-five. The Oregon Trail. Pa and Ma, young then and blooded and unwed. Somewhere, some night, some man, on the long grind from Missouri. Take the word of a lying old blackguard of a grandfather!

The door opened and let in Tom Ping. It opened again and let in Carmichael. Ping's eyes swam around the room and fixed and, having fixed, swam on. He hitched up the high side of his cartridge belt. His walk, as he went to the far end of the bar, was the bold gait of a man who'd had a few. His face, reflected in the rear mirror, looked loose and ornery. Carmichael had let himself down at an empty table.

"Set the bottle out," Ping said. "I'm howlin', Herb." He spoke so loud that a watching silence settled on the room. While it lasted,

Evans felt again, felt beforehand, the raw, unreasoning need of action. He breathed deep. He shook himself. He studied the bottles ranged beyond the counter. For what it mattered, Old Crow Whiskey was a favorite.

"Herb?" Ping had his glass lifted and was squinting at it. "Y'ever heard of a one-horse rancher?" The voice was still loud. "My ass to him!" He swung around. "Drink up, boys!"

The words took Evans down the bar. "What you have to say, you can say to me, Ping."

Ping turned his head. "That talk of yours, now, is hard for common men to understand. Ain't it so, Herb?"

Herb's eyes went to the floor and moved uneasily along it.

Behind him Evans heard the stir of movement. He said, "Go on!"

"I'm particular who I talk to."

Evans kept silent, watching Ping, waiting to catch and hold his gaze, knowing only that what came must come at last. He could hear his own breath, hard but even. It seemed to him he could hear the held breath of the room.

Ping jerked around. "You're a goddam high-winker."

"Get it all off your chest."

"You never made good on a friendship yet."

Beyond the dark face, behind the waiting

time, Evans for an instant was in Fort Benton again. He had come from the bank, and Tom was heeling from him with hurt and anger in his look and on his lips a foul goodbye; and McBee came from the years to say there'd been a bastard in the family. "Go on," Evans said.

A little twitch had begun to work at the side of Ping's mouth. He put up a quick hand to smooth it out. The hand was unsteady. Ping said, while the twitch worked again, "Do I have to tell you what you really are?"

As if unseen before, Ping's face came sharp to sight, scarred and trembling with its ancient wound. There, too, were the poor and later years and the ways of a life that his upbringing had blazed in advance. The thick black forelock, close up like this, looked thin and showed hairs of silver, and his eyes might never have laughed.

Evans said, "You'd better tell me, Tom."

"All right. You're a son-of-a-bitch!"

Evans heard the scuff of feet, the scrape of a chair, the opening whine of the rear door. "That says it, I guess," he answered without moving.

"Well?" Ping had taken a step from the bar and stood with his hands clear. Time passed. Out of the unsteady mouth came, "I never took you for a coward before."

Evans nodded and turned away and walked slowly to the door.

Watching, while men too afraid to sit tight and too curious to leave had shied off, Carmichael had thought without comfort that his was the right hunch all along. Or one of his hunches was right. No shot had come from the dark, fired by friends of the rustlers. No put-up job had been tried. But here was Tom Ping as imagined, made too big for his britches by a favor and whiskey and a loco quirk of the mind, and here was a set-to closed to third parties.

Lat had called Ping's hand. Not that he'd had too much choice, but still he'd forced the showdown. Then something had come over him. Carmichael didn't know what. He only knew it wasn't fear. He only knew the Senate was gone sure enough then. He only knew, this above all, that Lat could have killed Ping — and didn't.

Now, as Lat passed on his way outside, Carmichael had an impulse to get up and take his arm. Lat went by unseeing, his step heavy but unhurried, his gaze fast on the door, his shoulders held back as if beneath a burden. Something in his face, in the mold and set of it, stirred Carmichael more. A man laid bare, he thought, peeled to the bone, without explana-

477

tion or apology carrying his skull on the skeleton that was left of him. There was a word for it. Magnificent. That was the right and crazy word.

The door closed. Somebody snickered. Somebody said, "Senator!"

Ping flung around. "He's not a coward," he shouted at them. His mouth worked. "You cheap chippies, he's a better man than all of you."

Crying jags, they called them.

37

The wind was hard, so hard that Evans had to hold to his hat going home. Even the stars looked wind-blown, soiled by the leavings of winds. In his mind, it seemed to him, were only leavings, only the tatters and dusts of old storms, whirled again by the gale that was blowing.

Nothing mattered; all explained. Now was then, and then was now. Old wounds into new. A man tried. He kept trying.

To be right, he told himself, but to be right for the right reasons! To square things up, he told himself, but to square them only by squaring himself with himself! He couldn't go farther. He was too played out even to walk.

He went on. In winter the wind would have been welcome. It tore at him now, trapping his breath, driving grit in his face. He turned his back to a gust and walked backwards, holding tight to his hat. In the southeastern sky, over the old Oregon Trail, the stars were bright. When he turned, they were bright over Fort Benton. Old stars. The trusted stars! To the west, over the dark mountains, reared the dark mother cloud of the wind.

Home was a little star, not fallen yet. He stopped at the gate and wiped the hard dust from his eyes. He could see only shadows inside. He went to the door. It opened before his hand reached the knob.

He couldn't make out her face at once, only the hand that came out in a gesture brave and little and pitiful. The loved voice came to him, reciting. " 'Entreat me not to leave thee, or to return from following after thee: for whither thou goest...' "

He saw the face then and the smile that couldn't hold to its smile. He never had thought her ugly before, or so beautiful.

Her voice cried to him, "Come in! Come in out of the wind!"

For just an instant he waited. The wind whipped him, the warm wind, the sweet wind, the wind with the bone of winter in it unnoticed till now.

Then he went in.

480